Sarah Dreher

BAD COMPANY

To all our villains.
What would writers do without them?

Acknowledgements

No writer creates in a vacuum. Ideas are all around us, waiting to be picked up. Overheard scraps of conversation. The way a person stands at the check-out counter at the supermarket. A sudden memory. A dream. The color of a stranger's jacket. Newspaper stories. Television. Anything can jog a realization, or a thought, or a solution.

Those of us who are truly blessed know people who are gold mines to a writer, people who have an instinct for *what works*, people who can think around corners for that elusive answer, people who can follow a train of plot and find where it went off the track. When we get bogged down in our own words, or fall in love with a moment or scene that doesn't really belong, they can find it and gently help us to let go.

I have been and continue to be deeply grateful to Elisabeth Brook for being such a person. Her editorial sense and intuitive inspirations are always invaluable, and once again she has gotten me and Stoner out of some real messes. And she does it while walking that very delicate and dangerous line between tact and honesty.

Published in Great Britain by The Women's Press Ltd, 1996
A member of the Namara Group
34 Great Sutton Street, London EC1V 0DX

First published in the United States of America by New Victoria Publishers, 1995

British Library Cataloguing-in-Publication Data
A catalogue record for this book is available from the British Library

ISBN 0 7043 4469 6

Printed and bound in Great Britain by
BPC Paperbacks Ltd

Sarah Dreher is the author of the Stoner McTavish series of novels, which includes *Bad Company* and *Stoner McTavish* (The Women's Press, 1996). She is also a clinical psychologist and award-winning playwright. Sarah Dreher lives in Amherst, Massachusetts.

Also by Sarah Dreher from The Women's Press:

Stoner McTavish (1996)

CHAPTER 1

"Dear Stoner McTavish..."

The letter was typed on business stationery in bold, enthusiastic print. The business was an inn and resort near Sebago Lake, Maine. Probably another promotional letter, which she'd have to answer. Ever since she and her friend and business partner Marylou Kesselbaum had decided to forsake Boston winters and a city clientele, and move Kesselbaum and McTavish, Travel Agents, to the wilds of Western Massachusetts, they'd been deluged with promotional letters. And they had to answer them all because they couldn't afford to lose the contacts, now that they were starting over.

Marylou insisted the sudden attention had nothing to do with their leaving, but with the region's continuing economic uncertainty. "They all have to hustle now," she was fond of saying, as she jangled her silver bracelets for emphasis. "Even the cruise lines, curse their souls. Better they should lower their rates, if you want my opinion."

Nevertheless, she had to read them all, even if it meant opening mail over dinner in a public restaurant with Gwen.

"I was given your name by someone at the Cambridge Women's Center," the letter went on.

Cambridge Women's Center? Her old stomping ground. That caught her attention.

"I know you must be terribly busy, and I'm reluctant to intrude on your time and privacy, but I think I need your help.

"I'm the owner and manager of The Cottage, an historic inn providing lodging and resort facilities for women only."

Women only? Her attention deepened.

"For the past month, we have had a wimmin's amateur theater group rehearsing here. A *great bunch!* We're all *crazy* about each other. (I'm the producer, by the way.) But lately things have been going wrong. Unexplained accidents, injuries, that sort of thing. Nothing too serious yet. But we're all afraid it might mean something, and everyone's nerves are on edge, as I'm sure you can understand. I was told you have some experience with helping people in trouble, and might be able to help us. Do you think you could? I would, of course, provide you with free room and board for yourself and anyone you might want to bring along to assist you.

"I haven't told the theater wimmin about this, as I don't want to alarm them —or to give anything away, in case the perpetrator is one of us (Goddess forbid!). If you were to pretend to be a guest of The Cottage, and then volunteer to help with the production, I feel you could fit in and be inconspicuous.

"Do you think you'd be interested? I do hope so. It would be a tremendous relief to me (and to all of us, of course).

Yours in Sisterhood,
Sherry Dodder"

"You're practically drooling," Gwen said with a laugh. "What is it?"

Stoner handed the letter across the mosaic tiled table and built herself another chicken fajita.

"Looks good," Gwen said as she scanned the letter. "Tempted?"

"Maybe, but..."

"But?"

"I can't just run off and leave Marylou with all the cleaning and packing. It wouldn't be right."

"I'll bet she wouldn't mind."

She shook her head. "She'd say it was okay, but she wouldn't mean it."

"Stoner, my love," Gwen said, "I don't know quite how to tell you this, but..."

"What?"

"Well, packing really isn't your long suit."

"There's a brochure," she said quickly, hoping to divert attention from the fact that she felt like a fool. She spread it out between them.

It was printed in sepia on textured cream colored paper, tasteful. The front showed a stone building with French doors leading onto a flagstone patio. Inside, a formal-looking living room with wing chairs arranged into conversation nooks and stiff antique throne-like seats lining the walls. The dining room appeared (as far as she could tell from the photographs) to look out over gardens to rolling hills beyond. The tables were set with linen cloths and napkins, each table centered with a carnation-filled bud vase. The Cottage was unquestionably elegant. And disturbingly formal.

"The Cottage," the brochure read, "was modeled after the elegant 'cottages' built in the Adirondacks and Berkshires by wealthy New Yorkers around the turn of the Century. Gracious living in a rural setting, with all the amenities of a first-rate New York hotel."

"Have you ever noticed," Gwen asked, "how people always say, 'around' the turn of the century? Never 'at' the turn, or 'during' the turn. Always 'around.' Do you think it's the word 'turn' that does it?"

"Beats me," Stoner said, staring at the dining room picture. It didn't look like any Women's Inn she'd ever seen. Women's Inns, or hotels, or B&B's were usually sparsely furnished, run-down, and in need of repair which guests were encouraged to provide in partial payment for lodging. Short on amenities, but long on privacy. The Cottage looked like the sort of place where you were expected to mingle. "I don't know about this. It may be kind of rich for my blood."

Gwen leaned across the table for a better look. "Hard to tell, really."

"All that stuff about 'elegant' and 'amenities.' Sort of gives me the willies."

"It's not exactly the kind of place you see advertised in *Lesbian Connection*," Gwen agreed. "I wonder if they do much business."

Stoner thought about it. "I guess they could. I mean, there are probably a lot of lesbians around who'd go for elegant amenities. We just don't happen to know them."

"It doesn't say lesbians only," Gwen said as she chased the last of the extra hot sauce around the stoneware bowl with a tortilla chip.

"Yeah, but how many straight women are going to go to a women-only resort?"

"Marylou would. After all, these are the 'nineties.'"

"Marylou would do anything."

"True," Gwen said. "Do you want the rest of your guacamole?"

Stoner shook her head. She gazed at the brochure, mixed feelings tearing at her. If she did this...and she was sorely tempted. Hard to turn down a request for help from a Sister. She couldn't imagine it. And the outside really did look fine. She could see herself, sprawled on one of those carved wooden benches scattered here and there among formal flower beds, feet propped up, contemplating the scenery and her next move. But the inside...How could she think in a dining room with hard wooden chairs that made you sit with perfect posture, and flowers on the table? Or take charge of things—which, she had learned to her dismay, one inevitably had to do when solving mysteries, or rescuing people, or finding missing persons, or whatever it was she did—in that formal, over-stuffed Queen Anne living room. How can you think clearly when you feel inferior to the furniture?

Of course, she knew what the real problem was. The Cottage, despite its deceptively rustic name, was exactly the sort of place her mother would love.

Well, she'd love the inside, anyway. Nothing like rooms stuffed with antiques to make her mother's eyes sparkle. And she'd know which ones were genuine and which copies, and which ones were safe to sit on...

Stoner was sure *she'd* break the first chair she landed in. Even one of those big, heavy-looking things. She had a way with antiques. She always had. It wasn't that she was careless. She just had a perverse inability to do the right thing around them. It was probably a curse from a past life.

And why did she care what her mother would do? She was pushing forty, for God's sake. She'd hardly seen her parents, much less lived with them since she ran away from home at sixteen. They'd given up trying to contact her, apparently feeling her Aunt Hermione...with whom Stoner lived and whom she loved with all her heart...deserved what she got for taking her in. So what difference did it make, anyway, whether her mother would go orgasmic over The Cottage?

Besides, her mother would be utterly appalled at the prospect of an inn for women only. To say nothing of what she'd think of a women's theater company. If there was one thing Dot (her real name was Dorothy, but she believed "Dot" made her seem fun and "with it") McTavish couldn't see the point to, it was anything that involved women only.

The Women's Movement had had minimal impact on the adults in the McTavish household. In fact, Stoner was willing to bet her mother, who had never joined anything in her life except the D.A.R. and Colonial Dames, was a card-carrying, lifetime supporting member of Concerned Women for America. Her father's awareness of the feminist revolution had been limited to the nasty jokes he read in the *American Legion Magazine.*

"So," Gwen asked, "what do you think?" She had found an uneaten fajita wrapper amid the dregs of Stoner's dinner, and was piling it with left-over lettuce and cheese and onions and guacamole and salsa and frijoles and whatever else she could find on their plates. She rolled it tight, folded the ends over, and took a bite. "God, that's good."

"You are the only person I know," Stoner said with an affectionate smile, "who eats garbage."

"Not true," Gwen said. "Edith Kesselbaum eats garbage."

"That's just Marylou's opinion. Daughters' opinions don't count."

"Trust me," Gwen insisted. "Taco Bell is garbage. Have you made up your mind, or is it too depressing?"

Stoner fingered the brochure. "My thoughts are depressing. About this...?" She gave a shrug. "What do you think I should do?"

"I already said. Take her up on it. What's the problem?"

"I don't think..." She hesitated to say it. She was ashamed to admit why she was hesitant, even to Gwen—after all, she firmly believed all lesbians were Sisters in oppression, and had the same pains and fears—and it wasn't her place to tell someone else how to live, when she hadn't walked a mile in their moccasins...

Gwen was looking at her. "What?"

"The people who probably go here...well, sometimes I have a hard time with Yuppie Dykes in high heels."

"Nobody calls them Yuppies any more. These are the 'nineties.'"

"Will you please stop saying 'These are the 'nineties' every two minutes?"

"We're supposed to say it every two minutes. After all, these are the 'nineties.'" Gwen took a drink of water. "Do you know the first time I heard that expression? On January 1, 1990, at 12:01 am."

Stoner narrowed her eyes and faked a scowl. "I'll bet you were with that man, weren't you?"

"What man?"

"That Bryan Oxnard person."

"My husband?" She calculated. "I guess so. We weren't married yet, but we were working on it." She laughed. "I think the beginning of a new decade made more of an impression on me than he did. Unlike the impression *you* made on *him*."

"I didn't mean to kill him," Stoner said. "It was an accident." She glanced up to see the waitress—wait*person*, or maybe wait*ron*, after all, this was Cambridge—poised beside their booth. It wasn't the same young woman who'd served them. They must have sat through the shift change again.

"Ready for me to clear these?" the woman asked cheerily.

"Uh, yeah, sure," Stoner muttered. "Listen, what you just heard...it wasn't what you think...I mean, it was self-defense. He was trying to kill her, and..."

"That's cool," the woman said, and reached for Gwen's plate.

Gwen grabbed the plate in both hands and pinned it to the table. "Not until it's so clean you can see yourself in it," she growled.

"Anything you say, Ms. Owens," the waitperson said with a laugh. "I'm glad to see you haven't changed."

"I'm glad to see you *have*," Gwen said. She patted the young woman's arm affectionately. "You were one of the most...unfocused...adolescents I've ever taught."

"And you were the scariest teacher."

Stoner looked up in amazement.

"I had to be a *little* intimidating," Gwen explained. "Junior High students can't even control themselves. If the teachers lose control, anarchy reigns. Did you ever settle down enough to think about college?"

The young woman nodded. "U. Mass. Boston. Starting my third year next month. I want to be..." She hesitated and blushed slightly. "...a history teacher, like you."

Gwen put her head in her hands. "I've failed."

"As you always used to say, Ms. Owens, it depends on your point-of-view. Can I get you anything more?"

"Coffee?" Stoner said.

Gwen nodded.

The waitperson withdrew.

"I think you scared her," Stoner said.

"I doubt it." She took another bite of her creation. "You know, I really am pleased. Carol always worried me a little. She was so flighty, almost hyperactive. I was sure there was trouble at home, but I couldn't get her to open up. The only way I could get through to her was to play the heavy."

"She seems to be doing okay," Stoner said. "And, considering how she blushed when she told you she wanted to follow in your footsteps, I'd guess you reached her."

"Uh-huh." Gwen gazed off in the direction of the kitchen. "Teaching's such a strange business. You have these intensely emotion-filled relationships with kids for a couple of years. Every day a crisis or a triumph. Every minute, every little thing you do or say, seems so terribly important...a matter of life and death. And then June comes and they disappear, and most of the time you never see them again."

"I don't know if I could do it," Stoner said.

"It'd be hard on you. You get so attached, you'd want to keep up with every kid you'd ever met."

Stoner shook her head. "I meant that I'm afraid of kids. They're too—well, too *sudden*."

"They are sudden, that's a fact."

Sometimes Stoner tried to imagine what it would have been like if she'd had Gwen for a teacher. During most of her adolescence, having a crush on a teacher had been an incentive to do well. Which was why, she supposed, she'd gotten such a strange scattering of grades—A's in English one year, math the next, while English fell to a B. There was one half-year in which she sparkled in Social Studies, but that ended abruptly when Miss Collins left to get married. She had no innate aptitude for science, but her first look at Mrs. Lurie turned her into a genius, thereby proving that innate ability didn't count for everything. Of course, her other subjects were likely to suffer when all her attention was diverted by one teacher, but she didn't care. Her worst year had been tenth grade, when she hadn't had a crush on anyone and ended up with a nice, dull B minus average.

But if *Gwen Owens* had been her teacher…

It probably would have been a disaster. Because Gwen was so softly beautiful, so smart and wise, had such a wonderful, soothing voice, and brown eyes you could get lost in…Stoner knew, given her adolescent awkwardness and insecurity, she'd have been paralyzed with passion and anxiety. Sometimes she was even now. Like right here, at this very minute, in the middle of Chili's in the middle of Cambridge, on a Friday night, with the place filling up with beer-guzzling summer school students.

"So," Gwen said as she finished off her fajita, "what *are* you going to do about the letter?"

"I don't know."

"Want to stop by Marylou's and run it past her?"

"I know what she'll say," Stoner said. "She's been trying for weeks to get me to go away, so she can get us ready to move."

"She *WHAT*?"

"She's been…"

"I heard you," Gwen said. "It was a rhetorical *WHAT*. Then why haven't you at least taken a vacation?"

"It wouldn't be right."

Gwen choked on a shred of lettuce and sour cream. "Oh, God, I really *am* in love with a crazy person."

"It really wouldn't be *right*," Stoner repeated, a little hurt.

"Stoner, my love, nobody on the face of the earth would question your ethics or your manners. But sometimes you have to take into consideration how people *feel* about things."

"I know that," she grumped.

Gwen took her hand. "I love you to death, Pebbles, and I didn't mean to criticize you or hurt your feelings. But don't you see…?"

"Yeah, yeah," Stoner said, feeling like a real jerk. "You're right. You're always right."

"That's not true," Gwen said. "*I* married Bryan Oxnard. *You* didn't."

"Well, you're always right about small things."

Gwen thought about it. "Yes," she said, "I do believe *you're* right about that."

Stoner looked over at her and felt a rush of emotion sweep over her like a gust of summer wind. "Gwen, I…I feel so much for you it scares me."

"And I love you so much," Gwen said in her low, velvet voice, "it terrifies me." She laughed affectionately…and sexily…and tightened her grip on Stoner's hand.

Stoner's body responded on cue, her skin opening and tingling.

Great, she thought. Lust in the middle of Cambridge. She cleared her throat. "I'll bet that student of yours can't wait to get home and call everyone she knows and tell them her former history teacher was holding hands with another woman in public."

"*I'll* bet she can't wait to tell them her former history teacher was holding hands with the woman who murdered her husband."

"I didn't murder him, Gwen. It was self-defense."

"I know," Gwen said, giving Stoner's hand a little squeeze and withdrawing her own. "But it's more fun this way. After all, these are the 'nineties.'"

Dessert and coffee…served by yet another waitperson…didn't bring her any closer to a decision.

"Look," Gwen said at last as she counted out the money for the tip, "you know you're going to do it, so let's stop by Marylou's as long as we're in Cambridge, and you can reassure yourself she won't care."

"Well…"

Gwen looked closely at her. "It's something else, isn't it? In addition to guilt."

"Sort of." She couldn't remember when she'd stopped being able to fool Gwen. In their four years together as friends and then lovers, Gwen had gotten to know her pretty well. Actually, that wasn't completely accurate. Stoner had *let* Gwen get to know her pretty well. She didn't regret it, but sometimes it was a little unnerving. "To be perfectly honest…"

"Always a good idea," Gwen said in an encouraging way.

"It's not just the Yuppies or whatever…I really am kind of afraid of the furniture." She brushed her hand through her hair. "I mean, the kind of place that has that kind of furniture."

Gwen took another glance at the brochure. "I see what you mean. On the other hand, it might help you get over your fear of history."

"This is *not* the way to do it. Honest. I'm from Rhode Island. Rhode Island is full of history. Rhode Island *reeks* of history. Being around history is not going to get me over my fear of history."

"Well," Gwen said with a sigh, "I guess I can't help you. Back home in Georgia, history is what we do best." She got up and took the check. "Stoner, you know and I know you're going to do it."

Stoner took a deep breath. "Yeah, okay, but only if..."

"If?"

"If you'll come along."

"I thought you'd never ask," Gwen said.

Marylou was delighted. More than delighted. "You don't know," she said, "how I've been praying for this. Now I can get our mess straightened out."

"There's still the missing Tidrow suitcase," Stoner began.

Her friend dismissed it with a gesture. "I put a trace on it yesterday."

"The charter to Naples is falling apart..."

"I can handle it, Stoner."

"Remember the Morocco disaster? The hi-jacking?"

Her friend looked at her patiently. "That was the work of terrorists, not travel agents." She got up from her desk, nearly knocking over a stack of mysterious paper slips that looked suspiciously like the copies of airline tickets for the past six months.

"Marylou, if those are what I think they are..."

"They are."

Stoner felt hysterical. "We're supposed to turn them in, Marylou. Those things are like money. If they start checking our records..."

"Oh, calm yourself." She rummaged through a cardboard box marked "fragile" and pulled out a box of Snackwell's Devil's Food cookies. "Those are copies of copies. You know I send the original copies in every week."

"Oh."

"I'm more organized than you think I am, Stoner. I'd think you'd have noticed that in nineteen years."

Stoner was amazed. "Have we known each other that long?"

"We have, indeed." Marylou extracted a cookie and consumed it lovingly.

"And in all that time you've never offered me a cookie."

"That's right, and I never will. Sugar isn't good for you."

"It's good for you?"

"Of course it is." Marylou rubbed her fingertips together to brush off the crumbs. "*I* have a metabolism."

"Everyone has a metabolism."

"Not like mine."

Stoner turned on her computer, just to see what American Airlines was up to. There seemed to be an inordinate number of available seats. She brought up the screen for Friday. Same thing. "What's with American?"

Marylou came around the desk and peered at her CRT. She smelled of chocolate and Dewberry bath and shower gel from the Body Shop. "Beats me. I haven't heard any rumors. Try United."

She punched up the United Airlines data base. They were booked solid. She tried Delta. Same result.

"Curious," said Marylou.

"Yeah. Are you still speaking to that guy that runs the American ticket counter out at Logan?"

"Of course I'm still speaking to him," Marylou said huffily. "I haven't been out with him."

Marylou firmly believed that the best way to get rid of a bothersome admirer was to date him. "It destroys the mystique," she was fond of saying.

Stoner found that hard to understand, since the better she got to know Marylou the more she liked her. Even after all this time, Marylou could surprise her. She supposed it was because Marylou liked to change and grow, and you never knew what direction she was going to do it in. On top of that, her loyalty to Stoner was as solid as rock, something Stoner treasured above everything else.

Men, she supposed, were interested in other things. Not only sex...though they were certainly interested in that to a pathological degree...but they seemed to want otherworldly, almost mythic qualities in a woman.

"Nonsense," Marylou had once said. "They want the mother they think they had but didn't."

Since Marylou Kesselbaum wasn't about to be any man's mother, real or otherwise, she was frequently a disappointment to them.

"Why don't you give him a call?" Stoner suggested. "See if he knows what's up."

"Good plan." Marylou grabbed another Snackwell and made a dive for the phone.

Stoner turned her attention back to her desk. The pile of things to do hadn't decreased since she'd been looking the other way. In fact, it seemed to have grown, and was at the point of reaching critical mass. The worst of it was the sorting, deciding what was vital to keep and move, and what could be thrown away. She knew the minute she decided something had outlived its usefulness—like the receipts from the money they'd paid back to a group of charter passengers when Pan Am went belly-up—and threw it away, the IRS would descend like crows on a corn field demanding to see documentation for their ten-year-old tax returns.

So the receipts went in the "To Be Moved" box. Which placed them under Marylou's jurisdiction, since the movers would be there on the fourteenth of the month, exactly five days after Stoner had abandoned the travel agency like a rat leaving a sinking ship, to go off and play detective for a group of people she'd never met. Guilt, and then worry, washed over her. It wasn't fair, no matter how much Marylou said it didn't bother her, to leave her with all this responsibility. Not fair at all. Besides, she'd probably get into conversation with the movers and talk them into taking her to lunch at one of her favorite restaurants and leave all their valuable documents sitting on the street in the rain or something...

"You're kidding," she heard Marylou say into the phone. "You're not kidding? You *must* be kidding."

"What?" Stoner mouthed silently.

"Hang on," Marylou said into the phone. "There's someone on the other line." She covered the mouthpiece with her hand. "Strike rumors."

"Really?"

"Just rumors."

"Who's striking?"

"Get a grip on your bra straps," said Marylou. "This one's a shocker." She paused for dramatic effect. "Food service."

Stoner guffawed. "No one stays away from an airline because they might not be fed. Not airline food."

"You're right." She turned back to the phone. "Sorry to keep you waiting. Okay, you've had your little joke. What's the real poop?" She listened. "Oh, them. Well, it's always something, isn't it?" She glanced in Stoner's direction and indicated 'bomb threat.'

Bomb threats. If it wasn't one thing these days, it was another. She wished people would just calm down and go about their business and stop trying to involve innocent by-standers who didn't even know what the issues were. But testosterone poisoning was at an all-time high on Planet Earth, and violence reigned.

Aunt Hermione's spirit guides assured her it was the last gasp of the dying Patriarchy, unwilling to give up without a fight, and that better days were ahead. The New Age dawning with birth pangs as the Earth came out of the Dark Ages and into the Era of Love, Light, and Life. Trouble was, the Guides had no sense of Time-as-we-know-it, and couldn't give any estimates as to how long they'd have to wait. "Maybe not in this lifetime," Aunt Hermione said, "though of course that's an artificial concept, too, since all time is happening simultaneously so it's really dawning right this minute."

Talking about Time and Space always made the inside of Stoner's head feel like a television screen when the cable's gone out—all gray snow and static.

"God," Marylou blustered as she hung up the phone, "I wish they'd tell us those things. What would it take, to type it into the Main Frames? What are we supposed to do, sit around watching CNN all the time so we'll know what to tell our clients? What if we'd gone ahead and scheduled people on those flights? And they'd gotten to the airport and discovered their flights weren't happening? Who'd they blame? Those of us who serve in the trenches, that's who."

"I absolutely agree," Stoner said. "I don't know what's going to happen after we move. We'll be even more remote than we are now. The whole industry could close down, and we probably wouldn't know it."

"It'll be better," Marylou insisted. "News gets around quicker in small towns."

"Yeah," Stoner said, "but what if it's all local news? I mean, people in Shelburne Falls might not be into airline gossip. We could end up totally out of the loop."

"Nonsense," Marylou said with breezy optimism. "They're into all kinds of gossip. Didn't you ever read Sinclair Lewis?"

She hadn't, but she had read Shirley Jackson. And what she'd read in Shirley Jackson didn't give her a good feeling about small towns.

The anxiety about their decision that she usually kept at bay came flooding back. "Marylou? Do you think we're making a mistake?"

"Not in the least. You hate the city. Gwen wants a break from teaching. Aunt Hermione's longing for a place with better psychic vibes. This building's going condo...a good five years after the end of the condo craze, a prescription for disaster if you ask me. And I have to start learning to live on my own."

Stoner smiled. "You won't be exactly living on your own. All of us in one huge old house."

"Yes," Marylou said, "but it'll be *my* house, not my mother's. That does seem like a step forward."

She had to admit it was. Though she'd never had the feeling there was anything wrong or neurotic about Marylou's living arrangements. No more so than her own, with Aunt Hermione. Marylou and Edith actually liked one another, the way Stoner and her aunt did. It was convenient, and there was no good reason not to. What did worry her, though, was living with Gwen—the first time she had ever actually shared living space with a lover. True, they had all agreed that they wouldn't look at the arrangement as LIVING TOGETHER, but all of them sharing a house. But that didn't change the fact that they would be under the same roof, every day, for meals, taking out the garbage and doing the dishes and cleaning and hearing each other's music and knowing who watched what on television, and how long everyone took in the bathroom...

It made her want to scream.

"You look awful," Marylou said.

"I'm frightened."

"It'll be *fine*," Marylou said with a wave of her hand. "We'll be a huge success." She took a bite of cookie, dribbling crumbs across her desk top. "One look at you and Gwen, and the entire lesbian population of Western Massachusetts will be flocking to our door."

"Maybe," Stoner said. "But maybe it's not politically correct to use a travel agent out there."

"Then we'll target the elderly population. Elderly people take to you. I think it's because you're always so polite."

"What if the only time they leave home is to go to Florida for the winter?"

Marylou wet her finger and set to work picking up chocolate crumbs. "They have to get there, don't they? And Aunt Hermione can bring in business from her clients and other psychics. Surely they don't all travel out-of-body." She gathered the crumbs into a little pile. "*My* contribution will to be to volunteer for civic-minded activities and meet wealthy and important people. I might even be invited to address the Rotary Club."

In spite of her apprehension, Stoner had to smile. She could picture

Marylou organizing bake sales for the Lassie League. Helping with the SPCA benefit flea dip. Going on overnights with the Girl Scouts. Pitching in at the Happy Sunset Nursing Home Christmas Bazaar…

"Well," Stoner admitted at last, "whatever happens, it won't be dull."

"Not for a minute. I promise." She rolled the pile of crumbs into a soft ball and popped it in her mouth.

Stoner grimaced. Gwen was only half right. *Both* of the Kesselbaums ate garbage. "You're going to miss her. Your mother, I mean."

"No doubt," Marylou said. "But you have no idea what it's like having a psychiatrist for a mother."

"No, but I know what it's like having your mother for a psychiatrist. She was very understanding."

"That's what I mean," Marylou said with an animated jangle of bracelets. "She's too understanding. She understands and understands until I want to scream."

"I always thought that was a good quality."

"In a shrink, it is. *Not* in a mother. My God, adolescence was hell. There was nothing I could do to get a rise out of her."

"When you were kidnapped, that got a rise out of her," Stoner suggested helpfully.

"Sure," Marylou countered. "And if she thinks I'm going to go around putting myself in harm's way just to get a rise out of her, she can go to her grave unrisen."

"People usually do. It's afterward they rise."

Marylou tore open a pack of Raptor Bites and threw one at her.

"Where in the world did you get this?" Stoner asked. Raptor Bites were definitely not Marylou's style.

"Some heathen child left it on my desk. Its mother was trying to arrange a trip to the Mall of America, and it wanted to go to Jurassic Park."

"I don't blame it," Stoner said.

"The Mall of America," Marylou declared, "is my idea of Heaven."

"Maybe you'll go there sometime."

"After I die, no doubt. If I don't rise." She began to sort the travel brochures into two piles, one on her desk and one on the floor.

Stoner watched her for a while. "Interesting system," she said at last.

"It's simple. These…" She indicated the pile on her desk. "…are the keepers. And these…" She pointed to the floor pile. "…are the losers." She tossed a couple of garishly colored folders onto the "losers" pile. "How's the packing going at home?"

"Fine. Aunt Hermione's very organized. I just do what she tells me."

Marylou glanced up. "You do what *she* tells you, and I might as well slit my wrists as give you even the tiniest suggestion?"

"It's not that I don't trust your judgment," Stoner said quickly. "Most of the stuff in the brownstone's hers, that's all."

"It never ceases to amaze me," Marylou remarked as she sorted another handful of folders, "how you can accumulate so much office stuff, and so few personal items."

Stoner thought about it. "I guess it's because I *know* what's important in my stuff, but this..." She waved her arm in a gesture that took in the office. "...we could need anything at any time."

"I see," said Marylou with great seriousness. "The operative concept is, whatever causes you the most anxiety gets to stay."

"Something like that, I guess."

"Then Gwen and I had better start working on our intimidation styles."

She couldn't help laughing. "That's not what it's about, Marylou. It's *things. Things* frighten me."

Marylou looked at her as if she were crazy, and silently offered her a stick of Clove gum. She turned it down.

It was true, though, no matter how crazy it sounded. Things did frighten her. They had a life of their own, and operated under rules that were different from people's rules. For instance, they could transform themselves into totally different entities on a whim. She had seen $20 bills turn into ATM machine receipts in her very wallet. They could appear and disappear at will. Music tapes and CDs were especially good at that. Once, a strange record had appeared in her collection. She'd never bought it. No one had given it to her. It didn't belong to anyone she knew. It claimed to be classical music, by a composer she'd never heard of, played by artists she'd never heard of. It was on top of the stack, and hadn't been there the last time she'd looked.

Aunt Hermione told her it was called an "apport," and had slipped through from a parallel universe.

This was not comforting.

But the worst thing about *things* was their ability to disguise themselves right in plain view. Get five or six things together, and they could combine themselves into senseless piles of color and shape, so dense you couldn't separate out the one you wanted—the unanswered letter or unpaid bill, for instance, from the stack of junk mail.

About this phenomenon, Aunt Hermione took a surprisingly terrestrial viewpoint, and suggested that Stoner might be getting to the age where she needed to think about glasses.

"Stoner."

She looked up.

"Do you realize you've been sitting there, motionless, for the past ten minutes?"

"I have?"

Marylou came over and perched on the edge of Stoner's desk. "Look," she said, "if this move has you crazy, we'll cancel it."

"It's too late. We've made all the arrangements..."

"Arrangements aren't carved in stone. Or, if we can't change them, we'll move and then turn around and move back."

She'd do it, too. Stoner felt a huge upsurge of affection and gratitude for her friend. "It's not the move. Not entirely. It's just…I don't know."

"Well," said Marylou conclusively, "*I* know. It's the change."

"The Change of Life?"

"Of location. You're afraid of change. Always have been."

Stoner looked down at her desk. "Maybe."

"No 'maybes' about it." She brushed her fingers through Stoner's hair. "Once you find something or someone who makes you feel safe, you hang onto it like a dog with a T-bone steak."

"How would you know?" Stoner said irritably. She knew Marylou was right, and it embarrassed her and made her prickly. "You never had a dog."

"No," Marylou said, and moved behind her and massaged the back of Stoner's neck, "but I'll bet you, within one month of the move, I'll be living with one." She tucked one finger under Stoner's chin and pulled her head up to look her in the eye. "Won't I?"

"Maybe." A dog. They were going to live in the country, and she could have a dog.

"Or is it something else?" Marylou asked.

"Is what something else?"

"What's troubling you."

Stoner shook her head. "I'm okay."

"You are *not*," declared Marylou, "okay."

She knew Marylou was right. She wasn't okay. She wanted this move, that was the trouble. Wanted it so much she might have forced it on the rest of them. Wanted it so much she might have manipulated…

"Responsible," Marylou guessed. "You feel responsible for all of us. You think we don't want this, and we're just doing it to please you, and you'll have our unhappiness on your hands for the rest of your life."

"You know too much," Stoner grumbled, and glared at the floor. "I'll bet you've been reading your mother's case notes."

"No can do. She keeps them locked in the trunk of her car. I *know* you, old pal. It's as simple as that. And you know me. You might as well get used to the idea. Frankly, I rather like it."

"Well," Stoner said reluctantly, "I guess I do, too."

"So let it go, Stoner. Go solve the Mystery of the Troubled Theater. By the time you get back, the worst will be over."

Stoner faked a frown of cautious disbelief. "Famous last words," she said.

CHAPTER 2

The lobby of The Cottage, torn between its casual function and its formal atmosphere, had thrown its vote to the side of formal. Instead of a check-in counter, there was an antique writing desk bearing an open registration book (leather bound), a blotter, a quill pen with ball point tip, and a tap bell. There was no one in sight.

Marylou removed her white elbow-length gloves one finger at a time and looked around with palpable approval. She usually hated to travel—"Being Carried Along," she called it—but her curiosity had gotten the better of her. Once she had made the commitment she had, as she pointed out every five miles between Boston and Bangor, dressed for the occasion. Old-fashioned duster, wide-brimmed hat with flowing veil, and sunglasses. Gwen claimed it had given her second-hand Honda a new lease on life.

Stoner, struggling into the room under the weight of her suitcases, reminded herself that she was dressed for driving, too. Especially if she had to change a tire. She'd spent the majority of the morning washing and ironing her favorite 70s regulation Feminist work shirt and polishing her regulation Feminist hiking boots. Her jeans were new, but not stiff. "I'm making a statement," she'd explained to Gwen. "I refuse to be intimidated by furniture." Trouble was, she suspected she looked exactly as if she were intimidated and trying not to show it.

In fact, Gwen was the only one of them who really looked appropriate. In her slacks and light weight shirt and running shoes, she was dressed for summer. For hot, un-air-conditioned summer.

The Cottage was hot. And it wasn't air-conditioned.

Marylou swept off her hat, made a quick appraising trip through the living room and declared The Cottage "Perfect."

"I'm glad you like it," Stoner said. "You can take my place."

"Nonsense," said Marylou. "It's you they want. Besides, I can't imagine sleeping under the same roof with strangers."

"You slept under the same roof with strangers at Walt Disney World," Gwen pointed out.

"Yes, I did. And, as you might recall, it was a highly unpleasant experience."

"I thought you enjoyed being kidnapped."

"There were anxious moments," Marylou said. "This is not my year for anxious moments."

Stoner put her suitcases down with a thud. "I'll see if I can find someone."

"One does not..." Marylou announced, "...scurry about the corridors in this sort of place demanding service."

"She's been reading F. Scott Fitzgerald," Stoner explained to Gwen.

"In that case, we certainly have to do what's appropriate, don't we?" Gwen said. She slammed the palm of her hand down onto the tap bell.

Stoner cringed.

A door banged in the distance. A cheery voice sang, "Coming." Footsteps pit-patted along a hallway.

Stoner steeled herself. All right, she was here to do a job, to help out a group of lesbians—or at least wimmin—in need. Regardless of the surroundings, or how much her mother would like them, she had to rise above her insecurities and take charge.

"Sherry here!"

The woman was short and thin, with round cheeks and round eyes. Her curly, reddish-blonde hair formed an aura around her head. A rather healthy aura, Stoner thought. Plenty of color, plenty of depth. Still, it verged on the side of red, and Aunt Hermione always recommended caution when interpreting a red aura. "Sometimes a sign of vigor and passion, but often signifies rage," she was fond of saying. "One must judge each case by its merits. As in the visible world, so in the invisible. Or is it the other way around?"

Sherry was dressed in a long, flowing brocade skirt—roses on a black background—and a white silk blouse with long sleeves and pearl buttons. She wore a pink scarf around her neck, and patent leather Capezios. Amazingly, she wasn't even perspiring. Like a painting, a Nineteenth Century portrait of a Lady. Right at home in The Cottage. All she lacked was a bouquet of roses tossed lightly across one arm.

"I'm so sorry I wasn't here to meet you," Sherry said. "A minor disaster in the kitchen."

Marylou nodded smugly, giving Stoner a 'I knew only an emergency would keep the proprietor of a place like this from greeting us at the door' look.

"The dairy delivered salted butter. Can you imagine it? I've told them a thousand times, 'We do not use salted butter at The Cottage.' It's so low-rent. Would you like a glass of wine?"

"Yes, indeed!" Marylou nearly shouted with enthusiasm. Obviously, Sherry Dodder was Marylou's kind of people.

"Burgundy or chablis?"

"Please, chablis," said Marylou. "It's much too hot for burgundy."

"A woman after my own heart." Sherry took an ancient key from her pocket and began unlocking a small porcelain-knobbed door beneath the stairs. She looked questioningly at Stoner and Gwen.

"No, thanks," Gwen said.

Stoner shook her head. She was going to feel completely out-of-place here. The Cottage was a dreadful place, no doubt packed with dreadful people. Whatever this women's theater group was, they probably spent their free time reading Moliére, and discussing Art, and whether Shakespeare's 47th Sonnet followed a rhyme scheme common in its day or broke new ground, or something like that.

The small, heavy door swung open noiselessly to reveal a miniature cupboard. It was well stocked with glasses, bottles of liquor, and exotic snacks like honey-roasted almonds. "There's a nice little one in here," Sherry was saying. "But it's really not at its best without Boursin, is it?"

"Absolutely not," Marylou said. Her eyes were glittering. She turned to Stoner. "This is what we need in the new office." She indicated a refrigerator under the mail cubby holes. "Look, Stoner."

Sherry wheeled around. "Stoner McTavish?" She held out her hand. "I'm so sorry. I should have recognized you right away."

Stoner wondered what there was about herself that should have been immediately recognizable. Her clothing? Intensity? Was there a problem-solving sort of air about her? She felt Gwen nudge her and took Sherry's hand for a shake. "Nice to meet you," she said.

She hadn't expected the woman's handshake to be so firm and steady. She seemed like the grasp-and-let-go type. Or the keep-a-pocket-of-air-between-your-palm-and-mine type. Or even the limp fish type. But Sherry Dodder's handshake was...well, frankly, butch. "And this is Gwen Owens," she said quickly, out of politeness and eager to cover her confusion. "And my business partner, Marylou Kesselbaum."

Marylou pulled a business card out of her string purse. "Kesselbaum and McTavish, Travel Agents. We make travel almost as much fun as staying home."

The woman took the card and laughed. "That's wonderful. And you must be the Senior partner."

Stoner looked at Marylou. "You must?"

"The order of the names," Marylou explained patiently. "Actually, we're equal partners. We chose the order because it was more rhythmic that way."

"I see," Sherry said. She looked back to Stoner. "Stoner. An unusual name."

"I was named for Lucy B. Stone," Stoner said.

"Oh, I envy you. I think I was named for an alcoholic drink." She turned to Gwen. "Gwen Owens, was it?"

"Yes," Gwen said. Stoner thought she sensed a bit of electricity in the air around her.

"That's an English name?"

"Welsh." Yes, definitely electricity, and more than a bit of it. Gwen was annoyed, with anger rising.

"I'm very sorry," Sherry said, and seemed to mean it. "That was really awkward of me. Nasty business, that whole England-Wales thing. Remind me not to toast the Queen at dinner." She gave a hearty laugh. "Just kidding."

Gwen presented her with a tight-lipped, insincere smile.

Sherry didn't notice. She poured a bit of wine into a thin-stemmed glass and handed it to Marylou.

Marylou tasted it and sighed with delight. "Perfect. Exactly the right temperature." She perched on the edge of a straight-backed, horsehair-stuffed chair. "Cheers."

"I can't tell you how relieved I am that you could make it," Sherry said. "I've been half out of my mind with worry."

"I'm so sorry," Gwen said, her voice dripping ice.

Stoner gave her hand a warning squeeze. "Have you had other incidents?" she asked.

"Nothing I can put my finger on. The usual theater crises, of course. Yesterday there was a bench that had been painted. The day before, we thought. But when our lead actor sat on it, it was fresh. Her clothes were ruined. No one would own up to having done it." She shrugged. "Minor things like that. Not dangerous, but annoying and time-consuming. We're already three days behind schedule."

"How long have you been doing this?"

"This is my first year as producer," Sherry said. "That's because we rotate, so every woman gets a chance to learn and share."

"And last year you did...?"

Sherry looked down at the floor as if shy. "Well, I don't like to brag, but I had the lead."

"Don't you miss the attention?" Gwen asked.

"Good Heavens, no!" Sherry exclaimed with a little laugh. "It's a tremendous amount of responsibility."

"So is producing," Stoner pointed out.

"But the mistakes you make aren't made in front of an audience. Besides, it's not so different from running The Cottage. Organizing, dealing with details and people. It comes more naturally to me."

"Yes," Gwen said, "I can see where that might be the case."

What was going on here? "Are you okay?" Stoner mumbled to Gwen.

Gwen seemed startled. "Sure."

"Probably tired from the trip up," Marylou said, eaves-dropping. "It was endless." She held out her empty glass. "May I have just a touch more wine?" she asked. "To fortify me for the drive back."

Sherry refilled her glass eagerly.

"Marylou doesn't like to travel," Stoner explained. "It takes a lot out of her."

"Would you like to spend the night?" Sherry asked with a concerned knitting of the eyebrows. "We have plenty of room."

"Thank you, no," Marylou said. "My mother's picking me up. She's doing a workshop over in Bangor."

"Dr. Kesselbaum's a psychiatrist," Stoner said.

"Well," said Sherry, "I'll certainly have to watch what I say around her."

"Just don't tell her any of your dreams," Marylou warned. "Two sentences of dream fragment and she knows your entire life history."

"Of course she knows yours," Gwen said. "She's your mother."

"So you can imagine how precise she can get," Marylou said with a roll of her eyes.

"Are there other guests here, besides the theater women?" Stoner asked. "If not, we're going to be conspicuous..."

"Not to worry," Sherry said perkily. "On the third floor we have a young couple. They just went through a commitment ceremony, so I don't imagine we'll see much of them. Also a group of five from Dyke Hike."

"Dyke Hike?"

"A backpacking and mountaineering support group. Sort of like an outing club. Though I suppose nowadays 'Outing Club' could have very different connotations."

Even Gwen had to laugh.

"If they're here to backpack, I don't suppose we'll see much of them, either," Stoner said.

"You'll see them," Sherry said. "They come here every year to plan the next year's schedule of events. Sort of like a retreat." She turned to the registration book. "I've put you in room 214, on the second floor. Most of the theater women are on that floor, so you'll get to observe them without arousing suspicion. We have a few rooms on the first floor, but they're reserved for our elderly and disabled guests." She smiled apologetically. "I'm afraid we're not politically correct, no elevator. But I plan to renovate next year and bring The Cottage up to A.D.A. standards. I just hope it won't disturb any of the sleeping ghosts."

"Ghosts?" Stoner asked. "Is The Cottage haunted?"

"Not as far as I know. Nothing there to hang a reputation on. But these old places..."

"Stoner likes ghosts," Marylou said. "Her aunt's a medium."

"She's not a medium, Marylou, she's a clairvoyant. And I don't like ghosts, they make me uneasy. And I wish you'd call them 'spirits,' not 'ghosts.' It's more...more..."

"Politically correct?" Marylou suggested.

"Dignified. Respectful."

"Well, I don't think we have any," Sherry said.

Stoner hesitated. She hated to bring up anything as crass as money, but there was a worry she had to get off her chest. "Look," she said, "I really appreciate you offering to let us stay free, but...well, isn't that cutting into your income, giving up a room like that, to say nothing of the meals..."

Sherry laughed. "No problemo, my dears. As you can gather, the Cottage isn't even filled, so you'd hardly be displacing a paying guest. I make the majority of my profit during the winter. We're close to a number of downhill areas, and we have cross-country right here. I open the inn to families then." She gave them a conspiratorial wink. "You might say I let the hets subsidize the women's community. A nice irony, don't you think?"

"Very nice," Gwen murmured.

"And the theater pays me a bit—not enough to cover expenses, really more like an honorarium. I suppose that means the Patriarchy is subsidizing alternative art. Jessie Helms would be beside himself."

Stoner had to laugh. "Tell me about the theater group," she said.

"It's called *Demeter Ascending, a Women's Theater of Affirmation and Empowerment*."

"Catchy title," Marylou said.

"That's the name of the group. The play's *Not Quite Titled*."

"Well," Marylou said, "I don't know much about theater, but I do know you have to start your publicity early. And you're already into rehearsal. Don't you think you should have a title by now?"

"That is the title *'Not Quite Titled*, an original sophisticated satirical Feminist musical comedy in the tradition of Noel Coward.' "

"I see," Stoner said. Noel Coward? They were looking to a man for their inspiration? A talented and funny one, and reputed to verge on gay, not exactly Normal Mailer…but a man?

"It's being written collectively," Sherry said. "We've been working on it since last year."

Stoner nodded sympathetically. "I know how gruelling that can be." Support groups, self-help groups, even twelve-step programs had broken up over less.

"But loads of fun," Sherry said. "We're in hysterics half the time. Who said Feminism has no sense of humor?"

"Not me," Marylou offered. "I never said that. Did you ever hear me say that, Stoner?"

"Only when you lost the local N.O.W. chapter election."

Somewhere in the back of the Inn a screen door slammed. "Uh-oh," Sherry said, looking around and dropping her voice. "We have company." She handed Stoner the quill pen and indicated the register. "If you'll just sign in, Stoner and Gwen, I'll show you to your room," she announced loudly. "We have a women's theater company staying here. If you like, I'll see if you can sit in on a rehearsal."

"That would be nice." Stoner handed her back the pen and mouthed "Good thinking."

"I don't think anyone will bother you," she went on as Gwen signed in. "Now and then things get a little boisterous, at the end of the day. Theater is such demanding, disciplined work that we need to let off a little steam…"

"Endorphins," Marylou said in an explanatory way.

"But we generally do our partying in the barn."

"Very wise," Marylou approved.

Sherry turned to her. "By the way, you're welcome to stay for dinner if you like."

"Thank you, but it depends on when my mother gets here."

"If it's awkward for you," Stoner said eagerly, watching Marylou's hand creep toward the menu that lay beneath the register on the little writing table, "Marylou can have my place. I'm not at all hungry. Seldom am. It's just how I am."

"Oh, you are not," Marylou said. Her fingers touched the menu. "You're afraid there'll be things you can't pronounce. You hate food you can't pronounce."

"Well," said Sherry with a smile, "I'm sure you'll find the food here very pronounceable." Gwen handed her the pen. "That should do it. You're in room 214. Follow me."

As Sherry turned to lead them away, Marylou snatched the menu and slipped it beneath her voluminous duster.

"So," Marylou said as she lounged on one of the two single beds with the pineapple bedposts and perused her purloined menu, "what's your opinion?"

"It seems nice enough," Stoner said. She looked around the room, and tried to get a sense of it. The floor was polished wood, its hardness broken by a large braided rug. The rug was old, bits of straw or horse hair or something poking through. Single beds with white candle wick spreads...she really didn't like single beds. They'd mastered the art of making love in them without falling out. But single beds made cuddling awkward and uncomfortable.

"I was referring to your hostess."

Stoner shrugged and held two pairs of socks up to the light. Inspired by Gwen, Goddess of Impeccable Packing, she had vowed to be neater and more organized, and was arranging her socks in the drawer in descending order of brightness. It wasn't easy, as most of her socks were black or navy blue. "I guess she's okay. Hard to tell after only fifteen minutes."

"Not for Gwen," Marylou said. "She made up her mind in ten seconds."

"I don't like her," Gwen muttered. She slammed a handful of underwear into a drawer and attacked a shirt with a hanger.

"Clearly," Marylou said.

"That business with the wine, Lucy B. Stone, the Welsh-English thing. The woman panders."

"Of course she panders. She's in business. In business, you pander. These are the 'nineties.'"

"I'll bet Stoner doesn't."

"Stoner can't pull it off. That's why she gets to track down the lost luggage and reconfirm cruise reservations. It doesn't require pandering."

"It does, too," Stoner said, not wanting to be thought deficient. "I'm so good at it you never notice."

Gwen jammed the shirt and hanger into the closet and brutalized another. "Well, I hate it. It's so...so..."

"American?" Marylou suggested.

"Sleazy."

"I suppose. But hardly up there with drug dealing. Why does it annoy you so much?"

"It's dishonest," Gwen said. She took aim at another shirt. "Manipulative."

"Manipulation," said Marylou, "is also American."

"You don't mind because it was you she was pandering to," Gwen snapped.

"Actually," Marylou said calmly, "I think she pandered to all of us equally."

Gwen shoveled the rest of her underwear into a drawer and grabbed her empty suitcase and stalked into the closet. "I don't like her, and I don't have to like her if I don't like her."

"Of course you don't," Stoner said. She looked around for a place to put her books and note pad and camera and pens and all the other things she never used back in civilization but was sure she'd be miserable without. The only writing table was nearly covered by a large antique pitcher and basin. "I'm only doing a job for her, I'm not bringing her home."

"Thank God for small favors."

"If you don't mind my saying so," Marylou opined, "you're over reacting just the teeniest bit."

There was only silence from the closet.

Stoner found herself in the strange position of agreeing with Marylou. Gwen was over reacting, and in a very un-Gwen-like way. Gwen was usually the one who trusted and liked people on sight, whether she had any reason to or not. In fact, it usually took a considerable amount of concerted effort to arouse Gwen's dislike or suspicion. It had gotten her into serious trouble on more than one occasion.

"Gwen?" Stoner dropped her arm load of personal articles onto the bed Marylou hadn't commandeered. She went to the closet entrance. "Is something wrong?"

"Fine. Everything's just fine," Gwen replied in a tone of voice that said it clearly wasn't fine at all.

"Come on, what's wrong?"

"It's just such fun," Gwen said, "being the only person who sees what everyone else doesn't."

"I know," Stoner said, having been in that position herself. "Look, maybe you're right. Maybe something's uniquely wrong with Sherry. It's not a big deal."

"If it's not a big deal, why is Marylou harping on it?"

"You're both harping on it."

"I'm harping worse than Gwen's harping," Marylou offered as she snatched Stoner's pen and made a note in the margin of the menu. "I don't know why."

"Well, I wish you'd both stop," Stoner said. "This is an uncomfortable enough place. I count on the two of you to keep me sane in places like this. So if you don't mind..."

Gwen peered out of the closet. Marylou looked at her. They both looked at Stoner.

"I'm sorry," Gwen said, and touched her arm. "I don't know what got into me."

"Neither do I," said Marylou. "Maybe the place is haunted. Evil spirits lurking about, giving off negative vibrations, causing dissonance among friends, the whole spooky bit."

Stoner tried to open herself to the subtle vibrations in the room. She couldn't pick up anything. "I don't feel it." Not that that meant anything. She really wasn't good at sensing unseen energies—other than those emanating from people in bad moods. She was very, very good at sensing those. But Aunt Hermione assured her she could develop the skill if she practiced and believed. "Nothing," she said, trying to believe.

"Doesn't surprise me," Marylou said. "With a menu like this, there can't be anything wrong with the place." She thought for a moment. "Unless the cooking is terrible, in which case this menu is a cruel hoax and I shall personally see to it that no one ever comes here again."

"I'm sure the food is fine," Stoner said. She wandered over to the window. Beyond the ivory lace curtains, she could see across the circular drive and carefully mowed lawn to the woods. They were deep hemlock woods. The lower branches of the trees had been pruned and removed, giving a clear view of the forest floor, softly carpeted by pine needles. A rough barn stood at the edge of the sloping lawn. Through the trees, a lake glinted in the distance. If things got too awful, she could go over there and smell the trees and earth, and touch the water, and cleanse her soul of history and formality.

As she watched, a large, long, very white Lincoln Continental convertible pulled into the drive and circled the sundial. Its tires crunched luxuriously over the gravel. It stopped, the motor purred to silence, and a tall, wiry woman in gauzy slacks and blouse floated from the driver's seat like a cloud. Stoner raised the screen and leaned out. "Hi, Edith!"

The woman shaded her eyes with one hand and squinted in her direction near-sightedly. "Stoner, dear. Is my next-of-kin with you?"

Behind her, Marylou sighed heavily.

"She's here," Stoner called. "Can you stay for dinner?"

Edith slipped her gauzy scarf from around her neck. "I'm afraid I wouldn't be good company. The workshop was dreadful, and I'm in a foul mood. I can't think of anything but Burger King."

Marylou let out a soft, sobbing groan.

"What was the problem?" Stoner asked.

"They were silent. Utterly silent. The entire Mental Health Department of Maine is suffering from collective verbal constipation."

"For God's sake," Marylou whispered, "tell her to be quiet. She'll disgrace us in front of everyone."

"Don't be silly," Stoner said. She knew it was immature and probably neurotic and nasty of her, but she couldn't resist enjoying the sight of Marylou—whom she loved with all her heart, but who constantly made her want to crawl down a hole and pull it in after her with embarrassment—discomposed herself. "Nobody's going to judge you by your mother's behavior."

"They are."

"Are not," Gwen said. She came to stand beside Stoner and gave a wave. "Hey, Edith."

"Hey, yourself, Miss Jefferson, Georgia." Edith ran both hands through her hair. A soft breeze caught her scarf and set it fluttering. "Long time no see."

"Too long," Gwen said.

"Is Marylou coming?"

Stoner glanced around. Marylou had covered her head with a pillow.

"In a minute," Gwen said.

"Come on," Stoner said, going to the bed and shaking Marylou by the shoulder.

"I don't want to go to Burger King," Marylou whimpered.

"Maryloooo…" Edith's voice floated on the late afternoon quiet.

Marylou grabbed Stoner's sleeve. "Don't make me go, please, I'll do anything you want, forever. Just don't make me go to Burger King."

Stoner laughed. "You know you can't get out of it. Once her mind's made up…"

"Marylou! Please hustle your butt! I'm hallucinating a Whopper!"

That did it. Marylou jumped from the bed, grabbed her duster, and scurried from the room.

"She's on the way," Gwen called down.

Edith Kesselbaum grinned. "I can always get what I want from her," she said, "by quoting junk food menus in public."

"I'll remember that," Gwen said.

Downstairs, a screen door slammed. Marylou emerged at a flat-out run and hurled herself into the Lincoln's passenger seat.

"Have a nice vacation," Edith called.

"Will do," Stoner said.

"Y'all come back and see us real soon," Gwen shouted. "We'll go to Dairy Queen for Brazier Burgers."

Marylou ducked down into the leg well under the dash.

With a brisk wave of her arm, Edith climbed in, slammed the car into gear and negotiated the circular drive on two wheels.

"You know," Gwen said, slipping her arm around Stoner's waist, "it's hard to imagine Edith as your therapist."

"It was pretty scary at times," Stoner agreed. "But she kept me alive. She made life seem manageable."

"Edith doesn't manage life," Gwen said with a smile. "She browbeats it. It's a skill we should all cultivate."

Stoner leaned her face against Gwen's hair. It was soft and smooth and smelled of salt and freshly cut grass. Unconsciously, her hand found Gwen's, a gesture that had become as much a part of her life as breathing. She felt the warmth of her. "I wish we didn't have to leave the room," she said.

Gwen nuzzled closer to her. "Is that lust, or fear of the social life?"

"A little of both, I guess. Do you mind?"

"Don't be silly," Gwen said. She was silent for a moment, looking out over the lawn. Late afternoon sun made long shadows of the sun dial and concrete urns filled with petunias. "Let's find out."

"It's this place," Stoner explained over dinner. "I couldn't get my mother off my mind."

Gwen nodded sympathetically. "I know what you mean."

Stoner glanced up at her. "You didn't seem to be having any trouble."

"Just because it's such a Yankee Magazine kind of place. If it had anything Southern about it, you'd have seen trouble."

"I'm sorry, anyway."

"Will you please stop apologizing?" Gwen said. "Life is long and that was one hour of it."

"You know I love you."

"Of course I know. And sex isn't the Olympic Games of love. Now can we order?"

Stoner ran her hand through her hair. "I don't know what to order."

"Use the menu Marylou left for you. She marked everything you'd like."

"She marked escargot. I can't eat snails. They live under rotten boards. People trap them in gardens. They drown them in saucers of beer. In the dark."

Gwen took the menu from her and looked at it. "She didn't mark the escargot, Stoner. She marked the item beneath it." She handed it back.

"Oh," Stoner said sheepishly. "Broiled swordfish with garlic and lemon sauce. I can eat that. I think."

"Thank God," Gwen sighed. She motioned to the waitress and ordered. "This place really does give you the heebie-jeebies, doesn't it?" she asked when the young woman had withdrawn.

"Really."

"Know what I think? I think you had a very nasty childhood."

"No worse than yours. Not as bad. My father didn't beat up on me."

"That's true," Gwen said. "But I didn't live in a constant atmosphere of disapproval. Besides, I didn't have to go through adolescence with them."

"Yeah. You got to do that with a homophobic grandmother."

"She wasn't homophobic then."

"She didn't know you were a lesbian then."

Gwen laughed. "Neither did I, so it didn't make much difference." She pressed her finger into the bowl of a spoon, her thumb into the end of the handle, and lifted the spoon from the table. "Bet you can't do that."

"I'd just drop it on the floor and attract attention."

"You know what?" Gwen said as she peered at the spoon. "This is sterling silver. Not stainless steel, not silver plate. Sterling silver."

"Goes with the linen napkins and tablecloths, I guess."

"The rose buds are real, too." Gwen put the spoon down. "This is one fancy place, all right. I'm glad Sherry's paying our expenses."

"Doesn't seem right," Stoner said. "She's losing money."

Gwen shrugged. "Guess she can afford it. Anyway, the place isn't completely booked. It's not as if we're replacing paying guests."

Only half the tables in the dining room were taken. Two substantial, gray-haired women, one in a wheel chair, sat touching fingers by the windows that looked out on the lowering sun. Now and then they glanced at the flock of robins feeding on the lawn. Most of the time they gazed at each other as if in utter amazement and wonder at being together.

"Imagine what their lives were like growing up," Gwen said. "They must feel as if they've landed on another planet."

The Dyke Hike group—ruddy, rugged, and boisterous—had captured the table nearest the lobby. Five women in identical short khaki shorts, thick socks, heavy boots, plaid camp shirts, and deeply tanned, unshaven legs. They were drinking red wine and shrieking over a near-accident involving sheer granite rock. Clearly, the organizers had stolen a few hours from organizing and program planning to have a bit of adventure. They didn't seem to be at all intimidated by the furniture or silverware.

Dinner arrived.

"Has it occurred to you," Gwen asked as she lifted a fork full of Brook Trout Meunière, "...this is excellent, by the way. Want a taste?"

Stoner shook her head. It was one of those Trout things, cooked complete with head or tail. She'd never been able to eat meat that looked like what it really was.

Gwen took another bite. "We don't really know what we're getting ourselves into, do we? She said there'd been 'mysterious accidents,' or 'suspicious happenings,' or something. That could cover a pretty wide range of things."

" 'Unexplained accidents and injuries' was the way she put it," Stoner said. Her sword fish was tender and tasty and didn't look like what it was.

"Which could mean anything from skinned knees to attempted murder."

"She probably would have mentioned attempted murder." She tried the salad. It was light, crisp, and delicately flavored with dressing. The rolls were freshly made, warm and yeasty. "She runs a good kitchen."

" 'Unexplained accidents' could mean poisoning." Gwen scooped up a bite of Lyonnaise potatoes. "Food poisoning."

The French doors were open. From outside came the evening liquid chirp of robins. A power mower clattered in the distance. A screen door slammed.

"It's not like you," Gwen said. "You're usually so thorough. You'd want to know all the ins and outs of a thing before you took it on."

"I know." She had to admit it, she was a little puzzled by her own behavior. As Aunt Hermione would say, it just wasn't a Capricorn kind of thing to do. But this was a lesbian sister asking for her help. So what if she'd never met her? When a sister needs you, you help, simple.

Stoner couldn't keep from smiling at herself, a little wryly. Twelve years ago, when she was young and idealistic, every woman she knew thought that way. The pre-Reagan years, the years of Sisterhood and a brave new Women's World. Before the backlash and the burn out. Before the world moved on.

Like the rest of her generation, Stoner had learned—with a fair amount of pain—that being women didn't mean you'd exchanged penises for haloes. The trouble was, she kept forgetting it.

"You have that look," Gwen said gently.

"Look?"

"That Remembering the Women's Movement look, kind of sad and disillusioned."

"I guess so." She felt the familiar anxiety at being understood. She'd tried so hard to get over it instead of simply running away. But even now she could feel the mask trying to slide over her face. She pushed at it. "I miss it."

"So do I," Gwen said. "I wasn't as involved as you but there's a small hollow place in my heart, too." She took a sip of coffee. "Know what the miracle was for me? For the first time in our lives, it was all right to like women. I don't mean as lovers, necessarily. As friends. We'd never been allowed to like women before, remember?"

Stoner nodded. She recalled conversations between her mother and her mother's friends. Always about things like how much more interesting men were to talk to than women. Even though the women talked about who was doing what, and why, and wondered about Life—while the men mostly argued about the best series of roads to take from City A to City B, or whose car got the best mileage. She never did figure out what it was about road maps that made them more interesting than lives. But that was before she'd learned about the Patriarchy and how whatever It/They did was—by definition—all that really mattered.

"We were going to expose it all and change the world," she said.

Gwen reached over and took her hand. "You still might. I have great faith."

But before they could really get the Revolution going, Ronald Reagan was in the White House.

"How did Reagan get elected?" Stoner asked.

"I think," Gwen said, "it had to do with Iran, hostages, and the U.S. Olympic Hockey Team. Or, as we say in Jockdom, 'Team U.S.A.'."

"I never met anyone who voted for him, did you?"

"Not in the People's Republic of Massachusetts," Gwen said. "But I'll bet everyone in my home town did. He was the greatest thing to hit Georgia since Jefferson Davis."

Stoner thought about King's Grant, Rhode Island, where she had been raised. All the houses were set back from the streets, all the lawns mowed, no dogs wandering around. Lots of white paint, white lies, and white people. "He was in my home town, too."

"You know," Gwen said. She was stirring her salad with the tip of her fork and peering at it suspiciously. "You're always promising to take me to King's Grant, and you never do."

"I'd like to, but I'm afraid I'll see one of my old school mates or revert to the age of twelve or something."

"Well, that would be pretty horrible, wouldn't it?" She turned over a green leaf and peered closer. "This is organic lettuce."

Stoner leaned forward to look. "How can you tell?"

Gwen pointed her fork at a small black something that looked as if it might once have been alive. "Bug."

"Want to send it back?"

"No," Gwen said as she pushed the corpse aside. "It can't eat much."

"Not unless it has friends."

"Is there a problem?"

They looked up to see Sherry standing by their table. Gwen's smile turned stiff. "No problem," she said sweetly. "Just a little fauna in the flora."

"Oh, yuck!" Sherry snatched the plate and called across the dining room. "Michelle!"

Their waitress came forward.

"Take this back to the kitchen and bring us another. And, for God's sake, have them check the lettuce." She shoved the plate at Michelle. "I'll inspect it myself." She turned back to the table. "I hate bugs in the food."

"Listen," Stoner said as the waitress left, "it's no big deal. It happens all the time."

"Not here," Sherry insisted.

"My aunt's an organic gardener, and she says lettuce without holes or bugs is a really bad sign. Full of pesticides."

"Your aunt doesn't have to answer to the truly strange and particular in this world," Sherry said. "Or does she?"

"Only the Virgos. But she doesn't get many of them."

"Well, there you are," Sherry said with finality.

"Would you like to join us?" Gwen asked with cloying politeness.

"Yes, I would." Sherry pulled out a chair and dropped into it and turned to Gwen. "I feel as if you and I have gotten off on the wrong foot, and I'd like to try to fix it."

Gwen turned a little red and looked down at her lap, too honest to deny it but embarrassed at getting caught.

"Look," Sherry said, "I know I came on strong at first. Sometimes I'm kind of…well, kind of pushy, you know what I mean?"

"Pushy," Gwen said thoughtfully. "Maybe not exactly…"

"Too excitable, bouncy, eager to please."

"Eager to please is close." She looked up, ready to forgive and get back to her usual state of expecting the best from everyone. "But, really, it's not…"

Sherry rubbed the heel of her hand on the center of her forehead.

"Goddess, I hate it when I get like that. It always happens when I'm exhausted, like I have to pump up the energy and keep it pumped up."

"I understand that," Gwen said. "Running an inn must be kind of like teaching. You're on all the time."

"It's not one tenth as hard," Sherry said with a dismissive flap of her hand. "I wouldn't last five minutes in a class room. But it takes its toll." She fiddled with the edge of the table cloth. "And your friend Marylou...you know how, when you're strung out and off-center, anyone with a really strong personality can kind of set the energy level?"

"I can see that," Stoner said. Even though her own reaction when Marylou went high-energy was to become practically comatose, she'd seen her affect other people that way. And this afternoon Marylou had definitely been in overdrive.

"Not that I'm trying to say it's her fault," Sherry insisted as she moved the bud vase a millimeter closer to the center of the table. "Please don't think that. I'm just trying to...well, I hope you won't judge me by this afternoon."

"It's fine," Gwen said. "I appreciate you explaining."

There was noise from the distance. Banging, shouting, laughing. The theater women coming up from the barn.

Stoner leaned forward. "We really need to talk about...you know. Soon."

"True." Sherry frowned thoughtfully. "Tonight, after dinner. There's a small tavern off the living room. It's dark. We can talk there."

"Do the theater women hang out there?"

"Most of them. They like to let off steam after rehearsals." She gave a little laugh. "I already told you that, didn't I? To tell you the truth, sometimes they get...well, overly raucous. I find myself making excuses."

"I don't think the tavern would be the best place," Stoner said. "Someone might overhear us. At best, it would look suspicious, huddling there with our heads together." She turned to Gwen. "Don't you think so? Or would it be a good cover?"

"Suspicious," Gwen said. "Huddling. Heads. Dark place. Definitely suspicious."

Sherry looked at Stoner with large eyes. "You really think it's one of the women, don't you?"

"I don't have an opinion," Stoner said. "All I know is what you told me in your letter. But we should be on the safe side."

"You're absolutely right." She aligned the salt and pepper shakers to be parallel to the edge of the table. "There's the living room. That's hardly used at night. But you have to go through it to get to the bar."

"Maybe our room," Gwen suggested.

Sherry shook her head. "Someone might see me coming and going."

The voices were drawing closer.

"Is there any place away from the inn itself?" Stoner asked.

"The boat house! Perfect! I usually hang out with the guests after dinner, but I'll say there's something I have to do in town." Sherry checked her watch.

"It's seven-thirty now. I'll meet you there at nine. Just follow the path through the woods to the lake. You can't miss it. There's a security light that's always on. Do you need a flashlight?"

"I brought one," Stoner said.

"Okay, it's about a ten minute walk." The woman heaved a momentous sigh. "I can't tell you what a relief it is to have you here. The theater's been booked, the publicity comes out next week. Not that we'd need to do much publicity. We have a small but steady audience in the women's community, and our production is..." She cleared her throat modestly. "...well, frankly, one of the social events of the year on the North Shore. Our audience is counting on us. " She got up. "Time for my evening table-hopping." She glanced over at Gwen and smiled. "As soon as I check your salad."

"Was it awful of me?" Gwen asked.

Black water under a moonless sky lapped at the pilings of the old pier. From somewhere in the darkness came the deep bass boom of a bull frog. Stoner leaned against the rough wood of the boat house and felt the stored heat warm on her back. "Was what awful?"

"How I was about her this afternoon?"

Stoner shrugged and noticed an itch right between her shoulder blades. "Of course it wasn't. Anyway, I thought she was a little heavy-handed, too."

Gwen laughed. "You'd probably feel that way about Ghandi."

"I probably would." She slipped an arm around Gwen's shoulders. "You worry too much."

"I know." Gwen nuzzled against her neck. The stars trembled beyond the humid night air. "So do you."

"Worrying is what I do. It accounts for my great success in the travel industry. People who travel need someone to worry for them."

"Lucky you," Gwen said. "Teachers aren't supposed to let on we worry."

"Why not?"

"We don't want to do anything that might discourage teenagers from growing up." She was silent for a moment, thinking. "It's odd. I've never heard of *Demeter Ascending*."

"Neither have I," Stoner said. "But then I hardly go to plays." She grimaced. "The travel business is kind of like selling real estate. You work the darnedest hours."

"I noticed," Gwen said, and nuzzled closer to her.

Out on the lake, a sudden splash signalled a leaping fish. The bull frog fell silent. From far in the distance piano music drifted through the night. Stoner felt taken out of time. Bull frogs and leaping fish, and piano music in the distance had happened here twenty years ago, and forty years ago, maybe even at the beginning of the Twentieth Century, during the Civil War, even before. If they got up and walked back to the inn, they might find themselves in a different time altogether. Electric bulbs might have reverted to gas lights, and lamps to kerosene. They might find people talking about the Stock Market

Crash, or Abolition, or planning a trip to settle the west, or the upcoming election between Nixon and Kennedy. Maybe the Boston Braves would be making a run at the National League pennant. They might be talked into going along on the first coast-to-coast railroad trip, or going to the World's Fair in St. Louis…

Two beams of light swept across the lake, illuminating swarms of insects that hovered in the cool air currents at the top of the water. The lights went out. A car door slammed. Someone was coming toward them, hidden behind the yellowish beam of a flashlight. The beam picked up their faces.

"Stoner? Gwen?" Sherry's whisper snaked through the silence.

Gwen sat up. "Over here."

Sherry pattered across the dock and dropped down beside them. "For a minute there I couldn't find you. I thought you'd changed your minds."

"You need new batteries," Stoner said helpfully.

"This is just a pen light. We need new flashlights. All the ones we had were stolen."

Stoner sat up. "Your flashlights were stolen? Why would anyone want to steal flashlights?"

"Maybe it was the Cottage ghost," Gwen suggested.

Sherry laughed. "There's no Cottage ghost."

Gwen shrugged. "It just seemed to me, stealing flashlights doesn't make much sense, and ghosts are rather inscrutable in mortal terms…"

"Yes, I see what you mean," Sherry said. "Unfortunately, this does make sense, if someone's trying to sabotage the theater group. We actually use the flashlights a lot. Coming and going from the inn to the barn after dark. Moving around back stage. And we often have power outages in the barn—the lights are on a generator, an old one."

"What other things have happened?" Stoner asked.

Sherry sighed deeply. "Where to begin? Well, we've had pages disappear from scripts. That's not all that unusual, actors can get sloppy, we have one woman who reads a page, then whips it out of her notebook and drops it on the floor. We spend the last ten minutes of every rehearsal reconstructing her script. But there have been losses and mix-ups more than one would expect normally. Other things missing, like tools. Pieces of costume. We finally had to make every woman responsible for her own props."

"Did that stop it?"

"Pretty much so. Of course, there are things that have to stay in the barn, things like equipment and set pieces. We can't very well lug couches and tables to our rooms every night."

"Of course not," Gwen said. "Have there been any major thefts or bodily injuries? Threats against anyone?"

Sherry seemed to think about it. "Not that I know of. We've had money stolen from petty cash…our coffee and treats fund. But it doesn't amount to much. I've pretty much assumed someone needs a quick loan."

"And is the money returned?" Stoner asked.

"Not yet. But I'm hopeful." Sherry smiled shyly. "I'm an optimist, especially where women are concerned." She turned gloomy. "That's what makes this so disturbing. If it is someone inside the company, trying to destroy the project for whatever reason...well, it rattles one's faith in sisterhood, doesn't it?"

"Yes," Stoner said, "it does. But after all, we're only human. There are good sisters and bad sisters. Is there anyone..." She tried to think of a way to present it delicately. "...anyone you suspect at this point?"

"I'd hate to suspect anyone."

"I know," Stoner said gently. "But we have to start somewhere."

"Oh, I hate this," Sherry groaned.

"How about from the outside. Are there people who, for example, make deliveries here on a regular basis?"

"I pick up our groceries."

"Laundry delivery?" Gwen suggested.

Sherry shook her head. "We do our own right here."

"Garbage collectors?"

"Maybe. It's picked up Monday mornings."

"Okay," Stoner said, "we'll keep that in mind. Has there been any hostility toward you in the town, because this is lesbian space?"

"We're been here for years," Sherry said. "Nothing's happened."

Stoner was becoming increasingly bewildered and exasperated. There had to have been something, sometime that would shed some light. If The Cottage had coexisted for years near a small town in deep inland Maine with never an incident of nastiness or homophobia, they were witnessing a modern miracle.

"So what do you think?" Sherry asked.

Stoner shook her head. "It's much too soon to jump to conclusions." She reviewed what they knew. "You've had a series of petty thefts, minor vandalism, and that recent incident of the paint. Other than that, nothing?"

"Nothing but my feeling," Sherry said earnestly. "I have a clear, definite feeling something's going on."

"Sherry," Stoner said, "a 'feeling' isn't much to go on."

"I know, but it's such a clear feeling. That's why I asked for your help. Word around the Cambridge Women's Center was that you have some psychic skills. I thought it would give us an edge."

Her psychic skills—if you could call them "skills," they'd felt more like random curses to her—had never made Stoner feel as if she had any kind of edge. In fact, they made her feel distinctly edgy. "That's very complimentary," she said. "But I really don't..."

"You're not going to do this, are you?" Sherry said suddenly. "You're going to leave."

"Well, it seems like a waste of..."

Sherry clutched at Stoner's sleeve. "Please," she said. "I know it doesn't sound like much, but I really am frightened. I'll pay you for your time."

"That's not the point," Gwen said. "We don't want to..."

"Three days," Sherry said. "Give it three days, get to know the women. See if anything happens. If you still think it's all in my mind, we'll call it off."

Three days. In three days Marylou would have the office sorted and boxed. It was tempting. "What do you think?" she asked Gwen.

"Sure," Gwen said. "What's three days out of one lifetime?"

"Thank you," Sherry breathed. "You won't be sorry. I promise."

CHAPTER 3

"Stoner," Gwen whispered into the darkness, "are you awake?"

The half moon had risen and was setting. A rectangle of light, the color and texture of gray construction paper, crawled up the wall.

"Yes."

"Something's not right."

Stoner rolled over to face Gwen's bed. "I agree."

"But I can't put my finger on it."

"I keep going over it," Stoner said. "But all I can think of is, if all that's wrong is some petty theft and accidents with fresh paint, why in the world did she think it was dangerous enough to bring in help?"

"Yes, that's it. There's got to be something more than that. She's keeping something back. But why?"

"Maybe she doesn't trust us yet," Stoner suggested. "Or maybe she's afraid."

"What do you think we should do?"

"I don't know what we can do. Not until something happens."

Sheets rustled as Gwen sat up. "Just like the police," she said with a sigh. "Can't do anything until someone dies."

"What I don't understand," Stoner went on, "is why anyone would want to sabotage a play."

"Maybe it's a really bad play."

Stoner laughed. "Seriously."

"I am serious. I've seen plays I'd sabotage in a minute. Professional productions, at that."

A scream shattered the darkness. Terror and rage forged into a silver blade.

"Good God!" Gwen said.

Her heart racing, Stoner threw back her sheet and ran to the window.

Outside, the lawn appeared flat and smooth. The setting moon threw long, faint shadows of trees across the grass. Stars glittered through the humid air. Nothing moved.

"What was it?" Gwen asked.

"I don't know. It didn't sound exactly human."

"What it sounded like," Gwen said, "was a soul in torment."

Everything was still.

"I think we were the only ones who heard it."

"Really?" Gwen got out of bed and came to stand beside her. "In that case, it was probably a cwn annwn."

"A coon at noon?"

"Cwn annwn. It's a banshee or Hell-hound. Usually signifies someone's going to die. Usually the person who sees it. Or hears it."

"Thank you for that kind thought, Gwen."

Gwen leaned forward to peer out into the yard. "Do you see anything out there that looks like a large black dog?"

"It'd be hard to see, unless it was right under the window."

"Well," Gwen said ominously, "be glad it's not."

Stoner shuddered. "Don't joke about it."

Gwen slipped an arm across her shoulder. "It was just an animal."

"Animals don't start screaming in the middle of the night for no reason. And why just one shriek? Do you think it's dead?"

"What I think," Gwen said, "is that it was a screech owl, and someone disturbed it."

That made sense. "Who?"

A pinpoint of light flashed at the edge of the trees, moving toward the barn.

"There," Gwen said. "Someone's going to the barn."

The light flashed again, then disappeared. A faint glow passed a barn window from inside.

"Well, that explains the owl." Stoner watched the light moving back and forth behind the windows. "I wonder what they're doing."

"If we were normal people," Gwen said, "instead of mildly paranoid amateur detectives who don't know what we're doing, we'd assume someone forget something after rehearsal and was going back to get it."

"We're not normal."

"I'm normal enough to want to go to sleep."

Stoner gave her a quick kiss. "Go ahead. I'll watch for a while."

The moon had almost slipped into the lake before the prowler left the barn and started back toward the inn.

Someone was tapping on their door. Softly but quickly, urgently.

Gwen rolled out of bed and threw on her robe and opened it.

Sherry slipped inside. Her hair was wild, her clothes in disarray. She looked badly shaken. "Did you see anything last night?" she asked in a breathy undertone.

Stoner sat up and nodded. "Did you?"

"Lights in the barn."

"I take it it wasn't you," Gwen said.

"No. I don't know who it was. Or what."

"Or what?" Stoner asked as she reached for the long cotton shirt she used for a bath robe in the summer. "You think it was a 'what' ?"

Sherry looked as if she'd been caught with her hand in the cookie jar. "I mean 'who' ?"

"If you had meant 'what'," Gwen asked, "what would the 'what' you might have meant, but didn't, be?"

Stoner twisted the tap and let cold water into the wash basin and splashed her face. "Gwen, it's too early for that." She glanced at the pale light touching the sky, then at Sherry. "How early is it, anyway?"

"Going on seven." She plopped herself down on Gwen's bed. "Well, more like going on six thirty."

"I see," Gwen said, and sat beside her. "And how long has it been going on six thirty?"

Sherry traced the nubbed pattern on the bed spread with one finger. "A couple of minutes." She looked up in a basset-like way. "I know it's a horrible hour, but I was just so…so upset."

Gwen looked at her expectantly.

"About last night. People prowling around."

"Did you see them?" Stoner asked as she pulled the towel from its ceramic holder and dried her face.

"No. Just the lights."

"Couldn't it have been someone who left something behind after a rehearsal?"

Sherry looked at her with gratitude and admiration, as if she'd just explained the physics of time in one clear, easily understood sentence. "I guess it could."

"But you have other suspicions." Stoner was feeling increasingly ill-at-ease with what was happening here. She wasn't sure what it was, but it left her uncomfortable.

"Well…maybe…"

Stoner looked at her in a stern way. "Sherry," she said firmly, "we came here to help you."

"I know, and I'm really terribly grateful. Did I tell you I was grateful?"

She brushed the question away. "If I'm going to help you, you have to be completely open with me. If not, we're both wasting our time."

"Oh, I wouldn't keep anything from you."

"Wouldn't you?" Stoner went to her bed and sat. "Last evening you told us about some mysterious accidents. Now, I don't mean to minimize your fears, but any of those incidents could have a perfectly reasonable, non-threatening explanation."

"It's a feeling I have," Sherry said quickly.

Stoner held up a hand. "Please. Hear me out. Perfectly innocent explanations. Then, last night, someone went into the barn late. We don't know who it was or what they were after. I don't imagine you've had time to check for theft or damage, have you?"

Sherry shook her head mutely and miserably.

"Again, there could be a reasonable explanation. But it seems to have thrown you into a panic. Therefore, I have to assume…" She made her voice as gentle and understanding as she could. "I have to assume there are things you haven't told us. Things which would account for your fear."

"Oh," Sherry said. She got up and walked to the window, then back to the bed, then to the window, as if she were trying to make up her mind about something.

Stoner glanced over at Gwen, who nodded solemnly in agreement.

Sherry reached a decision. "You're right. It's time to put all the cards on the table." She crammed her hand into her pocket and pulled out a wrinkled, tightly folded sheet of paper. Without speaking, she held it out to Stoner.

It was a note. Written in blocky letters on plain notebook paper—college ruled—in an awkward hand. Possibly a child, possibly someone right-handed writing with the left to hide his or her identity.

"Stop this production," the note said, "or somebody's going to get hurt."

That it was correctly spelled and punctuated added to the use of the word production, not an everyday, childlike sort of word, suggested the writer wasn't just a child engaging in a prank. Stoner passed it over to Gwen.

"Not very original," Gwen said. "Someone's seen too many old, bad movies."

"How and when did this come into your possession?" Stoner asked, and thought she sounded a little like an old, bad movie herself.

"Right before I wrote to you. It was slipped under my door in the night. Why? Would it matter?"

"It might. If it had been tacked to the wall of the barn, for instance, the threat might be assumed to be directed toward the company as a whole."

"Nobody'd do that," Sherry said. "We don't put nails in the walls. Everyone knows that."

"We're talking about someone who's threatened you," Gwen said. "I don't think they're going to care about nails in the barn wall."

Stoner agreed. "So it's my hunch the threat is for you."

"Oh, Goddess," Sherry gasped. Her chin trembled.

Don't you dare cry, Stoner thought. It's much too early in the morning, and we have important things to think about.

She was a little shocked to find herself reacting in such an insensitive way. Truth was, she was beginning to get annoyed. If they were going to have to drag every incident, every suspicion out of her...

"Then you do suspect someone in the company," Stoner said.

Sherry looked at her with surprise. "I do?"

"You said nobody would tack it to the barn wall. You also said that was a company policy. So you must have the suspicion that this comes from within your group, or else it wouldn't have occurred to you to dismiss the wall-tacking so quickly."

"Uh," Sherry said, and glanced at Gwen for help.

"I know," Gwen said. "It's subtle and convoluted, but it's just Stoner's style of thinking. You do think it might be someone in *Demeter Ascending,* don't you?"

The woman picked at an invisible hang nail. "I hate thinking like that.

It's so unfeminist."

"If someone's out to sabotage your production," Stoner explained, "that person isn't very feminist, either." She read through the note again. "Let's assume it's directed to you because you're the producer. You're the one who has the authority to stop the show."

"Oh, no," Sherry said, and shook her head wildly. "We make our decisions collectively."

"But your input would have greater weight, wouldn't it? As the producer?" Gwen asked.

"I suppose."

"For instance..." Gwen wrinkled her forehead and thought. "...what does a producer do?"

"I oversee all the technical aspects of the production." Sherry looked at the floor modestly. "And co-ordinate the backstage and front-of-the-house crews. Like the ushers. Then there's renting the hall, doing the publicity outreach, handling the budget..."

"Sounds like quite a job," Stoner said.

Sherry nodded. "It used to be even harder. Before Joanna left for Oregon...she had the position before me...the producer made all the decisions. Joanna really ran the company. We were called 'Lavender and Lace' back then."

"I've heard of that company," Gwen said. "I even saw one of your productions. It was quite good."

"Thank you," Sherry said. "After Joanna left, we went through a major reorganization." She gave an embarrassed little laugh. "You know how it is—political differences, artistic differences."

"I know how it is," Stoner said. If there was one thing that could be said for the Lesbian Nation, it had its differences. Political, personal—and, apparently, artistic. "It can be wrenching."

Sherry's face took on a sad look. "It was. Anyway, after the dust settled, they decided to become a collective, so everyone makes the decisions."

" 'They?' " Stoner asked.

"I mean 'we,' " Sherry said quickly. She blushed a little. "I may as well level with you. We weren't all in favor of working collectively. It can be frustratingly inefficient." She shrugged. "But majority rules."

"Did you mind terribly?" Gwen asked. "It sounds as if you stood to lose a good bit of, well, authority."

"And responsibility," Sherry pointed out. "I have more than enough of that, thank you."

"So it seems," Gwen said. "In fact, if you pulled out there would be too many things to do for anyone else to pick up the pieces, wouldn't there? Especially if they had another function."

"Nobody has any more power or responsibility than anyone else in a collective," Sherry reminded her.

"I'm sure that's true," Gwen countered. Stoner could see the tiny tightening around her jaw that meant Gwen was beginning to clench her teeth.

Yelling was just down the road. "On the other hand, considering how important everyone's job is, the loss of any one person would leave a huge gap."

"That's just the point," Sherry said. "We're all..."

"Equally important, I know," Gwen muttered.

It was time to step in. "The thing is," Stoner said, "there must be special skills that you have that no one else does. Or few other people. Or other people who also have as much to do as they can handle."

"That's probably true," Sherry admitted.

"So, if you were out of the picture, what would happen that would make the production impossible?"

Sherry rocked back and forth on her heels and chewed her lip. "Well, for one thing, they wouldn't have a place to rehearse. I mean, if someone did me in, I suppose the police would seal off the whole area. And that'd be that, wouldn't it?"

"It certainly would," Gwen said.

"Therefore," Stoner went on, "you would be an important person to get rid of. Assuming the motive is to close down the show."

"I see your point," Sherry said. She gave a grim smile. "It's a dubious honor, isn't it?"

"I'd be willing to say," Gwen said, "they don't come much more dubious."

"In that case," Sherry said cheerfully, "I'll certainly have to watch my step." She brushed at her clothes, straightening out wrinkles. "I really ought to get down to the kitchen."

She started for the door. Stoner stopped her with a touch. "One more thing. Do you know why anyone would want to close the show down?"

Sherry frowned a little, thinking. "Haven't the slightest," she said as she opened the door. "Try the Eggs Benedict. They're excellent."

The sun was up full by the time they entered the dining room. Most of the tables were filled, but the guests were sleepily silent. The light was dim, the windows facing west and not yet in sunlight.

Stoner was grateful for that. She hadn't gotten to sleep until late, worrying senselessly about the light they had seen, anticipating the Soul-in-Torment shriek would happen the minute she let go of consciousness and send her into heart-racing insomnia. Then Sherry swooping down on them at the crack of dawn, all emotion and nervous energy. Not an auspicious start for the day. And she still had to go through her morning waking-up ritual. She had to do it every day, no matter what. Sometimes, when life was particularly hectic or quick, she didn't get to it until evening, but it had to happen or the entire day would be remembered as unreal. So, even though she had had to hit the ground running with Sherry this morning, she still had to do the ritual.

Sit quietly, drop back into herself, sip coffee. Let the surroundings come into slow focus. At first everything white-gray meaning "world," and "alive." Separating into colors, colors that signify things. Green, grass. Blue, sky. Eggshell, dining room walls.

Red! Blood? No, just a shirt, nothing to worry about.

Shapes forming out of the colors. Green grass and blue sky not seen through a window, but a painting on the far wall. Clumps of gray and brown and swirling rainbows resolving into human forms. Dyke Hikers. Table of women she hadn't seen before, probably *Demeter Ascending* women. The two silver-haired women, one in the wheelchair, over in their corner, still honeymooning.

"Feeling better?" Gwen asked quietly. She had learned about the ritual the hard way, spending an entire day with Stoner when she hadn't had the time for it. By evening, Gwen said, it was like being with someone from the Twilight Zone.

"Think so." Stoner wondered what she had done with Sherry's note, went through her pockets frantically, then realized she'd left it in the bureau drawer.

Was that safe? What if someone searched their room?

But why would anyone do that? As far as anyone knew, they were only guests here.

On the other hand, they had signed the guest register with their real names. Sherry had known enough about Stoner's reputation to contact her for help. What if someone else recognized her and guessed at why she was there?

But, other than Sherry, the only person who knew about the trouble was the person causing it.

So what did that do to their situation?

Obsessing was also part of the morning ritual. It always ended with her realizing, with all the surprise and joy of discovering for the first time, that obsessing was useless and only meant she didn't have enough information.

"We need to know more," she said.

"Agreed." Gwen dipped her spoon into her grapefruit. "It's probably time to infiltrate *Demeter Ascending*."

"Demeter was a pretty angry woman," Stoner said. "I hope it's not a bad sign."

"At least we're in it together."

That was something for which Stoner was filled with gratitude. She'd been in rough places before, but seldom with Gwen at her side. It made all the difference in the world. Not just because it gave her someone to bounce ideas off of, and someone to help fill in gaps. But because, when you loved someone as much as they loved each other, nothing and nobody could hurt you down to the bone.

"Have you decided on your cover?" Gwen asked.

Stoner shook her head. "It has to be something that'll let me come and go at rehearsals. That probably leaves out things I can really do, like building sets and stuff. What about you?"

"Props. Involving lurking back stage, with possible errands off the grounds with various persons."

"Sounds like a good choice." She thought hard. "Who else hangs around while a play's in rehearsal?"

"I'm not sure. At Watertown Middle School, there seem to be a lot of mothers hanging around."

"I don't think Stage Mother is a role I'd fit into."

"I've got it!" Gwen said excitedly, dropping her spoon with a clatter.

"Got what?"

"What you can do. Understudy."

That really made her laugh. "Understudy?"

"Why not?"

"Because I couldn't even act one part, much less all of them."

Gwen picked up a piece of toast and began buttering it wildly. "You wouldn't have to act. By the time the play comes off, we'll have the whole thing solved and be out of here. You just have to pretend to want to act."

"That's acting," Stoner said.

"Life is acting. I mean it, Stoner. It's perfect."

She had to admit it made sense. Being the understudy would probably give her plenty of freedom of movement, plus a reason to be around. And, if she needed to talk with any actor alone, there'd be an excuse for it—trying to understand her part, questions about character, things like that.

"Yeah," she said, "I guess you're right."

"Now all we have to do is infiltrate the company."

Stoner smiled. "Sometimes I think you like this cloak-and-dagger stuff too much for your own good."

"Hah!" Gwen said. "You don't?"

"Of course not," Stoner said, pretending to be insulted. "I only do it because it has to be done."

The Eggs Benedict arrived. They were as good as Sherry had promised. As good as Egg McMuffin, which Stoner secretly loved, even though she seldom ate them since she was trying to live Low Fat so as not to die of heart disease at forty.

"Gwen," she said, "you have to promise me something."

Gwen rolled her eyes. "Here it comes. 'Don't do anything dangerous, don't do anything rash, don't disappear without telling each other where we're going.'"

"This is serious. We're dealing with a potentially dangerous situation. Threats have been made..."

"I know. But you don't have to warn me every time we do something like this."

"Of course I have to warn you. You never pay attention."

"So why bother?"

"It makes me feel as if I've done my best."

Gwen leaned across the table and touched her hand. "You always do your best. It's one of the things I love about you."

Stoner felt herself go shy. She liked compliments, stored them up the way a squirrel stores nuts, to be dug up later and turned over and over and enjoyed. But she never knew what to do with them at the time. She used to brush them off, but Gwen was breaking her of that by reminding her it was rude and left the payer of compliments feeling rejected. So now she was less rude and more awkward.

Sherry came to her rescue. Bouncing across the dining room, all traces of her previous distress gone. Her innkeeper persona was firmly in place.

"Good morning," she said cheerily. "Did you sleep well?"

Not well, Stoner thought, and not long enough. "Fine," she said, and forced a smile.

"I don't know what your plans are for the day," Sherry said, not loudly enough to draw attention but loudly enough to be overheard. "But if you're interested, we have a little theater piece in rehearsal. I'm sure you'd be welcome to sit in."

"That would be nice," Gwen said, matching her tone. "But we wouldn't want to be in the way."

"You won't. We'd welcome an audience. It's a comedy, and we've all heard the jokes so often we don't think they're funny any more. A fresh point of view would be—well, refreshing." She gave them a clandestine wink. "We usually start around ten with warm-ups. Any time after that would be wonderful."

Stoner caught Sherry's sleeve. "Listen," she said quietly, "I'm sorry if we said anything to upset you this morning."

The woman looked at her. "Upset me?"

"You left our room so abruptly. I was afraid..."

"Oh, that," Sherry said with a tinkly laugh. She dropped her voice. "People were stirring. It wouldn't have done for me to be seen leaving your room, would it? Later."

She scurried away to greet the hikers.

Gwen looked after her. "At least we don't have to worry about working our way in. Sherry seems eager and capable."

"Yeah." That could be an asset or a liability. It all depended on how Sherry reacted when or if they had to act without her.

"I hate to sound 'unfeminist'...," Gwen began.

"Go ahead," Stoner said. "It's too early to be politically correct."

"...that woman is..."

"Strange," they said simultaneously.

"I wonder what Dr. Kesselbaum would think," Stoner said with a grin.

Gwen tossed an imaginary gauze scarf over one shoulder. "Strange, Stoner dear?" she said in a perfect Edith imitation. "Do you mean strange enough to be interesting, or strange enough to be in trouble?"

"Good question."

"She's exhausting. I keep wondering who I'm really talking to."

Stoner sneaked a look at the elderly women. "Of all the women here I'd like to meet," she said, "those two are my favorites."

Gwen glanced over their way. "Go ahead. You deserve a little pleasure."

"We have a job to do first."

"Oh, Stoner," Gwen said with a sad smile, "you're such a workaholic."

"Am not."

"What do you call it, then?"

"I just like..." She searched for the right words. "...to keep my priorities in order."

As it turned out, they didn't have to wait until the rehearsal to start meeting the Demeter women. Stoner decided they should languish about in the living room for a while, to do some casual observing as the women left the dining room. "To gather first impressions," she said. "Before we get cluttered up with knowing people's personalities."

"Easy for you to say," Gwen grumbled. "Your first impressions are usually right. Mine are usually wrong." She curled up in a corner of a hard horse hair sofa.

"We should look as if we're doing something," Stoner said.

"I am doing something. I'm going back to sleep."

She looked around the room. In the far corner stood a cloth-draped table with a coffee urn, hot water for tea, and tiny, demitasse-sized cups, saucers, and silver spoons. Little linen napkins lay in a row like soldiers. There was a tiny silver bowl of sugar, and another tiny silver bowl containing packets of Sweet 'n Low. Muffins, fruit, and bar cookies lay on a silver, linen-covered tray next to a stack of tiny plates and more tiny napkins. She should have known Sherry would provide all the niceties of civilization for her guests. "We could pretend to be having a second cup of coffee," she said.

Gwen looked around at the refreshments and diminutive china and dollhouse silver. "I feel as if I just fell into Gulliver's Travels," she said. "Or we're off to see the Wizard. You don't suppose she's getting ready for a conference, do you?"

Oh, great, just what they needed. More people. More confusion. Less chance for sneaking. People who'd never been there before and probably never would again, wandering through the halls, lost, showing up in unlikely and suspicious places...

A wild-looking woman sailed through the door to the upstairs like a two masted schooner taking the wind. Her hair was the color of lemons, and radiated from her head like rays of sun. She wore baggy, brightly colored cotton Arabian Nights pants, and a white peasant top and Birkenstocks. Her skin was pale and massively freckled. Her eyes were grey, her expression tight and slightly suspicious. Over one arm, she carried a huge straw Kenya tote bag. On her other hand perched a frog hand puppet. She tacked over to the refreshment table and poured herself a cup of coffee, much of which landed in the saucer.

She had to be a Demeter. In fact, she looked as if the group could have been named for her.

Stoner got up. "Back in a minute," she murmured, and went to the coffee urn.

"Hi," she said cheerfully and casually as she reached for a cup.

The woman gave a loud shriek and threw her packet of Sweet 'n Low into the air.

"I'm sorry. I didn't mean to startle you."

"'S all right," the woman said, fanning herself with one hand. "Nervous, that's all. Always been nervous. Maybe early menopause, maybe not. World full of danger, you know."

"I know." Stoner held out her hand. "My name's Stoner. We just checked in last night."

The woman engulfed her hand in a tight grip. "Rita." She held up the frog puppet. "This is Seabrook."

"Pleased to meet you." She wondered what the etiquette was concerning shaking hands with frog puppets. Well, better safe than sorry. She took one of Seabrook's feet between two fingers.

"Nuke Jane Fonda!" Seabrook shrieked, and pulled back violently.

"Sorry about that," Rita said, looking genuinely sorry. "He doesn't like to be touched. Early childhood trauma. Probably."

"I understand," Stoner said.

"Nuke Helen Caldicott," muttered Seabrook.

"Shut up, Seabrook," Rita said, and stuffed him into her tote bag. She pulled out a package of Fig Newtons and thrust them in Stoner's direction. "Fig Newton?"

"Fig the Newtrons," Seabrook muttered from inside the bag. "Fig Olivia Neutron-Bomb."

"Seabrook was active in the anti-nuclear movement back in the seventies," Rita explained. "Maced. Had a lasting impact. Banana?" She brought out a small bunch of bananas.

Stoner shook her head. "Thanks, but we just ate."

"Don't eat the food here."

"Why not?"

"Microwave ovens." She pointed to Stoner's watch. "That thing glow in the dark?"

"I don't think so."

"Radioactive. Use radioactive paint. Glows in the dark. Wear it long enough, you'll glow in the dark."

Stoner looked at her watch. "I didn't know that."

"Hah," said Rita. Her face grew progressively redder as she spoke. "Not surprised. People all over the world in trouble, don't even know it. Wear one of those glow-in-the-dark watches, you're a walking Chernobyl."

"Oh," Stoner said.

Rita plunged her hand into her bag again. "Apple?"

Speechless, Stoner shook her head.

"Gotta go," Rita said, and took a huge bite out of the apple. "Stay away from television sets."

She billowed through the front door and tacked across the lawn.

Stoner looked after her.

"Who," Gwen said at her elbow, "was that?"

"Rita."

"She's amazing. What on earth did you say to her?"

"I'm not sure."

"She looked angry enough to kill you alive."

"We were getting along fine," Stoner said. "I think so, anyway. She's disturbed about nuclear energy. Seabrook doesn't seem to share her politics."

"Seabrook?"

"The frog."

Gwen gazed across the lawn to where Rita was flowing steadily toward the barn. "She's a Demeter?"

"Looks that way."

The barn was huge on the inside. Deep and high-raftered, with the perpetual odor of dust and hay indigenous to old barns. The stalls had been dismantled, the openings that used to serve as Dutch doors to the outside converted into large, light-inviting windows. Some of the floor was still packed dirt, but a low stage had been built in the far end. Industrial-sized orange and tomato juice cans fitted with hundred-watt bulbs hung from beams and served as lighting. Gray metal folding chairs were scattered about in no particular order. Nearly every one was covered with bits of clothing, paper bags, notebooks, knapsacks, or unidentifiable clutter. A card table, probably the director's desk, sat squarely in front of the stage.

The actors were apparently finishing warm-ups. Some were stretching cat-like toward the ceiling, others making "puh-puh-puh" sounds and flapping out their cheeks. A small group was chanting "red leather, yellow leather," in rapidly increasing cadence and volume.

Stoner looked for Rita and found her, Seabrook in hand, reaching for the rafters and twirling about in a circle and coming dangerously close to the edge of the stage. Not a long drop, but sudden and deep enough to sprain an ankle. With truly amazing agility, she whirled forward, gyrated back to safety, swirled closer, pirouetted away. Despite her size, Rita was breathtakingly graceful.

"She's like a dancer," Gwen said admiringly.

"She certainly is."

"I'd like to have that much grace just for one hour."

"Yo!" A voice sailed toward them across the room. "Stoner. Gwen." Sherry detached herself from the "red leather, yellow leather" group and trotted toward them. She hooked her elbows through theirs and addressed the troupe. "Sisters! May I have your attention! Gwen and Stoner are guests here at the Cottage. I told them they could watch a rehearsal or so. Any problem with that?"

Nobody had a problem.

One woman, dark-haired and sultry, excused herself from "puh-puh-puh" and approached them. She was, simply, voluptuous, with the kind of cleavage many women went to plastic surgeons to acquire. But this woman's was clearly her own, and she drew attention to it with a low-cut flowered blouse. She was also wearing pale blue polyester slacks and straw sandals topped with straw daisies.

"Hi," the woman said. Her voice was as sultry as the rest of her. "Is your name really Stoner?"

Stoner nodded. "Stoner McTavish." The woman began to seem vaguely familiar.

"Name's Roseann," she said. "I have a last name but it's ugly and anyway it's my father's and I don't want to think about him more than necessary, if you know what I mean."

"I do," Stoner said.

"Anyway," Roseann went on without breaking stride, "I know your aunt. And I met you one day when you picked her up after a blue rinse."

It all came together. "Roseann," Stoner said. "Thelma's Cut 'n Curl."

"Yeah." She reached out and shook hands, casting a quick glance at Stoner's nails. "Good cuticles. Well, we call it the Galaxy Unisex Styling Center now, which shows you how long ago it was when you met me. Thelma says we got to keep up with the times. I dunno, feels like something out of 'Star Trek,' plastic all over the place." She turned to Gwen. "You must be Gwen. I heard about you having to kill your husband. Bummer."

"Thank you," Gwen said.

"Listen, next time you see your aunt, tell her she was right on the money with those cards. Boy, she's really spooky with those things."

"The Tarot?" Stoner asked.

"Yeah, the Tarot (she pronounced it like 'carrot'). Couple of months ago she was in for a perm, and while we were waiting for her to set—takes longer than usual, with that thick hair, you don't often see hair like that on a gal her age—well, she was fooling around with those cards so I asked her to tell my fortune. My 3:45 had cancelled, which was just as well. That old Mrs. Boggs, hair falling out by the handfuls, for which she somehow blames me. I keep telling her, 'Mrs.Boggs, honey, you got to quit drinking or eat more animal fat.'"

"Animal fat," Gwen said.

"Well, she gets all huffed up like I accused her of having VD or something, which I know she can't 'cause there isn't a man, woman, or child alive about to hop into the sack with a mean old face like that one. And old man Boggs—calls him 'The Mister,' can you believe it, is this the nineties, or what?—he can't get it up any more. She told me herself. Listen, I could have blushed clean out of my uniform, some of the stuff those old cards told her about me."

"Told Mrs. Boggs?" Stoner asked.

"Told your aunt. So I says, 'Ms. Moore, I just want to know what's going to happen in the future.' I mean, if she was working up to being any more personal—gosh, there's some things you don't want getting spread around the Galaxy Unisex Styling Center, even if it did used to be Thelma's Cut 'n Curl, you know what I mean?"

"Absolutely," Gwen said.

" 'Well, Roseann,' she says, 'you keep your eyes open, because one of these days there's going to be some excitement.' Now, that makes me a little nervous, 'cause there's some kinds of excitement I already got enough of, if you get my drift. 'No, Roseann,' she says, studying those cards, 'I don't mean anything like that. There will be a change in your life,' she says. Well, I can sure use a few changes, all right, but she gets this kind of mysterious look on her face. You know that look?"

"I know that look," Stoner said.

"'In the area of communication,' she says. Well, what does that mean to me, except maybe I can pay the phone bill on time for a change, but she says it's something I never thought of in my entire life, and then she clams up as tight as a Presbyterian on pay day. That kind of made the hairs on the back of my neck prickle, you know what I mean?"

"Only too well," Stoner assured her.

"So that Friday night I'm sitting around the Shamrock, having a couple of beers on account of the heat and all, and a bunch of us start in to singing, just passing the time like we always do. I got a decent voice, the nuns at Our Lady always said so even if they knew I wouldn't amount to anything, and I was doing one of those English music hall numbers—I got a couple of albums of them back home for parties, you know, when things turn a little naughty?"

"Uh," Stoner said. She could feel herself beginning to blush. Worse than that, she could feel Gwen staring at her. And laughing inside. "Yes."

"So I was entertaining the crowd," Roseann went on, not noticing that Stoner was as pink as a foam rubber curler, "getting our minds off the heat and the Red Sox playing like mules on this current home stand, which makes the guys kind of mean. And this gal Rebecca..." She pointed toward the stage and in the general direction of at least five other women, any of whom could have been a Rebecca. "...she was sitting in the back and up she comes to me, says a bunch of gals are putting on a show and would I like to try out for it? Geez-Louise, I felt like Lana Turner or somebody, which isn't such a bad comparison when you stop to think of it. I mean, boobs like these..." She hefted her breasts in her hands like melons. "...don't come thirteen to the dozen, do they?"

"They're very nice," Stoner said, and knew she looked like the main course at a lobster bake.

"Next day I go down to where they're having these tryouts, on my lunch break, Thelma kind of looking at me sideways out from under those black eyebrows of hers that aren't real I happen to know for a fact 'cause she says she's a natural blonde, and you get a blonde with black eyebrows, one or the other's got to come out of a bottle. Old Thelma's got her nose out of joint for sure, but I say to her, 'It's my lunch break to do with what I please and if you don't like it you can tell it to the Union.' That shuts her up for sure, she knows better than to get uppity with me, I got ten years' experience and plenty of offers, some of them even legit."

The crowd on stage had broken up. Some were lounging about in small groups, talking. Others were looking at scripts. Sherry was approaching a slender brunette in chinos and white shirt with the back of the collar turned up and her sleeves rolled to the elbows. They glanced back in Stoner's direction. The other woman nodded.

"So I go down and they give me something to read," Roseann was saying. "Everybody's looking at me and listening real hard, you know? Then this kind of spell comes over me. Next thing I know these fancy words are coming right off the page and out my mouth—it's like this made-up person I'm reading about has got inside me, talking through me, like in 'The Exorcist' or something. I'm telling you, Stoner, I was in another world. When I get to the end it's real quiet for a minute, and I thought, 'There you go, Roseann, bombed in

Boston.' It was disheartening. Then everybody starts jumping up and patting me on the back and clapping and yelling. Not like down at the shamrock, with the guys half drunk and trying to cop a feel. Just real nice, and a couple of them are crying, even."

Turned-up-collar was coming toward them.

Roseann nudged her. "That's Rebecca. She's the director." She turned to face Rebecca with an expression of apprehension and awe. Stoner was sure she'd learned it at Our Lady.

"Hi," Rebecca said. "Sherry says you'd like to hang out for a while."

"If it's all right with all of you."

"No problem. I'm Rebecca, by the way."

Stoner and Gwen introduced themselves and explained that they were on vacation.

Rebecca turned to Roseann. "Are you warmed up?"

Roseann gave a throaty chuckle. "Wound up is more like it."

"We'll start with Scene 4."

"Great." She watched Rebecca walk away. "Isn't she neat?"

Stoner had no idea whether Rebecca was neat or not, but she couldn't bring herself to take even the slightest amount of wind out of Roseann's natural high. "So you got the part," she said.

"Right then and there they tell me I'm going to be the star of this show. Acting and singing. 'Course by then I'm late getting back to work, but I feel so good I treat myself to a taxi. I stroll into the Galaxy Unisex Styling Center that used to be Thelma's Cut 'n Curl like I'm Bette Davis making a personal appearance. And there's my one o'clock trim flipping the pages of People Magazine waiting to ram it down my throat, and Thelma madder'n hell. And I'm just old Roseann Nobody again. But I remember how it was, all these gals sitting there listening so hard and all, and I tell her I'm gonna do this show, I'm gonna leave work at 4 pm every day, and I'm gonna take my vacation for an entire month in August. And if she doesn't like it, she can tuck her plastic curlers where the sun never shines."

CHAPTER 4

By the time they stopped for lunch, they had met most of the visible members of *Demeter Ascending*. They were invited to join the group in the dining room, but Stoner drew Sherry aside and requested a picnic for two. It would give them a chance to get away and compare notes. Gwen came up with a fresh legal pad and ball point pen, and they walked down by the lake.

In some parts of the country, Stoner supposed, it would be called a pond. A small body of water, too wide to swim across easily but you could probably reach shore from the middle if you were a particularly good swimmer. The woods ringing the lake were mostly red pine and hemlock, interspersed with birch. Toward the north end, a small, sparkling stream cut through tall grass to feed the pond. In the shallows at the south outlet, tall reeds rose from the swampy ground beside the water. A red-winged blackbird teeter-tottered on a cattail stalk and "muck-er-deed" to anyone who wanted to listen.

The water was calm, a few insects lazily riding the air currents over the surface. A flash of blue darted from a high pine and dove into the lake, reappearing with a small silver fish dangling from its bill. Droplets of water like liquid diamonds dripped through the sunlight. The kingfisher flew back to its nest with its prize.

Stoner spread a blanket on the ground at the edge of the water. A young hemlock cast a spikey shadow. Honey bees buzzed in a clump of pale blue early autumn asters near by. She unpacked the sandwiches and boxed juice drinks, and anchored paper napkins against the tentative, casual breeze with small stones.

"Okay." Gwen sat cross-legged on the corner of the blanket, her brown eyes large and deep behind her reading glasses. She was wearing shorts and running shoes without socks. Her legs were tan and firm.

"Yeah," Stoner said, forcing her eyes to focus somewhere other than on the sight of Gwen in the sunlight. "Okay."

Gwen clicked her pen and picked up the tablet. "Let's go through the cast of characters, no pun intended. First, there's Rita." She wrote her name on the pad.

"And Seabrook."

"I really don't think Seabrook's a threat."

"Unless he's Rita's alter ego," Stoner pointed out. "In which case he could be very dangerous."

Gwen glanced at her. "You think Rita's disturbed?"

"No. But she does strike me as a little unstable. And there's something going on between her and Marcy. Did you notice the way Rita glared at her? I wonder what that's all about."

"Bad history," Gwen said. She picked up a sandwich and bit into it. "Marcy ran off with Rita's lover. Rita took to drink and was hospitalized briefly. But that was a couple of years ago. She's been fine since."

"How do you find out these things?"

"I ask questions, silly."

"So do I."

"Not really," Gwen said. "You ask polite questions, and you don't follow through. You have to keep after it until there aren't any more questions to ask."

"That seems so rude," Stoner said.

Gwen laughed. "If you were a teacher, you wouldn't think of it as rude. You'd think of it as survival."

"How do you know when there aren't any more questions?"

"Their eyes lose that 'can I go now?' look."

"So who told you about Marcy and Rita?"

"Sherry."

The hemlock was oozing a small stream of sap. A column of ants trudged up and down the trunk.

"Okay, let's talk about Marcy," Stoner suggested. "What's your opinion of her?"

Gwen chewed the end of her pen for a moment. "I don't have one, really. She's lively."

"Bouncy."

"Helpful."

"Intense." She glanced at Gwen. "Did you find her intense?"

"Not particularly. What do you mean?"

"Well, I only spent a couple of minutes talking to her..."

"More than I spent," Gwen said.

"There was something about the way she looks at you. It's just very...intense."

"Intense," Gwen repeated, and wrote it down. "Anything else?"

Stoner shook her head.

"Moving right along. Who was the short butch with the tool box?"

"You thought she was butch?"

"Yeah, didn't you?"

"I've seen butcher."

"Dearest," Gwen said with a little smile, and patted her knee, "you've been butcher. On several occasions. But she did have that baby butch air about her."

"Are you sure it wasn't the tool box?"

Gwen sighed. "I may not have been out as long as you, Stoner, but I have learned a little something in the past few years. And one of the things I've learned is that tool boxes do not necessarily butches make."

"Okay." She nibbled off a corner of her tuna sandwich and looked up at the tiny white clouds casually drifting through the sky. It was turning hot, even for Maine, and she felt lazy. "Did you catch her name? The baby butch?"

"Boneset," Gwen said.

"That should be easy to remember. Baby Butch Boneset."

"So associate to her."

"Quiet, serious, task-centered..."

"With access to tools and ability to use them," Gwen added. She made a note beside "Boneset."

"Barb, the technical director," Stoner said.

"I couldn't tell anything about her, could you? She just sat there and wrote things."

"She was making a map or chart of some kind."

"I think it was a lighting design."

Stoner looked over at her. "Can you read those things?"

Gwen shook her head.

"Neither can I. I did notice, though, that the paper she was using matched the paper that was used for Sherry's note. And that the pad was half empty. If I could get my hands on it for a few hours, maybe I could match the tear lines."

"Good idea," Gwen said, and made another note. "How are you going to do that?"

"I'm not." Stoner grinned. "That's your job, Ms. Props Person."

"Thank you." She opened a box of juice. "Now, may we take up the subject of the playwright?"

"Playwright?"

"The play recorder, if you insist on being accurate. The play scribe. The woman who's writing down what the others create."

"Oh," Stoner said. "You mean the African-American woman."

"The very tall, very powerful, very colorful, very statuesque African-American woman who has had you drooling since you first laid eyes on her."

"Well, her name's Divi Divi, and she's..." Words failed her.

"Magnificent?" Gwen suggested.

"That's it. I haven't talked to her yet, have you?"

Gwen shook her head. "I didn't want to deprive you of the pleasure of interviewing her."

Stoner glanced at her. "You're not jealous, are you?"

"Of course not."

"I'm not lusting."

"Not even a little?" Gwen asked. Her eyes sparked mischievously.

Stoner raked at the grass, causing the line of ants that were headed their way to declare an earthquake emergency. "Well, just a little. I know it's not very politically correct."

"I don't think feelings can be politically correct or incorrect," Gwen said as she unwrapped a second sandwich. "Only behavior."

"You're probably right."

The day was turning hotter. There was a soft splash from the lake, where the kingfisher dove for another morsel. The sun made her sleepy and comfortable. She didn't want to go back to the barn. It was all noise and motion in the barn.

"Let's run through what we have," Gwen said. "There's Sherry. Producer. She called us in, which doesn't make her innocent but decreases the probability of her guilt. Seems fairly open..."

"I'd hardly say that," Stoner pointed out. "She didn't tell us about the note until we dragged it out of her."

"True. But she was very open about the fact that she was hiding something." She added to her notes on Sherry. "Not open but transparent. Okay?"

"Okay," Stoner said.

"Rebecca's the director," Gwen went on. "We don't know her yet. Roseann, who's playing the lead and apparently the only one who's new to the company. Was that your impression?"

Stoner nodded. The sun was making little drops of perspiration run down between her breasts. Her skin smelled of heat and salt. Store it up, she thought, store up all the warmth and the good smells and the sunlight, because winter's never far behind.

This winter they'd be in a new place. Away from the city with its dirty slush and constant drizzle and impossible parking and people in bad moods. It might be colder out in the hill country, but at least the air would be clean.

"Barb," Gwen said as she wrote and reviewed. "Tech director. Quiet and businesslike. May have paper that matches the threatening note. Rita and Seabrook, possibly unstable. Marcy of the wandering eye, bouncy, intense, and helpful in her own way. And, last but not least, Divi Divi. Plus a few assorted women of unknown name and function, extras, stage hands, probably both."

"See any suspects?"

"Not yet. Of these..." Gwen flipped the page and started another list. "...the actors include Marcy, Divi Divi, Roseann, Sherry and Rita."

Stoner opened her eyes. "I didn't know Sherry was acting."

"Minor part, according to her. Does it change things?"

"I guess not. It just makes her a more likely target. If someone wants to sabotage the show, they could get rid of the producer and an actor by getting rid of her."

Back in the forest, a woodpecker hammered furiously at a hollow tree.

"We need to know more about these people," Gwen said.

"Yeah." An ant was creeping across her leg. She felt too lazy to chase it.

"Time to start infiltrating."

"Uh-huh." She was almost asleep, suspended outside of time and space.

"I'll approach Barb and offer my services. Techies are great at back stage gossip."

"Okay." Everything was receding into the distance. She could feel herself drifting down, down...

"I think you should try to connect with Rebecca."

Stoner didn't bother to answer.

"Motive," Gwen said, and poked her with the pen.

Stoner started, nerves fluttering wildly, and groaned. "It's a beautiful day. Can't we just enjoy it?"

"We can enjoy it when we've earned it," Gwen insisted. "Motive."

The woodpecker stopped drumming. It was probably taking in the sun and soft air. It had probably decided work could wait. It knew the days of warmth and leisure were limited. It didn't have Gwen nagging.

"Motive," Stoner said. "Okay. Someone has been forced into doing this play. Or maybe they wanted to do it, but right now they don't feel like working that hard. But there's another person who keeps pushing, sending our suspect into a murderous rage..."

"Greed, revenge, jealousy," Gwen wrote, ignoring her.

"Suspect, whose pleas for mercy have gone unheeded, strikes out in blind fury and destroys everything and everyone in her path."

"All right, Stoner." Gwen put her notebook down and stood up. She peeled off her shirt and shorts and underpants and kicked her shoes out of the way. "Race you to the water."

It was mid-afternoon by the time they got back to the barn, warm, damp, refreshed, and—in Stoner's case—placated. The coolness in the old building actually felt good. It was a relief to be out of the blinding sunlight.

The cast and crew were sitting in a circle on the stage, while Rebecca talked from notes on her clip board. Stoner found chairs away from the center of activity.

"All in all, it was a pretty good rehearsal," Rebecca said in a winding-up voice. "Div, any script changes?"

"Nope," said Divi Divi.

"So the script is set as it is?"

"Unless we come up with some big holes."

"Okay. Swell. Good. Let's take five minutes, then do a quick line run-through to establish continuity." Women began talking, standing, stretching. Rebecca lifted a whistle that hung from a plastic lanyard around her neck and gave a short, shrill blast. "Sisters, please." They sat back down. "Before we break, are there any announcements? Anything we need to process?"

Everyone looked blank and thoughtful. Marcy raised a tentative hand.

Stoner thought she saw Rebecca heave a resigned sigh.

"Yes, Marcy?"

"I have a problem with a line on page 16."

Everyone picked up her script and turned to page 16.

"The one about the hamburger."

Rebecca closed her eyes.

"I thought we agreed," Marcy persisted, "this character was a dyke. I don't think a dyke would just go and eat a hamburger."

"Nukeburger!" Seabrook roared. "Dyke the nukeburger."

Marcy gave him a dirty look.

"Well," Rebecca said with infinite patience, "it's up to the collective. But I think there are a lot of lesbians who eat hamburgers."

"But I don't think we should validate that," Marcy insisted.

"Oh, come on," one of the extras/stage hands shouted. "Let's just rehearse."

"Suppose we take a vote," Rebecca suggested. "How many..."

"Wait a minute," Marcy broke in. "This is a collective. We go by consensus."

Boneset pulled herself to her feet. "Go ahead and consense. I have work to do." She picked up her tool box and strode to the back of the barn.

Rebecca tried again. "Look, is there anyone who objects to us changing the hamburger to a...a what?"

"Tofuburger," Marcy said.

Nobody seemed to mind. "Div," Rebecca said, "will you make the changes?"

"Uh-huh," said Divi Divi.

"Five minutes," Rebecca repeated. "Then a line run-through. Then we'll work on rough spots. And remember, we have our first tech rehearsal tomorrow. That's with props, costumes, and, we hope, with lights. Barb?"

"We'll have 'em," Barb said, "if I can get some help this evening with hanging them."

Stoner nudged Gwen. "Volunteer," she said under her breath. "Both of us."

Gwen nodded.

"It'll be long," Rebecca went on, "and boring, so..." She broke off as Sherry stood and started toward the door. "Sherry, where are you going?"

"To change."

"We're about to do a line run-through."

"No sweat. I'll be back. If I'm late, work around me. I only have a small part."

"There are no small parts," Rebecca said. "Only small actors."

Sherry gave a laugh and a wave. "Whatever." She scurried through the door.

Rebecca turned back to the others. "Okay, about tomorrow's tech run-through. Barb will tell us what she needs, so take direction from her. The most important thing is that you be on time, ready to work..."

Marcy began to contort herself into a series of peculiar and improbable positions.

"Marcy," Rebecca said, "can you tell us what you're doing?"

"I have to stay warmed up," Marcy said. She expelled a series of sharp, loud grunts.

Rebecca looked as if she wanted to walk out. She hesitated, looked at Barb, looked at Marcy, looked at the others, and decided the show had to go on. "They have to check sight lines and focus the lights, which means they need you to be ready to be anywhere you're going to be on the stage at any time, which means we walk through. Stop and go."

Marcy uttered a shrill wail, like a cat in heat, and settled into a round of chicken clucks.

The rest of the cast was growing very still and very quiet. Stoner could feel the air stretching tight and hard. Any minute now there'd be that moment when time stopped, the world stopped—the moment right before the powder keg blew.

"I'm going to kill her," Rita said. "We'll take a vote. Who wants me to kill her?"

The cheer that erupted broke the tension. Apparently oblivious, Marcy rolled on the floor, arching her back and hissing.

"Even if you're not on stage," Rebecca pushed on, "please keep yourselves available. Any props or costume pieces you've offered to lend or have borrowed should be here. Any questions? Okay, let's start our line run-through."

"Hey!" Marcy yelled. "I'm not through."

They all waited patiently, morbidly fascinated, while Marcy did a few more stretches and moans. At last she got up, panting and sweating.

"Anyone got a towel?"

Boneset tossed one from the back of the barn. Marcy inspected it with some distaste, finally found a corner that was clean enough to suit her, wiped her face and arranged her hair. She dropped the towel on the floor.

"You're welcome," Boneset called.

"Listen," Marcy said, "I don't see why we all have to sit around while they focus lights. Not all of us."

"Because they asked us to," Rebecca said tightly.

"And waste a whole lousy day?"

"You have something better to do?" Rita asked.

"Of course I have something better to do."

"Sandbag her!" Seabrook ordered.

Rebecca made one last try. "I realize it can be annoying, but they need all the help we can give them."

"It's their job. If they can't do their job..."

"Marcy, please. They wouldn't ask if it weren't important."

"It throws my timing off to sit around," Marcy whined.

Rita gave her a sarcastic smile. "What timing?"

"I'll explain it to you later," Rebecca said to Marcy, and silenced Rita with a gesture. "Can we move ahead now?"

"What about the energy circle?" Marcy asked. "We have to raise the energy."

"Douche-bag," said Rita.

Rita might be "all right" now, but there was still a lot going on between her and Marcy. Stoner made a mental note of it.

Rebecca gestured the cast forward. They all joined hands in a circle. All except Divi Divi, who crossed her large arms across her large chest and wandered over to Stoner and Gwen.

Up close she was even taller, even more imposing, even more…

"Either of you got a drink on you?" she asked.

"Sorry," Gwen said. "I'm Gwen Owens, by the way. And this is Stoner McTavish." She held out her hand.

Divi Divi swallowed it up in hers and turned to Stoner. "I'll bet folks are' always asking you where you got a name like that. They're always asking me."

Stoner smiled. "I was named for Lucy B. Stone. How about you?"

"I was named for a beach on Aruba. No. I'm not from there, I was conceived there. Or so my mother claims."

"It must have been memorable," Stoner said.

Divi Divi shrugged hugely and gracefully. "I guess so. I wasn't around at the time." She gestured toward the company. "What do you think of the play?"

"We haven't really seen the play," Gwen said. "Just the preliminaries."

"What's it about?" Stoner asked.

"Beats me. I knew when I started, but there's been so much input it doesn't make any sense any more."

The playwright, seeing her creative child torn apart by dozens of hands, each with an agenda, decides to end the show and save herself from disgrace.

Stoner hoped that wasn't the case. She really hoped that wasn't the case.

From the stage came a very loud, unanimous, "Ooooooommmmm."

"What are they doing now?" Gwen asked.

"Mingling auras," Divi Divi explained. "A little something Marcy picked up in a Feminist theater sharing, caring, and growing workshop."

"Does it work?"

Divi Divi gave a deep, rolling laugh. "You look at that bunch and tell me if you think it works."

Gwen watched them for a moment. "It doesn't work," she said.

"You two girl friends?" Divi Divi asked abruptly.

Stoner said, "Uh…"

Gwen said, "Yes."

"How long?"

"I'm not sure," Gwen said. She glanced at Stoner. "About four years, I guess?"

Stoner calculated and nodded.

"Seems like a funny thing not to be sure of."

"Well, we met one summer in Wyoming, and made love in Iowa, and again in Maine. I guess we really became lovers in Maine." She glanced at Stoner. "Didn't we?"

"I guess so."

"It was on a dirt road, outside of Castleton."

"Must have been uncomfortable," Divi Divi said.

"It was late winter," Gwen went on. "I was driving, and we had a fight about something and I made her get out of the car in the middle of the woods, and she leaned up against a tree and started to cry, and that's when I realized I was being an idiot and I told her I loved her, and we went back to the awful motel and made love on the pink chenille bedspread. Several times."

"Gwen," Stoner said under her breath, "I don't think she's interested in the details."

"Sure I am," said Divi Divi.

"She's a writer," Gwen explained to Stoner. "Writers are always interested in things like character and motivation and..."

"No," Divi Divi said, "I'm just nosy."

"The next night," Gwen went on, "I was mugged in an alley behind the drug store, and we made love again. We had to be really careful that time because I wasn't feeling too well."

"You were mugged in an alley?"

"It was a very dark alley," Gwen said.

"Well," Divi Divi said with a little smile, "I hope it went better in Iowa."

"Actually, that was the trip to Wyoming, when I was on my honeymoon, with my husband."

"And what happened to your husband?"

"Stoner killed him," Gwen said.

Divi Divi turned to her. "Girl, you don't mess around."

"She didn't really kill him in cold blood," Gwen explained quickly. "He was trying to kill me. It was sort of self-defense."

"Mugging, killing. Sounds like men give you a rough time," Divi Divi said.

Gwen nodded solemnly. "I never had much luck."

Divi Divi slipped an arm around Gwen's shoulders. "For what it's worth, doll, I give men a hard time."

"Good," Stoner said. "Someone has to."

"Okay," Rebecca said loudly, "let's run through the script. Off book if you can. Don't think about expression or phrasing. Say your lines as fast as you can, and pick up your cues. Barb will cue you. Div?"

"Coming, boss." She strode back to the stage.

Rebecca detached herself from the group and came toward them. There were spots of bright red on her cheeks and the tip of her nose. Either she had acquired a severe sunburn, or she was about to have a heart attack.

"Are you all right?" Stoner asked.

"Just need some air," Rebecca said tightly. She left the barn.

Stoner followed. Outside, Rebecca was pacing back and forth across the packed-dirt barn parking lot. Stoner fell into step beside her. "Anything I can do?"

"Do you have a cigarette?"

"Sorry. I don't smoke."

"Neither do I. At least, I haven't for six years. I may start again."

"I can't imagine doing what you do," Stoner said. "It must be gruelling."

Rebecca paused in her pacing and ran both hands through her hair, pushing it back from her ears. "Every time we do a show, there's a point at which I want to kill either myself or them."

Stoner smiled. "I guess you've reached that point."

"Nope. Three weeks from now. Then I'll have reached that point." She dropped to the ground in the sun, back against the side of the barn.

"When does the show open?" Stoner asked, sitting beside her.

"October 1. If ever."

"Then you still have five weeks."

"Guess so." Rebecca pulled a blade of grass and split it with her thumb nail. "If things stop going wrong."

So Rebecca had noticed it, too. "What kinds of things."

"Oh, nothing big. I'm just frustrated."

"Really, what kinds of things?"

"The flashlights, for one." She held another blade of grass between her thumbs and blew through it. It made a satisfyingly lewd sound. "Someone took all the flashlights. Big deal, huh? Except it is a big deal when you have to stumble around back stage and can't find anything. Or when you have to feel for the light sockets because they're up on the rafters and there's no light up there."

"That could be annoying," Stoner agreed. "And dangerous. Any idea who took them?"

Rebecca shrugged. "Kids, probably. A lot of hikers come through here in the summer. There's a cut-off from the Appalachian Trail just beyond the lake. They don't mean any harm, really. It's just a darn nuisance."

From here, she could see the Cottage in its entirety. A large, rambling building made of stone. French doors leading onto the terrace. A tall chimney with tendrils of vine crawling up the sides. A few women sat at the white wrought iron tables, reading or having cool drinks. "Do you always rehearse here?" she asked.

"For the last two years. It's a great place. And Sherry's been so generous with us. I don't know what we'd do without her."

Aha. More evidence of Sherry's importance to the company.

"Rehearsal space has completely dried up in the city," Rebecca went on. "Even places that used to let us use empty rooms want to charge by the hour. It's the recession, I guess."

Or they're still operating under an 80's "Greed is Good" mentality, Stoner thought. Grab as much as you can while there's grabbing to grab.

"Sometimes I think we should just pack it in," Rebecca went on. "Between the no-budget and the fits of temperament, I honestly don't know why we do it. Masochism, I guess. We draw pretty good audiences, enough to cover our expenses so we can start the next year with nothing, but at least no debts. Theater rentals are going up, though. And the audiences are getting smaller. People just don't seem to want to do anything any more. I remember when we first started, we had so many people wanting to help we couldn't find jobs for them all. Now we're doubling up. Maybe it's time to see the handwriting on the wall." She glanced over at Stoner and gave a small laugh. "I'm sorry. Here I am talking your head off, being pathetic, and you don't even know me."

"It's fine," Stoner said. "I need to let it all hang out from time to time, myself."

"Yeah? What do you do?"

"I run a travel agency."

Rebecca nodded. "Well, you probably have a pretty good idea of what it's like living on a tightrope."

"Sure do," Stoner said. She liked Rebecca. More than liked her, trusted her. Maybe it was instinct, or maybe it was the way the woman had let her collar deteriorate, one end folding under, the other standing as straight as a rabbit's ear. She hoped she wouldn't turn out to be their perpetrator.

If there was a perpetrator, she reminded herself. So far, they had only the missing flashlights to go on, and Rebecca's explanation was as good as any. And there was Sherry's note. But that could be a prank.

They sat for a moment in silence, feeling the sun and the slight uprising breeze that whispered of oncoming evening.

Rebecca had slipped her whistle off and was twirling it around one finger.

"That's a nice touch," Stoner said. "Makes you look very authoritative."

"Maybe authoritative, maybe authoritarian. Potato, po-tah-to. To tell you the truth, I think it's a little crass. Sort of camp-counselorish. But sometimes it's the only way to be heard."

"That's what we needed back at the Cambridge Women's Center," Stoner said. "That and a referee."

Rebecca looked at her. "You know CWC?"

"I practically lived there when I first came out," Stoner said. "I went from one support group to another. Some of them got pretty raucous. Especially the ones where we tried to define Feminism."

"The last time I was there," Rebecca said, "the only groups they had were for women with eating disorders and lesbians with babies."

Fifteen years ago, they'd had dozens of groups. Women entering the work place. Women reentering the work place. Consciousness raising and values clarification. How to fix your own car. Whether to fix your car, or convert to the less patriarchal and more environmentally sound bicycle. How to organize a demonstration. Organic gardening. Passive resistance. Organic gardening as passive resistance. Communal living. Class and race consciousness. Self-defense for women. Turning the contents of your purse or knapsack into lethal weapons. The list was endless.

But the world had moved on. Women burned out. Funding dried up. The Religious/Political Right sharpened its back-lash tools. Women's Centers, if they existed at all, did so now through the reluctant generosity of colleges and YWCA's, and services were restricted to the absolutely necessary-for-survival. Women no longer had the time or energy to fix their own cars. They were too busy just trying to make ends meet. The younger women looked at the old revolutionaries as dinosaurs, and cringed at the use of the word Feminism. Even lesbians, that ever-contentious tribe, seemed to be satisfied to call themselves "gay women," and spend their evenings at gender-free dances.

It made Stoner feel sad, and kind of middle-aged.

Someone left the Cottage and crossed the terrace, stopping to chat briefly with two women who seemed to be writing letters. She began to trot toward them across the grass.

"Hi," Sherry said cheerfully. "Hope I didn't keep anyone waiting."

"It's okay," Rebecca said. "But from now on, I wish you'd plan to stay once we get started. It really throws off the rhythm."

Sherry's face took on a whipped-puppy look. "Gee, I'm sorry. I wanted to change into jeans so I could help out the tech people. I didn't mean to inconvenience anyone."

"I appreciate your wanting to help," Rebecca said. "Next time, just tell someone, will you? It'll save you a lot of grief."

"Everyone was busy," Sherry said earnestly. "I didn't want to interrupt. I'm sorry if I upset you."

"You didn't upset me. Go on in now. They're probably waiting for you."

"Do you think they're angry?"

"No, I don't think anyone's angry. Maybe Rita..."

"She's always angry," Sherry said brightly. She gave Stoner a quick smile and slipped into the barn.

"Mother said there'd be days like this," Rebecca muttered under her breath, "but she didn't say when or how many."

Stoner laughed. "You're amazing, the way you keep it all calm on the surface. Are you an ex-nun?"

"No ex-any-nun I ever met," Rebecca said. "You must be Protestant." She pushed herself upright and stretched. "I'd better go referee."

Time to make her pitch. "Listen," she said, "I'd really like to help out, and you look as if you need all the woman-power you can get. I don't have any experience..."

Rebecca grinned. "That's the best. With experience comes Attitude."

"But I could maybe hold the script during rehearsals, and help the actors with their lines or whatever. We'll be here for a week, at least."

"Great." Rebecca squeezed her shoulder. "As of now, you're our temporary assistant director. Which is a fancy term meaning you get all the jobs no one else wants to do."

Temporary assistant director. It sounded a lot easier than understudy.

"It's your line, Roseann." Marcy's face was red and blotchy with anger. She saw Rebecca and Stoner enter and spun around to address them. "She's throwing my timing off."

Roseann looked as if she were about to cry. "You never gave me the cue."

"I did so."

"I never heard that line before."

"It was close enough."

"It didn't make any sense," Roseann said. She showed Marcy her script. "It's supposed to be..."

Marcy barely glanced at it. "It was the general idea." She addressed her frustration to the rest of the cast. "If she's going to be like this on stage, we're fucked. One misplaced comma, and the lead goes up on her lines." She flapped her arms. "This really makes me feel secure. This is really safe."

"I can't even find the line in the script," Barb said.

"I didn't recognize it," Roseann said. She was beginning to shake.

Rita moved over to stand beside her. "Forget it. She never gives the right cues."

"Personally," Divi Divi said, "speaking as the playwright, even though I didn't really write this turkey, I'd like it if you'd say the lines the way they're written."

The Goddess of Discord was in charge. Rebellion was right around the corner.

"Marcy," Rebecca broke in, "you really ought to have your lines down by now."

"I'll be ready when we open," Marcy said. "I never go up on a line on stage."

"You don't go up on them," Rita said, "but nobody can recognize them."

"Can we just move along from here?" Barb said. She picked up a few pages of script from the floor. "Shit, I don't know where I am."

"Well," said Marcy, "there goes my timing."

Barb threw up her hands. "I'm out of here," she said, and thrust her chaotic scrip in Rebecca's general direction. She stalked to the silence and sanity of the back stage area.

"I always get the sense of a speech," Marcy whined.

Rita gave a huge, weary, condescending sigh. "You don't even have the sense of the play."

"Because the play doesn't make sense," Marcy retorted.

Rita addressed herself to an invisible, sympathetic audience. "Wonderful. A general understudy who can't even remember her own lines." She blew the hair off her forehead. "Chills and thrills."

General understudy? So, if someone—like maybe the lead—drops out, Marcy gets the part. The plot thickens.

"Okay," Rebecca said brightly, "let's try to pick up where we got stuck. Stoner is going to hold book." She handed Stoner the stack of loose pages. "Marcy, please go over your pages tonight. We all know you'll be ready by the time we open, but your sister actors need to hear their cues in rehearsal, too." She turned to Roseann. "Roseann, you need to think in terms of what you can do if something goes wrong on stage."

Roseann looked as pale as fog, even under her suntan. "Huh?" she said.

"The most important thing is, don't break character. Think of how your character would respond to..."

"Can we do this later?" Sherry interrupted. "I have to break to meet with the kitchen crew at four thirty, and I really need a line run-through."

"Fine," Rebecca said. She turned to Roseann. "Let's meet after dinner and we'll work on this, okay?"

Roseann nodded. She looked terrified, frozen.

Stoner's heart went out to her. She couldn't imagine what it would be like to be on stage for the first time, with a group of people she'd never met, with the responsibility of the lead on her shoulders. Well, actually, she couldn't imagine what it would be like to be on stage at all, but she was pretty sure she wouldn't enjoy it.

"Let's back up a bit and start at the top of page 25," Rebecca said.

Stoner pawed wildly through Rebecca's script, which was badly Xeroxed, out of order, and covered with pencil notes and boxes and arrows and something that looked like short-hand and cryptic messages like MxR and RoxUL. She couldn't find page 25.

"I can't find page 25," she said.

Everyone looked around on the floor, under chairs, in their own scripts. No page 25.

"It was here yesterday," Sherry said. "I was on book, remember? I know I saw it."

Rebecca was beginning to gnaw on her lanyard. "Can someone lend Stoner a script?"

"Here," Roseann said. "Take mine." She handed it over.

"I'll run one off for you tonight," Sherry said. "And an extra page 25."

Stoner hoped someone had copied down the arrows and boxes and MxDC's. They looked important.

"Okay," Rebecca said. "Lets go." She turned to Stoner. "I want you to correct them even if there's only a misplaced 'the' or 'and'."

"Got it," Stoner said. She felt a little self-conscious and overwhelmed with the importance of this. Stoner McTavish, who can find lost luggage, deal with surly airline booking agents, pick her way through the intricacies of multiple main frame computers, arrange around-the-world tours for forty—panics at the sight of a play script.

But this was Theater. Magical, Mystical Theater.

They were looking at her expectantly.

"I'm all set," she said. "Go on."

"We need you to give us the first line," Sherry said.

Oh. She did.

Three lines later, Divi Divi went blank.

Stoner read out her line in what she hoped was a clear and commanding voice.

"Something's wrong," Divi Divi said. "I didn't hear my cue."

Roseann, whose line it had been, repeated it.

Divi Divi shook her head. "That's not the line."

"You're the playwright," Marcy said. "You should know the right lines."

"Honey, I just write 'em, I don't read 'em." She came over and took Stoner's script. Looked through page 25, then page 24, then page 26. She picked up her own script and Roseann's script and compared them. Picked a page at random from the early and late parts of the script and studied them, and shook her head. "Where'd you get this script?" she asked.

"Rebecca gave me the new pages last night," Roseann said, looking embarrassed and frightened, "the same time the rest of you got yours. I memorized all the changes, just like you asked us to."

"Well, it's not the same script."

"Maybe it's an earlier version," Sherry suggested.

Rebecca looked them over and shook her head. "I had them run off in town last evening. All of them. From the master. The only changes are the ones we wrote in today."

"Can we please move along?" Marcy yelled.

"Right." Rebecca said.

"Use my page 25," Divi Divi said to Stoner, and handed it to her. She smelled like vanilla.

Stoner flashed her a polite and—she hoped—warm "thank you" smile.

"Stoner," Rebecca said, "you keep an eye on Roseann's script. When they don't agree, make a check mark in the margin. We'll update them later."

She felt sorry for Roseann, who was already pretty shaky and was now faced with the prospect of saying the wrong line every time it was her turn. Life upon the wicked stage was, she decided, even more of a nightmare than she had thought.

It wasn't so great off-stage, either. Juggling two manuscripts, neither of them bound, comparing both, and trying to keep everyone's lines compulsively exact. Then there was the strange pattern to Roseann's mistakes. She'd go along letter-perfect for two or three pages, and suddenly everything would go wrong for a page. Stoner didn't know a lot about learning curves, but she knew it had something to do with first and last and then the middle. Roseann's learning curve looked more like buckshot.

After a while she settled into a rhythm that kept her a little ahead of what was happening on stage. Which gave her a chance to study Roseann's script a little more closely, and compare it to Rebecca's. It was very clear which of Rebecca's pages were new. The old ones were marked on, erased over, words scratched out and replaced, even some punctures that looked like tooth marks. At first glance, there didn't seem to be any difference between the pages Roseann had right and those she missed. Both were new, only slightly dog-eared. Roseann clearly took care of her script.

Something was a little off, though. She looked more closely, holding both pages 35 side-by-side. No difference in the paper or the handling, but there was something…

The print. The letters on Roseann's page was just a little darker, hardly noticeable unless you knew you were looking for something.

She puzzled over it, but not for long. Clearly, someone had substituted different pages for the real ones, and Roseann had faithfully learned them perfectly. No one else had had script trouble. So Roseann was the one being targeted. And it wasn't a prank like the missing flashlights, attributable to roving bands of adolescents. Or like Sherry's threatening note, which could have been a joke—though in fact it was a little hard to understand what was funny about it.

This was definite, malicious mischief, perpetrated by someone who had access to the scripts (and therefore probably someone in or around *Demeter Ascending*), and who wanted to make Roseann look bad.

Who was it who had had the scripts run off?

Rebecca.

It seemed unlikely that Rebecca would do this, unless her directing duties gave her a great deal of leisure and boredom.

Stoner was willing to bet that wasn't the case.

Sherry and Roseann had both been targeted.

Her first impulse was to take Roseann aside and talk to her, try to find out who might have had access to the script. Maybe there was someone in the company that Roseann had sensed had it in for her. But she couldn't do that without giving away her own interest in the matter, and blowing her cover. After all, Roseann was as viable a suspect as anyone right now. Just because something had been done to her was no proof it hadn't been done by her.

As usual, the best thing she could do was sit back and wait.

If there was one thing Stoner hated, it was sitting back and waiting.

CHAPTER 5

The first of the serious incidents happened that evening.

They were in the barn, hanging the lights. Long, heavy metal pipes were suspended from the highest beams on massive chains. Electric cords as thick as garden hoses were wrapped around the pipes and attached to a main electrical board at the back of the barn. The pipes could be reached only by climbing a tall, A-shaped ladder with round rungs. Then the lighting instruments themselves, each weighing at least fifteen pounds not including the cumbersome attaching cords, had to be hauled up the ladder and fastened to the pipes with heavy clamps.

Of all the things a person could do with her spare time, Stoner thought, this was the absolute bottom of her list.

Boneset was the official Goddess of Hanging Lights. She wore a heavy leather belt, from which dangled an assortment of wrenches and pliers and wire cutters on lengths of cord, low on her slim hips. Grabbing a clamp in one hand and a skein of string in her teeth, she started up the ladder.

Near the top Boneset seemed to hesitate, a questioning expression on her face. Then she shrugged off whatever was bothering her and went on. She attached the clamp, checked her alignment, and came back down for the light.

Barb handed it to her.

She clambered back up.

With a sudden rifle-shot "crack," the third rung from the top gave way beneath her. Boneset teetered for a moment, struggling to catch her balance, trying to hang onto the light.

"Drop it!" Barb ordered.

The instrument plummeted to the ground and shattered. Glass exploded in all directions.

Everyone jumped back.

Stoner saw Boneset grab for the ladder sides and miss. She threw herself forward. The woman tumbled down. Stoner broke her fall with one shoulder as they both collapsed amid the crunch of broken glass.

Gwen was the first to reach them. "Are you all right?"

Stoner nodded. "Boneset?"

"Shaken up," the woman said.

Barb helped her to her feet.

"Shit," Boneset said, "I'm getting too old for this kind of thing." She looked at Stoner. "Thanks for catching me. It was an insane thing to do, but I'm glad you did it. I'd have been road kill by now. Not a pretty sight."

"No problem," Stoner said. She felt shaky, and things hurt.

Boneset came over closer to her. "Are you sure you're okay?"

"Yeah, really."

The woman pointed to the floor. "Is that your blood, or mine?"

Blood? Stoner looked down. Yep, it was blood, all right. Not a lot of blood. Just a few spatters. But definitely blood.

"It's yours," Gwen said.

She sat up and inspected herself. Streamlets of red trickled across her right palm and the soft part of her forearm. Bits of glass glistened below the surface of her skin.

"First aid kit," someone called, and handed Gwen the blue metal box.

"Anything seem broken?" Rebecca asked.

Stoner shook her head. Something told her this hadn't been an accident. She wanted to get a look at the ladder.

Gwen took her by the unbloodied arm and helped her to stand. "Come on," she said, "let's clean you up."

She got to her feet. Sparkles of glass covered her clothes. She should probably go up to the inn and change, before it ground into her. But she didn't want to leave that ladder…

"Sherry's going to have a fit," Boneset said. "You know how she is."

Stoner glanced up. "How is she?"

"Like one of those overprotective collies. You know, the kind that bark their heads off every time a kid makes a potentially dangerous move? She's usually right on top of us when we do this stuff, standing in the middle of the room, barking. You feel nervous or anything?"

"A little," Stoner said. "How about you?"

"You have to be kidding," Boneset said with a laugh. "Soon as we're finished here, I'm heading for a hot tub and calming tea. Want some?"

It wasn't a bad idea. Aunt Hermione usually recommended a warm bath and chamomile tea for a case of the nerves. "Sure."

"Are you going to sit down?" Gwen asked. "Or do you prefer to stand there and bleed?"

Actually, standing there and bleeding seemed like a good plan. She knew what Gwen was leading up to, and that involved picking the glass out of her hand with a pair of tweezers, and that didn't sound like a whole lot of fun. "Where is Sherry?" she asked, hoping to divert Gwen's attention. Which, of course, was a ridiculous waste of time, since Gwen in her care-taking mode had the tenacity of a pit bull.

"Working," Rebecca said. "Problems with one of the suppliers, she said." She shrugged. "The last shipment of carrots wasn't up to standards or something."

"It was the paper towels," Barb corrected. "They sent paper towels with drawings of geese with blue ribbons."

Stoner couldn't blame Sherry for being upset. She hated that phony-Colonial cutesy New England motif herself. To say nothing of the fact that the ink in painted paper towels presented an ecological nightmare.

"Sit, please," Gwen said.

Two women were sweeping up glass, setting the dented light instrument aside. Two more hauled the offending ladder into the back of the barn, out of sight, where anything could happen to it. "Where are you going with that?" Stoner heard herself demand.

"We still have to hang the lights," Barb said. "There's another ladder. Why do you ask?"

She thought fast. "Well, don't throw it out or anything. I might be able to fix it."

"Hah!" said Boneset. "The Goddess Herself couldn't fix that mother so I'd get on it again."

"Indulge her," Gwen said. "It's kind of a hobby." She turned back to Stoner. "Sit."

She sat.

Gwen took her hand.

"Maybe we should wait on this," Stoner mumbled. "I want to look at that broken rung before anyone fiddles with it."

"Nobody's going to fiddle with it." With her free hand, Gwen rummaged through the first aid kit and came up with tweezers and first aid cream.

Stoner tried to pull away. "I mean it. If someone tampered with that rung, they're going to want to destroy the evidence before anyone sees it."

"If someone tampered with the rung," Gwen said, grasping her firmly by the wrist, "they're not going to try to cover their tracks with ten witnesses." She pressed Stoner's arm against her own lap. "Stop wiggling."

"You're not going to dig, are you?" Stoner said in a small voice.

"Not unless you keep stalling, in which case you'll clot, and all these nice, lightly embedded bits of glass will become firmly entrenched. Then I won't just dig, I'll have to excavate."

Stoner closed her eyes and clenched her teeth and tried to think of something else. Okay, who was here tonight, and who was missing? The actors, but Sherry had suggested they do an extra line run-through, once she finished dealing with…

A tiny stab of pain bit her hand. "Ow," she said.

"Sorry."

"Boneset probably got glass in her, too. Why don't you go torture her?"

"Boneset didn't hit the floor. She landed on you." Gwen looked up at her, and rested her hand against the side of Stoner's face. "I know you hate this."

The softness of her touch, the softness of her voice brought tears to Stoner's eyes. "It's okay," she said brusquely. "I'm fine."

Gwen smiled. "Sure, you are, toughie." She brushed her hand through

Stoner's hair. "You have glass chips in your hair. They look like stars in mahogany."

As usual, Gwen's tenderness reached her and made a warm place around her heart, and reduced her to a child. She wanted to curl up in Gwen's arms for the next fifteen years. She shoved it down. "I ought to shower and change," she said. "But I need to look at that ladder."

"All right," Gwen said with a little indulgent laugh. "You can be the big, strong, independent type for now. But later I get to give you a bath."

She knew her face had turned the color of strawberries. She was glad no one could see the flood of heat that flowed over the pit of her stomach and the insides of her thighs. "Okay," she squeaked, and looked up to see Rebecca standing near her—maybe within hearing distance, maybe not. She turned a shade redder.

"Is there anything I can do to help?" Rebecca asked, and added, "Now, that is, not later."

She'd heard, all right. "Yes," Stoner said. "Take me out and shoot me."

Rebecca ignored that and sat down beside her. "Listen," she said hesitantly, "I don't know how to approach this, but..."

Another pin prick of pain shot through her hand. "Spit it out," Stoner said, and winced. "Any diversion is welcome."

"I was talking with Roseann after dinner," Rebecca said hesitantly. She toyed with the simple silver chain she was wearing around her wrist. "She happened to say she knows your aunt."

"Aunt Hermione."

Rebecca nodded. "She says you have a reputation for being good at...well, puzzling things out."

Uh-oh. What did she mean, "puzzling things out?" If Roseann had mentioned her trouble-shooting reputation, it wouldn't take Rebecca long to figure out what was up. They weren't ready to have anyone know what they were really doing there.

"Puzzling things out?" Stoner said noncommittally.

"Right. She said if I needed to talk something over, you might be a good person to do it with."

Gwen glanced up from her work. "She's absolutely right."

"Well, the problem is..." she twisted the bracelet around one finger. "I think there's something funny going on here. Nothing I can really define, just a funny feeling. I don't want to say anything to the rest of the company, because I don't want to make them nervous or hurt anyone's feelings or anything." She laughed a little. "Maybe I'm just being paranoid."

"Maybe," Stoner said. "Maybe not."

"That ladder thing makes me nervous," Rebecca said. "I know Barb checked all the equipment yesterday. She always does that the day before we hang the lights. It's dangerous..."

"I'd noticed," Stoner said, and suppressed a grimace at a bee-sting of pain. If she were left-handed, she could do that herself. It didn't hurt so much when you did it yourself, when you were in control.

"And the thing about Roseann's script. Obviously, someone changed some of the pages. They must have had access to the script. And to Div's computer discs and a printer."

"Foul play," Gwen said.

"That's what I think. But it doesn't make any sense. The company's been together for years. Sure, we have our problems and our personality clashes. You should have been around for the Rita-Marcy wars. But nothing like this has ever happened before." She looked down at the floor. "The thing that really bothers me is, there's only one new member of the company."

"Roseann," Stoner said. She winced at another pang.

"Yeah. You have no idea how much I want it not to be Roseann."

Stoner's heart went out to her. "There are other guests at The Cottage, you know. There are the hikers, and the Crones..."

"You think that's possible?" Rebecca asked, and looked at her hopefully.

"Entirely possible."

"But why would anyone do that?"

"I know it sounds crazy, but sometimes people like to make trouble just to make trouble."

Rebecca nodded grimly. "I've known a few."

"So have I." But this much trouble? Boneset, or anyone, could have been killed. Tnat was a lot of trouble just for the sake of trouble. If this was merely for thrills, they were dealing with a sick mind.

"The thing is, I don't want the company to think I suspect anyone. Partly because I don't, really. But I also don't want people getting nervous. We have enough problems as it is." She frowned. "I'm really bugged about that ladder."

"I think," Gwen said, "Stoner should take a look at it, if she can do it without attracting attention." She pried another splinter of glass from the soft place at the base of Stoner's thumb. "That way no one would think you're suspicious."

"Sure," Rebecca said. "But don't you think they'd wonder why Stoner was so interested?"

"I don't know about you," Gwen said, "but when something hurts me, I certainly want to give it the once-over."

Good old Gwen. Always quick to see an opportunity and capitalize on it.

"Great," Rebecca said, and stood up. "Well, I'm glad you're okay," she said loudly. "Let me know if you need anything." She went back to the group.

Gwen yanked one last piece of glass from her hand. "That's done," she said, and spread some first aid cream over the nicks and scratches. "Can you keep from getting dirt in that, or do I have to bandage it?"

"I'll be careful." She let herself breathe normally again, and felt a little sick. "I'm such a baby."

"You're not a baby," Gwen said. "When things hurt, they hurt."

Stoner wiggled her hand to try to get some circulation in it. "Most people wouldn't half faint over a little thing like that."

"You aren't most people," Gwen said. "For which I'm extremely grateful." She packed up the first aid kit and snapped the lid. "Besides, I've never seen pain keep you from putting yourself in harm's way."

The ladder was old, the wood grayed and a little splintery. But it was as stable and solid as the day it came off the assembly line. Stoner set it upright, shook it, climbed up a few rungs, bounced up and down. It felt secure. She went up further, testing each rung. No problem. When the broken rung was at eye level, and about as high as she ever wanted to go on any ladder no matter how sturdy, she stopped and looked it over.

It hadn't been cut. That would have made it too easy, a nice, smooth, obviously-man-made cut halfway through the wood. The way things happened on television. Something anyone with a double-digit IQ could see.

But not in real life, Stoner thought. Things are never tidy in real life. Not my real life, at least.

Okay, time for problem-solving technique #1: stare at it until something occurs to you.

She stared at it.

Something occurred to her.

The rung had shattered into splinters, leaving nice, bristled ends where the break had happened. Just as you might expect.

She climbed up another step into insane and life-threatening territory, and inspected the top of the broken rung. And found what she was looking for. A slight, crescent-moon indentation right at the edge of the break. As if someone had hit the rung with a hammer. A very large, very heavy hammer, from the looks of it. Sledge hammer, probably. Carefully done, it would crack the rung to the point of weakness without necessarily breaking it in a visible way.

It would take real skill to do it, she thought. And a lot of practice, plus some luck. But it could work. Anyone climbing up to that level, especially carrying something as heavy as a lighting instrument, was bound to provide the last small bit of stress.

It meant this accident was no accident.

She looked down at the floor a hundred miles away, and felt a little sick. Someone wanted to do real harm. A prankster—even one on the sick side—would have broken a lower rung. No way you could fall from this height without risking life and limb.

Not only intentional, but directed at a member of the light crew. The chances of anyone climbing that high were remote, unless they were going to the top. And who would be going to the top but one of the tech women hanging lights?

Stoner leaned back and looked up and down the length of the barn. There was no hay loft, no tool or storage area off the floor. Nothing up there but the pipes and the lights.

Did that mean Boneset was the target? Anyone knowing the company would know Boneset was the Goddess of Hanging Lights.

Or was it just another attempt to create anxiety and distress in *Demeter Ascending* as a whole?

Sherry, Roseann, Boneset. Producer, actor, techie. The only pattern, if there was one, seemed geared toward the whole production.

From her perch near the top of the roof beams, she could see the other women at work. Lifting, carrying, steadying, handing. They worked together smoothly, like a team. More than that, she thought as someone said something she couldn't hear and the rest broke into gentle laughter. They worked as a loving team.

It wasn't any overt show of affection. But the energy wafting from them was warm and caring. They were easy with each other, and sure of themselves. If one woman needed a tool, another was beside her with it before she could ask. If one needed an extra hand, another magically appeared to help. Their actions were like a dance, carefully choreographed and well rehearsed.

Boneset offered to take over the light hanging again, but they pushed her back.

"Not without a Feminist analysis of the dialectic of the situation," Barb said in a loud and professorial tone.

The rest "booed" her.

It was hard to imagine any woman in that group wanting to harm any other.

Boneset cornered them as the entered the living room from the darkened patio. They'd taken a walk down by the lake to clear their heads and try to make sense of what had happened tonight. They hadn't succeeded at either.

Stoner was still nerved up. Her shoulder was beginning to ache and go stiff. She was working on a dull headache. Even Gwen's promised bath was beginning to lose its charm. She just wanted to take an overdose of aspirin and go to bed.

Three incidents so far—four, if you could count the missing flash lights. And the whole thing showed no signs of making sense. Threatening notes were one thing, easy to do and requiring little planning, adequate for a spontaneous expression of disgruntlement. She'd been tempted to write threatening notes, herself, though not since she was eleven. Still...

But it wasn't so easy to tamper with a manuscript. First you had to get hold of the original, and that had only become available last night. Then you had to match the typing, probably by using Divi Divi's computer disk and printer. Finally, have your counterfeit pages reproduced on matching paper and get hold of Roseann's script to make the substitution. Strictly from a convenience angle, that made Divi Divi the logical suspect for this part of the caper.

Gwen made a note for them to find out exactly who had taken the script to the copy shop. And what time the copy shop closed, and where it was, how far away, which would narrow down the time frame a little.

When they applied the means-and-opportunity method to the ladder, most of the tech crew came under suspicion. Except for Boneset. Even if she'd done the other deeds and wanted to deflect attention from herself by appearing to be a victim, she seemed too intelligent to rig such a potentially disastrous accident. Because, if Stoner hadn't broken her fall, Boneset would have quite a few bones that needed to be set.

Then there was the matter of the paper on which the threatening note, serious or not, had been written. It seemed to match the pad on Barb's clip board.

It was beginning to look as if half of *Demeter Ascending* was turning on the other half.

None of it fit together. She couldn't even figure out where they should start to look for clues. It gave her a helpless, depressed feeling. Who did she think she was, accepting Sherry's offer, letting her believe Stoner might be able to help her? Who did she think she was, pretending to know what she was doing?

"Hey," Boneset said in greeting. "I was just on my way to your room." She had changed into short seersucker pajamas and bare feet and was carrying a mug of steaming liquid. "I wanted to thank you again for saving my life."

"That's okay," Stoner said. "It was my pleasure."

Boneset giggled. "I doubt that. Anyway..." She held out the mug. "Here's the tea I promised you. I just had some. Sherry let me use the kitchen tonight."

"Thanks," Stoner said, and took the mug. The tea was a kind of greenish-dishwater gray. "What's in it?"

"Chamomile," Boneset said. "And valerian. That's what gives it that awful color and odor. And some other herbs. You're not allergic, are you?"

Stoner shook her head.

"Well, I have to hit the sack. Don't drink that until you're ready to go to sleep. It packs a wicked punch, but no hangover. See you in the morning." She disappeared up the stairs.

Stoner wrinkled her nose. "I don't know about this. It looks awful."

"I disagree," Gwen said. "It looks evil. But most of Aunt Hermione's potions look evil."

"Most of them are evil. Aunt Hermione doesn't know what she's doing with herbs. It's some kind of mental block."

"She cured one of my headaches once," Gwen said as they started up the stairs.

"She gave you plain parsley tea, and went in the other room and did a healing chant. She doesn't do well on the material plane. I'll bet a lot of psychic people have that problem. We'll have to ask Edith Kesselbaum."

"That's an idea," Gwen said, coming to a dead stop.

Stoner, following, nearly crashed into her. A few drops of tea spattered on the stairs. She wiped them up with a tissue, and was relieved to see they didn't eat into the wood or pulverize the tissue. "What idea?"

"Call Edith. Tell her what we know. Maybe she can give us an idea of what to look for, psychologically speaking."

"It couldn't hurt. And we'll call Aunt Hermione, too. She might be able to focus in on someone psychically."

"Good," Gwen said, turning back to the stairs. "Now that we have a plan, we can get some sleep. After bath time, that is."

Stoner doubted it. Unless Boneset's tea was a miracle drug, pain, worry, and frustration were going to combine to give her another sleepless night.

Sherry was lounging on Gwen's bed reading a magazine.

"Hi," she said cheerfully. "Hope you don't mind my just coming in. I knew you'd be along soon."

Actually, she did mind, but Sherry seemed to think it was the most natural thing in the world. She didn't want to appear selfish or tight-assed, so she said, "It's fine."

"So," Sherry said, swinging her feet to the floor and tossing the magazine aside. "What have you found out?"

Stoner hesitated as Gwen closed the door tightly behind them. They didn't have anything to report, really. And she found herself resenting Sherry's assumption that they'd tell her everything. On the other hand, she had hired them. At least she'd asked for their help and was supplying them with room and board. So maybe she did have the right to know…

"I'm sure you heard about the ladder," Gwen said.

Sherry nodded, and a frown crossed her face. "It's really scary, you know. All the stuff that's going on. I don't know what to make of it."

"Neither do we," Gwen said. She pulled her pajamas from the bureau and made a great display of taking off her shoes, giving the definite Going To Bed message. "It's a miracle no one was badly injured."

"I know," Sherry said. "I can just picture the law suits. And it would have been terrible if someone had been hurt," she added quickly. "I feel so responsible."

"To the best of your knowledge," Stoner said, taking her cue from Gwen and lifting her robe from the back of the bathroom door, "was that ladder in good shape?"

"I think so. The only time it's used is when we're picking apples down at the little orchard. Nobody's ever complained. Do you think there was something wrong with it?"

"There was obviously something wrong with it," Gwen said with an edge of irritation. "It broke."

Sherry glanced over at her. "You mean you think someone tampered with it?"

"We haven't the slightest idea," Gwen said. "What do you think?"

"I don't know," Sherry said, her voice a little shaky. "The whole thing really scares me."

"Well," Stoner said, and began to unbutton her shirt, "I wish we had news for you, one way or the other. At least everyone escaped unscathed."

"You didn't." Sherry's eyes were big and round.

Stoner gave a little laugh. "My injuries aren't exactly of law-suit quality."

"Do you really believe that's all I care about?" Sherry's lower lip trembled a little. "I'm sorry if I made you think that. These are my sisters. You're my sisters. Nothing's more important than your safety."

"We know that," Gwen said kindly. "We're tired and cranky, that's all."

"Oh." Sherry brightened. "That's okay."

"How did it go with the suppliers," Stoner asked, determined to be kind and hospitable if it killed her.

Sherry laughed and shook her head. "Boys. They just can't understand the importance of things. When we say we have only organic vegetables here, we expect our vegetables to be organic. To boys, a carrot is a carrot. Do you think they're trainable?"

"Carrots?" Stoner asked.

"Boys."

"Trainable," Gwen said. "Probably not educable."

"I'm getting a reputation as The Bitch who runs The Cottage."

"It's probably just as well," Gwen said. "You'll get better service." She took her soap and toothbrush kit from the drawer. "I really hate to rush you, but we were headed for bed. Okay if we talk again some other time?"

"Oh, wow, sure, I'm sorry," Sherry bubbled as she jumped to her feet. "Let me know if you figure anything out." She started for the door.

"Wait," Stoner said. "I was wondering about the scripts."

Sherry turned back. "Yes?"

"Where did Rebecca have the script changes run off last night?"

"She didn't. Div took them in when she finished writing them."

"Where did she take them?"

"Kinko's, in Bangor. Anything else?"

Damn. Stoner shook her head.

"Well, good night, then. Sleep tight. Don't let the bed bugs bite." She closed the door firmly behind her.

"Kinko's," Gwen said grimly. "Bummer."

"Yeah." Of all the hundreds of copy shops in a fifty-mile radius, she'd gone to the one that was open 24 hours. So much for narrowing down the time. So much for anyone seeing her come or go, or anyone slip into her room. If Divi Divi was like most writers, it was probably 3 A.M. when she went into town. Which meant she was probably the only one with access to the script changes.

Gwen went into the bathroom and started running water in the tub. "Come on," she said. "Take your bath and drink your tea. We've done everything we can tonight."

A little breeze had come up. Just enough to lift the curtains and move like breath across her skin. The night was dark and silent, the moon already gone down behind the lake. Stoner felt herself relax, felt the soft warmth of Gwen's hands gently massaging her back. She tasted the smoky flavor of Boneset's tea on her tongue. And drifted off to sleep.

Something woke her deep in the night. A solitary metallic click, like the sound of a single typewriter key.

She listened to the darkness. Gwen's breathing was soft and deep, sleep sounds.

Must have been her imagination, or the random sound of an old house responding to changes in temperature or barometric pressure.

She tried to get back to sleep, but her ears were alert as foxes' ears.

Minutes drifted by, and still no sound.

Something was happening to the light outside the window. Not dawn, but an occasional pulse of gray, so faint she wasn't certain it had happened. She waited and focused her attention.

There. And again.

Slipping from her bed, she sidled to the window. The lawn was black as velvet, the moon gone down, the stars cold.

There. Someone with a flashlight, just like last night, slipping from the parking lot and heading toward the barn.

The parking lot.

Her mind shifted into gear. If Divi Divi had left the new scripts in the car, and hadn't locked the doors...there seemed little reason to lock car doors at The Cottage, and no one would expect a thief to go after script changes, not even whole scripts...

That was how it could have happened. Take Roseann's new pages, and substitute the fake ones.

But then the perpetrator would have to find a way to ensure that Roseann got the wrong script. The new pages were probably handed out at random, first come first served.

Maybe not. Maybe the only changes were to Roseann's and a couple of other scripts—Rebecca's, of course, and probably Barb's, they were the people who would have to have the scripts intact. And the lighting people. And maybe props women would need to have all the right cues. Assistant director, who would be—as we theater folks say—on book.

No, yours truly was temporary assistant director, and she hadn't been given a script at all.

But there had been plenty of scripts around which needed to be up-dated. Getting the right one to Roseann would be a problem.

On the other hand, if the purpose of messing up the scripts was to disrupt the company in general, and Roseann herself wasn't necessarily the target, it wouldn't be difficult at all.

Assuming Divi Divi had left the new scripts in her car.

Assuming the perp had access to Divi Divi's car.

Assuming Divi Divi wasn't the perp.

Stoner sighed. There was one aspect of this situation that was becoming increasingly clear: whoever was causing the problems with *Demeter Ascending* was working from the inside.

The light flashed into view again, lighting up the barn door. It opened, and closed again on darkness. Again the pale glow, indistinct as moth wings in the windows.

Stoner pulled herself up. If she slipped out now, she could creep across the lawn under cover of night. She might be able to see who it was lurking around the barn. Might even catch them in the act. Red-handed.

No, said Gwen's voice in her mind, if you find anything, you wait to act until you have help. No heroics here.

Okay. Surveillance only.

Quietly, she slipped her jeans over her boxer pajamas. Struggled into a dark tee shirt. Slipped her feet into running shoes—not the safest things to go creeping about in the dark, with their reflective heels. But the darkest she could find.

There was always the possibility of going bare-foot. And the possibility of stepping on night-crawlers wriggling out of their subterranean caves to lap up a bit of dew. She'd stepped bare-foot on all the night-crawlers she cared to by the age of five, thank you very much. Not as sudden as snakes, but much slimier. Better seen than slimed.

Opening the closet door very, very slowly, she fumbled for her knapsack. Touched canvas. Only canvas knapsack left in America, no doubt, things having turned more and more toward weird, smooth, brightly-colored petroleum products—and how in the world could you feel as if you were really camping when your gear looked like something out of the Magic Kingdom?

She found the buckle and the flap, let her fingers do the stumbling through the collection of necessities inside. Small first aid kit. Sewing kit—never knew when that would come in handy. Compass-whistle-waterproof match box combination. Swiss Army knife that she never used because she didn't want to dull the blades. Swiss Army knives were plentiful right now, but anything could happen, better be safe. She should probably pick up a second knife, for emergencies. Small packet of paper napkins, so fingered and frayed they weren't good for much. A collapsible drinking cup. Personally, she enjoyed drinking from her own cupped hands, but once on a hike she had found a lost dog. In addition to being lost, the dog was thirsty, and they had both been considerably frustrated while she tried to pour water from a canteen with one hand and provide a drinking dish with the other. As soon as she had returned the lost dog (it turned out to be a Dandy Dinmont Terrier/Beagle mix, very high energy) to its tearfully grateful family, she had gone directly to the camp store and purchased the collapsible cup.

She found what she was looking for at the bottom, of course. Her very own, personal, handy flashlight.

Standing, she winced at the "pop" in her left knee. Creaking, popping, what next?

Well, as a sweet young dental hygienist had once told her, after 35 it's all down hill.

Twerp.

Gwen stirred a little, muttering in her sleep. Stoner leaned closer.

"Stoner?"

"Don't wake up. I'm going out."

"Out where?"

"To the barn. Someone out there."

"Oh. Be careful. Love you." Her breathing deepened as she fell back asleep.

Stoner grinned to herself. If Gwen woke up and remembered that little exchange, there'd be hell to pay in the morning.

She touched Gwen's hair for luck and slipped from the room.

The furniture made huge haystack chunks of gray, but they reflected enough light so she could move around them. Creeping to the windows, she looked out toward the barn. Whoever was inside was still there, moving back and forth in the stage area.

Okay, first we check the inn registry for a description of Divi Divi's car, then try to sneak up on our Barn Visitor.

Shielding the light with one hand, she turned the pages in the guest book until she found Divi Divi's name. Last name, Jones. Divi Divi Jones? Seemed like a waste of a good first name. Should be something exotic, like the woman herself. Jones, indeed.

She was in luck. In keeping with the quaintness of The Cottage, Sherry had written all the registration information in the book. Name, address, phone, car description...If she'd had to look it all up on the computer, she'd waste precious time. She could work it just fine, but sometimes people picked very odd names for their files. Marylou always claimed they didn't need password protection for their files at the agency as long as they were creative in naming them. The result was that they had files named things like "IGO-POGO," which Marylou found descriptive of tours to Atlanta. It worked, though. No one had ever broken into their files. And that included Stoner, who always had to call Marylou when she needed information after hours.

At one time she had toyed with the idea of getting them beepers and interrupting Marylou every time she went out to dinner—or later, if she had gone out with a man she was interested in. But it really didn't seem worth the trouble, and probably wouldn't annoy Marylou, anyway.

It was very difficult, trying to annoy someone who wasn't annoyed by much. Very frustrating.

Lt. blue '85 Chevy Blazer. Okay.

She closed the book and crept over to the door that led out into the parking lot. Turned the knob.

The door opened.

She slipped through and was about to let the door swing shut when she realized she'd probably lock herself out. Easing back inside, she swept her flashlight beam across the shelves behind the desk. Aha. A large roll of Scotch tape. Just the thing. Tearing off a long strip, she opened the door again, pushed the buttons that released the old lock, and taped them down for good measure.

It was the best she could do. If she couldn't get back in, she'd have to sleep outside until someone showed up, and pretend she'd gone for an early-morning walk and ended up locked out.

Stoner nodded to herself. Her mind was working amazingly well, considering the hour of night. She'd have to ask Boneset for the recipe for her tea. No sedative hang-over.

The car was easy to find, sitting at the edge of the parking lot under a choke cherry tree. She winced as the gravel made little crunching sounds beneath her feet. She stopped and listened for signs of stirring.

The silence was deep. No night birds twittering and fluttering. No bull frogs calling from the lake. It must be the dead of night. The witching hour. The stillness before the first silvery glint of dawn.

Holding her breath, she tried the handle on Divi Divi's car. The lock gave in response to her pressure. She stopped. She didn't really want to open the door. That might cause terrible hinge noises that would bring Security on the run. And who knew, maybe Divi Divi had one of those car alarms that were always going off and being ignored in the city? She could bet it wouldn't be ignored out here in the wilderness.

And, speaking of Security, it seemed The Cottage was a little derelict in that regard. Here she'd been wandering around downstairs, going through the books, opening and closing the front door, and nobody had shown up to ask what she was doing. She made a mental note to speak to Sherry about that.

Standing on tip toe, shining her flashlight beam through the open windows of Divi Divi's car, she looked around for tell tale signs of...of what? She wasn't really sure what she was looking for, but she didn't find anything out of order. Just the usual car clutter. Gum wrappers. A map of Boston with a foot print superimposed over the Public Gardens. Various audio tapes tossed on the dash board. Glove compartment held shut with duct tape. Behind the front seat an ice scraper, some frayed rope, a well-thumbed copy of *My Lives* by Roseanne Arnold. The floor of the front seat passenger side held an uncapped ball point pen with a gnawed look, an empty Dairy Queen Blizzard cup, and a receipt from Kinko's Copies.

At least there was nothing incriminating. And she now knew that Divi Divi left her car unlocked. Anyone could have substituted the pages in Roseann's script.

Switching off the flash, she gave her eyes a few moments to adjust to the darkness. She could go around the inn to the right and cross the lawn to the barn, following the prowler's path. But that would mean walking across an open space, vulnerable to being seen. On the other hand, she could circle around to the left, where the trees pressed close to the building, stay close to the woods and maybe be invisible. Assuming she didn't trip over anything, walk into anything, or fall into anything. There could be all sorts of obstacles in the woods, not the least of which would be dry sticks, ankle-grabbing vines, and poison ivy.

Good time of year for poison ivy, too. Should be just about ripe, viscous, and potent. She'd already had two attacks of poison ivy in the past five years. The first was relatively mild—she hardly recognized it, since she'd been immune to it from childhood. The second was more serious, involving both hands, one knee, and a band of the stuff around her waist that she couldn't even explain to herself. The third time was bound to be fatal.

She supposed she'd have to get immunization shots against it, since they were moving out into the country where it undoubtedly ran rampant. She wasn't looking forward to that. Gwen had done it as a child back in Georgia, and declared they "pound that stuff into your arm with a jack hammer."

Excuse me, she asked herself, but why are you standing out here in the middle of the night thinking about poison ivy shots? While your prowler is undoubtedly doing serious damage and getting away with it?

I don't know. One thought just seems to lead to another. And, anyway, what makes you think that prowler is up to no good? It could just be a member of the company going to get something she left behind.

In the middle of the night?

All right, all right, I'm going.

She crossed the parking lot, stepping carefully, wincing at the way the gravel crunched like Rice Krispies. Loud enough to wake the dead.

Rice Krispies reminded her that she was hungry, even though dinner had been ample, tasty, and not particularly frightening. Rice Krispies would be good right now. Rice Krispie candy made with marshmallow would be even better. Add a few chocolate chips and she'd be in heaven. And maybe a handful of peanuts. Salted peanuts. Good mix of textures, soft, crunchy, chewy…

It really was dark out here. Dark enough to disorient. To make you lose your balance. She reached out, touching the hoods of cars as she passed. Hoped she wouldn't leave finger prints, if it came to that.

Came to what? Strange expression, "come to that." Who made up things like that? Were there people who sat around in a kind of think tank, coming up with strange expressions to confuse people whose first language wasn't English? Nasty little self-righteous people, probably hold-overs from the Reagan administration.

Something made her stop in her tracks. A physical sensation. Something out of place, wrong.

What…?

The car she was standing next to…The hood of the car she was touching…

…was warm.

CHAPTER 6

It was an off-white Lexus, no more than a year old.

It was still ticking as it cooled. So it hadn't been parked long. Long enough to belong to the prowler?

Maybe. Stoner tried to calculate time in her head. It seemed hours since she'd been standing in the window of their room, watching that light. But it could have been minutes. If it had been as long as it felt, the eastern sky would surely be showing signs of awakening. In the unchanging darkness, time seemed to be stopped.

She didn't like this feeling of disorientation. She wondered if Lexus felt it. But Lexus had a flashlight, and probably a watch, maybe even an Egg McMuffin.

The thought of an Egg McMuffin made her mouth water. Creamy cheese, salty ham, the yeasty crisp of English muffin…

What was going on here? She didn't even like Egg McMuffin. The yolks were usually hard-cooked and dry and made her feel like gagging. It was desperation food, the kind of thing you eat when you've been driving all night on the Interstate and know you'll fall asleep and kill yourself if you don't stop for breakfast. Or when you have to be up in the morning long before anyone with any sense would dream of getting up, and nothing's open anyway, so you might as well have an Egg McMuffin. Either that or kill yourself from the sheer misery of being awake before anyone else in the world. Egg McMuffin was definitely an alternative to suicide.

Stoner shook her head. Concentrate. The Lexus was her first decent clue, especially if the owner also happened to be the Flash Light Prowler. Now, if she was lucky, the doors would be unlocked and the registration right in the handy-dandy glove compartment. She reached for the door handle…

…and just in time noticed the blinking red light embedded in the dash.

Expensive, never-fail, car alarm. Designed not only to raise the dead but to alert the police, the fire department, the highway department, and the department of public works.

Well, Lexus wasn't the only person in the world with a flashlight. Not by a long shot. Cupping one hand around the lens to focus the beam, she aimed at the car's interior—then realized too late and with a start that the alarm might well be light-sensitive.

It wasn't. But there was nothing of interest inside the car. Clean as a whistle, whatever that meant. Clean as a rental.

Maybe it was a rental.

Damn, she wished she could get inside.

In some states, you had to have your registration attached to the steering wheel, or clipped to the sun visor and visible at all times.

Not here, though. No siree, not in good old secretive, mind-your-own-business Maine. Not in the Pine Tree Fine Free State of Maine.

Back to checking the guest register, then. Assuming Lexus was a guest, and not just a person of low moral character slipping into The Cottage at night for nefarious purposes.

Stoner looked around at the still-dark night. Clearly, her best bet was to try to see the prowler for herself. Eyeball the suspect. Which brought to her imagination a vision of her eyeballs hurtling across the lawn in hot pursuit of the perpetrator.

McTavish, she muttered to herself, you are sick.

Hop to it. Time's a-wastin'.

Actually, for all practical purposes, time was standing still.

Moving slowly, placing each sneaker on the gravel carefully, she edged to her left across the parking lot and into the trees.

On her second tree-sheltered step she snagged her foot. Good old northeastern woods, bursting with vines and brush and downed trees and generally annoying undergrowth. She recalled the forests she'd seen in the west, particularly in Arizona. The tall, thick, reddish-brown trunks, and branches that seemed to start at the sky and go on forever. The forest floor as clean and needle-carpeted as a park, and smelling of fresh pine and heat beneath your feet. But in New England, nature was allowed—even encouraged—to run amok. New Englanders thrived on green congestion.

Now, there was a disgusting thought if taken literally. Green lung disease.

Or would that be green consumption?

No, green consumption would be eating a salad or other leafy vegetable. Healthy things.

What is the matter with me? she wondered. Her mind felt like a dog on a long leash, wandering over people's yards, stopping to sniff endlessly at some singular, fascinating blade of grass…

A dot of light flashed from the direction of the barn.

Stoner focused her attention and waited. If she could lurk here, out of sight, until the person or persons unknown returned to his/her/their car, and opened the door and got in…

The light swept back and forth briefly, then disappeared.

Now what?

A moment later, a faint glow appeared wandering through the trees toward the lake.

Great. Wonderful. Terrific. The old McTavish luck was as bad as ever.

She had to follow.

The woods grabbed her ankles and snagged her clothes and complained with loud cracklings and snappings and rustlings. A branch came out of nowhere and slashed at her face, raising a stinging welt. The jagged end of a broken pine limb stabbed her forehead and sent her stumbling backward into a bramble bush that hadn't been there a minute ago but welcomed her with open briars.

She felt about as graceful as a bull moose.

The light ahead of her was gone now, but she didn't dare turn on her flash. Person Unknown could have sensed her, and turned to look. She couldn't give herself away.

Suddenly she had the feeling Person Unknown knew she was following. Wanted her to follow. Had, in fact, staged this entire event for her benefit.

Good. As if we aren't having enough fun, let's have delusions of grandeur.

She pushed on.

Finally, by some miracle, she was at the corner of the barn.

She looked toward the lake. Nothing there. Whoever had gone that way was either lying low, or had disappeared from the face of the earth. Slipped into the lake, maybe, back into the primordial ooze of which all lake bottoms were made. The Creature From The Black Lagoon.

Creature From The Black Lagoon in a Lexus?

Stoner listened hard. She couldn't hear a thing. No footsteps, no splashing water, no heavy breathing except her own.

All right, she'd lost her quarry. The question now was, what should she do? Go into the barn and check for damage? Go back to bed before someone else decided to look out a window and saw her light and came to check, and then someone else saw both their lights and…

They could turn the whole night into one big slumber party. Invite the entire population of The Cottage. Even the Crones. Crones always knew how to liven up a party.

And eventually someone as congenitally curious as herself would ask whose idea it had been and why she'd been out here in the first place.

Better to slink back to bed and wait.

Except that she really was congenitally curious, and the thought of sleeping without knowing what had happened here was inconceivable. She knew she'd be up at dawn, rush through breakfast, and make a very-uncasual beeline for the barn. Thereby attracting attention and arousing suspicion.

She had to know, and she had to know now.

Carefully, she turned the knob on the door. It wasn't locked. Bad idea. She'd have to speak to Sherry about that first thing in the morning.

To her amazement, the door opened smoothly and silently. She'd expected squeaks and groans at the very least. After all, this was a night for noises. But the hinges were well-oiled. Unusual. People didn't normally pay a lot of attention to barn door hinges. But someone had paid a great deal of attention to these.

On a hunch, she touched two fingers to the upper hinge. They'd been oiled, all right, and recently. She sniffed. Not just oiled. Sprayed with WD-40, the handyperson's magic elixir. Guaranteed to clean, derust, and lubricate all in one spray.

So the hinges had probably been neglected until recently. Why would someone suddenly care about silent hinges?

Because Someone wanted to sneak around, obviously.

Or, equally obviously, because one of the techies, who was never without her can of WD-40, had decided to do everyone a favor and silence the squeaking hinges.

She tried to remember if the hinges had squeaked this afternoon.

Yes, they had. She had noticed it right away, because she'd been afraid of interrupting the rehearsal.

And this evening?

They'd been squeaky then, too.

She was relieved to note that her mind seemed to be functioning normally again, without going off on a food tangent.

So Someone—her prowler, no doubt—had wanted to slip into the barn unnoticed, and had gone to some trouble to do so.

Wait a minute. The hinges were on the inside, of course, there being very little purpose to placing hinges on the outside of a door and inviting theft and unauthorized entry. So that meant they'd been oiled earlier, possibly so someone could enter silently in the dark of night. Which pointed the finger of suspicion back at the company.

Well, she might as well have a look around.

Narrowing the flashlight beam again, she ducked below the windows and prowled through the uninhabited barn.

At night, the rooms in barns and factories belong to inanimate objects. It's their time, and their place, their turn to use the spaces of the world. Taking over, they sit heavily and sharpen their edges. They fill their territory with their bulk, pushing back the walls and permeating open places. The metal-and-electricity odor of them saturates the air.

They resent intruders.

Stage lights, caught in her beam, flashed a glassy warning. Ladders rose up threateningly. Piles of rags seemed to pull themselves together and think of attacking. A portable radio smirked. Tool boxes stirred. Out of the corner of her eye, she caught the movement of wrenches.

Moving to the periphery, she avoided snaking orange coils of electric wire. Chairs shifted, so silently and slightly it might be her imagination. In one corner, the broken lighting instrument lay plotting revenge.

It wasn't my fault, she wanted to say. I didn't do this to you. You can't blame all humans for one bad one.

The saw horses moved a little closer together and glared at her.

"Bigots," she muttered. "Human-haters, huddling together in your anger like the Religious Right."

The saw horses simpered.

As far as she could see, there was nothing wrong in here. No more breakage, at least. No obvious acts of vandalism. If anything had been stolen, she wouldn't know it.

It didn't make sense, she thought, sitting back and turning off her flashlight so she couldn't see the sneers of the tools and instruments. This was a theater company. An amateur theater company. A women's theater company. What could possibly be a motive for the things that were happening? Certainly not money. They'd probably meet expenses only if they were lucky, even with everybody volunteering her time. And the show had little chance of making it to Broadway, or even off-Broadway. They certainly didn't represent any serious competition.

Maybe someone had a grudge against someone, though destroying the show seemed like a rather elaborate way to get revenge.

Maybe it was like climbing Mt. Everest. You just did it because it was there.

Sure.

Well, this was getting her nowhere. She flicked on her light and took one last look around.

Nothing.

She crawled to the door and slipped out and took aim at the house, its white painted stones glowing like fog in the darkness. As she started across the lawn, she thought she heard the chairs behind her, shifting their positions.

Sleep still on her, she felt Gwen slip into bed beside her, and turned herself lazily into the softness of Gwen's arms. "Tell me it's not morning already," she grumbled.

"I'm afraid it is."

Stoner groaned. "I feel as if I just went to bed."

"You did," Gwen said with a low laugh. "You were prowling all night."

She nuzzled against Gwen's shoulder. "Did I wake you?"

"Not for long. Boneset's tea packs a punch. I only had two swallows and I was out like a light."

"Not me," Stoner said.

"Well, from what you've told me about your reaction to pot..."

"Huh?" Stoner said, jerking upright. "There was marijuana in that tea?"

"Sure," Gwen went on as blithely as if nothing had happened. "So, since you told me it always used to energize you..."

"Boneset gave us tea made of illegal recreational drugs?"

"...even though it always made you funny in the head..."

"She could have gotten us in big trouble."

"...I'm not surprised you couldn't sleep."

"That stuff carries mandatory prison terms."

Gwen laughed. "Come on, Stoner, this isn't exactly Narc-ville. Nobody's going to find out."

"That's not the point. She should have told us. We might have...scruples or something."

"That's not likely."

"But if we did..."

"True," Gwen said thoughtfully. "It is a matter of etiquette."

Stoner scrubbed her face with her hands, erasing the last traces of sleepiness. "Assuming it was marijuana. Lots of things smell like that."

"Not exactly."

She picked up the mug from the bedside table and sniffed it. It was marijuana, all right. Even the valerian couldn't hide its sweet-smokey odor.

"So what did you find out with all that running around last night?" Gwen asked as she slipped her hand under Stoner's tee-shirt and stroked her back.

"Not much." She flopped over onto her stomach and gave into the feeling of Gwen's firm, soft hands against her skin.

"Incidentally, my love," Gwen said, "I don't exactly appreciate you running off in the middle of the night that way."

"Sorry," Stoner mumbled. Sleep was trying to drag her back. "There wasn't any other way to run off."

"You know what I mean."

"I saw something. I wanted to check it out."

"What did you see?"

"A light."

"What kind of light?"

"Flashlight light."

"And?"

"Nothing. I found Divi Divi's car—on account of the scripts and all—but all I could tell was that she likes Dairy Queen Blizzards."

"Definitely the sign of a criminal mind," Gwen said.

"I went down to the barn, but it didn't look as if anything had been touched."

"Then why did you go out the second time?"

Stoner twisted her head around and looked up at her. "What second time?"

"You went out, and then you came in, and then you went out, and came in again."

"I didn't."

Her hand stopped moving. "You did, Stoner. I heard you."

"You were asleep."

"I woke up, and then I went back to sleep. But I heard what I heard."

"I only went out once, Gwen."

Gwen was silent for a moment. "How would you know? You were stoned."

"So were you."

"Not that stoned."

Something was wrong here. Something deeply, seriously wrong. Stoner sat up. "You don't believe me, do you?"

Gwen looked away. "Of course I do."

"No, you don't." She waited. Gwen didn't answer. "Gwen."

"We're going to miss breakfast," Gwen said. She swung her feet onto the floor.

"Gwen."

"Okay, I believe you." Gwen glanced at her quickly, then away. "You didn't leave twice, or come back twice. It was my imagination."

"Why would I do that?"

"How should I know?" Gwen snapped. "After all, it wasn't really true." She slipped into the bathroom and locked the door.

Stoner felt anxiety like a fist in her stomach. This was crazy. Or maybe Gwen was crazy. She'd never lied to Gwen, not in all the time they'd been together. And even if she'd wanted to—which she really never had—she was no good at it, anyway.

Maybe she'd done something she didn't know about, accidentally, to make Gwen not trust her.

She tried to think, but couldn't come up with anything.

The shower was running.

They'd been together the whole day yesterday. There hadn't been anything.

This was wrong. They loved each other. They weren't supposed to be having secrets and strangenesses and unvoiced distrust.

Calm down, she told herself. This is just some morning weirdness. Some before-coffee whatever.

She dressed quickly, and tried not to think, and sat down on the bed to wait for Gwen.

The shower stopped. The bathroom door opened. Gwen peeked around. She looked as if she'd been crying. "I'm sorry," she said.

Stoner went to her and took her—wet naked body and all—in her arms. "It's okay." Relief ran through her veins like blood. "It was just a…thing."

Gwen hung onto her. "I don't know what happened. I must be premenstrual."

"That's probably it." Gwen's hair was wet against her cheek. She knew that wasn't it. But it was all right now. It had passed. Forget it. "Get dressed and let's go eat." She forced a grin. "Unless you're planning to go like that and give the whole dining room a thrill."

"It's just so strange," Gwen said as she tossed her comb onto the dresser and picked up the empty mug. "I know one thing for sure. I'll never touch Boneset's tea again."

Stoner punched the automatic lock on the door and started to pull it closed. Then she remembered. "Wait a minute. I want to bring that note Sherry gave us. I thought of a way to check it against Rebecca's book."

She opened her underwear drawer and rummaged through the socks. No note.

Puzzled, she searched the tee-shirt drawer. Nothing there, either.

"Gwen," she called, "did you move the note?"

"Nope."

"It's not here."

"It must be here." Gwen yanked her drawers from the dresser and tossed the contents onto the bed. "I don't have it."

"Neither do I."

They looked at each other.

"Stoner," Gwen said, "are you sure you locked the door when you went out last night?"

"I always do. It's automatic with me."

"But do you remember doing it last night?"

"Not specifically..."

Gwen frowned. "Then I'm not crazy, and I didn't dream it. Someone was in our room while you were out."

They ran into Boneset in the lobby. She was wearing a paisley granny-skirt and light-weight unbleached muslin vest. Her hair was pulled back and up, and formed into a bun. Yesterday's baby butch had become today's Earth Mother.

"Hey," she called cheerily, "how'd you sleep last night?"

"Great," Stoner said in what she hoped was a convincing replica of enthusiasm. "The tea was wonderful."

"It certainly was," Gwen agreed, and handed her the mug. She lowered her voice. "Incidentally, you don't have to worry. We won't tell."

Boneset looked at them quizzically. "Tell what?"

"About your secret ingredient."

"The dong quai? It gives it an odd flavor, but it's no secret."

"The other secret ingredient," Stoner said.

"I don't know what you mean."

Gwen leaned close to her. "The marijuana."

The woman turned the color of strawberry ice cream. "There's no marijuana in that tea. I'd never do that."

"You wouldn't?" Gwen asked, puzzled and taken aback.

"Of course not. What if you had a drug problem or something? That'd be really tacky. And how'd I explain it to my AA group? 'I didn't slip, folks. But someone saved my life and I turned her on.' " She snorted. "That'd go over like a lead balloon, wouldn't it? Before you could say 'Higher Power,' everyone in the group'd be taking my inventory."

"Wait a minute," Stoner said. "You're telling me you didn't spike the tea?"

"That's what she's telling you," Gwen said.

"Besides," Boneset said, her voice rising, "one of those older women's an ex-cop. Who knows where her head's at. Do you know where her head's at?"

"I haven't met her," Stoner said, keeping her own voice low and intimate in the hope that Boneset would follow suit. "Look, we might have been mistaken..."

The woman sniffed the residue at the bottom of the mug. "It's pot, all right. Jesus! Maybe someone's messed with my herbs. Maybe someone's trying to set me up."

Maybe. If so, it meant that there had been two incidents directed at Boneset, which gave her the best score in the company. Boneset: 2. Roseann: 1.

"First the ladder, now this." Boneset wrinkled her forehead. "I assumed the ladder was an accident, but...You suppose maybe someone has it in for me?"

"I don't know," Stoner said. "Can you think of anyone who might?"

"Not in this lifetime. This might be some heavy Karmic shit."

Possible, but not helpful for our immediate purposes.

"What about someone you might have offended," she said, not sure quite how to put it, "when you were...doing whatever you were doing that you're in AA about ? "

"I doubt it," Boneset said. "I was living in Eugene, Oregon, at the time. Anyone who'd follow me across the country just to get even has a real problem."

"That's just it," Gwen said. "Whoever's doing this might have a real problem."

Boneset dropped into the nearest chair. It was a high-backed, stiff wing chair, the kind of miserably uncomfortable antique Stoner's mother aspired to. "Bummer," the woman said.

Stoner wondered if they had given away too much already. She wished she didn't have to work under cover. It made it nearly impossible to ask the kinds of questions she wanted, needed to ask. If she could do this openly, she could call everyone together, have them make anonymous lists of known or suspected enemies and see who got the highest score, have them all keeping track of suspicious incidents or persons. She could turn this ragged group of women into a lean, mean detecting machine.

Oh, God. She rubbed her face. She was starting to reason like the CIA. Her mind was still as loose and fluttery as a wind sock in a gale. She ought to know better than to think before coffee. Or try to think before coffee, since what she was doing fell somewhat short of rational thought.

"I don't know what to do," Boneset said. "I mean, this is truly scary."

Gwen patted her shoulder in a reassuring way. "Maybe it would be best not to mention it to anyone else—you know, let whoever's doing it think they're getting away with it. Stoner and I can keep an eye on things, sort of behind the scenes."

Boneset looked at her gratefully. "You'd really do that?"

"Of course," Stoner said.

"If anything happens and we don't see it," Gwen said, "just come tell me about it. We're teching together. Nobody'll suspect anything."

Gwen was amazing. She'd managed to put them on the receiving end of information without giving anything away. And she'd done it before breakfast.

"If it's not too personal," Gwen was asking, "what were you addicted to?"

Boneset rolled her eyes. "Everything. Alcohol, food, drugs, sex, love, you name it."

"Marijuana?" Stoner put in.

"Of course. If it altered your consciousness, I used it."

The Dyke Hikers swarmed by on their way to the dining room, hard, healthy, sun-tanned bodies impatient for exertion. They jostled and laughed and shouted to each other and filled the room with noise and activity. If that energy could be harnessed, Stoner thought, it would light all of Las Vegas.

"We'd better go in," Boneset said when the throng had passed and she could be heard. "We have a long day ahead. Feel free to join our table if you want."

"Thanks," Gwen said. "But something's not right with the plumbing in our room. We need to talk to Sherry about it."

"Good luck," Boneset said as she got up and headed for the dining room. "That woman's a maniac in the morning. I used to think she was on uppers. Then I realized she just gets high on crisis." With a wave of her hand she disappeared behind the French doors.

"I don't know how you do it," Stoner said when they were alone.

"Do what?"

"Make up things so easily. I mean, the way you size up a situation and come up with the perfect cover story...It's kind of uncanny."

"Thank you," Gwen said modestly. "It comes from being raised in the south."

"Kind of sociopathic, actually."

"Yankees," Gwen said with a sigh. "What's sociopathic to you is just gracious to us."

"Well, that's frightening," Stoner said.

Gwen squeezed her shoulder. "Don't worry about it. Remember, The Confederacy lost the War. It'll never catch on."

They found themselves jammed into a corner table that was too small to support a game of solitaire but set for two diners. Sherry was making the rounds of the tables. Gwen buried herself in her menu.

There was a pattern emerging here, Stoner thought in her morning-woozley way which sometimes gave her her best, if not most bizarre, ideas. Roseann's script had been altered, which made her look incompetent in front of the others. And Boneset had been frightened, which could make her go for her tea, which would put her in danger of being readdicted, or at the very least would be a blow to her self-esteem. Both women had been attacked at their points of vulnerability.

Whoever was behind this not only knew a lot about the women of *Demeter Ascending*, but was smart and very mean.

And how about Sherry? What was her Achilles' heel in this production?

The waitress was waiting. Stoner ordered coffee and a blueberry muffin. Gwen ordered a breakfast big enough to meet one's breakfast needs for a year.

"It's not fair," Stoner grumbled. "You eat breakfast like a trucker and never gain weight."

"All my metabolism happens in the morning." Gwen glanced up and flashed Sherry a smile.

Sherry made her way over to them, stopping by the other tables. Laughing at someone's joke, examining the rim of a glass. Jotting things in a tiny note book with a little silver pen. Obviously, Sherry made it her business to attend to all guest complaints personally.

She pocketed her note book and approached their table. "What a morning," she said with a heavy sigh.

"Problems?" Gwen asked.

Sherry dug out her note book and flipped it open.

To Stoner, it had a slightly theatrical quality, a gesture bigger than life. But it was morning, and everything seemed exaggerated to her in the morning. A car starting up on the street was an Army tank headed for her living room. A singing bird was a trumpet's blare. Sunlight was a spot light turned directly in her face. The odor of a cup of brewing coffee was like a warehouse stacked to the rafters with French Roast, going up in flames.

"Cobweb," Sherry read. "Corner of a bathroom on the second floor. Two chipped glasses, have to call the dishwasher repair people. It might indicate a malfunction. Sticky dresser drawer on one. Flowers need to be changed in the lobby." She closed it with an efficient snap. "The usual joys of innkeeping."

Joys? This went beyond joys. This was…was environmental harassment. So what if a cobweb showed up in a bathroom? It wasn't inhabited, was it? Dresser drawers stuck all the time, especially in August, especially in the Maine woods. As for chipped glasses, glasses got chipped, it was what glasses did. It kept you from getting bored with the old pattern. She wondered how desperate you had to be to work for Sherry Dodder.

"Do you enjoy it?" she asked.

"Actually, I do, in a perverted sort of way. How about you two, any complaints?"

"None," Stoner said quickly. The ceiling would have to fall in on their beds before she'd let their room go on Sherry's list.

"I guess you heard about last evening," Gwen said as she buttered her blueberry muffin. "The ladder?"

"I certainly did," Sherry said, noticing a smudge mark on Stoner's knife handle and adding it to her list. Someone would probably be fired for it. "Fortunate no one got hurt. I'm not sure our insurance would cover it. Unconventional use of building. Usual loopholes." She glanced up at Stoner from her writing. "Do you need me to file a claim for you?"

Stoner shook her head, a little surprised at Sherry's attitude. It seemed almost callous. "I don't know about Boneset, though. She was pretty shaken up."

"But not injured, thanks to you." A brisk smile crossed her face. "How are…" She leaned closer. "…things going?"

She thought about telling Sherry about the marijuana and the missing note, but decided not to. It made her feel as if she were reporting in, which always reminded her of having to answer to her parents, which she hated, which was probably why she had gone into the independent travel business, so she could work for herself and avoid authority. Why Marylou, who never seemed to have to answer to her parents, had decided to join her was another question. Probably, knowing Marylou, it had just seemed like a good idea at the time.

But there was more to her reticence here than mere parental baggage. She wanted to remain as autonomous as she could. Avoid potentially awkward alliances. Have to be objective. Can't get involved, lose your perspective. She'd never read a book on being a private detective, but she was sure they all offered that bit of advice.

She hoped Gwen, who was usually open and chatty as a wren in the morning, wouldn't spill the beans.

"There was one thing last night," she said, quickly grabbing on the event most likely to have been seen by others. "I saw someone crossing the lawn to the barn, with a flashlight."

Sherry frowned. "We don't have any flashlights. They were stolen, remember?"

"The place is probably loaded with flashlights," Gwen said. "People carry them in their cars. I'm sure at least one of the hikers..."

Sherry looked alarmed. "You suspect the Dyke Hikers?"

"No, I'm only saying there are undoubtedly more flashlights around than you think."

"I have one, myself," Stoner added. "But it wasn't me."

"Do you know what time it was?" Sherry asked.

"I'm not sure. I'd gone to bed, then woke up and saw it."

"I slept the whole night through," Sherry said. "I don't think I even looked out the window after I turned off the light."

"Well..." Stoner stirred sugar into the coffee that had finally arrived. "You might want to check out the barn. See if there's anything missing, and let me know."

"I will," Sherry said solemnly.

"Also," Stoner said, letting a bit of business-like gruffness slip into her voice, "who has access to the room keys?"

Sherry's eyes grew large and round. "Only the guests and the house keeper. Why?"

"No particular reason. Just checking."

"What about yourself?" Gwen asked as she broke into her omelet. "Do you have a pass key? For emergencies?"

"There is one," Sherry admitted. "We keep it in the safe."

"Who has the combination?"

"I do, of course. And the security people."

Stoner looked up. "Security people?" She hadn't seen any security people. Hadn't seen any security whatsoever, now that she thought about it.

"We use an electronic service, in town. They're very efficient. We had a robbery once, and they were here less than nine minutes after we hit the alarm."

Stoner had a mental image of Sherry pressing the alarm button and rushing to stand in the doorway, stop watch in hand, to time the arrival of the security service. She wondered how many minutes had to pass before they'd get written down in her little note book with her little silver pen. The woman was exacting to the point of obsession. It must be very unpleasant to work for her.

"You keep saying 'we'," Gwen noted. "Is there someone else?"

Sherry gave an embarrassed laugh. "I guess it's the Imperial 'we.' Though I had an actual partner when I first started, but it didn't work out."

Aha. Stoner wondered what the story was behind that. She was certain there'd be one. "How long ago was that?" she asked.

"At least…" Sherry pondered. "…at least five years." Her face brightened and she laughed. "You don't think my ex-partner's causing the trouble, do you? She's been living in California for years."

Maybe so, but some people could wait a long time to get revenge. She had a few old scores to settle herself, some day.

"Why do you want to know about keys?" Sherry asked. "Has something happened?"

"Routine," Gwen said. "In an investigation like this, we like to know who has access to what and where."

Stoner didn't think Sherry looked entirely convinced. "One more thing," she said, "do you know who owns the cream-colored Lexus in the parking lot?"

Sherry reached over to center the rose bud in the vase in the middle of the table. "I do. Why?"

"When I saw the light last night, I went out to check. Your car was still warm."

"Really? The alarm didn't go off when you went outside, did it? The police didn't come."

"No, they didn't."

Sherry whipped out her note book again. "I'll have to call them. Could be a malfunction." She glanced up. "It's happened before. Our wiring is ancient. Another thing I have to upgrade as soon as I have the money."

"So you were out late last night?" Stoner persisted.

The woman looked at her with a sheepish grin. "I had a date." She blushed a little. "I'm seeing someone in Green Lake. I got back late, about 2:00, I guess. Went straight to bed, you know how it is. You must have come outside right after that."

"I see," Stoner said. "And you didn't see anything?"

"Well, no. I had other things on my mind." She glanced toward Gwen and gave what looked like a meaningful wink. "Know what I mean?"

Gwen was paying close attention to her grapefruit half.

"Sure," Stoner said.

"Well, hey, gotta go. Catch you at rehearsal." She gave Gwen's shoulder a squeeze. "Right?"

Gwen glanced up. "Rehearsal. Right."

"What was that about," Stoner asked when Sherry had gone.

"What?"

"Meaningful looks, shoulder squeezes."

"Oh, Stoner," Gwen said with a little laugh. "You're such a nut."

Stoner felt a flash of anger. "You're denying meaningful looks and squeezes?"

"I'm not denying looks and squeezes," Gwen said. "I'm denying meaningful." She put her spoon down. "Stoner, are you jealous?"

She felt herself redden. "No, I just wondered what was going on, that's all."

Gwen reached across the table and took her hand. "I think you're jealous, and I think it's very sweet."

"I'm not jealous, Gwen."

"Okay," Gwen said, and looked at her with those soft, brown, bottomless eyes. "But if you were, I'd think it was sweet."

Stoner forced herself to pay attention to her blueberry muffin. She wasn't jealous. At least she didn't think she was. But something was bothering her, and she couldn't put her finger on it. She hated it. It made her feel crazy.

The muffin tasted like saw dust. She tried her coffee, and didn't like its taste, either. She felt stuck, and the only way to stop feeling stuck was to do something. Because if she didn't do something, the old Goddess of Insecurity About Relationships was going to take control, and she was going to pick a fight with Gwen.

"I'm thinking," she said aloud, "that I should have a talk with the Crones. Maybe the one who used to be a cop could help us out."

"You're suspicious of Sherry, aren't you?"

She felt her defenses go up. "Not particularly," she said, knowing there was some truth to it, but wanting to be absolutely, positively fair-minded and non-judgmental.

"Well," Gwen said, "she does have a key to the rooms. And we only have her word for it that she went right to bed last night. If I had to put money down right now, I'd put it on Miss Dodder."

"Why?"

"Because she's the only suspect we have."

Stoner had to smile. "I don't think that would stand up in a court of law."

"Life wouldn't stand up in a court of law," Gwen said. "Do you want that other muffin?"

"Help yourself." She felt her insides go soft with relief. Things were back to normal.

The Crones left the dining room and settled down out on the flagstone patio with books and writing paper.

Stoner pushed her chair back. "I'm going to try and talk to them," she said.

"Good," Gwen said as she signed the check. "I'll head for the barn and keep an eye on things there."

She poured herself another cup of coffee, as a cover, and went through the French doors. Standing a respectful distance away from the older women, she gazed out across the lawn as if contemplating the Universe.

What if it was Sherry?

Sherry had the master key to the rooms. She could have taken the note. She could have spiked Boneset's herbal teas.

And anyone could have gone into Divi Divi's car and tampered with the scripts. Anyone could have weakened the ladder. "Anyone" could include Sherry Dodder.

Sherry would hire her to catch herself? Like one of those serial catch-me-before-I-kill-more types?

But what better cover, than to hire a detective to solve the crime? Especially an amateur detective who didn't know what she was doing.

That made her mad. It was insulting. She knew perfectly well what she was doing, and she didn't like being used. If Sherry Dodder was doing it, she'd…

But Sherry hadn't been in the barn last evening, so she hadn't been the one to oil the hinges.

Really, the only thing that actually set Sherry apart from the rest was her ability to access the rooms.

Access the rooms? Access the rooms? She was starting to think like a computer freak. She knew it was a bad idea to computerize the travel agency, even though Marylou wanted it so badly she whined, and Gwen had sided with her. Next thing they knew, they were all going to start wearing baggy plaid slacks and horn-rimmed glasses and spend their days arguing about the relative merits of Nintendo vs. Sega and their nights watching the Sci-Fi Channel.

An ear-splitting whistle made her jump and set her heart racing. Glancing to her left, she saw the wheel-chair-bound Crone gesturing to her in an imperious manner.

Stoner trotted over.

"I'm Clara," the woman said. "This is Esther."

"Stoner McTavish," she said, shaking hands.

"After the Lucy B. Stoners?" Esther asked.

"After Lucy B. Stone," she said. "I don't know how it got to be Stoner. My aunt named me."

"Figured that," said Clara. "You're too young to've been born during the first Feminist wave, by about a hundred years."

"The Lucy B. Stoners," Esther explained, "were married ladies who kept their maiden names, the way Lucy did."

"Now we can only guess," Clara added, "how many of them were ladies of the lesbian persuasion."

Stoner grinned. "Were you involved in the Women's Movement?"

"We certainly were," said Esther. "Burned our bras at the Miss America

Pageant, protested the Republican convention in Miami Beach..."

"And everything else along the way," Clara said.

"It was a little later when I got involved," Stoner said. "I was pretty young at that time."

"Doesn't matter," said Clara. "At least you got there. Why have you been staring at us?"

"Uh..." Stoner said, feeling acutely embarrassed, "I'm sorry."

"If you're going to be sorry, don't stare," Clara said. "If you're going to stare, don't be sorry."

"I sort of wanted to get to know you."

"Why? Because we're old?"

"Well..."

"People always act like an old lesbian's some kind of rare jewel," Clara muttered. "Guess we're supposed to crawl off into the woods like stray dogs and die."

"That's not it," Stoner said quickly. "I mean, that's not it for me. I think all elderly women look like lesbians."

"You're right," Esther said. "They do. Once their husbands die off, they kind of butch up, don't they?"

"We've been watching you," Clara said. "You and your lady friend. Can't figure out what you're doing here."

Stoner hesitated.

"You're not with the theater bunch, they've been here for weeks." Esther motioned for her to sit down. "You're not with the outing club. And you're too young and healthy to want to sit and inhale the scenery like us."

"With all due respect," Stoner said as she sat, "I believe that's a stereotype. I've enjoyed scenery all my life. I've even been known to sit and stare at it for long periods of time."

"Well, you have my apology," Clara said.

"It's okay." She wondered how to ask them about themselves without appearing nosy. Admittedly, she was curious, but she didn't want them to think she found them to be curiosities.

"Good grief, woman," Clara said, "you're all wrinkled up in the face like a prune. What in the world is on your mind?"

"I was just wondering," she stammered, caught, "how you met, and what it's been like for you..." She shrugged. "You know."

"I know," Esther said with a sweet smile. "You want to know how two lesbians could find each other back in the Dark Ages."

Stoner nodded.

"I was a singer," Esther said. "Private parties, cocktail lounges. Fancy places, mostly. Grand pianos, evening dresses, no rough stuff. It was just after the end of World War II, and everyone was in a party mood, so there was always plenty of work."

"Tell the truth," Clara said. "You were good."

"I suppose so."

"And sultry. She had a voice that smoldered."

Esther laughed. "All the men thought I was singing just for them, of course, being men. And all the while I was making love to their girl friends with my voice. Some of them knew it, too, those girls. They made love right back with their eyes."

"And one night Clara came in with her date?" Stoner said eagerly, picturing the whole romantic thing.

"Not exactly. We'd had some trouble after hours at the club I was singing in. Female employees being accosted on their way home from work. A bunch of us got together and asked the Police Department to send someone over who could show us how to handle it. Maybe teach us a little ju jitsu."

"That got to be an ordinary thing during the Movement," Clara put in. "But in those days it was shocking. A woman was supposed to have a man to protect her, and if she didn't there must be something wrong with her. Working girls like Esther would be picked up at the stage door by their husbands."

"And most likely taken home to be raped or beaten, rather than having it happen on the street," Esther said. "So there was some resistance to bringing someone in to show us how to take care of ourselves. But we banded together and made a fuss, and there wasn't much the owners of the place could do. Well, we all expected some burly Irish cop to show up and laugh at us, but we were prepared to put up with a little humiliation if it got us what we wanted. Imagine our surprise when Clara comes sauntering through the door."

"Most of them had never heard of a lady cop," Clara said with a huge grin. "Much less a female Jewish cop."

"It was love at first sight," Esther continued. "For both of us. Every night Clara wasn't working the night shift, she'd wait for me outside the stage door..."

"Just like the other husbands."

"The other girls thought it was odd at first, but after a while they got used to the idea. And if one of the girls was having trouble with her man, Clara'd drop by in her uniform and have a little talk with him. That usually straightened the situation out pretty quickly." She paused for a moment, thoughtful and sad. "We never talked about what we were doing. I was a lesbian all my life, and even with Clara in my life I was afraid to say the word. We both were. When the Women's Movement came along...well, we hardly knew what to do with ourselves."

Clara reached across the sofa and took her hand in a firm and gentle way. She held it for a moment. "We've seen a lot of changes," she said, looking into her lover's eyes. "And been through ups and downs." She glanced over sharply at Stoner. "But I still want to know what you're up to."

She tried not to shift her eyes guiltily, but couldn't stop herself. "What makes you think I'm up to anything?"

"Forty years on the Boston Police force, that's what makes me think it. One of the things police work teaches you is to know who's up to something."

Stoner hesitated. She wanted to share what she knew. There were things she could learn from these women. At this point she could use all the help she could get. But…

"Well?" Clara rattled her coffee cup against its saucer. "Are you going to spill or not?"

"I don't know if I…"

"Indulge me, I'm old."

Esther tapped Stoner's arm. "Don't let her bully you."

On the other hand, older people often noticed things. They were often careful, living in a world that had grown complex and abrupt. Attentiveness was a survival technique.

She decided to be honest. "Yes, we're up to something. And I think I could use your help, but I don't feel comfortable saying too much."

"How about a compromise," Esther said, leaning forward eagerly. "You let us help you, and you can share on a Need-to-Know basis."

"That'd be great," Stoner said.

"Damn it, Esther," Clara huffed. "You sold out. We could have gotten a better deal."

"Probably not," Stoner said. "I'm just not sure what's the right thing to do here."

"If you always wait to be sure," Esther said, "you'll never do anything."

Clara rubbed her hands. "Know what this reminds me of? One of those murder-mystery weekends."

"We do them through our local AARP chapter," Esther explained. "They always hate to see us coming."

"Why?"

"Clara figures it out before anyone. But they don't dare ask us not to come. She threatens to sue them for disability discrimination."

"Sounds more like ability discrimination to me," Stoner said.

"So," Clara said, "what's our first clue?"

Stoner ran her hand through her hair. "Okay. We were asked to come here because some strange things have been happening in the theater group."

Clara nodded. "We noticed that."

"What did you notice?"

"Nothing you can put your finger on. People seem more tense. Laughter has a forced quality. Everyone's trying too hard."

"And it's not just theater nerves," Esther added. "I used to sing in cabarets, so I've seen theater nerves. You cry, you shake, you faint or throw up. But this isn't any of those things."

"Seems like it was just little accidents up to the time you got here. Oh, there was the business with the flashlights, but the gals seemed to dismiss that as a prank. It was Roseann and the script changes that really threw them. Then the ladder last night…The atmosphere's so thick this morning you could cut it with a knife."

Stoner stared at them in amazement. "You know all about it."

"Of course we do," Clara said.

"How?"

"When you get to be old," Esther explained, "people get careless around you. If you're in a wheel chair they think you're rooted to the ground like a tree trunk. They think you can't hear, so they don't lower their voices. They think you no longer have a mind or a memory, so they'll say anything in front of you believing you won't understand or remember it."

"Old age is very useful," Clara said. "You don't have to spend much time sleeping, and you can just sit in one place and observe. Most of the time they don't even see you. You'd be amazed at what you can find out."

"I see," Stoner said. "Have you drawn any conclusions?"

Both women shook their heads. "Not enough information yet," Clara declared.

"Would you be surprised," Stoner asked, "if I told you I think someone's been in our room?"

Clara guffawed. "I'd be surprised if they hadn't. These old locks. Give me your key and a file and I'll be in and out of every one of those rooms before lunch. Lock them on my way out, too."

"Clara was always especially good at breaking and entering," Esther said.

"So it wouldn't be hard for someone to make a pass key?"

"Simplest thing in the world." Clara gave her a deep look. "Have we eliminated your chief suspect?"

Stoner shook her head. "I don't have any suspects, really." But she would have, of course, if it took a special key to get into the rooms. That would pretty much narrow it down to Sherry Dodder. And Clara, of course, who admitted she was adept at getting through locked doors, and who may or may not be rooted to her wheel chair like a tree trunk.

"Sorry," Clara said with a laugh. "Not me. No motive."

"Am I that transparent?"

"Well," said Esther, "let's just say your eyes shifted in her direction about the same time your thoughts arrived there."

"The trouble is," Stoner said, frowning, "I can't think of anyone who'd have a motive. All of the women seem to want this to work. I haven't picked up any jealousy or antagonism between them…They get annoyed with each other at times, but it doesn't seem to go very deep."

"Rita doesn't seem overly fond of Marcy," Clara suggested, "but Rita doesn't strike me as the type to do this. More the plate-throwing sort, if you know what I mean."

Stoner knew what she meant.

The morning was moving along. They'd be expecting her. She stood and stretched. "I have to go. If you think of anything…"

"We'll pass a signal over lunch. If there's anything to report, I'll pretend to have trouble with my wheel chair. Then you come to our room as soon as you can. It's 108."

"Good. And if I have anything, I'll just come straight to your room."

She heard the sound of a screen door slamming and glanced toward the barn. One of the women was running across the lawn toward the inn. From the jerkiness of her movements, it was clear she was in distress. The door slammed again and another woman ran after her.

Roseann, with Sherry in hot pursuit.

Stoner planted herself in Roseann's path and held out a hand to stop her. "Hey," she said. "Is anything wrong?"

Roseann looked up at her. Her face was bright red and tear-streaked. "I can't do this any more," she blurted out. Tearing her arm from Stoner's grip, she ran into The Cottage.

CHAPTER 7

She was about to go after her when Sherry came trotting up, out of breath and frazzled.

Stoner stopped her. "What's going on?"

"She read Rebecca's notes," Sherry panted.

She brushed by them and ran into the inn.

Stoner looked at Clara and Esther, who shrugged in bewilderment.

"I'd better check this out," she said, and headed for the barn.

The screen door squealed behind her. Inside, the Goddess of Chaos had assumed full control of the situation. Boneset was hammering at a piece of scenery with an intensity that verged on homicidal. Barb was trying to cajole the rest of the technical crew, who were standing silently and staring at Rebecca as if paralyzed, into going back to work. Rita's hair had turned so frizzy and wild it looked as if her head had caught fire, while Seabrook called for Rebecca to be nuked immediately. Divi Divi, imposing in a brightly colored caftan, stood to one side making notes—maybe for a new play, maybe for a rewrite for this one, but apparently taking playwright's advantage of the drama unfolding in front of her. Rebecca paced back and forth waving a sheet of computer paper and demanding to know "who did this."

Marcy whined that all this emotional turmoil was ruining her concentration.

"At least," Gwen said with a nod in Marcy's general direction, "there's one member of this company you can count on for consistency."

"What happened?"

"As far as I can tell, someone got into Rebecca's computer and printed out her director's notes."

"These are *not* my director's notes," Rebecca shouted across the room. "These are *stupid* notes."

"So you keep stupid director's notes," Rita said helpfully. "It's nothing to be defensive about. I keep stupid gardening notes."

"Rita, Rita, my chiquita," Seabrook sang, "how does your garden glow?"

"They're not my notes!"

"Look," Marcy said with a heavy sigh, "are we going to rehearse this turkey, or not?"

Divi Divi pulled herself up to her full nearly six feet and sauntered across the stage. "Doll," she said to Marcy, "you may have had some input into this play, but most of the writing is mine and I've grown pretty attached to it. So, unless you want to have some real unpleasant interactions with me, just keep your opinions to yourself."

Marcy flung her arms into the air in a gesture of terminal frustration. She stalked to a chair and began filing her nails.

"Let's go outside and talk about this," Stoner said to Rebecca.

Rebecca's face had a dangerously unyielding look to it. The kind of look Stoner knew *she* sometimes got when she felt helpless and was refusing to cry. "We have a rehearsal to do," Rebecca said stubbornly. She raised her voice. "Okay, we'll work around Roseann's part."

Stoner grabbed her by the shoulder. "Outside, Rebecca. *Now.*" She turned to the rest of the company. "Take the time to go over your lines. Gwen can fill in for Roseann..."

"I should read Roseann's part," Marcy interrupted. "I'm her understudy."

"Only if she quits," Divi Divi said. "I'll hold book."

Stoner shot Divi Divi a grateful look and guided Rebecca toward the door.

"You're not the director," Marcy shouted after her. "You can't tell us what to do."

"The director's having a nervous breakdown," Stoner said. "I'm the assistant director."

"We have to process this," Marcy persisted.

"Oh, put a cork in it," Divi Divi said.

"And," Stoner added, "I'm naming Divi Divi assistant assistant director."

As the door swung shut behind them she heard Marcy say, "This isn't Feminist."

To which Divi Divi replied, "Life isn't Feminist. Start on page 5."

"If this weren't such a nightmare," Stoner said as she took Rebecca around the corner of the barn and sat her down, "it'd be hilarious."

"I'm quitting," Rebecca said. "Through. Kaput. Out of here."

Stoner dropped down beside her. "Sure."

"I'm sick of this play, I'm sick of these people, I'm sick of theater, I'm sick of the whole thing."

"Is this a *pout* ?" Stoner said, pretending to laugh. "Amateur City."

Rebecca turned to her and pushed out her lower lip in a real pout. "I mean it."

"Small-time stuff," Stoner said with a dismissing gesture. "I've pouted better than this over things I don't even care about."

"Well, I don't care about these people, or this play, or...or anything."

"Whatever you say," Stoner said. She wondered what approach to take. If she urged Rebecca to reconsider, reminding her that these women were her sisters and she couldn't let them down, not after all they'd been through together...chances were she'd make her feel trapped and desperate to get out. On the other hand, if she gave her breathing room, she might feel she could stay.

"If you want to get out, get out. After all, *Demeter Ascending* is supposed to be your recreation, isn't it?"

Rebecca laughed humorlessly. "Yeah. Some recreation."

"Wouldn't be bad," Stoner said thoughtfully, "if you were a masochist."

They sat side-by-side for several minutes, during which Rebecca pulled up enough grass to weave a Welcome mat.

"They think I'd say things like that," she said at last. "I'd never say things like that."

"Things like what?"

"Like what's on the printout." She pulled a crumpled ball of paper from her pocket and handed it over.

Stoner smoothed it out, resisting the near-compulsion to tear off the side strips with the holes punched in them.

It was easy to see why Roseann was upset. Under the heading "Roseann," someone—if not Rebecca—had written "this is hopeless. She can't learn her lines, she can't take direction, we'll be lucky if she can even cross the stage without making a fool of herself."

Stoner whistled. "Where did this come from?"

"My computer, I guess. I have a file I keep personal stuff in. It's just a place to let off steam. But I didn't write this, Stoner. I didn't even think it."

"Is your computer password protected?"

"Of *course* not," Rebecca snapped. "It's just a laptop, for God's sake. And I certainly don't expect my *friends* to go breaking into my files."

Stoner thought about pointing out that Rebecca was referring to "these people," whom she supposedly didn't care about, as her friends. But the situation might still be too sensitive. So she pondered for a while instead.

"Is it your printer?" she asked at last.

Rebecca shook her head. "It's Div's. I use it for the real notes."

"Then this might not have been done on your computer at all."

The woman took the paper back. "Maybe not," she said, studying it. "It's the font I use for my personal file, though. Palatino."

It wasn't an exotic font, but not one in every day use, either.

"Have you checked your personal file today?"

"No."

"Do it when you get a chance. See if this is still in it." She doubted it, though. Whoever did this would want to hide the evidence.

Rebecca looked at her. "What would that tell me?"

"Probably nothing," Stoner admitted. "It would just be...neater, somehow."

"You certainly have your own way of doing things," Rebecca said with a tentative smile.

"So I've been told." There was something she was missing here, something that might give them important information. She got it. "Does your computer have one of those applications that keeps track of your work time? With the date and all? We have one on our office computer, to track our time for taxes."

Rebecca shook her head.

Darn. She thought again. "I'll bet it has a Get Info function, doesn't it? That includes the date and time each file was last used?"

"I guess so," Rebecca said with a shrug.

It was a long shot, but so far the only shot they had. "Have you used your word processor yet today?"

Rebecca shook her head.

"Okay, when you get a chance, log on and get the information from your word processing application. But don't, under any circumstances, open the application until you have that information. If you do, you'll update it."

"All right," Rebecca said. She looked directly at her for the first time since they'd sat down. "You're a computer nut, aren't you?"

A computer nut? A *computer nut?* Stoner shuddered inwardly. It was Marylou Kesselbaum who was the computer nut. And Gwen, who liked to come into the office to play arcade games with Marylou. They had so many arcade games, between the ones they'd bought and the ones they'd downloaded from Compuserve or whatever it was called, that their computer screens looked like an ad for Computer Games 'R Us. And now Marylou and Gwen were talking about hooking up with the information superhighway. Marylou even suggested they get personal computers for their new home in Shelburne Falls, with access to Internet.

Stoner put her foot down at that. Even though she knew privacy in these United States was as much an illusion as the Easter Bunny and the Tooth Fairy, she also knew that if she could tap into the government's computers, they could tap into hers, and she had no intention of surrendering without a struggle. No Modems in the Home had become her motto.

Marylou gave in. Not, she said, because she was persuaded by the clarity and correctness of Stoner's argument, but because it was the longest speech she had ever heard Stoner make and thought it should be rewarded.

"We have one at work," she said. "Marylou—my partner, my business partner—and Gwen—she's my partner partner..." They *had* to come up with some better terms. If the Eskimos could have over two hundred or whatever words for snow, lesbians needed at least three hundred for their relationships. The lesbian linguists had better get on this. Though she imagined most lesbian linguists these days were busy fighting to keep the colleges and universities from cutting Women's Studies programs.

"...They're really into the computers. I can't help picking up a little."

Rebecca pulled up another blade of grass. "Stoner, how can I go back in there? They think I said those things about Roseann. How can I get them to believe I didn't?"

That was a hard one. It was one of the Laws of Nature that guilt rumored is always believed, while guilt denied is tantamount to a confession.

"The only way I know of," she said, "is to find out who really did it. What do you think Roseann will do with this?"

"I don't know," Rebecca said. "I know she feels out of place with us—she hasn't had any theater experience, and she's never thought politically in her life, or so she says. It might be the thing that makes her quit. On the other hand, she's very loyal, and feels a responsibility to the rest...I just don't know."

"Sherry's with her now," Stoner said.

"Good. Sherry's great at handling people. You should have seen her in action during the Rita-Marcy Wars. She kept this whole thing together."

People were constantly surprising her. From the little she had seen of Sherry, she'd have thought she was too bubbly to handle something as complicated and potentially nasty as heart troubles. Especially involving two people as volatile as Marcy and Rita.

"Even if she does come back, though," Rebecca went on, "she's not going to trust me. It'll be tense and awkward." She rubbed her face with the heels of her hands. "I had a chance to go canoeing across Alaska this summer. I should have taken it."

"I hear they have twenty-eight different kinds of mosquitoes there," Stoner said. "Some of them as big as sparrows."

"Sounds like a nice, restful change," Rebecca said wistfully.

Stoner laughed. "You're coming around."

"I'm afraid so. I have no moral character at all."

She looked up and saw, in the distance, Roseann and Sherry coming toward them through the sunlight. She nudged Rebecca. "Here's your chance."

Rebecca shot her a look of apprehension and got to her feet and went to meet them on the lawn.

The three of them stood in an awkward cluster, faceless silhouettes against the morning glare. Everyone looked at the ground. Then Rebecca raised her head, seeming to say something. Roseann turned away. Sherry gestured her back.

Strange, Stoner thought, she hadn't noticed how short Sherry was. Seen from a distance, she was only shoulder-high to the others, but Stoner hadn't experienced her that way. Most of the women she knew were either shorter or taller than herself in about equal proportions, so she wasn't always aware. But someone as short as Sherry...

Maybe it was her personality. She took up the psychological space of a much taller person.

Roseann and Rebecca were shaking hands.

She was skinny, too. Really skinny. Stoner hadn't noticed that before, either. If she'd had to describe her, she'd have mentioned her round cheeks and round eyes and round glasses and round curls...

Maybe that wasn't Sherry over there.

It was Sherry, all right. She could tell by her energy, the way her hands were constantly in motion, the way she kept shifting from one foot to the other, the way she had to keep touching the others...

An impression stirred deep inside her. She let it surface...

She didn't like Sherry Dodder very much.

Meaning, what?

Meaning she didn't want to get very close to her. Meaning something in her made her not want to say much around Sherry. Meaning Sherry wasn't someone she'd want to baby sit with her plants.

Meaning she thought Sherry was behind the goings on here?

Stoner shook her head. No, she didn't think that. Sherry was no more of a suspect in her mind than anyone else. And Sherry was no less a victim than anyone else. She just…

…didn't like her a whole lot.

Sherry detached herself from the trio and trotted toward her.

Stoner felt her protective shield snap into place. "How's it going?" she asked in a falsely friendly voice.

"Roseann's agreed to stay on," Sherry said. She threw herself down on the ground beside her.

Without being invited, Stoner thought darkly, and reminded herself of an overly-territorial, bad-natured dog.

"Good," she said.

"It was touch and go for a while there."

"I can imagine." She ought to ask Sherry how she'd talked Roseann into it. For some reason, she didn't want to. Maybe because she sensed Sherry was dying to tell her.

That made her feel mean.

"How's it coming on your end?" Sherry asked, big-eyed.

"Nothing new. At least, nothing you don't know about." It's only been about two hours since I last reported in, for God's sake. "Was there anything missing or destroyed in the barn?"

Sherry shook her head. "Not as far as I can tell. But I suppose whoever you saw last night was planting those directors' notes in the barn, don't you?"

That made sense. "Probably." Was it you, Sherry? Your car was warm. I remember that. "You're sure you didn't see anything when you came in?"

"I told you," Sherry said with just a hint of annoyance that pleased Stoner in a perverse way. "I had a date, I went straight to bed. End of story."

"Uh-huh."

"You don't think *I* had anything to do with it, do you?" Her eyes had gone from big to narrowed, and showing sparks.

"I didn't say that."

Sherry frowned. Her frown deepened to a scowl. A vertical line appeared and bisected the frown furrows. The indentations on either side of her mouth drooped, then eroded into gullies. She squinted her eyes, and deep rays shot out from the corners. Her skin went white, then red, then white again. Her mouth opened and turned down until it looked like a crescent moon dancing on its horns.

Stoner stared at her, fascinated, unable to look away. It was like watching a window shatter in slow motion.

She ought to feel compassion for the woman, or at least pity. She was obviously in distress. Her own detachment confused and disturbed her.

Sherry gave a huge, noisy, choking sob and grabbed hunks of her own hair in each hand. "I can't believe this," she moaned, shaking her head back and forth dramatically. "I *hired* you, and now you suspect *me*."

"I didn't say that," Stoner repeated reasonably. "I suspect everyone equally."

"I feel so *betrayed*."

Stoner wished Divi Divi were there to tell her to put a cork in it.

"Sherry..." she began.

Now Sherry was weeping without a break for breath. Huge, gasping, convulsing sobs.

Stoner touched her arm in what she hoped was a comforting way. "Look," she said, "it's not that big a deal. It's just the way I work. Please don't take it personally."

The woman turned on her, eyes tear-filled and silver with rage. "Don't take it personally? You accuse me of trying to ruin my own show, of doing terrible things to my friends, and then you tell me not to take it personally?"

She supposed Sherry had a point, but...She tried to remember exactly what she'd said. *Had* she suggested that Sherry was the perpetrator? She didn't think so. On the other hand, she might have said something so awkward it could be taken that way.

This whole thing was getting too complicated.

"Look," she said. "Maybe I'm not the best person to handle this investigation. Maybe you need someone more experienced."

Sherry threw her hands up in the air. "Now you're running out on me." She kneaded her face. "This is a nightmare, an absolute nightmare."

"I'm not running out," she insisted, thinking it sounded like a wonderful idea. "I only suggested..."

"You're not quitting?" Sherry asked in a small voice, turning tear-drenched eyes in her direction.

"I never said I was, did I?"

"Yes, you did."

"Well, I was only thinking out loud." Now she wasn't certain of what she *had* said. But she was pretty sure she hadn't used the words "quitting" or "running out."

"I *need* you. We all do. This whole thing will fall apart if you quit now. Everyone's suspecting everyone else. It's a mess. If we don't find out what's *really* going on, it's the end of *Demeter Ascending*."

Stoner took a deep breath and tried to smile. "Then we'd better get inside. We both have work to do."

As she got to her feet, Sherry clutched at her shirt. "Promise me something first? Please?"

"I'll try."

"Please don't talk about quitting again?"

"I didn't..." Oh, well. "I won't."

"And don't suspect me any more."

Stoner felt at a complete loss. She didn't want to make promises she couldn't keep. Everyone was under suspicion now. But Sherry was giving her that small-child-puppy-dog look again. She hated that look. It said, "Beat me, kill me, just don't reject me."

It made her want to scream, "Grow up and leave me alone!"

It made her want to do things she never did. It made her feel feelings she hardly ever felt.

It made her feel spiteful.

Sherry was still watching, waiting for her response.

"I won't suspect you," she said as gently as she could.

The woman jumped up and dusted off her shorts.

She hadn't noticed before that Sherry was wearing little, short-length overalls. They looked like a play suit. All she needed was a plastic bucket and shovel and they could all toddle down to the beach together.

"I really appreciate it," Sherry was saying. "No matter what happens, know I appreciate everything you're trying to do."

"Thank you," Stoner said.

Sherry held the screen door open for her. "Coming?"

Stoner walked through, feeling trapped.

The rest of the morning was uneventful. That is, there were no events. But it was stiff and awkward.

Roseann went through the rehearsal, but during the breaks she sat alone in the back of the barn and no one seemed to have the courage to face her. On stage, she kept her voice so low she was barely audible. Her movements were low-keyed, unsure, and Zombie-like. It was as if she were afraid to do anything that might be noticed for fear she'd be criticized.

Rebecca carried on as best she could, but she seemed reluctant to give directions to Roseann, even when she missed her blocking—as Stoner had learned to call being in the wrong place at the wrong time. As assistant director, Stoner had the job of providing missed lines and correcting movements. She had to do it so often she began to feel like a one-woman show.

It was affecting the others, too. Marcy's complaints were coming as quickly as labor pains in the final stages of child birth. Rita had taken to heaving deep, sharp sighs that sounded like "Hoh." They had even caught one another's eyes on several occasions and joined in mutual looks of frustration.

Nice for them, but hardly in the best interests of the show.

Only Divi Divi and Sherry seemed to remain above it all, but Divi Divi had entered another world and was filling page after page with large, scrawling writing. Sherry, real trouper that she was, actually seemed to be energized by the goings on, and was giving a consistent, sharp performance in her few scenes. Between times on stage, she came and sat next to Stoner, pulling up her chair to a closeness that invaded Stoner's preferred psychological space by about six inches.

Hardly a capital offense, but Stoner wished she wouldn't do it, and found herself subtly moving the chair away with her toe whenever Sherry left to go on stage. But when she returned to her seat, she'd pull it closer again.

By the time they broke for lunch, Stoner had decided she had to do something fast, before Roseann's anxiety and timidity became a permanent condition.

She caught up with Gwen at the entrance to the dining room and determined that there had been no incidents among the techies—who were beginning to seem like a placid, peace-loving bunch compared to the actors. Gwen had heard about the events of the morning. It had been discussed at length among the back stage crew, whose general consensus had been that "some really weird shit was coming down." But no one had had any idea who was doing it or why. Speculation had ranged from the Boy Scouts at the camp on the next lake over to the Cottage ghost. Barb had reported that there were some pages missing from her note book, and Gwen had managed to get a peek at the tear line. It *seemed* to match the tear line on Sherry's threatening note, but she wasn't sure. The paper matched, but since it was a standard sort of note book, available at every stationery, discount store and CVS pharmacy in the country, she didn't think it was much of a clue.

Stoner agreed, and told her of her concern about Roseann. "I'd like to have lunch with her and get her to open up a little," she said. "Maybe I can convince her that Rebecca didn't really say those things."

"Do you believe that?" Gwen asked.

"Yes. Do you?"

"I don't have a lot to go on, but, yes, I think I trust her. She reminds me of you. I'll bet that computer file is full of doubts and obsessing."

"Probably," Stoner admitted. The crew had been working outside through the morning, building sets where they wouldn't interfere with the rehearsal. Gwen's tan had deepened. The skin over her bare arms was the color of sandstone. "Will you be okay for lunch?" Stoner asked wistfully.

"Sure. Sherry asked us to eat with her, anyway. She'll have to settle for me alone."

More than anything else in the world, Stoner wished *she* could settle for Gwen alone. But she had work to do.

On second thought, she was glad Gwen would have some time alone with Sherry. She was curious to see if she'd make Gwen uneasy, too. She annoyed her at times, that much was clear. But this uneasiness, this sense of being in two places at once, of feeling two contradictory things—or feeling one and knowing you ought to feel the other—was just plain strange. It was like having one foot in each of two parallel universes. If Gwen noticed it too, she might be able to shed some light on Stoner's own reactions. She thought about mentioning it, but decided to wait, to let Gwen form her own impressions first. "I've been thinking," she said. "Maybe if I tell Roseann about the other things that have been happening, and why we're here and all...maybe it'll put what happened to her into perspective. What do you think?"

Gwen nodded. "I feel as if we're on the verge of having to bring it all out in the open, anyway, don't you? I mean, how far can we let this go before we have to warn people that they could be in real danger?"

"Do you think they don't know that already?" Stoner asked. "After last night and the ladder?"

"You would, and I would. But some of them need it spelled out. You know what Edith Kesselbaum says. Denial is the American Way. Besides, it might make them feel better to know someone's working on it."

Stoner ran her hand through her hair. "If I knew it was *me* working on it, it wouldn't make me feel any better."

"Glory, you are obtuse," Gwen said. "See you later."

Feeling lonely and abandoned, Stoner watched her go.

Looking back on it, she was glad she'd decided to talk openly with Roseann. Not only had the woman believed her, she'd been furious that someone was trying to make Rebecca look bad. "She's one of the nicest people I ever met," she's said. "Better'n ninety-five percent of the clientele of the Unisex Styling Center that used to be Thelma's Cut 'n Curl. Though I don't suppose she'd be caught dead setting foot in a dump like that. Strikes me as the type that gets her cuts from gay men—a little more flash for the cash, if you know what I mean."

Even though it was politically incorrect, Stoner had to agree with her.

Dessert was oranges which Roseann peeled for them both, having—as she said—superior orange-peeling fingernails which she insisted were more sanitary than Stoner's Swiss Army knife. "Vicious-looking thing," she declared, "and Lord knows what you've been hacking with it."

Stoner didn't dare tell her she'd only used it once, to cut off a length of thread when she'd sewed a button on her shirt and had lost the scissors in the bed.

"What I think I oughta do," Roseann said around a section of orange, "is apologize to Rebecca."

"Really?" Stoner took her own orange section and split the white, tough part with her thumb nails, in the middle where the seeds tended to gather. She squeezed them out onto her plate and touched her hands to her napkin.

"I thought some pretty mean stuff about her. I should have known she wouldn't do anything like that."

"You were a victim of circumstance," Stoner said. "You both were."

"Hah!" said Roseann. "If what you've been telling me is true, it's not any old abstract circumstance we're victims of. It's some mean person making trouble."

"True," Stoner said. She attacked another orange section.

"Want me to do that for you?" Roseann asked. "Your nails are all stubby."

"This part requires stubby nails. Yours'd break."

"Would not," Roseann huffed. She held up her hands and examined her nails. "Look at them. And they're all mine, too. No fakes."

"Lethal," Stoner said.

"You better believe it. They come in real handy. You never know when you're going to have to fight off some randy hooligan who said he wanted to take you out on the town when what he really had in mind was making a grab." She glanced over at Stoner. "Don't imagine you have that problem, though."

Stoner laughed. "You shouldn't, either. What are you doing, dating randy hooligans?"

Roseann shrugged. "You take what you can get."

"Tell you what." She milked the seeds out of another orange section. "I'll have Marylou get you a date. She knows a few men who aren't randy. And some who aren't even hooligans."

"I don't know." Roseann looked sad. "I probably couldn't keep up my end of the conversation."

Someone else might have been hinting for reassurance, but Roseann said it as if it were a matter of fact, one which made her unhappy, but one everyone would agree with.

"I haven't noticed you having a hard time," Stoner said.

"You're easy," Roseann commented, and handed her another orange section.

Stoner grimaced. "I don't know whether to thank you for the compliment or not."

"Yeah. World's a funny place, isn't it? You hardly know how to take things. Just when you think you have a handle on it, it all shifts."

The afternoon seemed endless. They rehearsed, and rehearsed, and rehearsed some more. The play still didn't make much sense to Stoner, but she assumed that was because they were doing it out of chronological order, skipping around Sherry's part while she finished in the kitchen. And the musical numbers. She hoped the musical numbers would add something to the play. Like clarity.

They probably would. Divi Divi had explained to her that ever since "Oklahoma!" musical numbers were supposed to advance the story as well as entertain. She was about to launch into a quick run-down on the history of the American Musical Theater when Rita needed a cue and a blocking check. Too bad. She'd hoped Divi Divi could explain the endless appeal of *The Fantastiks.*

If the musical numbers didn't help, maybe she should take time tonight and read *Not Quite Titled* through from beginning to end.

If she had time.

What she really wanted to do was go into town on some pretext, call Aunt Hermione, and ask for help from the Astral plane.

Clara and Esther had presented her with a list of the comings and goings of everyone staying at the Cottage. She had witnessed most of them herself, and the rest didn't seem to have anything to do with anything.

Clara had made her a pass key that could open all the rooms. She'd made it from her room key and a nail file. It convinced her that anyone with a little ingenuity could get into the rooms.

Roseann had obviously believed what Stoner told her, and she and

Rebecca were having a reunion that resembled a courtship, with a great deal of laughing and touching and nudging and teasing. The rest of the company seemed tremendously relieved. Nothing made Marcy miss her timing, and even Seabrook couldn't find anything to complain about.

Gwen came back from lunch late and without Sherry. She looked spacey, the way she often did when she was confused. Stoner wasn't surprised. An entire lunch with Sherry Dodder was undoubtedly a confusing experience.

She wanted to ask her how it had gone, but just as she was about to slip out, the blocking got completely mixed up and everyone ended up on the right-hand side of the stage...stage right, Rebecca explained. Having everyone on the same side of the stage was apparently a theater taboo. As was having everyone on the same level, all standing or all sitting or all at the front or the back...the taboos were endless. This particular one had happened every time they got to this part of the play, and Rebecca declared it had to be straightened out once and for all before the actors "set" it, meaning becoming incapable of moving any other way. This involved finding the exact moment where things went off, and required following the script word for word while Rebecca sorted it out.

Gwen's impressions of Sherry would have to wait.

Sherry herself didn't show up until about fifteen minutes later, then spent the next fifteen minutes apologizing and explaining a kitchen crisis in minute detail until Rebecca's eyes began to roll up in her head and she asked if they could *please* get back to business.

By the time the afternoon was over, everyone was hot, exhausted, and ready to either play or fight. Boneset announced that she would be conducting a healing ritual in the clearing by the lake at moon rise for anyone who was in need or just interested in raising healing energy, please bring songs, drums, and stories to share. S'mores would be provided around the ritual bonfire.

This shocked Rita, who found it sacrilegious, but Roseann explained—to everyone's surprise—that it was common practice for Wiccan festivals to end in singing and dancing and feasting. After all, all acts of love and pleasure were the Goddess' rituals, she declared.

Marcy looked at her funny and asked how come she knew that.

Roseann explained that one of her customers, a Ms. Moore, was a Witch and had told her all about it.

Stoner cringed, afraid she was about to add that Ms. Moore was also Stoner's aunt. It would arouse suspicion about her motives for being there. And, while the time was fast approaching when she might have to tell all, she wanted to be able to time it for maximum impact.

Fortunately, Roseann was diverted by Boneset, who said there was one little part of the ritual she was unsure about, and maybe this Ms. Moore had said something that would help her sort it out. They went off together.

Gwen came forward from the back of the barn and dropped down into the chair next to her. There was sawdust in her hair, and spatters of paint on her face and arms. She was sweaty and droopy and limp as a wrung out towel.

Stoner thought she looked adorable.

"Do you think that lake water's really swimmable?" she asked. "The other day, I thought there might be *things* in it."

"Things?" Stoner asked.

"Disgusting things. Things that nibble at our legs. Squishy things piled up on the bottom. Blood-sucking things."

"Beats me." She caught Sherry's eye and waved her over.

"No nibbling things," Sherry said. "But, yes, we have a few blood-suckers. Only a few."

"Only a few," Gwen repeated tonelessly.

"The Peking ducks keep the swimming area pretty clear, but they can't get them all."

Stoner didn't remember seeing any Peking ducks when they were at the lake. But perhaps they'd been laying low. On a nest or something. Hatching dozens of Peking ducklings which would go on a feeding rampage and rid the lake of leaches forever.

She wondered if the Peking ducks in Chinese restaurants were fed on leaches, and was immediately sorry she'd let her mind wander.

"Listen," Sherry was saying, "if you're squeamish about the lake bottom..."

"We're not squeamish," Stoner assured her.

"Stoner isn't squeamish," Gwen corrected. "I am congenitally squeamish."

"There's a canoe in the boat house. Paddle out to the middle of the lake. You can't even touch the bottom."

"Sounds good," Gwen said.

Sherry gave a little hop. "Have to go. Dinner prep."

"Right," Stoner said, and smiled warmly and insincerely.

"You don't like her," Gwen said as Sherry trotted away.

"She's okay, I guess. How was it at lunch?"

"Fine."

"Did you have any impressions about her?"

Gwen looked at her, one eyebrow raised. "Impressions?"

"Like..." She made circles with her hand. "Like, what kind of person she is or anything?"

"Nope. Nothing." She got up.

That was oddly abrupt, Stoner thought. Or maybe she was just being hypersensitive.

A hot, muggy air mass had moved in while they were rehearsing. It wrapped around her skin and felt like algae. Stoner hoped it'd be cooler out on the lake. She needed to talk to Gwen, but it was hard to concentrate when all you could think about was getting out of the sun. She was reminded of their times in Wyoming and Arizona, where it was even hotter than this. But there was no humidity there, and relief was as close as the nearest shade.

Gwen walked along looking at the ground, silent. Stoner was worried.

She'd seen her in this kind of brooding silence before, but not in a long time. It meant she was deeply angry, or deeply troubled.

She couldn't think of anything she'd done to provoke it. And there'd been no letters or phone calls bearing bad news. It might have been that lunch with Sherry, or something that happened with the tech crew.

She knew Gwen would tell her, sooner or later. But it made her nervous, uneasy—apprehensive.

Edith Kesselbaum would invite her to look for the transference. "This is obviously an old thing," she'd say.

Yes, it felt old. As old as time and something she'd always have with her.

"And when have you felt it before? Go with it, Stoner. Use the feeling to open doors."

Well, it was vaguely reminiscent of times when she was a child—an adolescent. Times she'd come downstairs in the morning to find her mother indulging in the Great Silence, which seemed to come out of nowhere and could go on for days, and usually ended with her mother screaming at her over something she'd done in all innocence, never thinking it was wrong.

Things had been like that a lot at home before she ran away. The rules changed from minute to minute, so something that had been okay ten minutes ago was suddenly the worst thing you could possibly do, and you had clearly done it on purpose to upset your mother. A deliberately malicious act planned to ruin her day, when she had so few good days, nasty child that you were.

It was Edith's professional opinion that Stoner's mother was mentally ill. Or, as she put it, "a psyche with more holes than Swiss cheese."

It wasn't much comfort to the kid she'd been, though. The one who'd been damaged. The one she still carried around with her. The one she wanted to care about, but who kept getting in the way…

"What's wrong?" Gwen asked.

Startled, Stoner said, "Huh?"

"You're so quiet."

"I was thinking about my mother."

Gwen took her hand. "Has she been after you again?"

"Only in my mind." Gwen's hand felt good.

"Do you think she'll come visit us after we move?"

"I doubt it." She let herself feel small for a moment, safe inside Gwen's hand.

"I'd like to meet her, the venomous old bag," Gwen said. She laughed her velvet laugh. "You, me, Marylou, and Aunt Hermione all under one roof. What a menagerie."

"Out in the wilds of western Massachusetts. My mother wouldn't go near Shelburne Falls on a dare."

"Then we're safe," Gwen said with a mock sigh of relief. "I won't have to change the locks."

"Gwen, we haven't even *seen* the locks *ourselves*."

"Well, the minute we do, I'm changing them." She slipped her arm around Stoner's shoulders. "That woman's not getting near you again, Stoner. Not until or unless you set the time and place."

They'd reached the door to the inn. The setting sun made long shadows, softened in the humidity-drenched air. The odor of freshly cut grass hung heavy.

Inside, Clara sat in her wheel chair in the coolness of the dark, seeming to sleep. Stoner closed the screen door carefully, so she wouldn't wake her.

"Really!" said Clara in a loud voice. She motioned Stoner over. "First you ask me to keep watch, then you go creeping around, trying to slip past me. Fine example you set. Now half the guests here will creep around out of deference to the old coot. How am I supposed to do my job?" She peered toward the door. "Who's that?"

Gwen came forward. "Gwen Owens," she said, and shook hands.

"Couldn't see you against the light," the older woman said. "You looked like an angel."

"Thank you," Gwen said. "I guess."

"*I* probably look like the devil." She pulled a tiny notebook from her pocket, lifted her glasses from their perch on top of her head, and read.

"Anything?" Stoner asked.

"Lots of ins and outs." Clara dropped her voice. "Nothing suspicious." She tore off the sheet of paper. "You can look it over. Most everybody who came through is travelling in pairs or more. Except for Gwen, here. And Sherry."

"What about Sherry?" Stoner asked, glancing through the list Clara had made. Her handwriting was so small, she could have engraved the Equal Rights Amendment on the head of a pin.

Clara took the sheet of paper back. "Came in with herself, here..." She pointed her pencil at Gwen. "...at 1:35. Dodder went to the kitchen. 2:04, Dodder left kitchen, went to her room. 2:27 Dodder went to barn. Came in with Rebecca and Roseann just now."

"How do you know she went to her room?"

"Followed her. It's right down the hall from ours."

"And she went straight from there to the barn?"

"Yep."

"Wait a minute," Gwen said. "Are you saying you suspect Sherry?"

"Suspect everyone and no one," Clara declared. "Leave no stone unturned, and no tern unstoned. Speaking of which, what's this I hear about marijuana in the herbal tea last night?"

Stoner whistled. "You don't miss much."

"I told you, people talk. Anything new on that?"

"Nothing. I don't think Boneset did it, but I have no idea who could."

"There's no problem getting it," Clara said. "There's a patch growing wild on the other side of the lake." She waited.

Stoner didn't say anything. She couldn't think of anything to say. Finding the marijuana patch didn't tell her anything, except that anyone in the Cottage had the opportunity to spike the tea. Anyone who knew about it, of course.

And if Clara had heard, it was probably dining room gossip.

"Well," Clara said, "don't you want to know how I know?"

"Sure."

"Saw it with my own two eyes. It might take me longer to get around than it used to, but I can still do it."

"That's good to know," Stoner said. "It makes you my prime suspect."

Clara looked appropriately shocked.

"You have means and opportunity. All I have to do is figure out the motive."

Clara grinned hugely. "That's what I like to see. Ingenuity. I might be able to teach you a few things."

"Always willing," Stoner said. The idea appealed to her. If she was going to continue to find herself answering calls for help—and everything seemed to point in that direction—it would be good to know what she was doing. But for now she just wanted to get away from it. Away from clueless mysteries, and artistic temperament, and people whose emotions were all over the place. Away from everything and everyone but Gwen. "Not tonight, though. Tonight I want to give my head a rest."

"Good idea," Clara said with a nod. "Helps to clear the brain. Sometimes you come up with an idea when you least expect it."

"If I come up with an idea," Stoner replied, "I can guarantee it'll be unexpected."

They went upstairs and stripped out of their dusty, sweaty clothes. The shower was too cramped for joint bathing, so Stoner went first. Wrapping a towel around herself, she stood for a while and listened to the sound of Gwen's voice singing above the water.

She climbed into her bra and pants and shorts, then reached into her t-shirt drawer. Her hand touched something that shouldn't have been there. Something hard and oddly shaped. She pulled the drawer fully open.

It was the note that had been missing this morning. But it was fastened to one of her shirts.

With a knife.

CHAPTER 8

She pulled her paddle from the lake and let it rest across the gunwales. Beads of water ran down the throat and dripped from the blade like slow rain. Circles widened from the falling drops, flattening to blend with the lake's own movement. Birds swooped low over the water and dipped to take a drink or veered sharply in pursuit of the moths that rode the slow breeze where air met water.

Swallows, she thought, or maybe swifts. The swallows should be leaving soon. She'd noticed them on the way up, perched in evenly-spaced rows on telephone wires. Learning to come together in flocks, preparing for the great migration as the evening light grew shorter and the air turned autumn dry.

In the bow of the canoe, Gwen shifted her paddle. It made a softly hollow "thunk," and Stoner was glad the canoe wasn't aluminum. The sound of wood on canvas belonged with cradle-rocking water and the purple-skyed evening.

Gwen had been silent through dinner and on the trip out. Stoner hadn't had much to say, either, thinking about the knife. They'd agreed to pretend they hadn't found it, and to try to see if anyone was watching them with particular intensity during dinner.

Nobody seemed to be.

Once again, she wished Aunt Hermione were here. She'd have held the knife, cleared her mind, and possibly picked up a clue or two from its vibrations. Stoner had tried it herself, holding it carefully in the palm of her hand, trying not to get fingerprints on it. The images that came to her hadn't told her anything: yellow light, anger mixed with pleasure, and a string of what looked like tiny bright green beads. Hardly a clue of major significance. So she'd turned it over to Clara. Maybe *she* could come up with something, using a more professional and less mystical approach.

And Gwen had sworn she didn't have the slightest association to it.

It made Stoner wonder why she'd gone a little pale when she'd shown it to her.

She knew it was best to leave Gwen to her own devices when she was turning things over in her mind. But the silent minutes had stretched into nearly half an hour now. She was growing impatient. More than impatient, worried.

"Gwen," she said softly.

Gwen turned to her.

"You thought something about that knife, didn't you?"

Gwen shook her head and looked guilty.

"You know something and you don't want to know it."

"Maybe." She fell silent again.

Stoner waited her out.

"I think I've seen it before," she said at last. "In Boneset's tool box."

Of course. That's what was odd about it. It looked like a pocket knife, but not really a pocket knife. The blades were heavy, the handle of black wood. The screw driver blade didn't have the bottle/can opener function of camping knives, but was long and sturdy. And there was a wire cutter. An electrician's knife.

But Boneset?

She was more than willing to admit people weren't always what they seemed. She'd known women who presented themselves to the world as helpful, caring, and dependable, for example, while behind the scenes they made terrible messes. Of course, nobody believed it except their victims, because they were so good at their public image. Street angels.

Were they dealing with a street angel in Boneset?

Possibly.

"When did you see it?" she asked.

"Last night, maybe, or this morning. At the barn."

"You mean just lying there in the box? And the box was open?"

Gwen nodded.

"Does she usually leave her tool box like that?"

"I think so."

"Then," Stoner said, "anyone could have picked it up. Besides, Boneset certainly didn't rig that ladder rung. She wouldn't take that kind of risk, even to throw people off her trail. At least, I can't imagine it. People are capable of anything, of course, but..." She'd expected Gwen to look relieved. She didn't. "Something else is bothering you, isn't it?"

Gwen looked away.

"Gwen."

"I'm fine, just hot and frustrated. It seems as if every time we get close to an answer, it just evaporates."

"True." She didn't believe her. She couldn't think of anything to say.

Gwen didn't say anything.

The evening deepened. Mosquitoes began to hum. Water patted against the side of the canoe. A sliver of moon rose in the east in a pewter crescent.

"You suspect Sherry," Gwen said at last, flatly.

"Among others."

"No, you think it's her." It sounded like blame.

"I don't, Gwen, really."

"She thinks you do."

Stoner shrugged. "I can't help that. I tried to reassure her. I thought I had."

"You're not being fair, Stoner. She's trying really hard to help."

"Fine." She was beginning to be annoyed.

"I wish you'd keep an open mind."

"My mind *is* open. If it were any more open, my brains would fall out."

"I don't think so."

"Okay, you don't think so." Her anger came into focus. She tried to deflect it. "Do you want to go to the ritual?"

"All right."

Stoner turned the canoe around and headed for shore. She felt stubborn and mean, and at the same time terribly lonely. "What did she say?" she asked, trying to keep her voice non-committal.

Gwen's voice drifted back through the near-darkness. "She didn't have to say much. I could tell she was upset."

Yeah, well, I'm upset, too. Can you tell that? "I asked her a couple of questions, that's all."

"Accusations?"

She fumbled a stroke and splashed them both with water and was glad. "They were *questions.* If she took them as accusations, it's not my fault. Maybe she has a guilty conscience."

"You made her cry," Gwen said as she wiped the water from the back of her neck with her t-shirt.

"She cries easily." She dug her paddle in the water roughly. "Did she *say* I made her cry?"

"No, but I could tell."

"You could tell she was upset, and you could tell I upset her. You're certainly perceptive today."

Gwen turned to look at her. Her face was a white balloon in the night. "Will you stop this? I know how you can be, Stoner. Once you have an idea, you just charge in. People can get hurt."

She couldn't believe Gwen was saying these things. "When did I ever charge in and hurt you?"

There was a brief pause.

Hah! Stoner thought. Can't think of anything, can you?

"In Wyoming," Gwen said. "When you said those things about Bryan, you hurt me."

"He was trying to *kill* you. I had to make you listen."

"Well..." Gwen seemed to be at a loss for words. "You could have been more tactful."

"You *hit me*. How tactful was that?"

Gwen didn't answer.

Somehow it didn't give Stoner much satisfaction to have won that round. "Gwen, this is ridiculous."

"I know. I'm just asking you to be a little kinder to Sherry, to try to understand where she's coming from, and you take it like..."

"I don't have the vaguest idea where she's coming from," Stoner said loudly. "That's the whole problem with her."

Gwen sighed. "She's only trying to keep the theater together, Stoner. *And* run the Cottage. So if she's not perfect, if she doesn't do and say things to absolutely convince you she has nothing to do with all this...Maybe you could cut her a little slack."

Cut her a little slack? Gwen never used language like that. Being around Gwen was being in a slang-free environment. Except for "these are the 90s," and she only said that to get a rise out of Stoner.

She started to point that out, but she didn't want to fight. Really, really didn't want to fight. "Okay," she said, "I'll try to be careful." She wanted to add, "of the baby's precious feelings," but stopped herself.

"Thank you," Gwen said. Her voice was formal.

It made Stoner want to cry. But there were already more than enough people crying around here, thank you very much. She wouldn't dream of up-staging Sherry Dodder.

The canoe touched the side of the pier and squealed against the old rubber tires that acted as bumpers. Stoner held it steady while Gwen got out. Gwen turned and offered her a hand.

"I can make it," Stoner said. "Just keep it still."

She wanted to take Gwen's hand, wanted it terribly. But she was afraid her touch would be as impersonal as her voice, and that would be too horrible.

They hauled the canoe from the water in silence, and stowed it on its rack in the boat house and hung the paddles against the wall where they belonged.

From the distance they heard the sound of drumming. "Sounds as if the ritual's starting," Gwen said. "Want to go?"

Stoner shrugged. "If you do." What she wanted was for this creepiness to go away and never come back.

"Stoner, I love you," Gwen said suddenly.

"What?" It was too dark to see her now.

"Love you. I don't want us to argue."

"Neither do I." She felt Gwen take her hand, and held on tight. "I'm sorry I hurt you in Wyoming," she said. "I never meant to."

"I was out of my mind," Gwen said. "To tell you the truth, I'm not even sure *what* you said." She slipped an arm around Stoner's waist and turned her toward her. "And I'm sorry I jumped on you just now. I really don't think you're insensitive. Sherry's probably premenstrual or something. Maybe I am, too."

"Probably." Which didn't address the fact that Gwen had accepted her accusations in the first place, or that she still thought Stoner had been too blunt in Wyoming. It made her wonder what else Gwen thought that she didn't know about.

Gwen's fingertips found Stoner's mouth in the darkness. "Forgive me?" she asked softly.

Stoner thought about it all. It wasn't worth arguing or worrying about. She loved her. That was what mattered. "Of course I forgive you," she said, and kissed her.

Women were coming along the path, talking softly, a few humming a chant.

"I think we missed the ceremony," Gwen whispered.

"No, we didn't," Stoner said. "What we just did was the Goddess' ritual. 'All acts of love and pleasure,' remember?"

Gwen pulled away a little and rested her neck on Stoner's arm. Night air rushed in between them, cooling them as it touched their perspiration-soaked nakedness. "Did Aunt Hermione tell you that?"

"Yeah. But she wouldn't tell me how she knew."

Gwen laughed. "Use your imagination. Grace D' Addario may have taught her about Wicca, but I think she taught her a few other things, too. I wish we'd brought a picnic."

"Hungry?" Stoner grinned in the darkness. Gwen was always hungry after they'd made love.

"Ravenous."

"Maybe we can raid the kitchen."

"In a while," Gwen said, and snuggled up to her.

Stoner toyed with Gwen's hair. It felt so good to be together and at ease again. Their love-making had been…

…desperate, something inside her said. A break in the strangeness. Time out of time.

She shoved the thought away. Things were okay…

…for now…

…and she refused to let her insecurities spoil it.

Gwen was reaching for her clothes. The path took her across Stoner, so they were skin-to-skin again.

She touched Gwen's back. She loved the feel of it, and the way she knew every bump and dip and tiny break in the smoothness. She even knew her freckles so well that she imagined she could sense the change in color, even in the darkness.

To know someone so well, to love someone in so many ways, made everything else irrelevant. Even Sherry Dodder was irrelevant.

Sherry Dodder was also just outside the boat house. They could hear her voice—perky, slightly demanding, insanely enthusiastic for the time of night. "Listen, guys. I'm calling a set-building session right now."

Various assorted groans and grumbles greeted the news.

"I know you don't want to do it," Sherry said with a cheery laugh, "but we're behind schedule, and the energy's high right now, so let's just do it."

More grumblings.

"One hour. Two, tops, and we're out of here."

"Sherry, I really don't think…" It was Barb's voice.

"Hey," Sherry said, "am I the producer, or am I the producer?"

Barb's voice took on an edge. "Am I the tech director?"

"We have to do it, Barb," Sherry said, her voice lowering and coming closer as she drew Barb toward the boat house. "We're falling farther behind every day. At this rate, we're fucked."

"Not according to my calculations."

"Look, you know we're having problems. Goddess knows what might happen next. I have to look at the total picture."

"The women are tired, Sherry. They need a night off."

"So we give them one, but not this one. Hey," her voice took on a hurt tone. "I'm only thinking of the good of the show."

"Sherry..."

"Good woman," Sherry said in a tone that had a pat-on-the-back feel to it. She raised her voice. "All *right*. Brewskis at the barn. Be there or be square."

There was a sound of people wandering away, then silence.

"Shit," Gwen said.

Stoner gave her a little squeeze. "What kind of language is that?"

"Southern Gothic." She pulled her clothes on. "That was the last thing I wanted to do tonight."

"What was the first?"

"Variations on our previous theme." She tossed Stoner's clothes in her direction.

"Well, so far I've been lucky," Stoner said as she sat up. "But much more action on this wood floor, and we'll be up all night pulling splinters out of my rear end."

"Damn," Gwen said in an accent that made two words of one. "She went and spoilt all mah fun."

Stoner giggled and pressed a hand over Gwen's mouth. "Calm yourself. They'll hear you."

"One hour," Gwen said. "We'll give her one hour and then we're on our own."

"Agreed," Stoner said. "And no 'Brewskis.' "

"No 'Brewskis.' 'Brewskis.' My God, everyone should grow up."

But, of course, one hour didn't do it. It was after midnight by the time they got back to their rooms. They were tired, and paint-spattered, and Gwen was still hungry.

"In spite of that lovely refreshment tray?" Stoner asked through the steam from the shower. She waved it away with her towel.

It had indeed been a sumptuous tray that Sherry provided for the techies. Cut-up vegetables and dip, sunflower seeds and salted nuts, popcorn which wilted quickly in the humidity. And more 'Brewskis' than anyone could want.

But carrot sticks and broccoli flowerets dipped in onion dip hadn't done much to satisfy the kind of hunger Gwen had. And Stoner had been so morbidly fascinated by watching the way Marcy ate sunflower seeds—holding them in the palm of her left hand, lifting exactly two between the thumb and forefinger of her right hand, raising them over her tilted-back mouth, and dropping them in, then immediately reaching for two more without breaking stride—that she'd forgotten to eat anything herself.

"This is the last time I stay in one of these quaint country inns," Gwen muttered. "From now on, I want soda machines and snack vendors."

"I'll go prowling," Stoner said as she rubbed her wet hair. She slipped into her pajamas. "I might be able to come up with a sandwich."

"Supermarket lunch meat," Gwen said. "On Wonder bread. With real mayonnaise would be Heaven."

"At The Cottage? I doubt it."

It was silent in the hall. And still. So still it almost seemed as if the yellow ceiling lights were humming. Only darkness showed beneath the doors of the other rooms. The threadbare carpet whispered beneath her feet. The faded wallpaper and dark woodwork gave The Cottage an eerie feeling, like slipping backward in time. She could almost hear the hiss of gas lights and the low creak of rope bed springs. Any minute now, someone would begin playing the harpsichord.

A good night for the Cottage ghost. If there was a Cottage ghost. She really doubted it. In her experience, if there were ghosts to be seen, she was likely to have the dubious honor of seeing them first. Sometimes they showed themselves to her alone. She supposed it was a gift, and she should be flattered to be considered worthy of other-worldly emanations. But, if there were gifts to be handed out, she would have preferred to be lucky with the lottery.

She went down the wide staircase into blackness. The moon had set. A few thin clouds reflected distant light, dimly, beyond the French doors. Chairs and tables were mounds of darkness.

Stoner felt her way along from chair to chair. Through the dining room, where the tables were set for breakfast, their linen cloths gleaming like phosphorescent mushrooms in a deep forest.

A night light on the stove cast a bluish glow. She felt a little guilty, prowling around someone else's personal kitchen. But this was a serious hunger emergency, and the kitchen *could* be considered public space. And besides, when you came right down to it, Sherry had brought her here to prowl.

All very respectable rationalizations. She was sure, given enough time, she could come up with even better ones.

The refrigerator was locked. Good, so if she found anything open, she could assume it was for general consumption. Of course, having the refrigerator off limits ruled out exotic lunch meats, unless it was so filled with artificial ingredients and preservatives it wouldn't go bad in summer, which was a possibility. Maybe the whole lunch meat industry was a scam, insisting on refrigeration just so the public wouldn't guess they were eating recycled building materials.

Who was she kidding? No way there'd be supermarket lunch meat in this Mecca of healthy gourmet dining.

She started in on cupboards. Plates, glasses, cooking utensils. No food. Not even canned goods or crackers. Not even peanut butter, which would make an acceptable substitute, though not as exciting as the real, politically-incorrect McCoy.

No luck. The closest thing she found to food was an entire section devoted to salt and pepper shakers.

Okay, where else do we find food?

Pantries.

She looked around for doors. There were three. The first opened onto a small lavatory. The second onto a set of stairs leading to the floors above. All right, let's see what's behind door number three. Trash or treasure? Trick or treat? The lady or the tiger?

The door was locked.

"Damn it, Dodder," she muttered, "this is downright inhospitable."

"The key's in the lock," said a pleasant voice that startled her halfway to the ceiling.

She whirled around as Sherry flicked on the overhead light.

The woman raised one eyebrow in amusement behind her round glasses. "I thought there were raccoons out here, but it's just a sneak-thief."

Stoner felt herself blush deeply. It made her furious at her autonomic nervous system. "I'm sorry," she stammered. "We were hungry, and…"

Sherry laughed. "*No problemo*. Actually, I should have left something out, just in case."

"That's very gracious of you," Stoner said. "But it doesn't make it right to break in here."

"Oh, break in, shmake in," Sherry said with a dismissive wave of her hand. "You needed something I hadn't provided. Very bad in the inn keeping business. The first fault was mine." She moved brusquely to the pantry door. "What can I get you?"

"Well," Stoner said, knowing she was about to humiliate herself even further, "some kind of lunch meat sandwich, if you have it."

"Done," said Sherry. She threw open the pantry door and tossed Stoner a loaf of bread.

Pepperidge Farm. For some reason, that pleased her. After all, there was such a thing as being *too* perfect. Wonder Bread would have been *too* perfect.

Sherry slipped a key ring off a hook just inside the door. "Here's where I keep the refrigerator key, in case you need it."

"Thank you," Stoner muttered.

"Pickle and pimento loaf?"

"Perfect." She'd always been drawn to pickle and pimento loaf. It was one of those meats so filled with preservatives that it dried out before it turned moldy. She liked that in a lunch meat.

"Now, what would you like on your sandwich? Mustard? Mayo? Something more exotic?"

More exotic than pickle and pimento loaf?

"Just mayo, thanks."

They carried the sandwich makings to a table in the center of the room and sat at high stools.

Sherry did the honors. "I'm kind of glad I ran into you like this," she said as she spread mayonnaise on bread. "I wanted to apologize for this afternoon."

"You did?"

"Getting all upset like that. It was really childish." She slapped three slices of pickle and pimento loaf on each slice of bread and flashed Stoner a quick smile. "I'm afraid I gave Gwen the impression you'd been unkind. I hope it didn't cause trouble between you."

"Not at all," Stoner lied, damned if she was going to share their personal discomforts with this stranger.

"I'm so glad. Wouldn't you know, when I got back to my room, I found I'd gotten my period. PMS was all it was. I guess I'd lost track of the date, with all the things that have been going on around here."

"That can happen," Stoner said.

Sherry eyed the sandwiches critically, slathered on more mayonnaise, added lettuce, got plates from the cupboard and placed them on a large serving tray. She took another slice of bread from the loaf and carefully trimmed the crust from it. Setting the crusts aside, she cut the bread into four tiny squares, took one, and set it up on its side. Carefully, she cut the square in half on the narrow edge, then prepared a postage-stamp sized bit of meat and slipped it between the bread slices.

Uh-oh, Stoner thought. Eating disorder. And a very bizarre sort of disorder at that. With anorexia, you didn't eat. With bulimia, you ate and purged. This was like...performance art.

She wondered if she should comment on it, or pretend she hadn't noticed. Which would be a little strange, since Sherry was doing it right in front of her. So would it be rude to notice, or rude not to notice? Maybe she should write Miss Manners for an opinion.

Meanwhile, Sherry was cleaning up as if nothing unusual had happened. Tossing crusts and unused bread into the garbage can, returning the meat and mayonnaise to the refrigerator. "What would you like to drink?" she asked.

Stoner shrugged. "Milk. Water. Anything."

"Milk it is. Help you sleep." She poured out huge glasses and put the bottle away.

"Don't you want any?"

"Water's fine for me," Sherry said cheerfully, and drew herself a tiny juice glass full from the tap.

"Uh...I guess you're not very hungry, huh?" Stoner suggested, indicating the miniscule sandwich completely dwarfed by its salad plate.

Sherry looked at her quizzically, then followed her gaze to the plate. For a second she didn't seem to recognize it. Then her eyes widened and she clamped a hand over her mouth. "Oh, my God," she said in dismay. "Oh, my *God*! I didn't even realize I was doing that." She grabbed the plate and thrust it onto the counter by the sink, out of sight. "I'm so *ashamed*," she said, wringing her hands.

"There's nothing to be ashamed of," Stoner said. "You just made a funny sandwich."

"It's a problem I have," Sherry said in a low, confidential voice. "I'm getting help for it. Or at least I was." She paused expectantly.

"Why did you stop?" Stoner asked, feeling as if she were responding to her cue.

"My therapist..." Sherry seemed to be trying to find the right words. "She...well, she...it just didn't work out."

"I see." But of course she didn't see at all.

"She was just so, so *withholding*. Do you know what I mean?"

Stoner nodded. She felt rather withholding around Sherry, herself.

"It was just getting me all screwed up." The woman seemed to shrink before her eyes. "I've never let anyone see me do that. I don't know what got into me. I just felt so, so *comfortable* with you." She looked up, tears glittering in the corners of her eyes. "Please, forget this happened. It's just so humiliating. If anyone else knew..."

"I won't say anything." What, was she going to rush up to the next group of people she met and start shouting, "You're not going to believe what I just saw?" Right. That was the Stoner McTavish way, all right.

"Not even Gwen," Sherry begged. "I'd be devastated if I thought she knew."

"Gwen wouldn't think anything bad," Stoner said.

"I couldn't bear it. You people are really, really special to me. I mean, I was thinking we might all be friends, once this is over. That's how special you are. But I don't think I can do that now."

"That's ridiculous, Sherry," Stoner found herself saying. "People do all sorts of strange things..."

"See? You think I'm strange." The tears brimmed up again. "Oh, God, I want to die. I just want to die."

Stoner wanted to shake her and yell at her to get a grip on herself. But that would be not only rude, but inappropriate. There was quite enough strange behavior going on for one night. "I won't tell her," she said. "Just calm down and let it go."

Sherry's face broke into a smile. "Oh, thank you, thank you." She gave a little laugh. "I'm indebted to you again. You're going to own me."

"I doubt that," Stoner said. She wanted to go back to her room, where things were calm and sane. "Look, I don't mean to run off, but Gwen's really hungry..."

"Go, go." She bounced down from the stool. "It's been really good to talk to you. I'm glad I thought you were a burglar." She started to leave, then turned and planted herself in front of Stoner in a manner that was obviously asking for a hug.

Stoner picked up the tray.

A cloud crossed Sherry's face.

It made Stoner feel like a mean person. After all, this woman may be unusual, but she was a human being, with feelings and needs. Just because she was a little hard to empathize with didn't mean she had to treat her like a pariah.

She put the tray down and reached out her arms casually. "Good night, Sherry."

Sherry clutched her in a bear-like grip that seemed to go on, and on, and on. It was amazing, the number of their body parts Sherry managed to get to touch. Especially considering the difference in their heights.

A great deal of time was passing, and Sherry was showing no sign of breaking the embrace.

"I really have to go," Stoner said, and extricated herself.

"Sweet dreams," Sherry said.

"Same to you."

"Give Gwen my love." She sighed. "You two are great. I have so much respect for your relationship."

As Stoner left the kitchen, carrying the tray of sandwiches Sherry had gone out of her way to make for them, and the glasses of milk Sherry had poured, she glanced back.

Sherry was standing very small in the middle of the very large kitchen, gazing after her with an abandoned look.

Gwen perched in the middle of her bed, toiling away with the blow dryer. "You were gone so long," she said, "I was going to come after you, but I was too weak with hunger."

Stoner set the tray down. "I ran into Sherry."

"Aha." Gwen grabbed a sandwich. "You got caught."

"Sort of. She made the sandwiches."

Gwen smiled when she saw what was in it. "She remembered."

"Who remembered what?"

"Sherry. What I told her about pickle and pimento loaf."

Stoner was puzzled. "There's something about pickle and pimento loaf?"

"My grandmother used to make it for me, back in Georgia. It was my comfort food when I was a kid."

"You never told me that," Stoner said. She felt cold inside.

Gwen reached for the sandwich. "I didn't?"

Stoner shook her head.

"I guess it never came up."

"I guess it never did."

Gwen looked hard at her. "Stoner, are you jealous of Sherry?"

She tried it on. A little, she guessed. Because stories of Gwen's childhood were precious to her, and it felt odd that this stranger would know one she hadn't heard. Which, she had to acknowledge, was rather small-minded of her. But what really bothered her was that she felt so unsure of herself. It was as if she and Gwen were talking about two different Sherry Dodders, and that was unusual between them.

"That's putting it a little strongly," she said.

"Because, if you are, there's really not a thing for you to be concerned about. We had a nice lunch and a few laughs, that's all. I'm not about to run off with her."

"That's a relief," Stoner said, pretending to tease. "I was really worried about that." She turned serious. "It's just kind of ironic. You didn't like her at first and I did, and now that I'm finding myself a little put off by her, you like her."

Gwen took a thoughtful bite of her sandwich and a swallow of milk. "Yeah, it *is* odd. I wonder what it means."

"Maybe she's just really changeable."

"No," Gwen said, "what I think is, I was put off by her public persona. And maybe you haven't had a chance to see beyond that yet."

Possibly. But she felt as if she *had* seen beyond that persona, and what she saw was disturbing. Anyway, it was late, and not worth arguing over. Tomorrow was another day, and on its way much too fast. She curled up on the bed next to Gwen and started in on her own sandwich.

"Know what I wish?" Gwen said.

"No, what?"

"I wish we had a television set in the room."

Stoner glanced at her. "It's nearly one in the morning. There's nothing on."

"Infomercials," Gwen said, "go perfectly with pickle and pimento sandwiches."

Saturday morning was overcast and damp. A "lowry" day, they called it in Maine, with the sky lowering pewter gray and clouds forming and shredding like tissue in flowing water. A heaviness seemed to settle over the Cottage. Even the Dyke Hikers were subdued on their final morning—highly unusual for them, according to Clara and Esther, who had witnessed more than one closing day of the Dyke Hike Retreat. According to Esther, the boisterousness was known to reach the level of fan reaction to a critical Red Sox win over the Yankees. Even the High Fives were a little slack-wristed this morning.

It was the kind of day, Stoner thought, when nothing much got accomplished, everyone made wrong decisions, and people got into arguments over things they didn't even care about.

Like whether Sherry Dodder was a Princess, or the pea under the mattress.

Actually, even Sherry was in a serious mood, though she had dressed in a bright yellow swirly rayon blouse and tropical print shorts. Clearly, she intended to counteract the day's gloominess if at all possible. At the moment, though, she was taking a break from her role as Cottage cheer leader and all-around good time girl to discuss the fine points of the Hikers' bill with their treasurer.

Smiles all around. Everything was apparently agreeable.

The honeymooners hadn't even bothered to come downstairs. In fact, in the three days they'd been there, Stoner had barely laid eyes on them. Their friends were probably complaining about how women acted when they became couples, joined at the hip. Give them six months, she thought. They'll revert to human beings again.

Gwen was packing away a breakfast that would have satisfied a trucker, giving no indication that she'd consumed one and a half pickle and pimento loaf with mayonnaise on white bread sandwiches only a few hours ago. Omelet *de jour*, with cheese, herbs, tomatoes, peppers, wild mushrooms, and something that looked like fiddlehead ferns but couldn't be since fiddlehead season was long past and Sherry *certainly* wouldn't sink to frozen or canned products.

Stoner searched her heart to see if there had been something unduly sarcastic or nasty in that last thought. If there was, she couldn't find it. Actually, she admired the choices Sherry made about the food she served her guests. It was healthy, unusual, and delicious. She never took the easy way, when it certainly must be tempting. And there was the daily array of assorted goodies on hand at all times in the lobby. Considering the rather odd personal relationship Sherry seemed to have with eating, the time and effort she took for other people was surprising—and, Stoner had to admit, admirable.

She chewed on her English muffin and sipped her coffee and contemplated the nature of innkeeping. As a career, it had a lot in common with being a travel agent. Lots of details, lots of people to satisfy, lots of things to go wrong. In the travel business you didn't have to worry about menu planning, an activity she found almost impossible to imagine without losing her sanity. On the other hand, Sherry probably didn't have to worry much about lost luggage.

Someone had said something about Sherry once having had a partner in running the Cottage. She wondered about that, and what had happened. Had they been business partners only, or friends or lovers? Had the separation been amicable or nasty? Had Sherry wanted to keep the inn, or had it become hers by default?

Could the current goings-on be an ex-lover's revenge?

"Penny for your thoughts," Gwen said.

"I was just wondering about the partner Sherry had."

"She talked a little about that. She said the other woman had wanted to go back to graduate school—chemistry or mathematics or physics or some other intimidating field—and Sherry bought her out. Marge wouldn't have had the money for school otherwise."

"That was her name? Marge?"

Gwen nodded.

"How long ago was it?"

"I'm not sure. Three, maybe four years ago. Why?"

"Just curious. It must have taken a pile of money."

"Sherry's grandparents had left her their house. She sold it and invested the money right away."

That made sense. Avoiding taxes was always a good idea, especially when you could do it legally. Doing it illegally was a little scary, even when you disapproved of what the Government was doing with it. It had been more than a decade since she'd been able to really get behind a Government program, but she still hadn't gotten up the nerve to become a tax resistor.

"Sounds reasonable," Stoner said.

"But there was something else." Gwen put down her muffin and leaned across the table to lower her voice. "Apparently they were lovers, and Marge..." A guilty look crossed her face. "Oh. I promised her I wouldn't tell."

Interesting. It seemed Sherry had more than one secret.

"Why?" Stoner asked.

"Well, it kind of slipped out while she was talking, and she didn't think it was the kind of thing she ought to spread around. And I think she was embarrassed about it."

"Was it the eating thing?"

Gwen looked at her quizzically. "Eating thing?"

"Yeah, she told me about an eating problem she has, but she didn't want me to tell you." She wanted to add, "*It* kind of slipped out, too," but didn't.

"No, it wasn't about eating." Gwen stirred her coffee.

Silence fell between them. Stoner didn't like it. This felt odd, not being allowed to talk freely. Especially when they hadn't made the rules themselves.

"Listen," Gwen said, "I'll tell you if you'll tell me, but we won't tell Sherry we told."

Stoner contemplated. "Is that fair?"

"Well, who would *we* tell? Besides, it doesn't feel right this way. We'd be talking around it all the time, and sidling up to it, and feeling guilty, and end up telling, anyway. So why not save ourselves all that agony?"

"Good point."

Gwen lowered her voice again. "She didn't actually *say* it, but she did imply that Marge was kind of abusive."

"Physically?"

"And emotionally."

"That's too bad," Stoner said. She wondered what was behind that. These things were usually complicated. She didn't want to blame the victim, but Sherry had already aroused feelings in her that she didn't ordinarily have and which she wasn't proud of. Before she was ready to condemn the unknown Marge, she realized, she'd have to have more evidence.

And Sherry? she asked herself. You seem willing to cast suspicion on Sherry for a variety of things, and you have no evidence that she's not what she appears to be.

And what's that?

For starters, one of the most bewildering, complicated human beings she'd ever met.

Clara and Esther came into the dining room. Clara aimed her wheel chair at their table, Esther in hot pursuit. "Here's your weapon," Clara announced as she dropped a small brown paper bag in Stoner's lap. "It's clean. I'd guess the perp wore gloves *and* wiped it off."

Well, it was about what she'd expected. In this world of television crime, and DNA testing and endless discussions of efficacies and legalities and constitutionalities, anyone who left finger prints anywhere had to be incredibly stupid or just escaped from a monastery.

Clara held out her hand. "Give me your room keys. Both of them."

Gwen wanted to know what for.

"I'm not going to go through your things. I'll fix the keys so you're secure. Seems there's enough free-wheeling coming and going in that room, if you want my opinion."

Stoner allowed as how it was her opinion, too, and they handed over the keys.

"Anything else I should know?" Clara asked efficiently as she secreted the keys in her pocket.

Stoner shook her head. "I'm floundering. Everyone seems to have the means and the opportunity for everything that's happened."

Clara cocked her head to one side. "In that case," she said, "I'd go for motive."

"I'm coming up blank there, too. There doesn't seem to be any point to it. I mean, why would anyone want to go around scaring people and making trouble for the theater group? Where would it get you? It doesn't make sense."

"She doesn't believe people go in for senseless trouble-making," Gwen explained. "She doesn't know many teen-agers."

Esther and Clara laughed appreciatively.

"Here's what I'd do," Clara said, lowering her voice. "I'd try to see if these incidents are focusing in on any one or two people, and look for any connections from there."

"I'm trying to do that, but these women have long, complicated histories with one another. It'd take forever to sort it all out."

"It'll take forever if all you do is sit on your duff and feel sorry for yourself," Clara announced briskly. "You're two young, healthy, and—I assume—fairly intelligent women. Split up, each of you take half and get to know them. Put your heads together. But, for God's sake, stop with the 'can't, can't, can't' and the 'don't know.' Drives me crazy." She turned her chair sharply and wheeled off toward their usual table.

Esther leaned toward them. "She's just as bewildered and frustrated as you are. But she's right. When you can't think of anything to do, that's the time you should do something."

"'When in danger or in doubt,'" Gwen quoted, "'run in circles, yell and shout.'"

"Exactly." Esther gave Gwen's shoulder a complimentary tap. "Meanwhile, we're keeping on with our stake-out. And figuring." She rolled her eyes. "Lord, how we're thinking!"

"I hate to have you using up your vacation with our problems," Stoner said.

"Don't be silly. This is the best time we've had in years. It's sort of like old times, don't you know?" She leaned closer. "If you need a decoy, I'm at your service. Had plenty of experience. I've played just about every role in the books—street walker, gun moll, drug dealer. They used to call me The Woman of a Thousand Faces. Of course, things were different then. They didn't have these automatic weapons. Clara'd have a screaming fit if I even thought of going under cover nowadays." She smiled. "To tell you the truth, I'd have a screaming fit if she went back to the job, too. She gave her legs to the fair city of Boston. I want the rest of my honey in one piece."

Clara was shaking out her napkin with an impatient flapping sound that carried clear across the dining room.

"She's impossible when she's working," Esther said. "We'll catch up with you later and exchange what we know. Remember, even if you don't know where you're going, you have to keep moving ahead."

Stoner watched her go. "I love older women," she said.

They decided Clara was right. If each of them spent some time with each of the theater women, alone, they might be able to put some things together. But they couldn't do it during rehearsals. It seemed the serious work of putting the play together was beginning, and that meant complete run-throughs, and working with scenery and props.

It was amazing to Stoner, and perfectly understandable, that a scene that had gone as smoothly as cream the day before could fall apart completely simply because the actors had to deal with glasses of water. Suddenly they didn't have enough hands—even though they'd had so many they didn't know what to do with them yesterday. They'd put a glass down and forget where they'd put it. Or just hold it and forget to drink, which drove Rebecca wild. Not as wild as actors who were supposed to be pouring coffee and would dribble a little in the bottom of a cup. "Nobody drinks a quarter inch of coffee," she said repeatedly. "Even if they ask for 'just a drop,' they expect a half cup at least."

But holding the glass and not drinking was the second deadly sin. "It distracts the audience. They keep waiting for you to *do* something with it."

Under her breath, she explained to Stoner that grabbing the audience's attention like that was known as "upstaging," and that if she really wanted to learn how to do it well, she should watch Marcy.

That gave Stoner an idea. Marcy was the general understudy. If someone—Roseann, for instance—had to drop out, Marcy would take her place. Giving Marcy the lead.

Uh-huh. Definitely something to check out. It didn't explain the attacks—if you could call them attacks—on Sherry, or the broken ladder. But maybe she shouldn't try to tie everything together. Maybe she should focus on one thing/person at a time.

The trouble was, she suspected she wasn't exactly on Marcy's list of favorite people, not after she'd put Marcy in her place at yesterday's rehearsal. But Gwen hadn't had any interaction, good or bad, with her. Gwen could try to get to know her.

Which meant Stoner should probably try to get close to Rita. Rita would be hard to pin down, but once she gained her confidence, Stoner had the feeling Rita would have quite a bit to say about everything and everyone.

She realized she was assuming Rita was innocent. Why? Because she seemed too disorganized and psychologically rumpled to plot and carry out this kind of mischief? A dangerous assumption, and not altogether fair. Just because Rita was flaky, it didn't necessarily preclude her being as evil as the next person. In fact, when you looked at it, Rita's flakiness could be a perfect cover.

Motive?

As yet unknown.

And, she reminded herself, "as yet unknown" does not necessarily mean "non-existent."

Rita it was, and as they broke for lunch Stoner grabbed Gwen, hurriedly filled her in on what she'd come up with, and arranged to meet her in their room after lunch.

Now all she had to do was find a reason to talk to Rita.

As it turned out, she didn't have to look for a reason. All she had to do was loiter about the living room before lunch. She'd wondered how to draw Rita away from the rest of the Demeters, but the cast and crew came through without her. Odd, Stoner thought, but maybe she'd had to go to her room for some reason like a change of clothes or a headache. So she decided to leaf through *Architectural Digest* one last time before she gave up.

She felt Rita's arrival even before she saw her, a swirling and spiking of the air. Electric energy, and the smell of ozone. Then dead silence, like the moment before a thunder clap.

A yellow-haired hurricane, Rita exploded into the room. Her face flamed. Her eyes flashed knives. Her lips were red as blood. She was Demeter personified. She was Medea. She was Cerridwen, and dragons. She was storms at sea that drowned ships and left sailors' bones to litter the ocean floor. She was War, and Fire. Hiroshima and Nagasaki. Gettysburg and Iwo Jima.

Rita was Rage.

"I'll kill the fucking bitch!" she declared to the universe, and headed for the dining room door.

Stoner pulled herself out of her temporary paralysis. "Rita!" She made a dive for her.

Rita flicked her to the side.

"Damn it," Stoner shouted. "Listen to me!" She grabbed the woman's wrist and dug her nails into the soft skin.

"Jesus!" Startled, Rita turned to her. "What the hell are you doing?"

"Keeping you from doing something you'll regret, I hope." She gave her a shove toward the nearest piece of furniture.

Caught off balance, Rita fell onto the sofa and wallowed, struggling to get up.

Stoner put her hands on the woman's shoulders and held her there. "I don't know what you're doing, or why," she said, "but from here it looks like a really bad idea."

Rita pushed her hands away.

Stoner figured the woman outweighed her by about seventy-five pounds, and had the strength of anger on her side. So she did the only thing she could think of. She sat in Rita's lap.

"For God's sake," the woman said, "are you some kind of nut ball?"

"Its been rumored," Stoner replied firmly. "I'll let you up if you'll tell me what's going on."

"She's gone too far," Rita said.

"Who has?"

"Marcy." She looked as if she might cry. "She wants to ruin everything I love, and I don't know why."

"Yeah," Stoner said, getting up. "I heard about her and your lover."

"Of course you heard about it. Everybody in the whole fucking world heard about it. Everybody in the whole fucking world feels sorry for me to my face, and laughs at me behind my back."

"I don't think so…"

Rita started to heave herself out of the sofa.

"Don't make me sit on you again," Stoner said. "It's rude."

"They made me look like a fool," Rita muttered as she settled back. "Jesus, don't I already look enough like a fool?"

Stoner studied her. "Actually, you look like a Leo."

"Well, I *am* a Leo. So what?"

"So…there you are," Stoner said. "Rita, what's going on?"

The woman hesitated, then dug down into the front of her dress and brought out Seabrook. The frog's head had been ripped nearly off. Sawdust trickled from behind a cotton ball Rita had stuffed into the wound.

"She killed him," she said, and began to sob.

CHAPTER 9

Stoner didn't know what to say. If this was someone's idea of a prank, there was nothing funny about it. It was cruel and petty.

On the other hand, it might not be a prank at all. It might be part of the pattern of accidents and intimidation.

Sitting down beside Rita, she took Seabrook into her hands gently. "He can be fixed," she said, and felt inadequate in the face of Rita's grief. "Look. It'd be easy."

The big woman wiped her eyes with a sodden, balled-up tissue. "That's not the point," she said. "She knew I'd react the way I did, and make a scene, and then I'd be so humiliated I'd have to quit the show."

"She?"

"Marcy."

"If it was Marcy, I guess she didn't figure on me stopping you before you hit the dining room," Stoner said. "Big surprise on her, ha-ha."

Rita smiled a little. She had a lovely, genuine smile. "Ha-ha on her."

She slipped an arm around Rita's shoulders. "How do you feel?"

"Shaky, but getting there."

"You're certain it was Marcy?"

Rita didn't seem to know quite what to do with Stoner's arm around her. She half leaned into her, then straightened up, not enough to lose contact but enough not to lean. "I hope nobody else hates me that much."

"Why does Marcy hate you?"

Rita thought it over. "I don't know. It's not as if I stole anything from her. She just thinks I'm shit. I mean, we had our problems, but she won, didn't she? It's not my fault it didn't work out."

Stoner hesitated. She didn't want to say too much. But, on the other hand, she couldn't let Rita think this was personal if it wasn't. It wouldn't be fair. "The thing is," she explained, "I'm not convinced Marcy did this, and I'm not certain it was only directed at you."

Rita looked at her.

"You've noticed the things that have been happening here. The problems with Roseann's script, the ladder, maybe even the flashlights. And maybe even before that. Remember the wet paint? It looked like a mistake at the time, but what if it wasn't? I could be wrong, but wouldn't it seem to you as if someone's trying to sabotage the show?"

"It occurred to me," Rita said. "But I figured I was just being crazy again. I've been crazy, you know. Locked up crazy. Sometimes I still get that way a little, if I'm around Marcy too much." She held up one hand. "I know what you're going to say. I should stay away from her if she makes me crazy. But these people are my friends. I'm not going to let her run me off, even if it *is* sick to stay around."

"I heard you call her 'douche-bag' at rehearsal," Stoner said. "That seems pretty healthy to me."

"That was Seabrook, ventilating. It doesn't bother her. She probably likes it. It makes her the center of attention." She sighed. "Damn her eyes."

Stoner nodded. "With some people you just can't win."

"So true," Rita said. She took Seabrook from Stoner and toyed with his head. "You really think he can be fixed?"

"Easily." And she was willing to bet there were half a dozen women in *Demeter Ascending* who'd be glad to try.

"I'll ask Div," Rita said. "She makes her own clothes."

Remembering Divi Divi's elegant dresses and caftan, Stoner was impressed. "She's very good."

"Sure is. She doesn't exactly like it, because her mother supported them by being a seamstress for Macy's. But she claims, with her size, the only clothes she can get in ofay stores make her look like a loaf of Italian bread." She pinched the edges of Seabrook's wound together. "He's lost a lot of sawdust. He's going to look skinny. Maybe I should try that."

"I think," Stoner said, "getting your throat cut would have a very different effect on you than it does on Seabrook."

It was beginning to rain. Fine, gentle drops that fuzzed the edges of the forest in the distance. It was the kind of rain that could last all day. That was all right. It would keep everyone in one place, instead of wandering off all over the grounds during breaks the way they usually did.

"Want a banana?" Rita was saying as she rummaged through her tote.

She realized she was hungry, and becoming more so by the minute. "Yes, thanks."

Rita handed her one. "Organic. Don't ever eat stuff that isn't organic. Full of radiation."

"Really?" She extricated her arm from around Rita to peel the banana. "I didn't know that."

"Didn't you see 'Silkwood?' " Rita asked, working on a peach.

"Yeah, it was a great movie."

"Remember where she worked, where they had all the radiation? Kerr-McGee. And what does Kerr-McGee make? Fertilizer."

"You're right. I never put it together."

"I figure what that was about was, they're hiding radioactive waste in the fertilizer. It all ends up inside us." Rita shook her head. "You have to be on guard all the time," she said. "They get you when you least expect it."

An organic banana wasn't going to do it. Last night's pickle and pimento loaf, loaded with nitrites and fat and probably radioactive, was beginning to look like Treat of the Year. Maybe the *last* treat of the year. But she didn't dare go into the dining room, where Rita was talking seriously and animatedly with Divi Divi, who had gone with her to a table in a corner and was examining Seabrook with all the solemnity of a brain surgeon. Rita was talking, but she wasn't eating. And while Stoner had no intention of spending the rest of her stay here avoiding dangerous foods, it seemed unkind to flaunt Rita's well-meaning advice only ten minutes after she gave it.

So she loitered about the living room until most of the other diners had gone upstairs or to the barn, tempted by the goody array but knowing any more sugar would send her into outer space. Finally, she crept out to the kitchen to take advantage of Sherry's Hostess with the Mostess hospitality and beg for food, any food. Which Sherry delivered with concern, nurturing murmurs, and characteristic cheerfulness. It almost made Stoner feel guilty for her lack of enthusiasm over Sherry. Almost, but not quite.

She checked in with Gwen, who hadn't been able to get Marcy aside for a chat, but who had volunteered to take the inn's pick-up truck into Bangor this evening and pick up some large sheets of styrofoam to be used in the scenery. She thought she had a pretty good chance of getting Marcy to come along.

She checked in with Clara and Esther, who handed over their surveillance reports for the morning. At a quick glance, it appeared as if the comings and goings in the Cottage were identical to yesterday's—although the honey-mooners had ventured downstairs for coffee around 10:30 am. Clara had underlined the event in red, and said they should always remember it as a Red Letter Day. A national holiday wasn't out of the question—Honeymooners Out Of Bed And Into The Dining Room Day. The Dyke Hikers had left, the Demeters had gone to the barn, and Sherry had joined them about a half hour later, after making a final check of lunch plans with the kitchen crew.

No, they hadn't noticed anything suspicious, though Clara had an idea or two and was planning to do a little spying during the afternoon. Stoner asked if it involved breaking into people's rooms. Clara informed her it was none of her business.

By the time she left the kitchen herself, brushing off the evidence of her gastronomic transgression—the left-over pork spare ribs were perfect, the chocolate cream pie to die for—Sherry had finished reviewing the dinner menus and walked her down to the barn.

Sherry was uncharacteristically silent, though there was a glittery excitement about her that seemed barely contained.

Strange. But maybe she'd come across the marijuana patch down by the lake.

Maybe she had, and maybe she'd slipped it into Boneset's herbal tea stash, and maybe...

Stop that, she reminded herself firmly. If you focus on Sherry, you might overlook something important. Keep the mind loose and open.

Rebecca had announced another complete run-through, with whatever props and costume pieces were available. Stoner was glad. This morning, what with having to straighten out blocking messes and watch for missed cues, she really hadn't gotten to see the play. She still didn't know what it was about, quite, though it was beginning to come into focus. Something to do with oppression of women and reclaiming our herstory. Famous women from every known era meeting at a soft ball tournament. Standard Feminist fare, except that the Demeters had included in their cast of characters famous women who had opposed the liberation of women. It made for an interesting mix, with poignant moments like Phyllis Schlafley lecturing Medea on the proper behavior for a wife and mother.

Medea, who was being played by Rita to Marcy's Schlafley in a brilliant stroke of type-casting, was not amused.

When the time came for the entrance of Everywomon—who roamed time and space dressed in Birkenstocks and a strappy-tee—Roseann didn't appear. Rebecca asked Stoner to look for her.

She found her outside, behind the barn, huddling under an overhang. Her face was pale, and she was shivering. Stoner hunkered down beside her.

"What's up?" she asked.

Roseann looked at her with dark eyes. "Guess I'm just trying to figure out what to feel."

"About what?"

"This." She held up a flannel shirt. It had been ripped to shreds.

"Isn't that your Scene 2 costume?"

"Yep."

"And I take it you didn't do this."

"Nope. But somebody sure did." Slowly, Roseann pushed herself to her feet. "Well, I'm out of here."

"Out of here?"

"Out of the play, out of Demeter, out."

Stoner reached for her. "Wait a minute."

"Forget it, Stoner. They don't want me here. I should have known better than to get above myself."

"Damn it, Roseann, listen to me."

"Hey, I'm not blaming you. You've been swell to me."

"*Listen to me*," Stoner said firmly, and pushed herself to her feet. "Some really bad stuff's going on around here, and it doesn't have anything to do with you." She told her about Seabrook.

Roseann's eyes widened. "Who'd want to hurt that cute little frog? That's really...really pathological."

"Exactly," Stoner said. "And I think it was the same person who did this to your costume."

"No shit?"

"No shit."

"You think it was one of the women?"

Stoner shook her head thoughtfully. "I don't know what to think, except it's time to bring some things out in the open." She took the torn costume in one hand and Roseann's wrist in the other and marched into the barn and up to Rebecca. "Call everyone together," she ordered. "We have to talk."

Rebecca blew a shrill blast on her whistle, breaking up at least four private conversations and ruining Marcy's timing.

All of a sudden Stoner was sorry she'd done this. It wasn't time to blow the lid off of everything, particularly her own role in it. But they were all waiting now, giving her their full attention. She had to make decisions fast, and move carefully.

"Go along with whatever I say," she mumbled to Roseann.

She held up the shirt. "We have a problem," she announced. "Roseann just found her costume vandalized. Can anybody shed any light on it? Did anyone see anyone unfamiliar hanging around the barn since last evening?"

She waited.

No response.

"Okay, has anyone else had something trashed or stolen?"

No response. Not even from Rita, who had apparently decided to keep quiet about Seabrook.

"I'd like you to check your things now. All your props and costumes. Any personal things you have down here."

Roseann nudged her. Stoner turned to her. "I didn't have it in the barn," she whispered. "It was in my room."

"In your room?"

Roseann nodded.

"Was your door locked?"

"Of course not," Roseann said in a normal tone of voice. "If I did that, the other gals would think I didn't trust them."

Marcy groaned and rolled her eyes.

Stoner made a mental note of it.

"If you ask me," Boneset said, "this was a clear classist act."

Sherry pushed herself forward through the shocked and silent crowd. She pulled something that looked like a check book out of her pocket. "Look, Roseann," she said, "I feel responsible for this. Let me give you a check to cover the damages."

Roseann looked bewildered.

"Well," Marcy said loudly to Rebecca, "I knew something was bound to happen, but I didn't expect this."

Stoner looked at her. "What do you mean?"

"There are some people in the group who resent her bringing in an outsider..."

"That's ridiculous," Rebecca cut in.

"...to play the lead."

"Marcy," Barb interrupted, "I don't think anyone in *Demeter Ascending*..."

"I'm telling you, there are some people who aren't happy at all." Marcy crossed her arms over her chest in a stubborn pose. "I hear things."

"We processed this," Rebecca said.

"You bulldozed us," Marcy insisted.

Stoner tried to think of a way to get Roseann out of the room. Actually, she wanted to get out of the room herself. It was turning nasty, and people were about to reveal parts of themselves she didn't want to know. She could feel it in the air.

Sherry ripped a check from her book and held it out to Roseann. "Here," she said.

Roseann took a step backward, looking hurt and confused. "I don't want the money."

"Take it," Sherry said dismissively. "I have insurance." She took Roseann's hand and squeezed it shut over the check. "Please, Roseann. I feel terrible about this."

Roseann twisted out of her grip and threw the check on the floor. "Why should you care?" she spat. "I'm just a hairdresser Rebecca picked up in a bar."

She stormed out of the barn, slamming the screen door. Gwen slipped out quietly behind her.

"Well," said Marcy knowingly, "it's obvious someone resents her, big time."

Stoner wanted to choke her. Rebecca got there first and drew her to one side. Stoner followed.

"Marcy," Rebecca said, "do you suspect someone?"

"I don't want to name names," Marcy said with an insincerely innocent look.

"We'll keep it between us," Stoner said.

Marcy glanced around. "Well, there's one person crazy enough to do this."

"Oh, come on, Marcy," Rebecca said. "Just because you two had problems..."

"Just because of that you think I don't know what I'm talking about."

"Rita wouldn't do anything to hurt the show," Rebecca insisted. "I've known her for years."

"But *I've* been in a position to see a side of her you've never seen. And, believe me, she can turn very, very nasty."

"Rita's been solidly behind Roseann from the beginning," Rebecca said.

Marcy threw up her hands in frustration. "I wish I'd never even *heard* of that bitch."

"Roseann?" Stoner asked.

"RITA!" Marcy shrieked.

From the front of the room, Rita shot Marcy a charming smile and a little wave which segued into a third-finger salute. Marcy stalked into the tack room and began nailing something together.

Rebecca looked around at the other women, who seemed to be in shock. "Well," she said as calmly as she could, "I guess we should take a little break. If anyone wants to go check her room..."

Nobody moved. The energy was rock-bottom low. *Demeter Ascending* was on the verge of falling apart.

Stoner was determined not to let that happen. She pulled Rebecca aside. "We have to do something," she said. "Something we can all do together, as a group. Maybe something physical."

Rebecca looked around the room. "We need to bring the piano down here from the lounge, but the grass is wet and it's drizzling..."

Sherry had picked up the check and was looking at it as if it were an alien life form. Stoner went over to her.

"I don't get it," Sherry said. "I was just trying to do the right thing."

"It's complicated," Stoner said. "You see, she was really hurt, and feeling rejected, and when you tried to pay her off..."

"I wasn't paying her off," Sherry said.

"Well, it looked that way to her." And to me, too, she thought. "The point is," she went on, "you took what was emotionally loaded, and *appeared* to put it on a material basis. Do you know what I mean?"

"But that's terrible," Sherry said. "How could she misunderstand me that way? I'd never be that insensitive." She turned to Rebecca. "Have you ever seen me be insensitive like that?"

The slight hesitation before Rebecca denied it told Stoner she had, indeed, but wasn't about to get into that now.

"The thing is..."

"The thing *is*," Sherry said heatedly, "she thought something completely crazy and mean about me. *Nobody's* done more for this group than I have. *Nobody* cares more about Demeter than I do, and I really resent some *outsider* coming in here and trying to make trouble for me."

Rebecca kneaded her face with her hands. "I'm sorry I brought it up," she said. "Nobody's trying to make trouble. Just forget it, okay?"

Stoner wondered how what had originally been an insult to Roseann had suddenly turned into an offense against Sherry. And why she felt a little guilty for even mentioning it, as if the whole thing were her fault. "Look," she said, "who did what to whom and why isn't really relevant right now..."

"It is to me," Sherry insisted petulantly.

"Of course it's relevant," Stoner agreed, "but we have a major problem here and we need to do something about it right away." She had a bright idea. "And you're the one person who can help."

It worked. The anger drained from Sherry's face and mood like water down the sink. "You think it has to do with...you know what?" she asked under her breath.

"I certainly do," Stoner said with deep solemnity. "And I want to look into it immediately. But I need the rest of the company to be diverted."

Sherry nodded. "I hear you."

"Rebecca says the piano has to be moved. But I know it's kind of damp out, even if we cover it. The grass..."

"No *problemo*," Sherry said. "Wouldn't be the first time. Anything else?"

"Not at the moment. I'll get back to you."

Sherry bounced away and across the room to the other women. "Come on, guys!" she trilled. "Time to check our rooms and move the upright. Be there or be square."

Rebecca watched them file out after Sherry, and turned to look Stoner directly in the eyes. "Who are you really?" she asked.

Nothing like moving a piano on a wet lawn on a drizzly day to bring a bunch of women together. Stoner put her shoulder to it and shoved. It was hard, hot, damp, dirty, miserable work. Like playing softball during the July heat wave. Anyone from another planet observing the goings on would conclude that suffering made Earth-lesbians absolutely cheerful.

Rebecca was the most cheerful of all, but not because she was moving furniture in the rain. Stoner had confessed that she was there, under cover, for the express purpose of finding out who was trying to sabotage the play. "I guess it's not very Feminist, hiring someone to spy on the sisters," Rebecca said, "but oh, Goddess, what a relief!" The back of her collar had seemed to stand up particularly high since then.

Sherry had apologized to Roseann, and had managed to do so without insulting her further. Roseann had accepted her apology, warily but graciously. Sherry went one step further by asking Roseann to please, *please* correct her if she committed any more classist acts. Stoner thanked the Goddess for small miracles, and for Roseann's innate generosity of heart.

Gwen had managed to talk Marcy into going into Bangor with her to pick up the styrofoam.

Divi Divi had actually approached Stoner and invited her to drive in to Green Lake after dinner. She said she had a couple of errands to run, and maybe Stoner would like to take in some of the local sights. "You don't often get a chance to see a place," she said, "with so little to recommend it."

Perfect. It would give her a chance to call Aunt Hermione without worrying about others listening in on the line. She needed some serious advice of a psychic nature. And she hadn't forgotten that Dairy Queen cup. A chocolate covered cherry Blizzard would be a real asset about now. There might even be a Brazier Burger to be had.

Gwen wished her well, and assured her there wasn't a thing on the potential menu that she coveted.

Which reminded her of something...some little bit of information she'd stored away, something that hadn't seemed significant at the time, but was tapping at her brain like raindrops trying to get in a window.

Menu. Menu.

Food.

Kitchen. Something about the kitchen.

She remembered, and detoured through the dining room.

The cooks were busy, and obviously resented her intrusion, just as she had always suspected real cooks would. Not like Aunt Hermione, who would beam a welcome and declare herself desperate for company, and before Stoner knew it would be curled up in the window seat blowing cigarette smoke out the window while Stoner finished up whatever slicing, dicing, or sauteing she had interrupted.

She found the salad prep woman, who had prepped the salad and was lounging against a cupboard. "Listen," she said, "when I was down here with Sherry the other night, she mentioned something about a back stairway. Do you know which door it is?"

"Sure," the woman said, and pushed herself away from the cupboard and went to the door and opened it for her.

"And this is unlocked at the top as well as in this room?"

"Wouldn't be much good if it wasn't."

No, it wouldn't.

"What's up?"

She started and turned. Sherry stood behind her, an open and vacuously innocent smile on her face.

"She was asking about the back stairs," said Salad Prep before Stoner could jump in with some transparent, trumped-up, lame explanation.

Sherry gave her a "don't you have something to do?" look.

The woman scooted back to her lounging point against the cupboard.

"I thought it might be a way someone might have gotten in and out of the Cottage to do things," Stoner said, and could see her eighth grade English teacher spinning in her grave.

"You're right," Sherry said thoughtfully. "It could." She leaned close to Stoner. "You know what this means, of course."

"What does it mean?"

"That anyone could be doing this. Sneaking out the back way in the night, sneaking in during a break in rehearsals when no one would notice. Anyone."

"Well," Stoner admitted, "anyone who knows about the stairs."

"And, if you were going to set out on a well-orchestrated campaign of terrorist acts, you'd plan it out ahead of time, and part of that planning would be to check out where the entrances and exits are. Right?"

"Right," Stoner said.

Sherry grinned. "Maybe I should go into the detective business. I'm beginning to think like a criminal."

Beginning? the voice in her head wondered.

"So what's next?" Sherry was asking.

Stoner looked around the room. The next logical step, of course, would be to interview the kitchen crew. But she could just imagine Sherry—budding detective that she was—leaping forward eagerly to do that job, and she couldn't think of a good reason to stop her. "I'm not sure," she said. "I'll let you know."

As she was heading up the stairs to shower before dinner, she heard Clara hail her. The older woman handed Stoner her room keys, and explained that during the afternoon she had re-keyed the lock so that only Stoner's and Gwen's keys would fit. Even the pass-key wouldn't work. That should take care of unauthorized entries. She advised against starting any fires or doing anything else that would require someone getting into the room to save their lives, as they were going to be a pair of cooked geese if they did.

Stoner wondered what Sherry would think of this, when she finally told her. But it was in the line of duty. After all, Sherry had invited them, hadn't she? She'd probably be glad, and think they were all terribly clever.

Oh, sure. And Jerry Falwell organizes Gay Pride marches.

As Divi Divi had promised, Green Lake had a lake but little else. The lake was green, too, choked with algae and duckweed that seemed incandescent in the late twilight. The town itself boasted a general store, a gas station, and a gun-and-fishing-tackle shop where you could also buy topographic maps, hunting licenses, and liquor. A small restaurant that had probably been someone's old living room was closed tight. It had chipping red paint, a sagging porch, and a trellis clogged with bittersweet. Split window shades hung against glass streaked by years of tobacco smoke and cooking grease. The hand-painted sign spelled out "Sue's" in awkward, primitive vines that most closely resembled poison ivy. A crayon-on-cardboard sign announced that "Sue's" would be open again for breakfast at six am.

Stoner wondered who in the world Sherry—who certainly seemed to aspire to sophistication, if you could judge by the ambience at The Cottage—could be dating in Green Lake.

As a matter of fact, she found it a little strange that Divi Divi would insist on coming to this tiny, weary town to have her Blazer serviced when there must be plenty of places in Bangor where the waiting was more interesting.

Bangor, it turned out, didn't have Hank Markle. Hank and the Blazer had met two summers ago during an alternator incident, and it was mutual love at first sight. Hank understood the Blazer with an understanding that verged on empathy. She was the car he'd been waiting for all his life, the car his mama had convinced him to save himself for. When he touched the Blazer, there was love in his fingertips. He could stand, eyes closed, listening while Divi Divi idled the motor, and tell within seconds just what was wrong with "his girl."

"It's kind of a Zen thing," Divi Divi explained when they had wandered out of ear shot. "I swear, if I took the car to someone else, he'd know it and sue me for contributing to the delinquency of a Chevrolet." She laughed deeply. "I can tell he hates to take money for fixing her. It makes him feel like a prostitute, and probably isn't respectful of their relationship. But he does good work and deserves to be paid. Besides, I'm neurotic about money."

"So am I," Stoner said.

Divi Divi shot her a quick glance. "Doll, you're neurotic about a lot of things. I'll bet you have all your insecurities catalogued."

Stoner laughed. "No, but Gwen keeps track of them for me."

"Looks like she might," Divi Divi said with a sage nod.

"What do you mean?" Stoner asked with a quick glance at her.

"It's pretty obvious that woman cares a lot for you. You might not notice it, being a little on the butch side and neurotic to boot, but she has a right protective air about her where you're concerned."

"Really?"

"Really. I know *I* wouldn't mess with you. Though there's some that might."

Stoner stopped walking. They were opposite Sue's and heading for the general store. "What do you mean?"

"Well, I don't like to spread gossip, but since there's already enough shit coming down and you seem to be trying to do something about it, I'll tell you. For what it's worth, I've seen Sherry shooting daggers at you from out of her eyes."

Stoner stared at the cracked and buckled pavement and hoped Divi Divi had more to say and would say it.

"She covers it up fast," the woman went on. "But it's hard to hide things from an astute observer of human nature like myself."

"What do you think it means?" Stoner asked.

"I think she's sorry she ever laid eyes on you."

"She kind of invited us here," Stoner said vaguely. "Because she was concerned about the things that had been going on, and she thought an outside observer..." She trailed off.

"Uh-huh. Well, it's my guess she regrets the day she ever did *that*." Divi Divi slipped her hands into her loose pockets and fluttered her skirt. "Seems to me it's all gotten worse since you arrived."

"Do you think we're doing it?"

"Nope. But you know what I do think? I think it's being done for your benefit."

There was a telephone on the corner, its dog-eared directory shedding bits of pages in the breeze.

"Go make your call," Divi Divi said. "I'll flounce my black ass around the general store and give the old guys hemorrhoids."

"Blessed be."

Stoner felt her face turn into a grin. "Aunt Hermione. I'm glad I caught you at home."

"I had planned to go to a movie with Grace," her aunt said, "but then Spirit informed me you'd be calling."

"Did Spirit tell you what time I'd call?" she asked. She absolutely believed that her aunt believed these messages came from her Spirit, but she couldn't resist trying to catch her in a lucky guess. It was a game they'd played for twenty years, and one they'd probably go on playing for the rest of their lives.

"No, but I was informed at about four thirty. Does that fit your time frame?"

Stoner sighed. "Perfectly. You know, we could save a lot of long distance money if we just communicated on the Astral Plane."

"We would," her aunt said. "But in order for us to do that you'd have to believe in it, and that's just not something you're ready for. Despite all your evidence."

She had to admit Aunt Hermione was right. She *had* had enough supernatural—or at least paranormal—experiences to qualify as a Born-Again Psychic. Trouble was, as soon as the experiences ended her belief in them started to fade, until she was left with nothing more than the conviction that Something Very Strange Had Happened.

"Be that as it may," Aunt Hermione went on, "I'm willing to be patient with you." She gave a low chuckle and lit a cigarette. "I've been patient through at least six lifetimes, if memory serves. Well, maybe the seventh time will be the charm."

Stoner wasn't sure about this reincarnation business, either. But she hoped she and her aunt would go on through eternity.

"Sometimes I think you can't wait for me to go away so you can smoke all you like," she said in an accusatory way.

"You're absolutely right," her aunt replied. "I love you dearly, but there are some advantages to your absence. At least I tell myself that. The first couple of days, I lounge around like a pig in mud doing perfectly disgraceful things of which you would never approve. But by Day Three, I'm afraid the hole in my heart where you belong begins to feel a little drafty."

"Me, too. What disgraceful things?"

"Disgraceful things?"

"What disgraceful things are you doing?"

"I would call them 'graceful,' not disgraceful. "

Stoner smiled. So things were still going strong between her aunt and Grace D'Addario.

"I know what you're thinking," Aunt Hermione said.

"Well, I know what you're thinking, too. *And* what you're doing."

"Just be glad I can still frolic at my age," her aunt said, sounding very pleased with herself, "and don't be stuffy."

"I worry about what's going to happen when we move." The sun had gone down. Even the humidity-lengthened twilight was fading. Darkness was coming on fast. "How will you and Grace get together?"

Aunt Hermione took a deep and satisfying drag on her cigarette. "Maybe I'll learn to fly. Do you think they have a little airport near Shelburne Falls?"

That struck terror into Stoner's heart. "You don't even drive."

"What good is a witch who can't fly?"

"Brooms are one thing," Stoner said. "Planes are another."

"We don't use *brooms*, Stoner. Not in this day and age. Never did, as a matter of fact. We went out of body."

"I don't think you want to go out of body for what you and Grace are doing."

There was a brief pause, at the end of which her aunt said, "Did you call for a particular reason, or just to harass me?"

She couldn't help grinning. It wasn't every day she could reduce Aunt Hermione to silence. "I win," she said.

"You do. Now, what can I do for you?"

Stoner ran her hand through her hair. "I feel completely at a loss. Things have been happening...Some of them could be just nuisance stuff, but it seems to be getting nasty."

"Give me a for instance," her aunt said.

"Okay. Sherry showed us a note she'd gotten, telling her to close down the show. We didn't think much of it, but we put it in my underwear drawer..."

"Where you always put things you're trying to hide. Honestly, Stoner, it's the first place people look. I know *you* wouldn't, but most criminals would."

"Well, they did. Because when we went to find it, the note was gone. Later, it was returned, with a knife stuck through it. Roseann's script was tampered with, and her costume torn. Someone planted marijuana in Boneset's herbal teas, and Boneset herself was almost badly hurt when the ladder broke, and it turned out someone had tampered with it."

"Boneset?" Her aunt interrupted. "Is she Wiccan?"

"I don't know, but I'll ask her."

"Please do. There's a subtlety about the Lammas Ritual that I just can't grasp. Unless you think she's your troublemaker."

"No more than anyone else. I have a dozen suspects and no motive. Everyone's had the means and opportunity to do these things, and I feel as if I could narrow it down if I could come up with a motive."

The older woman was thoughtfully silent. "I'm sorry, but I just can't pick up anything occult. Whatever this is, it's apparently without any astral component whatsoever. Purely material plane mischief. And fairly amateurish, as material plane mischief goes. But sincere. Quite sincere. Please be careful, Stoner. There's nothing quite so dangerous as a twisted soul who's clumsy."

"I know," Stoner said. "It feels dangerous to me, too."

"Surround yourself with a white light at all times. I'll send you all the helpful energy I can."

"Thank you."

She could hear her aunt lighting up another cigarette. "Dear, are things all right between you and Gwen?"

"Sure. Why?"

"I notice you slipped from saying 'we' to 'I.' I wondered if it meant anything."

She wondered why she felt uncomfortable. "I don't think so. We haven't had time to talk over the latest stuff, so I don't know her thinking on it, that's all."

"I see. Well, if it should turn out that there *is* a little something wrong, remember to approach it with an open heart."

"I will."

"And remember that I love you."

"I never worry about that, Aunt Hermione. I love you, too."

"You're certainly cheerful," Divi Divi said as they pulled out of the Dairy Queen lot. "I never saw anyone get such a lift out of a phone call. You win the lottery?"

"It was good to talk to the folks back home."

"Uh-huh."

Stoner savored a spoonful of chocolate covered cherry Blizzard. "You've been in *Demeter Ascending* for some time, haven't you, Div?"

"Some." She managed to drive and stir her Peanut Buster Parfait at the same time. "Days like today, it feels like my whole life. Days like today, I think I'm in that place my Mama used to tell me I was going if I sassed her. 'Somewhere hot and dry,' she used to say, 'and it isn't Tucson.' " She shifted gears. The Blazer's motor purred. "Damn, that boy's good with this car."

"Is it always this difficult, doing a show?"

"Do you mean are sawed-off ladders and ripped-up clothing an everyday occurrence? No. But it's always hard. Sometimes I'd like to quit, but I'm afraid they'd call me racist." She laughed. "Isn't that a kick? First we were all oppressed, now we oppress ourselves trying not to be oppressive. Is this what Liberation is all about?"

"Probably," Stoner said.

"It's just a passing thing, wanting to quit. Has to do with all the anxiety that goes into theater work. It's kind of like being in labor, I guess. Once that baby's there and grinning up at you, you forget all the pain. Besides, these women are my sisters now."

Suddenly Stoner felt like a spy, trying to get Divi Divi to squeal on her friends.

Except that someone in *Demeter Ascending* wasn't a sister, or a friend.

She squeezed her cup to crack the chocolate that had hardened onto the side and scraped it down into the Blizzard dregs where it belonged. "Do you have any idea about who's causing the trouble?" she asked casually as she scrounged with her spoon for the last creamy mouthful.

"Nope. Do you?" Divi Divi glanced over at her. "I thought that was what you were taking a particular interest in finding out."

Stoner felt herself redden. "Am I that obvious?"

"To someone with my superior powers of observation, yep." She glanced over again and grinned. "Rita told me. She said you were really nice to her about Seabrook, and let her in on your theory that this was all deliberate."

Oh, great. She wondered how many people Rita had told, and whom.

"Rita won't forget that, you know," Divi Divi went on. "She never forgets a kindness."

"Or an unkindness?"

"You suspect her?" She let the car steer itself and ate a spoonful of parfait. "Rita wouldn't try to ruin the show. It's not her way. You see how she is about Marcy, glaring and yelling. That's as far as Rita goes. And she goes there often. I'll bet every one of us has been called a douche-bag at one time or another. I keep telling her to broaden her vocabulary, but she doesn't listen to me. Nope, Rita's not our woman. Besides, she doesn't have the attention span for what we're seeing."

What Stoner was seeing at the moment was a totally dark, not very straight road with pine trees pressing close and deer no doubt lurking behind every bend waiting to fling themselves into the path of the car. And Divi Divi calmly eating a Peanut Buster Parfait with both hands.

"Would you like me to drive?" she asked. It came out in a kind of squeak. "I've finished my Blizzard."

"Am I making you nervous?"

"Well, you know, moose and all..."

"Don't worry," Divi Divi said. "I've driven this road a hundred times, never even came close to having an accident." She paused thoughtfully. "Well, there was that one time...but you don't want to hear about that."

"Divi Divi..."

"I'm teasing you, girl." She put her cup in her left hand and rested it on the steering wheel. "Will one-handed do?"

Not really, but she didn't want to say so. "Okay."

Divi Divi eased the car to the side of the road and stopped. "You drive. I only get a Dairy Queen about once a week, and your nerves are spoiling it for me." She opened the door and got out. "Get yourself over here before I change my mind."

Sitting up high, looking down at the road, sensing the Blazer's power in her hands gave her an invincible kind of feeling. She found herself looking around for male-driven black muscle cars to harass. The kind that liked to tail-gate and pass on the right, or blow their horns impatiently when you were lost in the bowels of Boston looking for a street that had been here yesterday but today had completely disappeared. She'd love to slip up behind one, real close, and hit the high beams...

"Calm yourself," Divi Divi said, sensing her mood. "The point of Preppy is to equalize the power, not get the advantage."

Stoner eased up a little on the accelerator. "Preppy? That's what you call the car?"

"Yep. Because it's a Blazer. Preppy Blazer, get it?"

Stoner groaned. "That's terrible."

"I was going to call her 'Circle Pin,' but it lacked punch."

"Preppy Blazer has punch all right."

"Anyway," Divi Divi went on, "I'd be real surprised if it was Rita making trouble."

They went through the others one by one. Boneset was, indeed, Wiccan, and believed in the Three-Fold Law. Whatever she put out into the universe, she believed, would come back to her three-fold. She wasn't likely to do anything to bring negativity on herself. Barb was pretty taciturn and kept to herself. But Divi Divi had no reason to think Barb would cause trouble, as she was completely wrapped up in making the inanimate objects of theater behave themselves. Besides, Divi Divi said, she didn't have "that kind of imagination," which Stoner took to mean Barb didn't have much imagination at all. It didn't make her the life of the party, but it didn't make her a suspect, either.

Marcy, surprisingly, was a bit of an enigma to Divi Divi, who had begun to suspect—only this year—that there was more going on with her than met the eye. She couldn't put her finger on it, though.

Which left Rebecca, Roseann, and Sherry. Divi Divi was inclined to reject the notion that Rebecca would sabotage something she'd put as much energy into as she had into *Demeter Ascending*.

Roseann hadn't been with them long enough to get it in for someone, and, besides, she'd been too much of a target.

"And then there's me," Divi Divi said. "What do you think of my chances?"

"Not much."

"I don't know if I should be pleased or disappointed."

"What's your motive? Unless you're trying to stop them from making a mess of your script."

Divi Divi laughed. "Doll, they *couldn't* make a mess of that script. I can't even get a handle on it myself. But it'll come together by the end. I'll shift the order of a few scenes, and suddenly the wit and brilliance—not to mention the deep political and philosophical significance—of *Not Quite Titled* will flash like a diamond. If you continue to treat me with respect and deference, I'll invite you to the Pulitzer Prize ceremonies."

"How about the rest of the crew?"

"I really doubt it. Barb brings the crew up during the last couple of weeks, after the softball season ends. They stay long enough to build the sets and get the props and costumes together and be general go-fers. Then they go back to Boston and wait until we're ready to go into the theater."

"So they haven't been here all along," Stoner said.

"No longer than you have."

"And the trouble started before that."

"Long before. If you want to throw every suspicious accident into the stew, it started right at the beginning."

Stoner glanced over at her. "Really?"

"Just about. Watch the road, please."

"Sorry."

"Just some weird shit happening," Divi Divi said. "Stuff disappearing from the barn…"

"Stuff?"

"People's clothing, books, scripts. But they always showed up somewhere else, so we figured we'd misplaced them."

"Showed up where?"

"In our rooms, or in the living room. Places we'd gone. And it didn't really matter about the scripts, since we were changing the play every day, anyway, and someone or other was running in to Bangor every night to get copies made. I guess that's why we didn't suspect anything, because it was all mistakes we could have made ourselves." She paused. "Or is it '*they were* mistakes?' If you ever decide to take up writing, try to do it in an easier language than English."

So no one had noticed. No one but Sherry, that was. But no one but Sherry had received threatening notes.

"I guess you and Gwen are above suspicion, too," Divi Divi went on. "Since the trouble started before you got here."

"Minor troubles," Stoner said. "We could have seen what was going on and decided it was the perfect opportunity to make trouble and not be suspected."

"What would you do that for? You didn't even know us. If you wanted to make *real* trouble, you could have tampered with the Dyke Hikers' equipment."

"But it wouldn't have been as much fun, or as challenging as trying to mess up a group that had worked together for years."

Divi Divi scraped the last bit of her Peanut Buster Parfait from its cup and stowed the trash in a plastic bin in the back seat. "You have a devious mind, Stoner McTavish," she said.

"So I've heard. We haven't talked about Sherry."

"Sherry." Divi Divi was silent for a moment. "Sherry," she repeated.

Stoner glanced at her. "Something wrong?"

"Just trying to get a grip on her. Watch the road, please."

"Sorry."

"To tell you the truth," the woman said after a while, "I don't know what to make of Sherry. Not that I think she'd do anything against Demeter, but in a general kind of way."

"How do you mean?"

"Well, most of the time she seems okay—a little bossy, a little too much of a cheer leader, and there are moments when I wonder if she knows the difference between a producer and a social director."

Stoner smiled. "I saw that in action."

"And sometimes she plays kind of loose with the boundaries, steps on other people's toes. Like the other night when she called a set-building session. Now, technically, that's was Barb's business to decide, not Sherry's. But I guess she'd say that's what being a collective means—people don't have rigid, assigned roles. On the other hand, there is such a thing as good manners. Not that Sherry's manners aren't good, exactly. She just kind of slips over sometimes. But maybe she doesn't know any better. Maybe she wouldn't mind if someone else did that to her, so it's not really important to her."

"Did she ever step on your toes?"

"Just once. We'd been working on some script changes, back before it was time for me to take over the writing and make it coherent. I wasn't quite satisfied with the new material, wanted to try a couple of other things the next day. Well, come rehearsal time Sherry waltzes in with new scripts, which she'd driven in town and had run off the night before without telling me. I clouded over and rained all over her." She fell silent again.

"What happened?" Stoner asked.

"Made a damn fool of myself, is what. She pointed out that she was only trying to help, and it wasn't as if she'd burned the barn down, she'd just had a few pieces of paper copied. I ended up feeling as if I was mentally ill for getting upset. Or is it 'were mentally ill?' Anyway, I dropped it and she didn't do it again."

"So it all ended okay."

"I guess. But, to tell you the truth, I still feel like a damn fool."

And I'll bet you haven't criticized Sherry again, Stoner thought. "That doesn't sound so bad to me," she said. "I've done damn-fooler things than that."

" 'Damn-fooler?' "

"Hey, you're the writer, not me. I can say anything I want."

A soft puddle of light appeared in the distance, the glow from the Cottage reflected on the undersides of leaves. Stoner slowed for the turn. "Sherry mentioned that she was seeing someone in Green Lake," she said. "After being there this evening, I find it hard to imagine."

Divi Divi seemed surprised. "Did she say that? I never heard anything about it. Of course, she might not tell me, since I'm..." She lowered her voice conspiratorially. "*...hetero...sexual.*"

Stoner reached over and patted her hand. "You can't help it, Div. You were probably born that way."

CHAPTER 10

She was surprised to see that Gwen hadn't come back yet. It was ten-thirty by her watch, and she doubted if even K-Mart stayed open much past nine. But they might have found a Wal-Mart, or stopped at the Dairy Mart, or the Food Mart, Fine Mart, Mini Mart, Smart Mart...

She decided to run down to Clara and Esther's room and pick up their observations for the evening. Maybe something had happened which would clear everything up.

Sure.

There was no light under their door. The "Do Not Disturb" sign hung from the door knob.

Darn.

She trudged back to the second floor, and looked both ways up and down the corridor. There might be someone up and about that she could talk to. Maybe she'd even come across a bridge game needing a fourth. She felt too wired to be alone, too edgy. She needed to pass the time until Gwen got in.

There was light toward the end of the hall, spilling out of an open door. She went toward it and tapped softly on the jamb so as not to startle anyone.

"Hey, hi," Marcy said, turning toward her and away from the mirror. "Come on in. I was doing some expression exercises."

"I thought you and Gwen were going into Bangor," Stoner said, puzzled.

Marcy rolled her eyes. "Would you believe, at the last minute I got a message that my ex-lover was going to call this evening, so I had to stay here. Naturally, she didn't call. Just like her, used to do that all the time. I can't believe I was taken in again. I really can't believe it. How many times do I have to fall for that before I get the picture?"

"That's too bad." Stoner sat on the edge of the bed. "So who did Gwen go with?"

"Sherry."

Stoner felt herself go cold.

"She is *so* great," Marcy went on. "Sherry, that is. Well, I'm sure Gwen is, too, but I don't know her. Sherry gave up all her plans for the evening—had a hot date, she said —just so we'd have that styrofoam for Barb in the morning."

"Wouldn't it have been more helpful," Stoner said, dry-mouthed, "if Barb had gone?"

Marcy turned back to the mirror and resumed her facial exercises, twisting her mouth into grotesque shapes, frowning and furrowing her eyebrows, scrunching her features into an excellent imitation of a Shar-Pei. It was fascinating, and kind of frightening.

"Barb's beat," she said around pursed-up lips that displayed her beaverish front teeth. "Sherry said she was hitting the sack early."

A snake of apprehension woke up in her stomach and began moving around. Something told her this wasn't a coincidence.

"How did you find out your ex-lover was going to call?" she asked.

"Sherry told me. I guess she called earlier, when we were still rehearsing. One of the other guests took the call."

"Which other guest?" A honeymooner? Esther? Clara? Someone from the post-softball tech crew?

Marcy shrugged. "What's the diff?" She sighed heavily. "I really can't believe I fell for it again," she repeated. "To quote a Rita-ism, Jennifer is a douche-bag."

"Uh," Stoner said, "how long does it take to get to Bangor?"

"Half an hour, max."

"Don't you think maybe they should be back by now?"

Marcy looked at Stoner in the mirror. "Didn't you get my note?"

She shook her head. "What note?"

"I left it in your mail slot."

"I didn't check the mail slot."

"They're not coming back tonight. They decided to stay in town."

Stoner was puzzled. "Did something happen?"

"They didn't say, just to tell you they'll see you in the morning."

Apprehension shed its skin and turned into something larger. Something kind of slimy, that made her feel a little sick. Look, she told herself, everything's okay. Gwen's not in any trouble, or they wouldn't have called. Maybe they had a car breakdown, or one of the headlights got burned out or broken and they didn't want to drive in the dark that way. Gwen's a grown-up. She can take care of herself. If she suddenly wanted to go to a late movie, or just stay in town for the heck of it on a spontaneous whim, she has every right. She couldn't call me, I wasn't even here. Everything makes perfect sense.

"What?" Marcy asked.

"Huh?"

"You muttered something about 'perfect sense.' What do you mean?"

Great. Now she was talking to herself out loud. In company.

"I was just thinking it makes perfect sense to stay in town. There's nothing going on out here."

"Nothing going on in Bangor, either. That place is dead." She rearranged her hair and went through her facial exercises again, looking at herself from a different angle. "You think I should wear my hair like this for the show?"

"Looks fine," Stoner said. "Do you think they had car trouble?"

Marcy turned back and forth, studying her reflection. "Possibly. That heap's fucked me up more than once."

Sure, that was it. Gwen *couldn't* have chosen, of her own free will, to spend the night in Bangor with Sherry Dodder. Not with Sherry Dodder.

"Hey," Marcy said, "as long as you're here, do you want to run lines with me?"

Stoner was shocked. "Do *what?*"

"Run lines. You know. Give me my cues and see if I know my lines."

"Oh," Stoner said sheepishly. "I thought you meant something else."

Marcy turned and looked at her, then burst out laughing. "You thought I was talking about doing coke, didn't you?"

Stoner nodded, feeling even more foolish.

"McTavish, that's known as *doing* lines, not *running* lines."

She felt her spirits lift a little. At least feeling like an idiot was better than worrying. And, since worrying was what she did best, perhaps the healthy thing to do would be to stay here for a while, until that eel got tired of swimming around in her stomach.

Not only that, but Marcy obviously didn't hold it against her that she was being cozy with Rita. She was glad. She hated feeling stiff and awkward with anyone.

"Sure," she said. "I'll cue you."

She actually enjoyed it. Marcy could be entertaining, once you got used to the idea that every mistake would send her to the brink of suicide. It was nearly midnight by the time she got back to her room. She'd have a long, hot bath while looking over her notes. That would make her sleepy. And, by the time she'd slept and had breakfast, Gwen would be back…

…or would have called if she couldn't make it back, and would talk to her personally…

…not have to settle for just leaving messages that could be shortened or garbled by anyone who happened to get them…

…who wouldn't be reliable or wouldn't understand the importance of writing down messages in their entirety…

…and being accurate and thorough and asking enough intelligent questions so people wouldn't get half-messages and end up nearly crazy with anxiety thinking all kinds of stuff…

Stoner shook her head at herself as she slipped the key into the lock and opened their door. Hard to believe she could be so nerved up over one little thing not quite going the way she'd expected. If she kept on like this, she'd end up never leaving her room, and spending all her time going through her things to make sure they were exactly the way she'd left them so there wouldn't be any surprises.

Actually, she *was* a little surprised at the way she was taking this. She'd never thought of herself as a particularly jealous or insecure person—well, no more jealous and insecure than any lesbian who'd been raised by homophobic parents and taught she didn't deserve anything in this world and would never be loved because of what she was, and besides "those people" couldn't be trusted, they'd play with you to get their way and leave you broken and broke by the wayside while they ran off with the next conquest...

Lovely. She was really having very mature and loving thoughts tonight.

She rummaged through her underwear drawer and found her notebook just where she'd left it, thanks to Esther and Clara and their skill with keys. Sitting on the edge of the bed, she jotted down a few thoughts. They weren't very useful thoughts, not even very coherent thoughts, but they made her feel as if she were doing something.

"AH says no occult involvement. Perp amateurish but sincere, therefore dangerous. DD doesn't suspect anyone, never heard of SD's mystery date in Green Lake."

That was it. The fruits of an evening. Well, it wasn't entirely wasted. She'd had a change of scenery—if you could call it that—and talked with Aunt Hermione, which was fun and took her out of herself a little. She'd had a chance to get to know Divi Divi better. And pretty much eliminated her as a suspect. Divi Divi just didn't *feel* right as a trouble-maker. And then Divi Divi had eliminated just about everyone else.

She went to the bathroom and turned on the water, letting it run against her wrist until the temperature was right. It seemed like a good night for soaking and thinking, so she added a handful of rosemary bath crystals. Taking off her clothes, she tossed them onto her bed. She was about to get into the tub when she realized she'd have to travel some distance across the cold tile floor on warm and wet feet to get her pajamas when she left the tub. Better to have them close at hand and ready, instead of hanging on the back of the door under Gwen's night shirt.

Reaching out, she looked toward the door, and went hard as stone.

Gwen's night shirt wasn't there.

Under her own pajamas, maybe. She took them down.

Nope.

It had been here this morning. She was certain of it.

The laundry?

She ran to the closet and went through the clothes bag. Then through Gwen's bureau, and Gwen's suitcase...

The night shirt really wasn't there.

Okay, okay, there had to be a logical explanation for this. Maybe Gwen had planned to stay in Bangor right from the start.

But why hadn't she told her?

Because, when Stoner had left the Inn, she was still planning to go with Marcy.

Maybe...

Then what? Marcy's plans change, and Sherry goes instead, and Gwen decides to go along and spend the night since it's with Sherry?

And what are the implications of that?

Maybe it all happened as a last-minute kind of thing.

So why hadn't Gwen left her a note? Why rely on the "plans changed while we were in town, see you tomorrow" ploy?

Obviously their plans hadn't changed after they got to Bangor. They'd planned to stay right from the start.

Maybe they'd even set Marcy up, telling her she had to wait for a call so they could go together.

Gwen and Sherry?

It had to be a mistake. A misunderstanding.

Then why had Gwen taken her night shirt? She'd obviously done it voluntarily. Their room was locked, and only *their* keys fit. Gwen *must* have done it. Deliberately and deceitfully.

Wait a minute, wait a minute. If Gwen was setting up a night on the town and a toss between the sheets, she wouldn't need to take her night gown. She could buy something special and filmy and sexy in Bangor. Or go with nothing at all.

So was the taking of the night gown for Stoner's benefit? Like a message, maybe? Like "I'm tired of you," or "Shape up," or whatever obscure messages lovers left for each other to figure out?

But that wasn't Gwen's style, either.

On the other hand, she only knew Gwen's style in relation to herself. Maybe she had a very different style with other people. Maybe who she was with determined her style. So, if she was with someone who was subtle and sleazy, maybe she'd be subtle and sleazy, too.

This was ridiculous. She'd known Gwen too long for her to change suddenly like that. If she kept on thinking this way, she was going to drive herself crazy.

But she couldn't stay here in this room. It was too small, and too quiet. It made her thoughts bounce off the walls and back at her.

Maybe she should take Gwen's car and drive in to Bangor.

And what? Make the rounds of the motels, checking out the parking lots like some stalker?

And suppose she found them. Break down the door shouting, "I caught you, you cheating little worms!" and beat their brains out with a tire iron? That would certainly be cool. Very, very cool. It would certainly make the Bangor papers. And probably the Boston papers, having that local interest of her being from Boston. She could see the headline on the *Herald*, that bastion of conservative righteousness and prurient appetite: Lezzie Love Nest Murder.

No, driving in to Bangor wasn't a good idea.

Go down to the living room. Maybe someone else will be there, someone you can talk to, someone else whose lover has taken her night shirt and gone into Bangor with Sherry Dodder…

She bathed quickly, threw on her pajamas and robe, and headed for the stairs.

The living room was dark as the bottom of a coal mine, the only light coming from the night lamp that always burned on the registration desk. Stoner flicked on a table lamp.

So much for finding someone to talk to. She sighed and paced a little.

Look, she told herself, even if Gwen *is* momentarily taken in by Sherry, it's obviously just because Sherry is probably one great manipulator and trouble-maker, and Gwen is trusting and a little naive. It doesn't mean anything.

Well, not much of anything. There's always the missing night shirt.

She felt shaky inside, like a wall that's starting to crumble.

Somebody had to be up. There had to be *someone* she could talk to.

She went upstairs and prowled the hall, looking for light. Nobody was up.

What was the matter with these people? Didn't anyone stay up past ten, for God's sake? Didn't they realize the dark night hours were the best for doing all kinds of creative things? For intimate conversations? For listening to near-strangers who are freaking out and obsessing themselves into psychosis?

Maybe on the third floor. Maybe there'd be a sane person up there, reading or having a thought.

She scurried up the stairs, and knew before she even got to the top that all she'd find was darkness.

All right, the rooms on the first floor, then.

But they were dark, too.

She went back to the living room.

The stupid night light was still glowing, just the way Sherry left it every night.

Damn Sherry Dodder. And damn Marcy's ex-lover, that Jennifer-rat who was responsible for all of this, who had arranged for Marcy to stay home in the first place.

But maybe there hadn't been a call from Marcy's ex-lover. Maybe Sherry had made it up so she could take Marcy's place on the Bangor trip. Marcy hadn't talked to her herself, she'd gotten a message. And it was Sherry Dodder who had given her that message. The sneaky, conniving…

And maybe, just maybe, Sherry and Gwen had cooked this up together right from the start, so Stoner would go off happily to Green Lake with Divi Divi. Gwen knew Stoner would be wary if she said she was going with Sherry, they'd already had awkwardness around their impressions of Sherry. The only awkwardness there'd been between them in forever, as far as Stoner could remember, had been around Sherry.

Be fair, she warned herself. You have absolutely no evidence that Sherry Dodder is anything but a perfectly nice, slightly strange individual. After all, what had Sherry done that was so bad? Happened to learn about Gwen's childhood love of pickle and pimento loaf, and provided some in case she wanted it. What was so bad about that? Been overly sensitive when she thought she was being criticized, and underly sensitive about Roseann's feelings? But they'd made up.

So she had some pretty bizarre habits around food, but that didn't make her a sleaze.

Nobody else thought there was anything suspicious about Sherry Dodder.

Just yours truly. The whole rest of the world thinks Sherry Dodder is a saint, and I don't trust her as far as I could spit her.

It was the loneliest feeling in the world.

Sherry, Sherry, Sherry.

Screw Sherry.

Which could be what Gwen was doing right this minute.

No! This was ridiculous. There was a perfectly logical explanation for it, she just couldn't think of it on her own. Besides, even if Gwen *had* decided on a romp with Sherry, it was her body, her life. Loving someone didn't mean you owned them.

She found herself over by the liquor cabinet and decided to have a drink. She hadn't had one in months. It would take the edge off her anxiety. Maybe even make her sleepy.

Except that Sherry kept the cabinet locked.

She checked anyway.

As luck would have it, tonight it was open.

Swinging the doors wide, she looked at the neat rows of bottles, all bright and shiny and business-like and eager to please. Mostly wine, which wouldn't meet her needs and would leave her with a headache and other ailments in the morning. What she wanted was a Manhattan. A Manhattan like she'd had back in Wyoming, in the bar at Timberline Lodge in the Tetons, where she'd gone to save Gwen from her husband.

She didn't want a Manhattan. She wanted Gwen, or all the Manhattans in the world.

Sherry, of course, wasn't supplied with pre-mixed Manhattans. Of course not. Pickle and pimento loaf, but no Manhattans.

It was the last straw. She closed the cabinet and sat down on the floor and cried.

I'm losing my mind, she thought as she pulled herself together and rummaged through the desk for a tissue. She found them in the bottom drawer, then decided to go through the rest of the drawers again, slowly, to see what she could find.

Nothing but loose pencils, paper clips, cheap ball point pens, pads of paper, anything the guests might need while checking in or out.

She found a roll of stamps and stole two, just for the hell of it.

The credit card machine sat on the corner of the desk. She thought about vandalizing it and creating untold complications for the elegant Ms. Dodder, but decided that was childish and would only inconvenience guests who wanted to check out.

Marcy's message was still in Stoner's box. She tore it into tiny pieces and was about to scatter them over the entire living room when she realized how much satisfaction that would give Sherry. Finding an envelope, she dropped the pieces in and sealed it and tossed it in the waste basket.

But Sherry might see that, and be curious and open it, and that would give Sherry even more satisfaction.

She fished the envelope from the trash, folded it up small, and slipped it in her bathrobe pocket. As soon as she got upstairs, she'd burn it.

This was getting crazier and crazier. She needed help.

The phone on the wall gave her an idea. She checked the time. One-forty-five. Chances were Edith Kesselbaum was still up. Edith was working on a paper for the Boston Psychoanalytic Society fall meeting, and always stayed up late when she was working on a paper. Sometimes she didn't actually work, but watched Infomercials—her current favorite was Jane Fonda's new treadmill ad. But staying up late, she insisted, was part of the creative process whether she actually did anything productive with the time or not. "Incubating," she would explain.

Stoner picked up the receiver and punched in Edith's home number. She thought of using her calling card, and charging it to her own phone, but changed her mind. Let Sherry Dodder pay for this call. It wasn't much, but it was a small act of revenge.

Edith had declared war on telemarketers and phone solicitors, and either monitored all her calls, or answered and let them give their spiel while she put the phone down and went into the other room. She liked to help them run up their phone bills. But sometimes she couldn't bear to do even that. Tonight was one of those nights, and she'd set her answerer to Call Screen Plus. She wouldn't even hear the ring. Stoner called again and entered her by-pass code. She listened through the message.

"Edith, it's Stoner. If you're there, please answer. I need to talk to you."

"Stoner," Edith said immediately, "what's wrong?"

Just the sound of Edith's voice made her feel more sane. "I'm okay, I guess. How are things there?"

Edith declared that she was fine, though especially uncreative tonight, and was looking for a more inspiring Infomercial. "I'm almost desperate enough to call Psychic Friends, but I fear Hermione would never respect me again."

"You're probably right," Stoner said. "Have you seen the new Popiel Pasta Maker?"

"No, I haven't. But I'll certainly look for it."

"How's Marylou?"

Marylou was fine, too, not at all resentful of being left with the packing, and had decided to interview various movers, pretending they hadn't already settled on one. It had netted her two dinner dates already.

"They can't have been very good dates," Stoner said. "I doubt that movers go to very exotic places."

"On the contrary," Edith said. "These are teamsters. They have a great deal of money and don't mind spending it. Although I have to admit their taste runs peculiarly to overly decorated Italian restaurants."

"It's okay to wonder," Stoner said. "But it might be wise not to wonder out loud."

Edith was silent for a moment. "Oh," she whispered at last. "I see what you mean. Do you suppose any of them might know my husband from his old F.B.I. days?"

"Anything's possible. But I really wouldn't worry."

"I'm not worried," Edith assured her. "The only times Marylou has ever gotten herself in real trouble was when she was with you."

"Edith!"

"It's true, Stoner. I know you're insulted, but it's only reality. What's on your mind? Are you homesick, or merely troubled?"

She hated being coy, but found she couldn't bring herself to spell it all out. "I'm just frustrated by this case."

"I hear more than that in your voice. Is everything all right between you and Gwen?"

She withdrew a little. "Fine," she said with forced cheerfulness. "Great."

"That was very enthusiastic. Not your style at all."

She withdrew a little more. "No, really." Edith's silence told her more was required. "The case is driving me nuts."

"You're oblique. That's always a bad sign."

"We're *fine*, Edith."

"You are not fine. Whatever's wrong between you, I'm sure it's temporary and not really serious."

"There's nothing..."

"The important thing is not to panic. You know how you are when you panic, all sense and reason fly out the window."

"Edith..."

"Now, tell me what's wrong, without panicking."

"You don't have to be my therapist any more."

"Stoner, dear," Edith Kesselbaum said, "you once paid me a great deal of money...not by today's obscene standards, of course, but a great deal for the times...to be your therapist. You're entitled to a little extra help now and then."

She felt irrationally furious. "You were my therapist. I didn't buy your *prying* services for a lifetime."

"Aha," Edith said in a satisfied tone, "we've struck a nerve. Now we're getting somewhere."

Her defenses were beginning to crumble. Edith Kesselbaum had an annoying habit of doing that to her. "Things are just strange. I mean, nothing's happening, but...I don't know."

"Not knowing," Edith proclaimed, "is a step up from knowing the wrong things."

"It's nothing I can put my finger on." She tried to keep her voice calm, but she felt very shaky. No way was she about to break down in the middle of the darkness in the middle of Maine, with no one for comfort but the overstuffed furniture and viscous dark and a few perseverating crickets on the patio. "It's just kind of...as if we're running on parallel tracks, but not the same track."

"You feel alienated from her?"

Right. Alienated. "Uh-huh."

"But not actively disagreeing."

"Uh-huh." She was beginning to sound like a child. She was beginning to *feel* like a child.

"Just kind of 'off,' as one might say?"

"Yeah, off."

"Have you talked about it?"

The helplessness she'd been keeping under wraps began to ooze to the surface. "I would, but I don't know how."

"I see."

"Edith, I don't know what to do. Everything's okay…I mean, it seems to be…but there's this big…I don't know…windy space."

"It's called 'loneliness,' Stoner," Edith said gently. "It happens all the time, when people disagree or don't see things exactly the same way, or aren't in the same mood at the same time. It's uncomfortable, but it doesn't have dire meanings."

She felt tears burning behind her eyes and tried to make herself cold. "Are you sure?" It came out with a little hiccup.

"Positive. It's just that you're so afraid of being rejected, and so devastated by it, you're overly sensitive to the little ebbs and flows of human interaction. You've been like that as long as I've known you."

"I'm sorry," Stoner said.

"You should probably be glad. Some people are so insensitive, they don't realize there's anything wrong until it's too late. What I find truly amazing is that you're willing to care about people at all. It must take tremendous courage on your part."

"Not really. It just happens."

Edith Kesselbaum laughed in a warm and affectionate way. "Now I find myself in the embarrassing position of taking Hermione's viewpoint: it may 'just happen' to your conscious self, but your Higher Spirit is one of great valor."

Stoner didn't know what to say.

"I hope," Edith said, "that your silence means you're weighing the wisdom of my words and it's changing your life forever. But I fear you're either confused or chagrined."

"She went into Bangor with one of the other women," she blurted out. "She took her night shirt."

Edith's silence was suspiciously long by a half second. "I know what you're thinking. But you have to avoid jumping to conclusions."

"Why? You just did."

"That's my job," Edith said.

"It is not. You're always telling me a shrink has to keep an open mind."

"Well, that's true, but we always jump to conclusions along the way. We just let go of them easily."

"Edith…"

"All right, I think it's very strange behavior and not at all like Gwen, which makes me believe there's a large chunk of this puzzle that you don't have. So, until you find that chunk, I suggest you chill out."

"Chill out?" she said.

"Forgive me. I had that adolescent group out at HRI today. You know, the eating disorders one."

That reminded her of something. "Edith, did you ever run across anyone who made a sandwich by slicing the crusts off the bread and cutting the bread into four pieces and then slicing one in half sideways and throwing away the rest?"

"Goodness! I probably have, but I don't remember at the moment. Actually, I'm sure I'd remember if I had. We're talking about an eating disorder, of course, but a pretty bizarre one." She paused. "Well, maybe not entirely bizarre in the run of things, but if this person did this in front of you…"

"She did."

"Then *that* is strange, and I would suspect there's something more going on. Something for your benefit."

"You really think so?"

"The majority of women with eating disorders are ashamed. They don't make a display of it."

"Maybe she slipped."

"You don't understand the depth of humiliation these women feel," Edith said. "They're not likely to make that kind of a mistake. Especially since control is one of their biggest issues."

It made sense.

"What else do you know about this person?" Edith asked.

"She's the one who hired me. The one Gwen's with tonight."

"Uh-oh. Stoner, you might be way out of your league here."

"No kidding."

"I hate to say it, but it really begins to sound as if your trouble-maker is a 297.3."

"A what?"

"That's a diagnostic designation. I really only use them for insurance purposes, but sometimes it helps to remember what you might be up against."

"What I might be up against?"

"Would you like me to come up there?"

It was tempting. She could bounce her ideas off of Edith, who would at least understand her frustration. And Edith would be comforting, and help her put things into perspective…

But it would also change the dynamics of the situation, and put people on their guard. She had a hunch she could get to the bottom of it better if she didn't do too much to rock the boat.

She said as much to Edith, who sort of agreed, with the qualification that Stoner keep in mind her own tendency to believe she had to go it alone.

"I know," Stoner said. "But this is one of those times I think I'm right."

"Well, you know how to reach me if you need me."

Stoner rested the phone against her shoulder and rummaged through the refrigerator beneath the mail boxes. She found a Dr. Pepper, and was about to open it when she remembered that Dr. Pepper was loaded with caffeine, and she might need to sleep for an hour or two tonight. She settled for a Ginger Ale instead.

"Edith, do you think this woman would want to wreck the theater company she's an integral part of?"

"It's possible," Edith said hesitantly.

Stoner knew that hesitation. It meant Edith knew she was verging on making clinical judgments without proper evidence and was trying not to.

"I really couldn't say," Edith went on, "without knowing her better. Contrary to what the insurance companies and HMO's would have us believe, it's impossible to know what a person's *real* problems are in three sessions. If I thought I could do that, I'd get a job as a call-in shrink on a talk show."

Stoner smiled to herself. She found it warmly reassuring, having Edith Kesselbaum behave like Edith Kesselbaum. It made the world seem safe and predictable.

"Let's take a hypothetical example," she suggested.

"Good," Edith said eagerly. "Let's."

"Suppose someone inside *Demeter Ascending* is trying to sabotage the production. Why would she do that?"

"I assume you've ruled out material gain."

"Yes."

"Fame?"

"Hardly likely."

"Personal vendetta?"

"Possible, but the women here who are most likely to want to get back at each other aren't the type. They'd rather announce each other's deficiencies in public."

"Okay." Edith made a crinkly, rustling sound in the background. "This is complicated, so pay attention."

"I am."

"There are some twisted individuals…I know you won't believe this, but bear with me…some people who might do a thing like this simply for the thrill of setting people at one another's throats. Or for a reason so obscure no one else would think of it. An imagined slight, for instance. I've encountered a few in my practice. They can turn a capable, well-trained hospital staff into spitting, name-calling children in no time at all. A women's theater group might be just the place for someone like this to find entertainment."

"Ah," Stoner said.

"The trouble is, these people are very hard to spot. I've personally worked with them for months, sometimes years, before I realized what's happening. They're very good at covering up their manipulations. It's usually only when they involve a third party that their pathology comes to light."

"How would that happen?"

"In a setting such as yours? Let me see." Edith's voice turned muffled. "Forgive me," she said. "I'm eating a Jolly Rancher. It helps me to concentrate. Now. I would look for three things. First, no two people will experience her the same way. To one, she'll appear to be an absolute angel. To another, the incarnation of evil. Very *dramatically* different impressions, you see."

Check, Stoner thought.

"Second, they try to create walls between people. I remember a client I once had, who convinced me that she was so embarrassed by her family that I must never, ever tell *anyone*, not even a colleague or peer supervisor about them. Not even anonymously. Not even during her brief and dramatic hospitalizations. Foolishly, I agreed, in the interest of sustaining the therapeutic relationship. Later, I found out that everyone who had ever met her had heard the same stories. But, by swearing us all to secrecy she had us not communicating with one another."

How many people, Stoner wondered, had been sworn to secrecy, and about what? She'd agreed to be silent on at least one occasion, herself.

"They're geniuses at coming between people, even in casual settings. It's almost a compulsion. Put them with two other people, they'll try to get one off in a corner paying attention only to them. Couples seem to be especially challenging, since one is completely taken in and flattered, while one is left out in the cold. You should see what they can do to a marriage."

"This is complicated," Stoner said.

"Well, it would be particularly difficult for you to comprehend, since you tend to be rather direct and open. Deviousness isn't second nature to you. To these people, deviousness isn't second nature, either. It's first nature."

"Is there anything I can be looking for right now? The way things are escalating, I don't think I'm going to have time to study the group dynamics."

"There's one thing that might be helpful. It's not sure-fire, as it depends on how good your manipulator is at covering up. But sometimes, when everything is falling apart around them...if you happen to catch them off-guard, they appear almost cheerfully excited."

The penny dropped. The gears meshed. She had it now.

One last question. "There is 'someone' here...hypothetically, of course...well, it's odd," she said. "I mean, sometimes she gets very upset, but I don't feel anything for her. Do you know what I mean?"

"I know exactly what you mean," Edith said. "Thank your lucky stars you're not her therapist. When I get a client like that, my tendency is to fall asleep, just to get out of the room. No matter how hard I try, I nod off. And, believe me, in the world of psychotherapy, falling asleep in the presence of a client is considered *very* bad manners." She paused. "I think you've found your villain. Hypothetically, of course."

Stoner grinned. "I think so."

"Listen to me very carefully," Edith said. "Be very, very cautious when you decide to move on this. People like this can make a great deal of trouble when they're cornered."

"Two-ninety-seven point threes?"

"Among others."

"Well, I can make trouble,too," Stoner said, feeling almost giddy.

"I'm serious about this, Stoner. Their desire to win is so great that nothing is beyond these people. They don't really expect to be caught. Once trapped, there's no telling what they'll do. And when they turn on you, they can be very dangerous."

"I'll watch my back," she said. "Thanks, Edith. You've saved my sanity."

She hung up the phone and curled her hand into a victory fist.

Got you.

"No motive necessary," she wrote in her notebook. "Trouble an end in itself. May be cheerful when things are falling apart..." and realized she didn't have to write any more. She wasn't about to forget what she knew.

Now she had to lay the trap. Up until now she'd been playing catch-up with their perpetrator. The time had come to try to get ahead of her.

It wasn't going to be easy. It was essential to trick her into doing something in front of the others. Because if Edith was right, this woman would be expert at turning them against one another. The more out in the open this could be, the better. Let them all see the same behavior.

So what Stoner had to do was think like a manipulator. And not just any manipulator. She had to think like the Grandmother of all manipulators.

But she had the identity of her perpetrator.

And she had the motive.

Now all she had to do was prove it.

CHAPTER 11

What was left of the night crawled by. Exhausted in mind, body, and emotion, she turned out the lights and crawled into bed, grateful for the smooth sheets and soft, comforting pillow.

She became aware of the silence. Suddenly. It exploded like a fire cracker. Her eyes flew open. Her heart pounded as if she'd been thrown down a well.

Take it easy, she consoled herself. Gwen may be momentarily transfixed by Sherry Dodder, but as soon as she knows the truth…

…if she believes the truth…

She'll believe it, because I'm going to set up such an air-tight, fool-proof, alibi-resistant trap, she'll never be able to squirm out of it.

Oh, yeah? Let's hear a few brilliant ideas along those lines.

She stared at the ceiling, her mind blank. Edith Kesselbaum was right, she wasn't good at things like this. She needed to talk with someone with a devious mind.

And who would that be?

She couldn't think of anyone. No one in her personal life, and no one in *Demeter Ascending*.

That's pathetic, she thought. I have to start hanging out with a worse class of people.

Well, there was Divi Divi. She was a writer. Writers were probably devious, at least in their heads. How else would they make up plots? She'd have a talk with Divi Divi in the morning, first thing. As soon as she got some sleep.

She closed her eyes and waited. Sleep showed not the slightest interest in her.

Trouble was, Divi Divi might be too close to things. And she might not like the idea of setting up a sister.

So put Divi Divi on the short list—the extremely, ridiculously short list—of helpful plotters, and think some more.

Sleep helped her think by remaining a thousand miles away.

Devious. Have to think devious. Like a criminal…

Clara.

She sat up in bed and turned on the light. Clara was perfect. She'd spent a lifetime out-thinking criminals.

All she had to do was wait for morning...probably early morning, elderly people usually got up early...and find Clara.

Now that she had an idea, she *really* couldn't sleep.

Getting up, she slipped into her bathrobe and went out into the hall. Maybe there'd be something to read in the living room. Something really boring and difficult. Maybe something by Charles Dickens—not too difficult, but truly boring.

On the other hand, maybe she could find a detective novel that would give her ideas.

Where do people get ideas, anyway?

She walked the length of the hall and started down the stairs.

J. B. Fletcher never had this kind of trouble. J. B. Fletcher could come up with a plot to entrap without even thinking hard, as quickly as you could make a pitch for switching from AT&T to Sprint. And J. B. Fletcher wasn't even a cop, just a writer.

Which brought her once again to Divi Divi. She turned and walked back to Divi Divi's darkened room and stood there, as if she could catch cleverness by osmosis.

She couldn't. And she couldn't spend the rest of the night standing in the hall like an idiot. Back to the living room.

The sky was beginning to tarnish, the stars fading out. The viscous night grew less dense as dawn purple diluted the black. Any minute now, the birds would start up, each in its assigned, raucous place. Already she could hear an occasional "peep" as the thrushes tested their voices.

Well, it was useless to try to sleep now. She stretched out on a couch and watched the trees take shape. As soon as things were moving, stirring around—as soon as she heard the kitchen crew begin their metallic symphony—she'd go upstairs and dress and come back and wait for Clara. But for now, she didn't want to face that empty, night shirt-less room alone.

Before the thrushes had yielded to the warblers, she was asleep.

Michelle the waitress woke her, coming in to set up the coffee urn. Stoner jumped up, murmured apologetically about "couldn't sleep - fell asleep," and was about to go upstairs to dress when she had an idea.

"Has Sherry come back yet?" she asked.

The waitress shrugged "I don't know, could care less," and arranged packets of Sweet 'n Low in a tiny silver dish.

"Doesn't she usually check in with you before every meal, to make sure things are running smoothly?"

"Nope." Michelle looked as if she were one of those people who couldn't function before noon, and who found herself in a job that demanded action and sanity by six a.m.

"I thought she did," Stoner said in a deliberately puzzled way.

The woman just looked at her.

Right. Her mind isn't engaged yet. Have to be direct. "She's always telling us she has to confirm arrangements with the kitchen crew."

"Well, she doesn't. We get our orders Monday morning, and she doesn't talk to us again until the next Monday, unless something goes wrong."

Stoner frowned. "That's odd. I've seen her go into the kitchen after meals on more than one occasion."

"Snooping," the woman said. "Trying to catch someone making a mistake. Sometimes she goes upstairs, through the back. Probably trying to catch the housekeepers off guard."

"I take it," Stoner said carefully, picking up on the waitress' disgruntled tone, "Sherry Dodder isn't your all-time favorite employer."

"Nope."

"How come?"

She shrugged again. "Dunno. Just never took to her."

Stoner couldn't help admiring and envying the woman. Life would be so simple, if you could just shrug off your dislikes with a "Dunno. Just never took to her." But she couldn't do that. Oh, no. She had to analyze and rationalize and chase down her motives and try to justify every rude or unkind or negative thought. It made everything complicated and confusing.

Michelle had finished laying out the endless array of tiny little silver spoons and little linen napkins next to the little cups and saucers. She gave the table a grudging look of approval and moseyed back to the kitchen.

So, Stoner thought, all those conferences with the cooks never really happened. She was only buying time to make mischief.

She was almost humming as she ran up the stairs.

By the time she got back down, dressed and ready for action, Boneset was curled up in a wing chair, waiting for the dining room to open and reading the Sunday paper.

"It's Sunday?" Stoner said. "I didn't know it was Sunday. I've completely lost track of the days."

Boneset looked up at her and smiled. "Want to look at the *Globe*? The travel section's interesting this week."

"Spare me!" Stoner said with a groan. "I'm a travel agent."

"Yeah? I didn't know that. I don't know what I thought you were, but I never would have guessed travel agent."

"Neither would I."

"It must be really interesting work."

"Only if you love endless, repetitive, mind-deadening details."

Boneset shuddered. "Not me. Did you ever notice how many boring occupations there are in the world?"

"As a matter of fact, I did."

She waved the Classifieds section. "Look at this. There's not a thing in here I'd like to do."

"What *do* you do?" Stoner asked.

"I'm a healer."

Well, naturally. What else? "Herbal?"

"And crystals. Candle healing. Energy balancing, Bach flowers. I might get into Reiki, but it takes a lot of time to learn. And money. What do you think?"

Stoner threw up her hands. "Don't ask me. My aunt would say do it if your Higher Spirit agrees."

"Mine doesn't have anything to say on the subject. I've asked. I've asked the Goddess for a sign. Tried the Tarot, the Runes, the Ogham cards. Can't seem to get an answer."

"I guess that's your answer, then."

"Guess so." She dropped the Classifieds onto the floor. "Looks like you had another bad night."

"Sort of."

"Your aura's muddy. Want me to clear it?"

"Later, maybe." She poured herself a tiny cup of coffee. "Has Sherry come back yet?"

"No. I wouldn't look for her until at least eleven."

Stoner sat on the couch. "Really? Why's that?"

"She never gets back before late morning on Sundays. We think she has a little something going for her Saturday nights in Bangor."

She certainly did last night, Stoner thought with a dark feeling in her stomach. She'd been keeping that information at bay, shoving it back with plans and schemes. Now it leapt forward to the place of honor. If Boneset thought her aura was muddy, she should take a look at the color of things inside her psyche. Dark, heavy, and on the horizon flickers of yellow anxiety like distant heat lightening on a muggy night.

It'll be okay once Gwen gets back, she told herself. We'll talk, and I'll find out I was crazy, and everything will have a logical explanation.

What was important now was to stay around people, stay busy so she wouldn't have time to brood.

Speaking of time..."Boneset, do you know what time it is?"

Boneset glanced out the window. "A little after eight, from the shadows. See, this time of year, when the shadow of the Inn reaches the edge of the patio, it's exactly eight-thirty."

"That's interesting." Only a little after eight. They probably wouldn't be back until nine at the earliest. Even if the got up with the birds and dressed right away—if they dressed right away—and then got something to eat...There's no way Gwen would go even ten miles, much less however long it took to get to Bangor, in a car without something to eat first. She was always convinced, once on the road, she'd never eat again. And Stoner was one of those people who could go on driving forever without stopping, or until the gas ran out. It had made for some interesting trips.

So, nine o'clock. You can start to worry at nine o'clock.

Meanwhile...

She glanced up as Roseann came into the room. She seemed frightened.

Roseann saw her, made her face go blank, and slipped onto the couch next to her, sneaking a peek at Boneset out of the corners of her eyes. "I have to talk to you," she whispered.

Stoner looked around. They could go out by the reception desk. That way they'd have a little privacy, and could see if anyone approached. She signalled to Roseann to get some coffee and follow her.

"You told me to tell you if anything happened," Roseann said when they were safely ensconced in front of the front door, at an angle to the stairs, where they could see people coming and going.

Stoner nodded. "What happened?"

"Well, nothing, exactly. I mean, something might have happened, but I'm not sure it was anything."

"What *might* have happened?"

"Someone was walking up and down outside my door last night."

Stoner smiled. "That was only..."

"At first I didn't think much about it. We're all kind of on edge, what with all the stuff that's been going on and all. I figured, hey, I'd be walking the halls, too, except you told me to be careful, and wandering around in the night didn't feel like careful to me."

"Roseann, it was..."

"It gave me the creeps, you know what I mean? Could have been some really bad person, even a crazy old ghost pacing around out there, even though they say the Cottage ghost is only a joke. Well, that's what they said when Ronald Reagan wanted to be president, and you see where that got us. Some joke."

"Roseann, that was *me I* was walking past your door."

"What for? Jesus, Stoner, if you wanted something, you could have just knocked."

"I needed to think. I didn't want to wake you."

"Of course," Roseann went on without listening or stopping for breath, "if you'd just walked in without knocking, you'd have been in for a rude surprise. I got a glass of permanent wave lotion propped on top of the door frame. If you'd knocked that down, you'd stink for a month."

"I wouldn't have walked in."

"You wouldn't have walked in twice, that's for sure. Look, I've been thinking, like you asked. Like who might want to get rid of me and why? At first I thought it might be anyone, on account of I'm not like them. I mean, I don't have a lot of education and I sure don't have much political...political..."

"Consciousness?" Stoner suggested.

"Yeah. Shows, huh? Then I said to myself, 'Roseann, you're just thinking this way because your feelings are hurt, and it isn't fair to get down on all these gals who have been real good to you on account of one rotten apple in the barrel.' I mean, a person can take a dislike to you for no reason, maybe you remind them of some mean old school teacher they once had. 'You can't know what's in another person's mind,' I said to myself, 'unless they care to tell you.' Do you think I should apologize?"

Stoner frowned. "To whom?"

"Everyone."

"I'm sure that isn't necessary."

"Sure," Roseann said with sudden cheer, "how do they know what I've been putting in my own mind? I must be getting a fat head." She pulled a scrap of paper from her pocket. "But I did sit down and ask myself, 'who stands to profit?' like you said. You know, Stoner, that's a really valuable way of looking at things. It'll come in real handy, you know, when things turn a little weird, I'll just ask myself 'who stands to profit from this?' "

Stoner gritted her teeth. This was making her edgy again. "And what did you come up with," she asked as evenly as she could.

"I figure someone wants my part. I mean, that's the only profit anyone's gonna get from me turning tail, right? Now, Divi Divi doesn't much like to act, so that leaves her out. Rebecca and Barb aren't going to make any more trouble for themselves, they have enough already. Besides, they're the ones who 'discovered' me. What kind of sense would that make, trying to get rid of me?"

You have no idea, Stoner thought, what senseless things can make sense to a twisted mind.

"Rita doesn't care about anything but not getting blown up," Roseann pressed on, "and anyway she figures hanging around in spotlights too much she might get radiation."

"From spotlights?"

"Who knows what she knows?" Roseann said. "Too much, if you want my opinion. I mean, if we all knew everything about everything, we'd never get out of bed in the morning. It makes you crazy. Boneset—well, she'd figure if the Goddess wanted her to have the lead, she'd have the lead. Marcy, she knows she's up next in the rotation and she has the almost-lead now."

"I didn't know that."

"Yeah, she doesn't talk much. I mean, she talks a lot, but she doesn't say much. Did you ever notice that?"

Stoner shook her head.

"Still waters run deep, they say. I don't know. Thelma doesn't say much, either, and I'm sure there isn't much going on in *her* head. Most of what she says I wouldn't use to wrap the dog's throw-up."

"And Sherry?" Stoner asked.

"Well, Sherry can be sweet as pie one minute, and spit in your eye the next. But she's aiming for the Jet Set, you can tell just by looking around. I don't think she'd do anything down and dirty, soil her lady's hands, so to speak. And this sure is down and dirty. Stealing's one thing, you can figure maybe the person has a bad need for the stuff, or some kind of mental illness. But tearing stuff up? The down can't get much dirtier than that."

"Maybe," Stoner said.

"Besides, Sherry's in this up to her tush already. Where's she going to get the time to play the lead?" She put down her little coffee cup and little saucer and folded her arms proudly across her chest. "I got it narrowed down so there's only one person that might want to get my part."

"Who?"

"You."

The room turned upside down. *"Me?!"*

"You're assistant director, aren't you? Listen, I saw 'All About Eve.' Six times."

"But I'm not the understudy, Marcy is."

"Yeah, but you see, you have to get me out of the way first. Then you deal with her."

"Roseann..."

"You think it came like a snap for Eve Harrington? Go rent the movie."

"Roseann, believe me, I don't want your part."

Roseann broke into peals of laughter. "I really got you going, didn't I? I'm only kidding. You wouldn't try and put one over on me. You have principles. Principles up the wazoo."

"Thank you."

"If there's one thing I am, it's a good judge of character. You stand around all day with your hands in people's hair, you get to be a good judge of character." She reached into her pocket. "Anyway, I wrote down some notes for you, like you asked. Anything funny that's been happening to me. But mostly you know it."

Stoner took the sheet of paper and glanced over it. She turned to the other side.

Someone had written, "Get out of the show or else," in the same childlike block printing as Sherry's note.

"Roseann, where did you get this paper?"

"I don't remember. Why?"

She showed her the paper. "It's a threatening letter."

"No kidding?" She took the page and studied it. "Jeez, I've never seen a threatening letter before. Sounds like some little kid wrote it, doesn't it?"

"That isn't the important thing..."

"Look at the handwriting. Whoever wrote this never saw the inside of a convent school, that's for sure. The nuns would've rapped our knuckles."

"People sometimes write like that," Stoner explained, "to disguise their identity."

"Yeah?" Roseann wrinkled her nose in distaste. "You'd think they'd take more pride in their work. I wonder who did it?"

Stoner shook her head. She wanted to tell, so they could speculate together. Despite her rough edges, Roseann did indeed seem to be a fairly good judge of character. But it wasn't time yet. Now it was just time to collect evidence, as much and as specific evidence as she could.

"I don't know any little kids," Roseann went on, still staring at the note. "Except my brother's two, and they live in Dubuque, Minnesota."

"Try to remember where you got the paper. Was it in your room, or…"

"Why would my brother's kids want me to get out of the show, anyway? They don't even know I'm in it. I mean, why should I tell *them*? They'd just smirk."

"*Think,* Roseann. Maybe someone broke into your room."

"I remember. I was looking for something to write on, and I put my hand in my pocket and there it was."

"Okay, who might have been in your pants?"

Roseann looked shocked. "Look, Stoner, there's no need to talk dirty to me. I have principles, too, you know."

Roseann had been wearing these slacks yesterday, she thought. If it had happened while Sherry was away, they were back to square one. On the other hand, this was the U S of A, and you were considered innocent until…etc., etc. If there was another suspect…"Can you remember, at any time in the past 24 hours, leaving your pants in a public place?"

"Boy, you really have your mind in the sewer this morning."

"Roseann…"

"Well, we had that costume parade thing yesterday afternoon, remember? I probably left them in the back of the barn for that."

And there were people coming and going there all afternoon. Darn, she should have been watching more closely.

"How'd you like that little chartreuse number I wear in the second act," Roseann asked. "Pretty, isn't it?"

She tried to reconstruct four hours of comings and goings in her mind, but it was impossible, of course.

"You don't think it was too revealing, do you?" Roseann asked. "I don't want to look like some floozie out of *Vogue Magazine.*"

Under hypnosis, maybe. There wasn't time for that.

"My Dad would've beat me to a pulp if I ever dressed like some of those girls in *Vogue Magazine.*"

"Did you see anyone lurking around back there, more than necessary?'

"It's a good thing he died."

"Please, Roseann, concentrate."

"Dropped dead right in the middle of the third inning of the Red Sox-Yankees game. In the bleachers. It's the only thing that ever happened in the third inning in the entire history of Fenway Park."

"*Roseann, think!*"

"I *am* thinking," Roseann said. "Talking is how I think. No, I didn't see anyone in there except people who should have been there. The actors and costume girls, and Gwen, and Sherry…"

"Sherry?"

"Well, sure. She's the producer, isn't she? Has to have her nose in everything."

"I'm not positive," Stoner said, "but from what I've heard, very few producers take such an active part in the day-to-day activities of the company."

Roseann thought that over. "Well, she's kind of a nosy-newser, isn't she? Sort of like a stray dog, sniffing in all the garbage cans."

Well put, Stoner thought.

The dining room doors opened. Eight-thirty and no Gwen and Sherry in sight. She supposed she ought to go on in, sit with the other women, pretend nothing was wrong, or she didn't suspect anything, or didn't care…

But she did care. She couldn't hide from that, or from the feeling that she was being chewed to pieces inside.

All right, if Gwen wanted to have a fling, okay. She could live with that.

But she couldn't live with the fact that Gwen had lied to her, had sneaked behind her back, had contrived with Sherry to set the whole thing up. She couldn't live with the fact that Gwen *liked* Sherry Dodder, *trusted* Sherry Dodder, *believed in* Sherry Dodder.

It put a gap between them as wide as the Grand Canyon.

"Hey," Roseann was saying, "you coming?"

Stoner shook her head. She couldn't go in there and pretend. "I have some stuff to do first," she said. "I'll catch you later."

Unfortunately, the conversation with Roseann had made her doubt herself. She had to think realistically. She wanted Sherry to be the one, more now than she had even last night. But what if it was jealousy making her think like this? What did she have, really? That funny glint in Sherry's eyes, caught off guard, when everything was falling apart. Hardly solid evidence of guilt. Adequate to fuel a therapist's hunch, but they weren't dealing with hunches here.

She poured herself another miniature cup of coffee.

It was all too damnably complicated. Maybe she ought to pack up and get out right now. Just take Gwen's car—if she didn't want Stoner to take the car, she shouldn't have left the keys behind—and start driving. At this point, she didn't care where she ended up. As far as her money would take her.

Flopping down on the sofa, she put her feet up in the upholstery and took a measure of satisfaction from possibly marring the furniture.

It was a very small measure.

She wished Clara and Esther would show up. They could talk about the case and get her mind off things. Maybe they could even talk about "things" and come up with some other possibilities than the junk she was torturing herself with.

What she got instead of Clara and Esther was Rita and Seabrook.

Rita was looking radiant this morning. Dressed entirely in yellow and stepping briskly along. When she spotted Stoner she ambulated over. "Good morning," she said cheerily. "Your lady not back yet?"

Stoner shook her head. "They had to stay overnight. Car trouble."

"She used to make up better ones than that," Rita said. "Age must be taking its toll." She reached into her tote bag. "Want an apple."

"No, thanks." She wanted her to go away.

Rita settled onto the couch and took a huge, crunchy bite from her apple. "That bitch has seen the inside of every motel room between here and Tiajuana."

She really didn't want to hear this. "I guess they'll finish the set today, huh?"

"Especially the ones with double beds," Rita went on, ignoring her.

Stoner felt tears leap into her eyes, and thought frantically about how to make an exit.

"I may be a frog, Rita," Seabrook said loudly, "but *you* give *me* warts."

"Shut up, Seabrook," Rita said.

"Know what I think?" Seabrook persisted. "I think you've had your teeth X-rayed once too often."

Rita drew back in horror. "Seabrook!"

"Oh, stuff it. If you weren't crazy, you'd be boring." He turned his head and looked at Stoner with his black, round button eyes. "I want to tell Stoner a story."

Much as she wanted to leave, Stoner found herself fascinated.

"She doesn't want a story," Rita said.

"*This* isn't one of your garden variety, dull cocktail party, good God isn't it time to leave yet stories. *This* is a frog fable."

Rita tapped Stoner's leg. "You'd better listen. Frog fables are quite rare."

"This is for you," Seabrook said, leaning close to her. "Not for Rita, may her warts clone." He cleared his throat several times, and tried out various postures. "Once upon a time...when I say 'once upon a time' you have to listen very carefully, because what you're about to hear is true and important. Are you listening?"

Stoner nodded.

"Once upon a time there was a woman named Rita, who had a lover named Jennifer. They lived in a depressing little apartment on the third floor of a building that also housed a second-hand furniture store and El Carbo Carry-out Grinders and Subs. They were very much in love. Well. One day along came a wicked witch, disguised as a beautiful princess, and she sang her songs and weaved...wove?...weaved her magic spells and fluttered her eyelashes. And before Rita knew what had happened, beloved Jennifer had run away with the wicked witch, leaving behind a Christmas cactus that wouldn't bloom, a lean and hungry pregnant cat, three months' worth of unpaid phone bills, and an overdue book from the Boston Public Library."

"That's terrible," Stoner said.

"Don't interrupt. Now, Rita had many friends. Not enough to elect her Woman of the Year, but many good friends who loved her. Did she go to these friends and say, 'My heart is broken?' and let them take her to dinner and to sad foreign films? No. Do you know what she did, Stoner?"

Stoner shook her head.

"She sat in her depressing little apartment above the second-hand furniture store and El Carbo Carry-out Grinders and Subs, and watered the Christmas cactus that never bloomed, and raised the kittens that were born to the lean and hungry cat, and only went out to return the book to the Boston Public Library. And she drank. And drank. And drank. And when her friends called and asked, 'Are you okay, Rita? We never see you any more,' she told them she was busy, and they grew discouraged and went away. She locked all her tears and her softness deep down inside, until she went crazy."

He stopped talking and made a little bow.

Stoner looked up. Her eyes met Rita's. Rita held out her hand. "Sure you don't want an apple?"

She took it, turning it over and over. She touched the smooth skin. She smelled the fresh-apple odor. She felt the tears running down her face.

She felt Rita's arm slip around her, and buried her head against Rita's pillowy, comforting chest.

"The important thing," Rita said, handing her a tissue, "is to not just let it eat you. Fight back. At the very least, scream and yell. This isn't a time for good manners. Think up nasty names and make sure everybody hears them."

Stoner had to smile a little. "Like douche-bag?"

Rita shrugged. "It works for me. Though I kind of have the copyright on that one. How about…" She thought for a moment. Her eyes lit up. "Cunt breath!"

"I don't think so," Stoner said quickly. "Besides, she has friends here. They might not be so understanding."

"Nonsense," Rita said, dismissing Stoner's hesitation with a wave of her hand. "Everyone knows what Marcy's like. I made sure of that, once I got my head clear."

"She isn't with Marcy. She's with Sherry."

Rita sat back, a look of astonishment on her face. "I thought she went to Bangor with Marcy."

Stoner explained what had happened.

"Oh," Rita said. She seemed to think very hard for a moment. "Then I guess you can use douche-bag."

And who should come waltzing in at that exact moment, Stoner thought, but the douche-bag herself? With a sparkling smile and a brisk, "Sherry here!"

Gwen wasn't with her.

"Where's Gwen?" Rita asked.

"Dropping the foam off at the barn." She beamed at Stoner. "Gwen Owens is one terrific woman, isn't she?"

"Have a nice time?" Stoner asked between clenched teeth.

"The greatest." She perched on the back of the couch. "I know I said it before, but I have to say it again. You two have a really terrific relationship. I have so much respect for you."

"Thank you," Stoner said tightly.

"And Gwen is really terrific. I don't think I've ever met anyone like her."

"That's too bad."

Sherry looked at her. "What?"

"It's too bad you've never met anyone terrific."

"Well," Sherry said with a laugh, "not terrific in exactly the way Gwen's terrific. Know what I mean? She's just one special lady."

"I'm not sure what you're referring to," Stoner said. She wanted to give the woman a good shove off the couch and watch her bounce.

"She's just so…I don't know…warm. And caring. And exciting, and fun. Everything about her, I guess."

Rita rolled her eyes.

Sherry jumped down. "Gotta check the kitchen. They can't make a decision without me." She disappeared into the dining room.

"Don't just sit there," Rita said, nudging her. "Do something."

Stoner got up. "She doesn't do a damn thing in the kitchen," she said. She could hear Sherry making the rounds of the dining room. Everyone was happy to see Sherry. Everyone greeted Sherry with glad cries and peals of laughter. "Cunt breath."

She stalked out of the room.

She knocked loudly on Esther and Clara's door. Esther opened it a crack, saw who it was, then opened it wide. "Stoner!" She turned back to the room. "Clara, Stoner's here."

The older woman wheeled her chair forward. "I have some notes for you," she said, and started to take out her note book.

"Not now," Stoner said. "I need the pass key you made."

Esther went to her bureau drawer and retrieved it.

"What are you planning?" Clara asked suspiciously.

"You don't want to know," Stoner said.

"Breaking and entering is illegal, you realize."

"I'm not going to break, I'm only going to enter."

"Well, watch your step," Clara said. "In police work, impulsivity can be your worst enemy."

Esther snorted. "You should know, dear. They didn't call you Officer Leap Before You Look for nothing."

Stoner wasn't in the mood. Not for arguments, not for humor. She took the key and left.

Sherry's room was at the end of the hall. Stoner rammed the key in the lock and turned it. The door opened.

She stepped inside. Looked around.

Going to the bureau, she pulled out one drawer after another. Carefully, she pawed through the contents.

She didn't know what she was looking for. Nothing. Everything. It didn't matter. She wanted to invade Sherry's life the way Sherry had invaded hers.

The dresser yielded nothing. She tried the desk. Papers, writing materials. A set of small keys that looked as if they went to lock boxes. Probably has stacks of them, Stoner thought, all holding love letters from admirers. Trophies from couples she'd destroyed, friendships she'd broken up.

She'd like to find those boxes. She was willing to bet she'd know a lot more about the elegant Ms. Dodder if she did.

She started to pocket the keys. A shadow fell across the desk blotter.

In a panic, she looked up.

There was no one there.

She slipped out into the hall. The housekeeper was just disappearing into the broom closet.

It would serve her right if she'd been caught, she thought, her heart still pounding. Letting her emotions run away with her. Letting herself grow careless.

And taking the keys would be the ultimate act of carelessness. She still had to catch Sherry in the act. It wouldn't do to give away her suspicions before hand. And if Sherry discovered the keys were gone, the first thing she'd do would be to get rid of those boxes, wherever they were. She put the keys back into the drawer and hoped she'd returned them the way she'd found them.

The closet was next. But it, too, was unrevealing. She'd seen some of the clothes that were hanging there. And some of the shoes. There was a suitcase on a shelf next to a pile of three sweaters. The suitcase was empty. Other than that, there was nothing.

Stoner gazed around the room. It looked pretty much like the other guest rooms, except for the desk. In fact, it was as undecorated as the other rooms. Odd, since this was Sherry's home. She'd expect to see pictures, maybe posters, personal knick-knacks or souvenirs stashed here and there. Stoner couldn't spend two consecutive days in a motel room without personalizing it in some way.

Maybe Sherry kept it like this on purpose, in case there was an overflow and she needed to use the room for guests.

So there must be another room. One where she kept her individual things.

As she was about to leave, she hesitated. Something told her those keys...or whatever they unlocked...could be important. They were the only vaguely personal things in the room. It must mean something.

She took the keys and slipped them in her pocket.

As she eased out into the hall and closed the door behind her carefully, she realized it was time to do something she dreaded with all her heart.

It was time to go confront Gwen.

They reached the living room at the same time. Gwen looked tired, a little gray around the edges.

Long night? Stoner wondered with a touch of bitterness. Or guilt, maybe.

Gwen saw her, and her face lit up. She ran forward and threw her arms around Stoner's neck. "I'm so glad to see you," she said.

"You are?" Tentatively, Stoner returned her embrace.

"Completely." Gwen laughed into Stoner's shoulder. "I'm such a jerk. One night away, and you'd think it had been months."

She didn't understand. "You would?"

"I promise," Gwen said as she squeezed her tighter, "I won't always be like this. It was just so frustrating."

Frustrating, Stoner thought, isn't half of it. If this was an act, Gwen had talent she hadn't begun to plumb. She extricated herself from Gwen's arms and took a step back. "Did you have a good time?"

Gwen shrugged. "It was okay. Bangor isn't exactly Walt Disney World. Come to think of it, it isn't even Death Valley."

"So," Stoner said as casually as she could, "what did you do with yourself?" And with Sherry, she wanted to add but didn't.

"We went to a movie. Some juvenile thing full of breaking glass and scenes in men's rooms and guns, of course." She looked at Stoner in a puzzled way. "Is something wrong?"

"Of course not. I just wondered if you'd had a good time."

"It was adequate."

"Good." Time to get into it. Time to start the argument. She couldn't bring herself to do it. She started for the stairs. "We'd better get to rehearsal."

Gwen took hold of her sleeve. "Wait a minute. Something's wrong."

"I missed you, that's all."

"You don't act like it."

"I'm sorry," Stoner said, "if my behavior is inconsistent with your expectations."

Gwen flopped down in a chair. "Oh, God. I've done something terrible."

"It's just...well, since you were planning to spend the night, it would have been nice if you'd left me a note or something. Nothing elaborate, just a 'see you tomorrow,' maybe. It's not required, of course, but it would have been considerate."

"I didn't know I was going to spend the night," Gwen said. "I sent you a message."

That made her angry. " 'Spending the night in town,' " she snapped. "Delivered through Sherry to Marcy. Yeah, that certainly is a loving, tender message. It certainly did warm my heart. I guess I should be glad I got it."

"That was the message?" Gwen asked.

Stoner nodded.

"She didn't tell you I love you?"

She shook her head.

"She didn't say we'd had car trouble?"

She felt herself lose control. "*Car trouble?* Jesus, Gwen, how stupid do you think I am?"

"We had car trouble." Gwen spread her hands helplessly. "We were starting back, and Sherry heard the motor start to ping, the way it does when the alternator belt's about to break. There weren't any gas stations open after nine, and we didn't want to drive back here and risk breaking down on a deserted road in the middle of the night. So we checked into a motel and Sherry got it fixed first thing this morning and here we are. Isn't that what you would have done?"

"Yes, that's what *I* would have done," she said, deliberately heavy on the sarcasm.

Gwen got up and came to her. "I can't believe Sherry didn't tell you..."

"I don't want to hear her name!" she shouted. "And I don't want to hear any more lies. I trusted you, Gwen. If you had a problem with me, or if you just wanted to...do whatever you wanted to do, I wish you'd had the guts to tell me the truth."

"I'm telling you the truth."

"I'm not stupid, and I don't like being made a fool of!" The silence in the dining room hinted that she might have spoken a lot more loudly than she really wanted to.

Gwen took her hand. "Dearest, what's wrong?"

Stoner flung her away. "Just *stop* it!"

"Stoner..."

"You want me to swallow this load of bull shit, and you know you had the whole thing planned."

"You're out of your mind," Gwen said.

"Did the two of you sit and giggle girlishly about it between pickle and pimento sandwiches."

"Okay," Gwen said, throwing up her hands. "Obviously something happened in my absence, which has left you psychotic. When you figure out what's *really* going on, we'll talk about it." She turned on her heel and went up the stairs, her jacket in one hand and a paper bag in the other.

No doubt, Stoner thought, the paper bag contains the famous night shirt. Or maybe the new lacy underwear.

"Is something wrong?"

She turned and looked to see Sherry standing at her elbow. Rage swept over her. "Nothing we can't handle. Alone."

"Oh, gosh," Sherry said, her face reddening, "I hope it didn't cause a problem between you, us staying in town last night. I mean, everything Gwen said—about how you are and all, you know, your understanding—I thought your relationship was...you know, open. Was I wrong?"

"People who think with their vaginas," said Stoner, "are nearly always wrong."

She brushed Sherry aside. Taking the stairs two at a time, she ran up after Gwen.

The door was just closing. It closed in Stoner's face. She shoved it open viciously.

"Okay, Gwen, you can stop the games. I know what happened."

Gwen's eyes were bright with anger. "Then you know more than I do. And I resent being treated like this."

"You and Sherry had yourselves a little prearranged fun last night, didn't you?" She sounded like a jealous lover. She *was* a jealous lover. She hated it, but she couldn't stop.

"I'm not even going to dignify that with a response."

"You maneuvered me into going to Green Lake just so the two of you could be together." She folded her arms across her chest. "Nice work, Gwen. But not nice enough."

"You're crazy," Gwen said flatly.

"She admitted as much just now."

"Then she lied."

"You took your damned night shirt!"

Gwen only looked at her.

"If this whole thing was just some accidental doo-dah, why did you take your night shirt?" She ran her hands through her hair. "Or maybe you had a premonition you'd have car trouble. Maybe you're the greatest psychic since Edgar Cayce. Maybe you should go get a job in the damned circus!"

"Maybe I should. It's probably more sane than here."

"She's been on the prowl for you from the minute we got here," she spat out.

Gwen's face was white. "You have a hell of a nerve, Stoner..."

"And you've played right along."

"I haven't played anything."

"At least you could have had the decency to tell me you were falling for her."

"Falling for Sherry?"

"You didn't have to parade it around in front of everyone."

"*Goddamn it!*" Gwen shouted, "I'm not going to defend myself to you. It's my Goddamned body, and my Goddamned life, and if I want to get involved with Sherry Dodder or Madonna or the Man in the Moon, it's none of your Goddamned business."

"Great." Stoner strode to the window and stared out at the empty lawn. "Let's just do anything we want. Fuck commitment. Fuck loyalty. Fuck honesty. It's just all one big, happy fuck."

"Yeah, well, how about trust?" Gwen's voice was shrill with anger. "We've been together all this time, and I've never lied to you, or kept anything from you. All this time, and it hasn't built up one ounce of trust in you. That makes me feel really great, Stoner. Really terrific. Like it's all really been worth while."

Stoner turned back to her. "How am I supposed to trust you, the way you've been acting. The minute we walk in, you hate her. Next thing I know, you're going out of your way to be nice. Meanwhile you're closing up on me. You don't want to talk one minute, you want to make love the next. I don't know what I'm doing with you. I don't know what you want from me..."

"*You* don't know what *I* want..."

She felt cold and hard inside, like a suit of armor and a sword with nothing human behind it, and right now she just wanted to swing the sword and mow down everything in her path. "You want to ride off into the sunset with little Miss Goody Two-Face? Little Miss 'You two have such a *great* relationship. I have so much respect for you. You're so *special*?' Go ahead. If *that's* what you like, you're wasting your time with me."

"Jesus *Christ*," Gwen blazed. "You're so damned stubborn. You make up your mind about what's real and what's not, and I might as well talk to the trees. You don't listen to me. You don't take me seriously. You get wrapped up in your own little world, and God forbid anyone would want to get in."

"It's not hard for someone to get into *your* world, is it?" She said bitterly. "You just let them in, it doesn't matter who, or who gets hurt. Live for the moment, right?"

"Has it ever occurred to you that I might sometimes feel closed out?"

Stoner looked at her. "You?"

"If Sherry was making you uncomfortable, you could have said so. You could have talked it over with me. But, no, I'm not important enough, or smart enough, or *something* enough..."

"How was I supposed to talk to you? You're so smitten..."

Gwen cut her off with a gesture. "This has nothing to do with Sherry. It's you and me. It's you keeping me out."

"Keeping you *out*? I've gotten closer to you than anyone in my life. Anyone in my entire life. I've always been afraid, and I guess now I know why."

Gwen was silent for a moment. "Okay," she said. "I'm out of here." She grabbed her suitcase from the closet and tossed it on the bed and began furiously ramming the contents of her bureau into it.

"Fine. At least your night shirt's already packed."

Gwen stopped and glared at her. "You're *obsessed* with that night shirt. Have you totally and completely lost your mind?"

"No, and I haven't lost my ability to add two and two, either."

"I didn't take my night shirt anywhere, Stoner."

"Oh, give me a break." Stalking to the bathroom, she grabbed Gwen by the arm. "Look." She pointed to the empty hook. "I don't see any night shirt. Do you?"

"Yes." Gwen extricated her arm. She reached behind the toilet and picked up the night shirt from the floor. "Is this what you were looking for?"

Stoner stared at it stupidly while the room turned upside down. "It wasn't there before," she said.

"Well, it's there now." She threw it at her. "Here, you want it? Since it's obviously the most important thing in your life, you might as well keep it." She slammed the bathroom door and turned on the water.

She sat down on the bed and buried her face in the shirt. It was soft, and smelled of Gwen.

She'd always known it would happen like this. No matter how hard she tried, she knew there was something in her that would break the things that mattered most. It would say or do the wrong thing at the wrong time. Or not say and do the right thing at the right time. Or take something wrong and ride it to death.

And she'd finally done it. That demon in her, the demon that waited to destroy whatever she loved had stepped in and crushed the very thing she cherished most. Smashed it into grains of sand she'd never, ever be able to put back together.

She didn't feel like crying. This went too deep for crying. All she could do, forever, was sit there holding Gwen's shirt.

"Stoner." Gwen touched her.

It felt very far away, a chasm between them she'd never be able to cross.

"Honey, we have to talk about this. Calmly."

She opened her eyes. Gwen knelt beside her, looking up at her.

"It's all so crazy," Gwen said.

Stoner nodded.

"Why did you think," Gwen asked, her voice low and loving, "I'd do a thing like that? And with Sherry Dodder, of all people?"

"I don't know."

"You must have *some* idea."

She shrugged. "Nothing that excuses what I did."

"That's for me to know and you to find out." Gwen took her hand. "Stoner, I love you. I wouldn't do that." She gave a little laugh. "And I certainly wouldn't do it in such a low-down, tacky, stupid way. Even if you don't trust me, at least give me credit for being more creative than a soap opera."

In spite of herself, she had to smile a little. She could feel Gwen's hand holding hers. "I'm sorry," she said.

"So am I. I promise you, if I ever go off and do something this crazy, it won't be with any old Sherry Dodder."

She tightened her grip on Gwen's hand. "I said some awful things to you."

"So did I. There was probably a grain of truth in some of them, but we can sort that out later, okay?"

"Okay."

"What can we do now to make it better?"

Stoner looked at her and said, "Hold me?"

"An excellent plan," Gwen said, and put her arms around her.

"I'm so sorry, Gwen. Honest, I really don't know what to say. I'm just so…sorry."

Gwen laughed. "Boy, you're *fierce* when you're angry. And incoherent. Fiercely incoherent, one might say."

"One might," Stoner muttered.

"I'm sorry, too." She brushed her hand through Stoner's hair.

It felt so good to hold her. It felt so good to be held by her.

"I love you so much, Stoner."

She clutched at her. "I love you, too. Gwen, I'm so…so…"

"Shhh," Gwen whispered. "It's okay."

"But some of the things you said about me…they're true."

"I know."

"I really try not to keep you out, but it just happens…"

"Stoner," Gwen said, and kissed her forehead and looked long and hard into her eyes, "we live in a hard, complicated world. Nobody grows up without damage. If it sometimes gets in our way…I guess that's why they invented forgiveness."

Stoner leaned into her and drew a deep, heavy breath. It felt like the first real breath she'd drawn since they got here. "I wish we could leave," she said.

"Well, we can't."

"This place is evil."

"Not the place, Stoner. This is a very human kind of evil. And we have to do something about it." She got to her feet. "There's something I have to show you." Taking Stoner by the hand, she led her into the bathroom. "Look." She pointed to the corner, behind the toilet. "That's where I found the shirt."

"It must have fallen. Maybe when I took down my robe. And I accidentally kicked it to the side. I guess I just didn't see it."

Gwen went and sat on the edge of the tub and looked back and forth into the corners of the room. Slipping off her shoes, she hopped into the tub and looked back and forth again. "Did you take a bath last night?"

Stoner nodded.

"It wasn't here," Gwen said.

"What?"

"Come over here." She pulled Stoner's head down to be on a level with her own. "Look. From here you can see that corner as plain as the nose on your face. In fact, it's impossible *not* to see that corner."

She looked. Gwen was right.

But…"Nobody but us can get in here."

"Maybe."

"Clara rekeyed the door, remember?"

"These are old doors with old locks," Gwen said. "I'll bet a child with a hairpin and a little skill could get in here." She brushed her hair back angrily. "Somebody's playing with us. What's worse, somebody's playing with your head. I won't have that, Stoner."

Stoner looked at her, at her sweet, angry face. She sat on the edge of the tub.

"We're being set up," Gwen said.

"You really think so?"

"I know so. And I resent it." Gwen counted off her points on her fingers. "First, why did *Sherry* end up going with me to Bangor instead of Marcy? Because Marcy had to stay home and wait for a phone call. Did she ever get the call, do you know?"

Stoner shook her head. "She didn't."

"And who told her about the call?"

"Sherry. But Sherry claimed someone else took it and told *her*."

"Did she say who?"

"No. Just some other guest."

Gwen dismissed that with a wave of her hand. "So that got Marcy out of the way. We go in to Bangor. Next, she claims to hear something wrong with the truck. I didn't hear it, but I don't know that truck, so I believed her. Three,

I wanted to call you, but she insisted you wouldn't be back from Green Lake, anyway, and she had to leave orders for the kitchen crew."

"She never leaves orders for them," Stoner put in. "Only on Mondays. Michelle told me. She doesn't like her."

"Michelle is a woman of great wisdom and sensitivity. Four, instead of leaving you a message of explanation and affection, instead of repeating exactly what I told her, she leaves a message that…what?"

"That you'd decided to stay in town. But that could have been Marcy's mistake."

Gwen snorted. "I doubt it. It's consistent with the rest." She held up her hand, fingers extended. "And five, to round it all off, she takes my night shirt so you'll freak out, and returns it while I'm delivering the styrofoam. That part was a little tricky. What if you'd been in the room?" She frowned. "But she was insistent we leave Bangor at eight, not before or after, now that I think of it. She must have timed it so we'd get here while you were at breakfast. Were you?"

"No."

"What were you doing?"

"Snooping around Sherry's room."

"Good woman! Find anything?"

"Only some keys," Stoner said. "They look as if they fit strong boxes. I took them."

"Bummer," Gwen said.

"I know, but I don't dare risk trying to return them. She could walk in at any time."

"On the other hand," Gwen said thoughtfully, "it might not be so bad for her to suspect we're onto her. It could make her careless." She grinned. "Besides, I want to see her squirm for a change."

"Yeah, and I really think there's something important in those boxes, but I don't have any idea where they are."

"All in good time. Something tells me the tables are about to turn."

"She's pretty good at what she does," Stoner said.

"You haven't seen me in action when I'm riled up." Her fingers curled into fists. "God, I hate being manipulated. My previously-alive husband was bad enough, but this…Even the lunch meat was a set-up to make you jealous. The little twerp."

"Well," Stoner said, "I played along. I fell for it. It takes two to tango."

"You know our problem? We're both too innocent. Even you, with your suspicious nature. We're minor league, dearest."

Stoner smiled. It was going to be a beautiful day. "Are you fierce when you're riled, too?"

"Formidable." Gwen thought for a moment. "I suggest, for now, we pretend we've had a fight. Let her think her little scheme worked."

"Good idea."

Gwen looked down at her surroundings. "Just goes to show you, I always do my best thinking in the tub."

Stoner leaned down and kissed her. "You better get out of there before I'm tempted to turn the water on again."

"Be my guest. I'm going to take a quick bath. I think it would be better if we went down to the barn separately."

"Okay." She got up. "Gwen, don't you think we should have a plan?"

"Probably," Gwen said. "But at the moment I don't have one, do you?"

"No. What I do have is a terrible appetite."

Gwen began taking off her clothes. "You always do when we've had an argument. For me, it's sex. For you, it's anger."

Stoner shook her head. "My anger isn't about anger, it's about fear."

"Well, *that's* normal." She was down to her underwear. "There's a bag of Dunkin' Donuts in the bedroom. I made her stop long enough to get them for you."

"I love you forever. Any vanilla creme filled?"

"Of course."

Gwen had thought of her. It really was all right.

Her grin was wide enough to permanently damage her face.

She could hear Gwen singing in the bathroom, over the running water. "You're certainly cheerful about all this," she called through the door.

"You better believe it," Gwen called back. "It's the first time in my life I've ever been right about somebody."

CHAPTER 12

They decided to go to the rehearsal separately, in keeping with their roles as feuding lovers. Stoner would go first. If they needed to talk during the day, they'd pretend to have an irresistible impulse to get in the last word.

Gwen agreed to try to fake friendly feelings toward Sherry, though it was going to be difficult. She insisted on being granted unlimited private bitching sessions, and other favors to be named later.

Carefully arranging her face in what she hoped was a look of cold rage and desperation, Stoner left the room. The hall was empty. Either the women had left for rehearsal right from the dining room, or they'd frightened them away with their shouting match.

The way things were escalating, there could be a new incident any minute. She wanted to be on the scene when it happened. But first she had an idea.

Detouring through the nearly empty living room and the French doors, she found Clara and Esther on the patio where she expected them.

"Well," said Clara when she spotted her. "You look as if you've been through the mill."

"I have. Can't explain now." She took the cluster of small keys from her pocket. "I found these in Sherry's room."

"Didn't get caught, did you?"

"No."

Clara glanced over at Esther. "I told you she had possibilities."

"If my memory serves," Esther said. "*I* told *you*."

"Our memories don't serve either of us," Clara huffed. "We're old, remember?"

"Of course," Esther said. "I forgot for a minute."

"See what I mean?" Clara turned back to Stoner. "Old age—no memory."

"I need a favor from you," Stoner said, "if you think you can do it. I'm kind of in a hurry."

"Youth," Esther said. "No patience."

"It's not my fault," Stoner said. "Our perpetrator's getting ahead of us."

"Do you know who it is yet?" Clara asked.

"I'm pretty sure it's Sherry Dodder. I don't know why she's doing this stuff, but I'm sure she's the one doing it. I only need to prove it."

Clara grinned and touched Esther on the leg with the tip of her cane. "Told you she'd figure it out."

Esther brushed the cane aside. "Batterer," she said in a bantering way.

"Did you suspect it was Sherry?" Stoner asked.

"I was getting there," Clara said. "She was the only person with periods of time when she was out of sight of the rest. Short periods, but time enough to do some mischief. The only snag was, she was supposedly in the kitchen during those times."

"There's a stairway from the kitchen to the other floors. Probably to an outside door, too."

Clara nodded. "There's our missing piece. We couldn't get to the kitchen without attracting attention."

"Not even at night?" Stoner was puzzled. "I was under the impression she left food available, in case anyone got hungry."

"The kitchen door was always locked," Esther said. "We've tried it three times."

So, they'd been manipulated even more than they knew. The night of the Pickle and Pimento Caper, the door had been wide open. Sherry must have planned that. Gwen had probably told her—having been carefully led in that conversational direction—about her night time cravings. Then, when Gwen had mentioned the childhood "comfort food," Sherry had laid in a supply and waited for Gwen to get hungry in the night, knowing that one of them would come looking for something, knowing it would cause trouble between them.

Sherry Dodder was an astute student of human nature.

But it would have required keeping watch, to be sure the kitchen was unlocked when Stoner got there.

No problem, if Bangor had a Radio Shack as well as a Kinko's. She could have wired their room with a sensing device. Every time someone opened the door, it would send a signal to Sherry's room.

Except she hadn't seen anything remotely resembling a receiver in Sherry's room.

Not in Sherry's designated room, anyway.

There was another room. She was certain of it. Maybe in the basement or an attic, but probably on the third floor, where it would seem to be just another uninhabited guest room.

"I need to know what these keys fit," Stoner said to Clara and Esther. "I have a feeling it might be important. They look as if they go to a locked box of some kind."

Clara examined. "Probably. Mid-security grade. Not cheap, but not the most secure, either. Even without the keys, I could get in there in…oh, ten minutes per box, more or less."

"The problem is finding them. I think Sherry has another room somewhere in the Cottage, probably on the third floor."

"I'm afraid that leaves me out," Clara said. "I can only go where I can go."

"Ahem," said Esther.

"Aha," said Clara.

"Perfect," said Stoner. "Gwen and I will be at rehearsal, right under her nose. She'll never suspect a thing."

"What am I looking for?"

Stoner frowned. "I'm not certain. Evidence of tampering with the theater things. A cache of flashlights. Stolen objects, maybe. A computer and/or printer. Anything else you find that looks suspicious."

"Generic evidence," Esther said. "A written confession would be exciting, but I'll bet I won't find one. Nobody keeps that kind of diary any more, except politicians."

"The boxes are important, of course. I suppose you could open them?"

"She could *not*," declared Clara. "That would be against the law."

"Breaking and entering isn't?" Esther asked, wide-eyed. "When did that change?" She gave Stoner a knowing wink. "She's afraid of being left out."

"Then just take the boxes," Stoner said. "We'll all open them together." She ran over the plan in her mind, in case they'd overlooked something. "And see if you can find a receiver, the kind that tells if a door's been opened."

"Motion sensor and console security system," Clara said. "Similar to the RS 2609."

"But it can't be the kind that sounds a loud alarm," Stoner added. "Don't most of them make a terrible noise and call the police?"

"Easy to disable once you have one. A simple matter of disengaging a few wires. Anyone with a simple knowledge of electronics, or the time to read the manual, could do it."

"Esther, you have to be careful. Her room's probably bugged, too."

Clara laughed. "That woman can get into places only a moon beam could penetrate. After all, she got into my heart."

"We'll keep Sherry under our noses as long as possible." She checked her watch. "It's 9:30 now. She can't really insist she has to go deal with the kitchen until 11 at the earliest. Do you think that's enough time?"

"Unless we're talking about secret passageways and hidden rooms, it is."

"We might be," Stoner said. "I'm beginning to think nothing's too elaborate for her."

"If you doubt her love of elaboration," Clara said with a snort, "take a look at the menus. This is back woods Maine, for heaven's sake. Not the Queen Elizabeth. Folks who come out here would as soon cook a lobster in the sand as pick snails out of butter. Probably rather."

Stoner grinned. "I guess she wants to make a reputation for herself."

"Well," said Clara, "she'll get her wish if we do our job right."

She arrived at the barn to find yet another crisis. Roseann had fallen from the stage while practicing a dance. The extent of her injuries wasn't yet known. At the moment, she was sitting on the floor moaning with pain and clutching her right ankle.

Sherry announced that she'd go for ice.

So she'd have time for a side trip to the secret room? Or to make more trouble? What if she found Esther?

Stoner caught Gwen's eye and tilted her head, indicating that Gwen should go with her.

Gwen got the message.

"How did this happen?" Stoner asked Barb, who seemed particularly distraught.

"She went past her marks. At least, I think she did."

"Her marks?"

Barb led her to the stage and pointed to two small crosses of masking tape a couple inches from the brink of the platform. "We set these to tell the actors when they're coming too close to the edge of the stage. She must have stepped over them."

Stoner glanced at her. "You don't look certain."

"I don't know. Those marks…if I hadn't set them myself, I'd say they weren't right."

Behind them, the other actors were lifting Roseann and helping her to a chair. Roseann was chanting, "Shit, shit, shit," like a mantra.

"I'd like to get a closer look," Stoner said. "Can you put some light on the stage?"

"Can do." Barb caught the attention of one of the techies, who was seated behind a console crammed with switches and dials. "Bring me up to half on three," she said.

One of the spot lights went on, spreading amber light across the stage. Stoner knelt by the taped marks. Her shadow fell across them. "I need the light more from the front."

"Take three out, give me full on four," Barb called.

The amber light went out. Soft blue flooded the front of the stage. "Spill," Barb said, squinting critically into the light. "Make a note to fix that," she called to the dimmer board operator.

Stoner pressed her face close to the floor and found what she'd been looking for. "Barb?"

The technical director knelt beside her.

"Look here." She pointed to the faint outlines of two crosses. "Someone…" She hoped she was using the right terminology and not making a jerk of herself. "…reset your marks."

The new settings were only off by a few inches. Not much, but enough to distort Roseann's sense of distance. Especially if, being inexperienced, she was depending on them. "Do the actors usually rely on these?" she asked.

"Some. Especially at first, until they get a feel for where things are. It keeps them in the right places relative to the lights. Once they're on stage, the last thing actors want to have to do is look for their hot spots. It throws them out of character."

"I see," said Stoner, having only a vague grasp of what Barb was talking about but willing to take her word that it was important. "Do you think

Roseann needed this in particular?"

"Sure. She's new to this. Doesn't know what she's doing. We're trying to make it as concrete as possible for her." Barb pulled a bandanna-type handkerchief out of her overalls and blew her nose heartily. "Excuse me. Allergies." She stuffed it back into her pocket. "I'd rather work with the inexperienced ones. It's the ones who think they know what they're doing who mess us up." She shook her head ruefully. "Actors."

Stoner nodded sympathetically. "Do you have any idea who might have moved these marks, or why?"

"Hey!" Barb bellowed to the back of the barn. "Who fucked with the marks?"

It wasn't exactly what Stoner had in mind when she thought of discreet investigations. She couldn't imagine women fighting each other for the privilege of being the first to admit to "fucking with the marks." In fact, no one seemed to want to claim credit. But she hadn't really expected them to. This was just another incident, and the alleged perpetrator was on her way to the kitchen.

With Gwen, who had the unenviable job of trying to appear friendly toward, even fond of, Sherry.

"Okay," Barb said loudly. "Joyce, want to fix the spill on four?"

The woman named Joyce, resplendent in strappy-tee, cut-offs, work boots, and the omnipresent techie wrench hanging by a piece of rope from a leather belt, scrambled up a ladder like a monkey up a palm tree. Perching precariously at the apex, resting on the top step, the one that always bore a "not a step, do not sit or stand" label, she set about adjusting the light with vigor, efficiency, and a great deal of grunting and banging. Whatever the "spill" was, it would never withstand the joint efforts of Joyce and Barb.

She turned her attention to Roseann, who had stopped moaning and now mostly looked as if she were about to go into shock. "How does it feel?"

"I don't think I broke anything, but it's tender." She got to her feet. "Let's see if I can walk."

Tentatively, she put the injured foot down. Stood for a moment. Took a step forward, winced, swore, and fell back into her chair. Rebecca moved to stand beside her protectively.

"Guess I won't be dancin' for a while," Roseann said sheepishly.

"Let's not jump to conclusions," Rebecca said.

Roseann uttered a short, barking laugh. "I'm not gonna be jumping *anywhere.*"

"What happened?" Stoner asked. "As specifically and clearly as you can remember."

"Well," Roseann said, rubbing her ankle. "I was just going along, doing the steps the way I always do..." She glanced up at Rebecca. "I was, wasn't I?"

"As far as I could tell." She raised her voice. "Barb, did Roseann have the steps right?"

"Perfect, as always."

"Barb's the choreographer, *and* the tech director," Roseann explained. "Can you beat that?"

"She has hidden talents," Stoner said.

"Yeah, I'll bet there's nothing she can't do. I'll bet she could even beat the gals from Thelma's Cut 'n Curl—excuse me, Unisex Styling Center—at Friday night Hearts. She's going to sit in, once the play's over. Aren't you, Barb?"

"Sure am," Barb replied, and shot a warm smile in Roseann's direction.

It looked as if there might be a budding romance here. At the very least, from the way Roseann was looking at Barb and blushing slightly, she had one heck of a crush on the technical director. Maybe Marylou wouldn't have to worry about finding the ideal date for Roseann, after all.

"I guess it wasn't my fault," Roseann said.

"What wasn't your fault?"

"Falling off the stage."

"No," Rebecca assured her, "it wasn't your fault."

"Well, that's a first." She thought for a moment. "Funny thing. Right before I fell, the floor turned all kind of eely, like there was egg white on it or something."

"What?" Barb shouted from the stage. "Egg white?"

"Felt kinda like egg white. Of course, you wouldn't necessarily know what I'm talking about, since you probably never gave anyone an egg white mousse."

"Not likely," Barb said. She blew her nose, then got down on the stage and sniffed the floor boards. She sniffed again, then blew her nose again and sniffed one more time. "God*damn*," she grumbled, and ran to the back stage area. She returned carrying an aerosol can. Popping the cap, she sniffed it. "Silicone," she announced. "Someone sprayed the floor with silicone."

Rebecca rolled her eyes. "What next?"

"I don't know about you," Roseann said through clenched teeth, "but I sort of hope they get back here with the ice before I get too much older, you know what I mean?"

"Hang on," Stoner said, and squeezed her hand. She turned to Rebecca. "What happens if she can't do the dances?"

"She can still do the show," the director said. "We can have someone else fill in for the dances. In the old musicals, they had separate casts for the acting and the dancing."

"They did?"

"Look at the 'Out of my Dreams' sequence on the movie of *Oklahoma!* some time. It works." She glanced over at Divi Divi. "What do you think, Div?"

Divi Divi shrugged. "That's the director's decision, not the playwright's."

"*I* think it would look doody," Marcy put in.

"Spoken like a true understudy," said Divi Divi.

That made her stop and think. If the point of all this was to give Marcy the leading part, and the seemingly unrelated incidents were a smoke screen…

All of a sudden she was doubting herself again.

"Listen," Roseann said loudly, "it's making me crazy, all of you standing around like this. Don't you have something better to do?"

Rebecca smiled. "I guess you'll live, huh?"

"I'll live."

Rebecca raised her voice. "Okay, let's run a light check. Barb, you set?"

Barb said, "Yo."

"Company, entrances and exits. Places."

The rest of the cast and crew went to their assigned stations.

"Ready? Cue 1, opening. One and three to half, area two full. Schlafley enters. Joan of Arc enters. Medea enters." One by one, the actors filed onto the stage.

"What's going on with you?" Roseann asked in a low voice. "Lips are flapping faster than at the Unisex."

"What do you mean?"

"You and Gwen? That was some blow-out you had this morning. We heard you all the way into the dining room."

"You should have heard us when we got upstairs."

"We did," Roseann said. "Your windows were open."

Stoner told her about the fight. "It was all a misunderstanding. It's fine now. But we're pretending we're still angry. We think we might get more information that way."

"Good idea," Roseann said with an approving nod.

"What are people saying?"

"Nobody knows what to think." Roseann rubbed at her ankle. "Some say you're out of your mind, others say Gwen and Sherry are a couple of sluts. Most are just confused, and a few don't care one way or another."

"Good." She didn't care what other people thought, as long as Sherry continued to believe they were still estranged. They needed to control and monitor Sherry's comings and goings, and to do that Gwen had to be around her at all times. "Don't let on what I told you, okay?"

"As Sherry would say, '*No problemo.*' Just let me know what you need me to do."

They should be getting back with the ice. Stoner glanced out the window and saw them, coming toward the barn. Gwen was talking excitedly, her posture angry. Sherry gave her a sympathetic hug. It was working.

"I need an amber gel on seven," Barb shouted.

Marcy complained that she'd come to rehearsal expecting a complete run-through, and it wasn't happening, and she could feel her timing going off.

The screen door squeaked. Gwen and Sherry crossed the room, Gwen leaning into Sherry a little as if for protection.

Stoner glared at them and moved to the stage.

"Want to hold book?" Rebecca asked sympathetically.

Stoner looked at the complicated system of light cues and shook her head.

"Hang in there," Rebecca whispered. "It'll pass."

"Page fifteen," Barb called. "Coming up on thirty-eight. Cue: 'I must be mistaken.'"

"I must be mistaken," said Rita/Medea.

All the lights went out. Barb turned to the back of the room. "Lisa, can you give me thirty-eight?"

"I am," said the woman at the console.

"It's not right."

"I have cross-fade to area three."

"That's not what you're getting."

"I don't understand," Lisa said.

Stoner had the feeling *she* understood. Understood all too well. "Try a few others," she said to Barb.

"Okay, Lisa, give me thirty-nine. Forty-two. Fifty-six." She turned to Stoner. "They're all wrong."

"Uh-huh. It's been sabotaged."

Barb pulled out her handkerchief and blew her nose loudly. "I can't believe this. We have to redo the whole light plan." She jumped up onto the stage and strode from one side to the other, peering up at the lights and down at the floor and making notes. "This is going to take us the rest of the day."

"You *can't* do that!" Marcy wailed. "We have to rehearse."

"Calm yourself," Rebecca said impatiently. "You'll get a chance to rehearse."

"If I have to take over for Roseann, I'd better get a lot of rehearsal time."

"I don't think you'll have to take over for Roseann."

Stoner tried to cast Marcy in the part of their villain, and couldn't. Marcy was much too impatient. There was no way she'd have the fortitude to construct the complicated plot they were dealing with here.

She glanced over to where Gwen and Sherry were tending to Roseann. Gwen was looking down, focused on holding the ice against Roseann's ankle. Sherry had glanced toward Joyce on the ladder, her lips parted in just the hint of a smile. The glittery look was back in her eyes.

Was she excited about what *had* happened, what was *going* to happen, or all of the above?

And if it was about what she had planned for the immediate future, how dangerous was that? How much farther was Sherry willing to go to accomplish whatever it was she was accomplishing? Physical injury wasn't beyond her limits. What about serious harm? What about murder?

It was time to put an end to this.

And how was she going to do that?

If Esther couldn't come up with some hard evidence, she really had nothing to go on. So the only way to trap Sherry was to get her to trap herself.

She was beginning to get an idea. Edith Kesselbaum had said that people like Sherry enjoyed setting people against one another. So why not give her the perfect opportunity? Bring the entire company together, accuse Sherry of being the troublemaker, and watch her try to manipulate the situation. In front of everyone. It would be a classic confrontation in the Miss Marple and Jessica Fletcher tradition. Everyone assembled and watching, while Stoner and Gwen outlined Sherry's dastardly plot from beginning to end, quoting times and dates, displaying irrefutable evidence. Leaving Miss Sherry Dodder sputtering with incoherence and guilt, while the rest of *Demeter Ascending* raised, as one, the angry voice of condemnation.

It was a great idea. Trouble was, she didn't have the slightest idea if she could bring it off.

Better pray Esther and Clara come up with something more concrete.

For now, she'd have to settle for collecting as much evidence as she could, and hope for the best.

But she couldn't do that in the middle of a rehearsal. And she had to make certain Sherry was being watched at all times.

Steeling herself, she marched over to Gwen. "I want to talk," she said gruffly.

Gwen glanced up. "I don't have anything to say to you."

"*I* have something to say to *you*." Good grief, she should have gotten Divi Divi to write better dialogue.

"Yeah?" said Gwen. "Well, I'm busy."

"Hey, listen, guys..." Sherry said, stepping between them.

Stoner stepped around her. "I want to talk to you, and I want to talk to you *now*. Or should I make a scene?"

Gwen emitted a heavy sigh and got up. "All right." She glanced at the others. "I'll be right back. *Right* back."

Stoner strode from the barn. Gwen followed.

"Can you keep close to Sherry for the next hour?" she asked when they were out of ear shot. She waved her arms a little in the way she thought people might wave their arms if they were having a shouting match.

Gwen planted her hands on her hips in an annoyed, stubborn way. "I guess so. What are you up to?"

She filled Gwen in on her thinking, and Esther's activities. "She knows I suspect her. If she planted the night shirt, she knows we rekeyed the locks. And she knows I don't have good feelings about her any more. We can't take the chance of her finding out what we're doing, and hiding some evidence."

"Just be careful, will you? I'll do my best, but she might slip away from me. We already know she's slippery." Gwen folded her arms across her chest and turned her back. "I love you."

Stoner grabbed her shoulder and spun her around. "I love you, too. We must look like Lucy and Desi."

"Don't you dare make me laugh." Gwen brushed her hand away.

It was hard not to smile. "Get out of here, will you, before I blow it?"

Gwen turned on her heel and stalked back to the barn. Stoner watched her for a moment, then began loping toward the inn.

She hesitated outside the door to their room. If she went in, and if Sherry was keeping track of their comings and goings, the opening of the door would register on Sherry's receiver.

Stoner had to laugh at herself. Sherry already knew she was under suspicion. She'd already been in their room, to take and return the night shirt, and knew they'd changed the locks. Face it, no one was fooling anyone any more.

She hoped Gwen was fooling Sherry.

Pulling her knapsack from the closet, she emptied the contents onto the bed, sorted through and decided on taking her knife, note book, and pencil. After all, this was an evidence-collecting expedition, not a camping trip.

A glance at her watch told her she had about an hour to see what she could come up with. She consulted her notes. The marijuana. Clara had said she found a patch growing wild down by the lake. If she could find it, along with evidence of recent harvesting, that would account for the Boneset Tea incident.

She slipped out of the inn through the parking lot entrance, and followed her previous path along the edge of the woods. There was a slight chance she'd be seen, if Sherry happened to be looking out a barn window at just the right angle. But that might be all right. It might make her nervous. She loved the idea of making Sherry nervous.

Problem was, it would probably just give her a thrill and add to the excitement.

It was warm in the sun, but cool under the trees. Yesterday's rain had washed away the humidity and left the air with a dry, autumn-like feel. The white furniture shimmered against the flagstone patio. Pines took on a deep green intensity, while the sky above them was light and high and the palest blue washed with wisps of cloud. The lake sparked silver through the trees. From everywhere and nowhere came the scent of ripening grapes. Women's voices drifted to her from the barn, indistinct and murmuring as a swarm of bees.

She reached the lake and looked for a path around. There had to be something, at least a fairly smooth area, to accommodate Clara's wheel chair. Water lapped at the shore and caressed dark stones. Across the pond, water lilies were in full bloom where the little outlet stream formed shallows. The marijuana patch wouldn't be beyond that spot, unless there was a bridge over the brook...

Suddenly she remembered the first night, when Sherry had met them by the boat house. She'd come by car, then left the car and followed a path. That would be the way Esther and Clara would come. Not to the right, where the pier jutted out over the water. There was too much traffic in that section for a marijuana patch to remain for long. Someone would have smoked it or reported it back in July. Left was the direction to take.

The path appeared almost immediately, and beyond it a thinning of the woods, where the road cut through. She passed the parking spot. The path was less worn here, but still passable for a wheel chair if you didn't mind a few bumps. Clara and Esther didn't remind her of women who minded a few bumps.

She glanced back in the direction of the boat house. A figure emerged from the building and stood for a moment as if looking back and forth along the far shore. Sherry? She wasn't certain, but ducked back into the dark tree shadows just to be safe.

Another figure joined the first, and this one she definitely recognized. Gwen, in her sleeveless pale blue work shirt and faded jeans. Then it was Sherry, all right. They talked for a moment, then turned together and went into the boat house.

Stoner decided to stay put.

A few seconds later they came back out, Sherry carrying what looked like a large hammer. Stoner noted her pink shirt and bibbed blue shorts. Another play suit.

They were gone. She slipped back to the path and kept walking.

A strange odor, the odor of old, wet, burnt wood came to her. She looked around and found a dead camp fire, to her left away from the lake and in a small cleared area ringed with stones. Bits of unburned logs lay in a jumbled pile. The remnants of Boneset's ritual bonfire? Stoner looked overhead, at the close-packed canopy of pine needles and birch leaves. Not here, certainly. A bonfire here would be much too risky.

But someone had made a fire here. Campers, maybe, hiking the Appalachian Trail and veering off for the night.

She knelt down to take a closer look.

Beneath the pile of ash and charcoal and burnt logs, she saw something that didn't belong. A round, turned dowel, at least an inch and a half in diameter. Man-made and half burned.

She found a stick and used it to poke deeper into the ashes. Another dowel, and another. The last one was nearly intact, but shattered in the center. And, near the point of shattering, those hammer dents she'd seen on Boneset's ladder.

That explained how Sherry had managed to break the stage ladder rung so neatly. She'd been practicing, and this was what was left.

Things were beginning to fall together in a nice way. Feeling a little optimistic for the first time in days, she gathered up the broken rung and stuffed it into her knapsack.

The marijuana patch lay only a few yards farther along the path, in a spot by the water that was sunny, dry and protected by some knee-high laurel bushes. A small patch, only about four or five plants, hardly enough to catch the attention of the narcs—though considering the way they pounced on a single plant on a window sill these days, no one was really safe. They were lovely, healthy plants, the flowers just on the verge of bloom. Each plant probably worth about a thousand dollars on the street.

She found what she was looking for. Scars and branching where leaves had been plucked off. Taking out her knife, she harvested the plant with the most tell-tale marks, and left the rest to turn to bird seed.

No doubt about it, this was turning into a fruitful morning. Stoner lashed her knapsack shut as tightly as she could. If she ran into anyone before she reached her room, she didn't want any tell-tale distinctive odors giving her away. As it was, she'd probably be high before she got back to the Cottage, just from being so close to the Devil's weed.

Taking a last careful look around, in case other clues were waiting to reveal themselves, she slipped her arms into the knapsack straps and walked forward along the path until she reached the stream. There was nothing new.

Stoner turned and trotted back to the inn.

She was just coming down the stairs, having left the evidence inside the closet, locked in her suitcase, as Sherry came through the French doors. "Where were you?" Sherry asked in a friendly, cheerful voice. "We missed you."

Stoner twisted her face into what she hoped was a wry smile. "Really?"

"Rebecca needed you on book."

She hoped Esther had finished up in her search for the missing room. She wished she'd thought of a way to secure their own room, because Sherry was here now, her alibi intact, and Stoner couldn't think of a single excuse not to go back to the rehearsal. She looked at her watch. It was a few minutes before eleven. "She'll have me for an hour before lunch. That should be enough."

Damn, damn, damn. She *knew* Sherry would be poking around their room the minute she was out of the building. That locked suitcase was a dead give-away, and wouldn't slow her down for a second.

"Sher!"

Stoner glanced up at the familiar voice.

It was Gwen, hot on Sherry's trail. She sidled up to Sherry and took her arm.

Stoner's stomach, not yet having processed the information that this was all an act, complete with affectionate nick names, turned over.

She brushed past them and out the door.

Clara and Esther were sitting on the patio, placidly drinking coffee and looking sun-sleepy and self-satisfied. From her lap, Clara flashed her a thumbs-up.

Esther had found the room. She'd found the boxes. It was all coming together.

And Gwen was hanging on Sherry's arm, making sure the only things Sherry could do for the next hour were the things she said she was doing.

As she walked across the lawn, Stoner wondered if Sherry had begun to be suspicious. She knew *she* would. But maybe Sherry was so impressed with her own brilliance she felt invulnerable. And so convinced of her own innate desirability she absolutely believed Gwen could fall in love with her overnight.

Stoner envied her that. It must be nice, to go through life like that.

Then she remembered something she'd read in an Agatha Christie, one of the Miss Marples, only she couldn't remember which one, something to the effect of, "Such people live dangerously. They just don't know it."

Well, Sherry Dodder was about to know it.

By the time they broke for lunch, it was beginning to be clear who felt what about the goings on between Stoner and Gwen. Rita fussed over her, offering her goodies from the tote bag and making comforting sounds. It touched her, and made her feel guilty about the deception. So guilty it was all she could do not to take Rita into her confidence.

Rebecca was keeping an open mind. Clearly, she didn't consider one twenty-four hour period to be any indication of long-term troubles.

Marcy was into herself and didn't give a damn one way or another.

Boneset, while pointing out that she didn't necessarily condone what was going on, stated that the Goddess moved in mysterious ways, and people had to do what they had to do.

During a break in a line run-through, Divi Divi passed by and whispered, "Scratch her eyes out."

Roseann, who knew the whole story, avoided Stoner's eyes so she wouldn't giggle.

A few of the techies looked uncomfortable, as if they weren't sure what was happening or what to do about it.

Joyce discovered they were out of amber gels, and took off for Bangor. Lisa spilled a cup of coffee on her light cue sheet.

Barb had troubles of her own. It was all she could do to take a moment now and then to blow her nose and check on the progress of Roseann's ankle.

"Okay," Rebecca said when they'd reached the end of the line run-through, "it's going well. We'll go through the songs after lunch. Okay, Barb?"

"If I can find my music," Barb said.

Stoner perked up her ears. "You can't find your music?"

"I thought I'd left it in my room, but I couldn't find it last night. So I figured I'd left it down here, but it isn't here." She shrugged. "It'll show up. I'm just a flake."

If there was one thing Barb wasn't, Stoner thought, it was a flake.

"If you can't find yours," Divi Divi said, "I have a copy. I sure don't need it, can't read a note. Want me to bring it down after lunch?"

Barb shook her head. "No need. I know I'll find mine."

"Better bring yours," Rebecca said to Divi Divi under her breath.

"Gotcha," said Divi Divi.

"Okay," Rebecca announced. "One hour for lunch. We meet back here at one on the dot." She blew a quick blast on her whistle and the company headed for the door.

Stoner caught her eye and grinned at the whistle.

"I know," Rebecca said as she dropped into the chair next to her. "To quote Marcy, 'It's so doody.' How are you doing?"

"Okay. I might be a little late getting back from lunch. Is that all right?"

"Of course." Rebecca patted her knee. "Just don't do anything I wouldn't do."

She waited until she was certain Gwen and Sherry had gone to the barn before approaching Clara and Esther's room. Gwen was doing a great job of dogging Sherry's foot steps. If Sherry had wanted to do anything with her lunch hour other than play innkeeper, she didn't have a snowball's chance in hell, the way Gwen clung to her. In fact, if she were Sherry, she'd be a little tired of Gwen's cow-eyed devotion.

You made your bed, Miss Sherry, Stoner thought. How do you like lying in it?

It gave Stoner a great deal of pleasure.

She tapped at the older women's door.

"Who is it?" Clara demanded.

"Stoner."

She heard the lock scrape, and Esther opened the door.

"Thought you'd never get here," Clara grumbled.

"Sorry." She turned to Esther. "Did you have any trouble?"

"Of course not. What I do, I do very well."

Stoner looked around the room. There was no sign of lock boxes, computer disks, flashlights, music sheets—nothing. "Was it the wrong room?" she asked, and tried not to sound too disappointed.

"It was the right room."

"Oh. Then there wasn't anything in it?"

"There was..." Esther's face broke into a huge smile. "...*everything* in it." She went to the closet door and opened it. "One security console, left in place to avoid discovery, but disabled. The only comings and goings it will record will be her own." She held up a small object. "The bug from your room. Over your door, in case you're wondering. Flashlights." She swung the door wide, revealing a small hill of silver flashlights, black flashlights, waterproof lanterns, and pen lights. "Assorted clothing. Hidden deep in the bowels of the closet. And the *pièce de résistance...*" With a flourish, she pushed aside a collection of sweaters on the shelf and revealed three iron gray metal boxes.

"Okay!" Stoner said eagerly as Esther handed them to her. "Great work!"

"I know," Esther said.

"Have you looked inside?"

"We were waiting for you."

"None too patiently," Clara added. She took the first box and settled it on her lap, brought the keys out from her pocket, and set to work. The lock popped open.

Inside lay a pile of legal-looking papers. Clara took them out one at a time and studied them.

"Birth certificate. Doesn't seem to be counterfeit. Well, at least she's who she says she is." She laid the paper aside.

"Deed to the inn, signed over to her by one Margaret Bankhead, in exchange for..." She whistled. "...two hundred thousand dollars. Where'd she get that kind of money?"

"I heard there was an inheritance," Stoner said. "Her grandparents."

Clara rooted around in the box. "Yep, there it is. And a sizeable mortgage.

All seems to be on the up-and-up. Our friend knows what she's doing."

"That's what I'm afraid of," Stoner said.

The older woman put the papers back in the box and locked it. She took up the second. "Let's see what this brings forth."

The next box contained insurance policies—house, car, life, health—and contracts from suppliers, security service, spring-and-fall house cleaners. Also warranties on the kitchen and housekeeping equipment. But not what they were looking for.

Stoner was becoming discouraged. She could go with what she had if she had to, but she really wanted to find more compelling evidence. Flashlights and clothing could be planted in a closet. It would be a little harder to squirm out of the contents of a locked box.

She sighed.

"Patience," Clara said.

The last lock gave. Clara opened the box. "Well, well," she said.

"Well, well?" Stoner asked, straining to see around Esther, who had bent eagerly over the box.

"Bingo," Clara crowed, and held up a 31/2 inch computer disk. "I wonder what could be on here."

Stoner took it. "I can find out." Rebecca's lap top would run it, she was certain. And probably Divi Divi's as well. She was willing to bet there'd be some nasty little remarks about Roseann in one of the files. And unauthorized script changes in another.

Maybe even a diary.

We should be so lucky.

She turned her attention back to the box.

A copy of the script, with light cues. She was willing to bet they were the correct cues, which Sherry had replaced with the wrong ones.

Samples of the handwriting of all members of the company, hers and Gwen's included, Xeroxed from the guest registry.

A wallet-sized pack with a zipper, made of black leather-like material. Clara pulled out a tissue and snatched it up before Stoner could touch it. "Lock picking equipment," she explained. "You don't want to get your finger prints on this. It's illegal to have them in some states, if you're not a lock smith."

A letter, addressed to Sherry. The handwriting wasn't familiar. Stoner compared it with the registry signatures. It didn't match.

And, on the bottom, a necklace made up of small green stones. Sparkly stones. It looked very familiar.

It was the necklace she'd seen in her vision, days ago, when she'd tried to "read" the knife.

Did this mean the necklace was intended to play a part in Sherry's scheme? And if so, what? Was it a card she hadn't played yet?

And what should they do about it now? Return everything and wait for Sherry's next move? See what she had up her sleeve next?

It was too late for that. They were down to the last few hours of this.

Sherry knew she couldn't cozy up to Stoner now. She knew she would be watched. And it wouldn't take her long to figure out that Gwen wasn't *really* devoted to her, just watching her.

But the necklace might come in handy when she forced the confrontation.

Clara was looking at the letter. "Well," she said, "this is terse and to the point."

Stoner took it from her.

"Sherry," she read. "I know about your affair with Rita. I trusted her, and I trusted you. But I guess it's open season now. So much for your 'respect for our relationship.' Jennifer."

Jennifer? Was this the famous Jennifer of Rita-Marcy fame? Jennifer who'd been Rita's lover, but left her for Marcy? If so, then Jennifer and Sherry were lovers, but Rita had left Jennifer for Sherry, which left Jennifer free and clear when Marcy came along, which meant...

But Rita thought it was Marcy who'd come between herself and Jennifer. Rita had never mentioned Sherry, except to say that she'd been helpful.

Everyone had thought Sherry was helpful.

Everyone but Jennifer, who apparently had a different slant on it all.

This whole thing was more complicated than "Days of Our Lives."

And what about "respect for our relationship?" That certainly had an all-too-familiar ring to it.

"What do you think?" Clara was asking her.

"I think," Stoner said, "if Divi Divi could write plots like this, she'd be set for life."

"Do you have enough to go on?"

"I hope so. Something tells me it's all we're going to get." She wished she had a way of taking a look at that computer disk. It could end up being exactly what she needed—definite proof that Sherry was involved in this. Add it to the handwriting samples, the letter, and all the other findings, and it would be nearly impossible for Sherry to claim innocence.

She realized she was being cautious, maybe too cautious. But she was dealing with a slippery one.

Well, she'd have to make her move, and make it tonight. She had a hunch time was running out.

"Can you return the other boxes right away? And the keys?" she asked Esther. "We'll keep this one, and the flashlights and clothing"

"Can do," said Esther. "What are you going to do?"

"Try to get her to trap herself."

Clara frowned. "This doesn't sound very safe or sensible."

"It's the best I can come up with. Do you have another idea?"

"Not me," Clara said. "I'm a cop. We can't do a damn thing until blood's spilled."

"Let's hope it doesn't come to that."

"Let's hope," Clara agreed. "And if you get in trouble, remember, I'm not as fast as I used to be."

CHAPTER 13

It was nearly eleven. Allow another ten minutes for Esther to return the things to Sherry's secret room. Even though Sherry had to know Stoner was on her trail, it seemed important to keep the extent of their discovery from her as long as possible.

She decided to drop by their own room and change from her flannel shirt to a lighter one. The day was heating up rapidly. Humming to herself, she climbed the stairs.

There was something on the floor outside their door. As she came closer, she saw that it was a small vase of flowers. Not just any flowers, but two pink roses. The card taped to the vase read, "To Gwen, lovingly, Sherry."

It had to be the corniest thing she'd ever seen. The "morning after" bouquet, right out of the movies. She was surprised it didn't read, "Thanks for last night." Of course, it was possible Sherry was totally smitten with Gwen Owens—anyone in her right mind would be—but she had the sneaky feeling it was intended to cause more trouble between them. And she had a pretty good idea why Sherry would want to do that. Because it was what she did best, for one thing. For another, she sensed them closing in on her, was nervous, and had decided to create a further diversion.

"Thank you, Sherry," she said to herself, "I'll take this as a compliment."

She added water to the vase, and placed the flowers in the center of Gwen's bed, the card facing her as she came into the room. It would drive her crazy.

Tossing her flannel shirt into the laundry bag, she slipped into a faded blue work shirt and rolled the sleeves up to the elbow. One last check of drawers and closet. Nothing missing. Okay, time to find out the latest developments from Rehearsal Land.

She smiled to herself as she crossed the lawn. It was a little after eleven now, and she'd been out of Sherry's sight for over an hour. Sherry must be nearly apoplectic, wondering what she was up to. And trying to get away from Gwen, whose devotion had her trapped.

Trapped and worried. The perfect situation for Sherry Dodder.

As a matter of fact, Sherry was coming out of the barn at this very minute, with Gwen in hot pursuit. Despite the smile on her face, from the way she was walking, sort of jerking along and coming down harder than necessary with her tiny feet, Stoner had a pretty good idea Sherry wasn't a happy camper.

Glancing over her shoulder, she was relieved to see Clara and Esther come out onto the patio. It meant Esther had finished putting flashlights and locked boxes back in Sherry's room. And just in time, no doubt. The room was the first place Sherry would check.

She veered to her left to pass close to them. Gwen spotted her and stopped, and set a look of anxiety on her face. Stoner strode by and said, loudly, "Slut."

Sherry smiled.

"Listen," Gwen said on cue, "if you have something *real* to say, say it."

She stopped and turned on Gwen. "I have plenty to say to you, but not in front of Miss Goody Two-Face."

"All right, we might as well have it out." She waved Sherry away. "I'll catch you later, Sher."

Sherry hesitated. "Maybe I should stay," she said in a protective, wrap-you-in-my-web voice. "You might need me."

"Go eat worms," Stoner snapped.

Gwen closed her eyes wearily. "I can handle this. You have things to do. We'll talk at lunch."

Reluctantly, Sherry turned and trudged toward the inn.

"My God," Gwen said, as she led Stoner away from people and buildings and toward the privacy of the woods, "that was the longest morning I've ever spent in my life."

"You did good work," Stoner said.

Gwen kneaded her face with her hands. "My face is frozen forever into this ridiculous, moon-sick smirk."

"If it's any comfort, you gave me the time I needed. *And* you made Sherry's life miserable."

"Small comfort." She scrubbed harder at her face. "Muscle strain," she explained.

Stoner looked around. "Do you think it's safe to kiss you?"

"I doubt it. People have been keeping their eyes on me all morning. We have to drop this charade soon, Stoner. My life's in danger."

"It is?"

"Some of your supporters are pretty angry. I fear the wrath of Rita."

"She has a little history with this kind of thing."

"Those," said Gwen, "are the most dangerous kind."

Stoner grinned. "I'll try to keep her at bay. We only have one or two loose ends to tie up. By tonight we'll be able to bring it all out in the open." She filled her in on Esther's findings, and her plans. "I want to see what's on the computer disk. After that..." She spread her hands. "I don't know what else we can do, do you?"

Gwen thought a moment, and shook her head. "There's something you should know. She did get away from me for a few minutes this morning. I found her in the boat house. She said she was getting a heavier hammer to work on the set. She got one, but I'm sure she had something else up her sleeve."

"I saw you. I was across the lake, in the marijuana patch."

"Stoned again. No wonder you're so full of yourself."

"Did you happen to see a phone in the boat house?"

"A wall phone," Gwen confirmed. "Why?"

So that was how she'd ordered the flowers. Stoner grinned. "You'll find out."

"Tell me."

"I can't bear to spoil the surprise."

"I hate you."

"Sure." She looked at Gwen and wanted to take her in her arms. Wanted to so badly she could feel her nerves reaching for her.

"Stop that," Gwen said softly and lovingly.

"Stop what?"

"Your aura is wrapping around me. It's not fair, having a fight and not being able to make up properly. We should be out on the lake in a canoe, gazing into one another's eyes and murmuring sweet nothings and apologies. I miss you terribly."

"Me, too."

Gwen turned away a little, out of temptation's path. "Can't we get this over with this afternoon?"

"I thought about it," Stoner said, back to business. "But I don't know how soon I can look at the disk. And if we were in the middle of a confrontation and it got too hot for her, she'd be able to escape with that 'have to check the kitchen' excuse. Once we're into this, we have to keep going to the end."

"Glory," Gwen said with a heavy sigh. "Another five hours of mooning after her. You owe me, pal. You owe me *big*."

Stoner knew there was nothing she'd rather do than pay that debt.

Roseann's ankle seemed to be better. At least she was standing, leaning on the back of a chair as they went through the songs. Stoner sat down next to Rebecca.

"How's it going?" she asked.

"Okay. How about yourself?"

"We're getting there. I see you found the sheet music."

Rebecca nodded. "Finally. Nobody can find anything today. Divi Divi had her copy stashed in her car, under the front seat."

"That's lucky." Luckier than she knew. If it had been in her room, chances were that copy of the music would have been missing, too.

"By the way," Rebecca said, "I checked the word processor on my laptop. You were right. It was used after I did my notes the other night. While we were at the evening rehearsal."

While Sherry was "consulting with the kitchen help," no doubt. Another piece of the puzzle fell into place.

"I'd have told you sooner, but I haven't had a chance to talk to you."

"That's okay. I've been hard to pin down."

"Look." Rebecca shifted uncomfortably in her chair. "If there's anything I can do…you and Gwen, I mean…"

"It'll be fine," Stoner said.

"I know it's really awkward and all. But I don't know how you usually do things between you…"

Stoner forced bitterness into her voice. "Not this way."

"If you'd like me to act as go-between…"

She shook her head. "We'll work it out."

"I don't know what's gotten into Sherry. This really isn't like her."

Oh, yes it is. It's exactly like her. "What I really need to do," Stoner said, "is focus on what's happening with the company. It…well, it helps me keep my mind off of things."

"Know what you mean," Rebecca said.

"So how about we eat lunch fast, and go up to your room? I'd like to use your computer."

Rebecca smiled and relaxed, clearly relieved that she wouldn't have to negotiate the Stoner-Gwen Wars. "*No problemo*, as Sherry would say." She caught herself and looked stricken.

Stoner laughed. "As Sherry would say."

They broke for lunch. Gwen, who had been keeping herself out of sight by working on the scenery in the back of the barn, emerged covered with paint and announced to anyone who cared to listen that she was going to scrub off before she ate. Stoner would have given her right arm to be in the room when Gwen found the roses.

Rebecca was subdued through the meal, not exactly moping but not cheerful. Her energy felt gray.

"Is something troubling you?" Stoner asked over salad Nicoise and iced tea.

"Nothing much. You have enough on your mind."

"What I have on my mind," Stoner said, "would welcome an intrusion."

Rebecca sent her a grateful glance. "I'm just a little down about the show."

"You've had a lot of snags," Stoner said. She didn't add that they were about to end, and that the outcome would be either snag-free sailing, or the biggest mess anyone could possibly imagine.

"It's not the obstacles. We always have plenty of those. The company doesn't feel right. It's not…I don't know…cohesive."

"Have you worked with outsiders before?"

"You mean, do I think Roseann's the problem?" She shook her head. "Everybody likes Roseann. She fit in right from the start. Marcy might be a little jealous, but Marcy'd be jealous of her own shadow. We go through that with every production. She knows she'll get her turn for the lead in the rotation."

Stoner sipped her tea. "Do you think it's the nature of the things that have been happening? That must play a part."

"Of course. But it should bring us together. Instead, it's as if we're splintering, suspicious of one another. Nobody seems to know whom to trust. This never happened before, not even at the height of the Rita-Marcy Wars."

"And now you have the Stoner-Gwen Wars."

Rebecca smiled wryly. "You mean the Stoner-Gwen-Sherry Wars." She leaned forward. "Tell me the truth. How seriously should I take that?"

Stoner felt herself in a found-out blush. "Not very," she said. "But keep it quiet, okay? All will be revealed."

"Goddess, I hope so," Rebecca said.

It gave Stoner an idea.

The laptop whirred in the tinny-plastic way of laptops, and ran through its repertoire of question marks and smiley faces and start-up icons. The desk top appeared, and Stoner inserted the floppy disk into the drive. She double-clicked, holding her breath, half expecting a warning beep and some horrible message like "This disk can not be opened because the application that created it is missing," or "This disk is unreadable. Do you want to initialize it?" or—the most dreaded of all—"This disk is password protected. Please enter password."

But it went through, and brought up files created by Rebecca's word processing program or an identical one. She clicked on the program itself, pressed control-I, and copied down the date and time the program had last been used.

"Okay," she said with a glance at Rebecca for luck, "show time."

There were two files showing. DN (director's notes?) and SC (script changes?). Stoner chose DN and opened it.

It was all there. Everything Rebecca had supposedly said about Roseann. And a few she hadn't read on the print-out, probably reserved for more trouble-making later. There were nasty comments about Marcy, too, and snide remarks on Rita's appearance. Complaints about Divi Divi's script, and gripes about Barb's lighting. Even a few questions in regard to Sherry's competence as a producer. All of which would be "found" by the right people and used against Rebecca. Sherry's reign of terror, it seemed, had barely gotten underway.

Rebecca was silent as she read the notes. Deadly, dangerously silent. The chill in the air was nearly solid.

"I know what you're thinking," Stoner said.

"Do you know who did this?"

"I have a pretty good idea." She hesitated. "Don't you?"

Rebecca nodded very slowly. "The only person with access to our rooms."

"I'm afraid so."

"It's so…so…"

"Disillusioning?" Stoner suggested.

"Right. I don't understand why she'd do it."

"It's complicated."

Rebecca's hands curled into fists. "I'm going to wring her neck."

"My sentiments exactly. But I think we should make this a group activity."

"It won't work. Half the women in the company think she's the greatest thing since Susan B. Anthony."

"And the other half?"

Rebecca shrugged helplessly.

"Surely this is proof, isn't it?"

"Stoner, the only computers on the grounds are Div's and mine. It'd be my word against Sherry's."

"Maybe it would, maybe it wouldn't. I'll see you later."

Her next stop was Divi Divi's room. Luckily, Divi Divi was in, lying on her bed and reading a copy of *Essence*. She welcomed Stoner to use the printer any time, as long as she didn't make *her* create what she printed.

She ran off copies of DN and SC, and showed SC to Divi Divi. SC and the bastardized script were a perfect match.

"Where'd you get that floppy?" Divi Divi asked.

Stoner grabbed up the hard copies and the disk. "I'll explain later. In a hurry."

She ran to her room. Gwen had been and gone. The flowers had been moved to the back of the toilet, the card placed aesthetically on Stoner's pillow. She was glad Gwen hadn't destroyed the roses. They were pretty, and it wasn't their fault. She hated it when people destroyed inanimate or barely-animate things simply because the humans involved had screwed up. It was such a male thing to do.

She stuffed the disk and papers into her knapsack and was about to go in search of Boneset, when suddenly it didn't feel safe leaving them behind. From now on, she had a hunch, she'd better keep all the evidence with her.

Boneset's door was closed. The odor of incense drifted around and through the cracks. From inside came the tinkling sound of New Age music. She was probably meditating. Stoner sat down in the hall and waited, playing with the straps of her knapsack, trying not to think about what lay ahead. Stay focused. Don't let your mind drift to "what if's" and "did she really's" and other things that can make you doubt yourself. It's time to be like a silver arrow, to fly straight to the target. Time to take the big leap off the rim of the Grand Canyon and hope the trail you think you saw below is really there. Time to Believe In Yourself.

The music stopped. Rustlings and throat-clearings came from behind the door.

She stood and knocked.

"Blessed be," came a voice from inside.

It reminded her of Aunt Hermione, and made her feel warm and safe. "It's me," she said as she opened the door.

"Hi." Boneset gave her a bright smile. "I was just leaving for rehearsal.

Want to walk along?"

"In a minute." She paused, wondering how to phrase what she wanted.

Boneset watched her calmly and expectantly.

"My aunt," Stoner said. "The aunt I live with. She's Wiccan, and she mentioned a kind of ceremony...well, you know the trouble that's coming down with Sherry and Gwen and me. And other stuff that has people up tight and kind of scrappy..."

Boneset nodded.

"I remember my aunt, Aunt Hermione, the witch, the one I live with...she said there was an ancient Goddess ritual of some kind that women did when there was tension building up in the community..."

"Stenia," Boneset said. "The Bitching Ceremony. It's very ancient. It was held during the Festival of Thesmophoria, or the Festival of Demeter, as some people know it."

"That's the one. I think maybe it would help us out, if the whole company took part. Kind of a clearing of the air."

"It might at that," Boneset said thoughtfully.

"Can you conduct it?"

"Of course. But we'd need Crones. Crones are absolutely essential to the Stenia. They keep things from getting out of hand."

Stoner thought of Esther and Clara. They'd probably think it was insane, but they'd do it. "I can get two Crones."

"Lesbian Crones?"

She nodded.

"Good. As the petitioner, you'll have to go through a purification rite beforehand. Actually, we all should, but getting *that* bunch to do anything all at once...Well, you know how that is."

"I do. Is it something we can do indoors?" She didn't want anyone wandering off into the shadows at a critical moment.

Boneset considered it. "I think so. There's one moment when all the complaints are burned in a bonfire, but I think we can substitute a cauldron and do it in the barn."

"Great. Is there anything you need, anything I can help with?"

"I have the herbs and candles and crystals. What *you* have to bring is a clear intention and an honest heart. Can you do that?"

Stoner felt a twinge of guilt. Her intention was clear, but she couldn't really say she was doing this honestly. Her motives were slightly devious, having less to do with healing than with entrapment.

"Well," she said sheepishly, "almost."

Boneset looked hard at her for a moment. Then she smiled. "I guess that's good enough," she said.

Everything was set. At the end of the afternoon rehearsal, Boneset had announced that there would be a "healing ritual" for the company that evening in the barn at sunset. The women agreed that healing was in order, and Sherry even declared that they should all "be there or be square."

Stoner wondered if Sherry had any idea what was up. It was hard to tell. If she'd known Stoner was behind it, she might have tried to stop it. On the other hand, given Sherry's by-now-legendary level of self-confidence, she might be welcoming the opportunity to turn things to her advantage. At the very least, it would provide the kind of excitement that made Sherry's eyes glitter.

Esther and Clara were delighted to play the part of Crones. It meant they wouldn't be left out of the excitement. They promised to bring all the incriminating items in their possession, and to play it cool.

As the petitioner, Boneset explained, Stoner would have particular tasks to do in preparation.

First, instead of eating in the dining room, she would accompany Boneset to the barn, where they'd construct the Crones' bower. It suited her fine. She needed to keep busy. If she didn't, she'd be overwhelmed with apprehension and lose what little self-confidence she had. For this to work, she had to be able to convince the others of the rightness of what she believed. And to do that she had to believe she was able to convince them. And that meant she had to believe she believed she was able…

"You're preoccupied," Boneset suggested.

Stoner looked up.

The woman stood with her arms piled high with pine boughs and trailing vines. She smiled. "I've been waiting for you to take these for the last five minutes."

"Sorry," Stoner said, blushing with embarrassment as she reached for the load of branches. "I'm a little nervous about tonight."

"However it comes out, it'll be the will of the Great Mother."

"Yeah. I just hope Her will and mine are running along the same track."

Boneset reached for a branch that had fallen recently from a silver birch. "Sometimes the Goddess works in ways we don't understand. But we have to trust in Her wisdom."

"I trust Her wisdom," Stoner said. "I just don't trust my own powers of persuasion."

"Ask Artemis to help you. Place your trust in Her hands."

"Is she articulate?" Stoner asked as she bent her knees so Boneset could add the birch branch to her pile. She was familiar with the Artemis manifestation of the Goddess, the Huntress, Mistress of the Hounds, Lesbian. But not with Artemis the Orator.

"No, but she's direct. Her arrow's swift and true." Boneset glanced at her. "I think what you're looking for is truth, not lies hiding behind pretty words." She turned her attention back to the forest floor. "Speak from your heart. Where other hearts are open, your words will take root. Seeds aren't praised for their beauty, flowers are. But without the common seeds, there'd be no flowers."

Boneset was changing as she went about the ritual gathering. She seemed older, more serious, more focused.

"All right," Stoner said.

"If you need to feel Her near you, carry a bit of birch bark in your pocket."

"Is that her sacred tree?"

"It is if you say it is," Boneset said. "That's the beauty of the Goddess. She's flexible." She filled her arms with fallen branches and partridge berry vines and leaves of wintergreen. "I guess we have enough. Thank the Goddess for her gifts and blessings."

She did.

They made their way back to the barn, to where they'd built a wooden lean-to frame on the stage. Laying down the branches, alternating north-to-south and east-to-west, they wove a roof of pine, then decorated it with the berries and fragrant leaves. Boneset pulled up a folding chair and covered it with a deep purple robe. "That's for Esther," she said. "I imagine Clara will come in her wheel chair." She got another robe and folded it and placed it on the folding chair. "This is for Clara. You only have to drape it around her."

Stoner nodded.

Boneset stood back and admired their work. "Not bad. Demeter will be pleased. She likes the younger ones to exert a lot of energy."

"Well, we certainly did that," Stoner said. "I'm so dirty and sweaty I couldn't face anyone, much less a Goddess."

"Then you're ready for the ritual bath. Do you want to use my room, or your own?"

It probably wouldn't do to risk running into Gwen. It would be too distracting, to say the least. She'd want to tell Gwen everything she'd been doing, and what it all meant. Time enough for that later, when they could be as mundane as they wanted. For now, she wanted to stay safe inside the mystical spell Boneset was weaving. "Yours," she said. "I'll go get clean clothes."

"You won't need them."

That brought her up short and caused a flood of panic. "I don't have to do this in the *nude*, do I?"

"Only your feet," Boneset said, an amused smile brushing one corner of her mouth. "As petitioner, you'll wear a white robe."

"I don't have a white robe. Only a plaid one."

"We'll use a sheet. And a belt made from rope. That should look humble enough."

Carrying a handful of left-over vines, she started for the door. Stoner ran to open it for her. She already felt as if Boneset were a Priestess.

"Do I have to prostrate myself?"

"Like a nun?" Boneset laughed. "Hardly. The Great Mother isn't interested in humiliation."

"Well," Stoner said as she walked along beside her through the dew-damp grass, "all I can say is, this is a far cry from Christianity."

"It certainly is. Didn't your aunt ever invite you to a celebration?"

"Yes, but we never quite got around to it."

"Then you'll have something to tell her, won't you?"

"Uh-huh. Life with her is going to be one big 'I told you so' for about three days. She always insists I'd take to the Old Religion like a fish to water."

"And are you taking to it?"

Stoner ran her hand through her hair self-consciously. "Like a fish to water."

The bath was hot and fragrant with the herbs Boneset had provided. Steam rose around her like a sauna, scented with rosemary and mint and lemon. She let herself drift and float outside of time, feeling protected, as if invisible hands were holding her. Visions of women played themselves out on the screen within her head. Mysterious women, darkly dressed, moving through a twilight forest. They carried small objects—one a sprig of yew, another a colored stone, a third a wheat stalk, a fourth a ripe apple. They seemed to float above the ground like fog, hundreds of them converging toward a lavender-lighted clearing. A feeling of joy went through her. These were the Old Ones, the ones long-gone but never gone, gathering to lend their succor and wisdom to the coming ceremony. As they were present but unseen wherever women joined to do the Mother's work.

A tinkling bell, bright as a spirit, brought her back to herself. "It's almost time," Boneset said.

"Coming." She dipped beneath the water, inviting the herbs to perfume her hair.

As she rose from the bath, Boneset came into the room. She carried a towel, and was dressed in a flowing black gown decorated with silver moons and stars. Around her neck she wore a pentacle whose center was a large aquamarine crystal. A rope of bright red braided and knotted wool hung around her waist. She took a towel and began wiping the water from Stoner's body.

"I can do that," Stoner said, feeling a little awkward.

Boneset shook her head. "We've begun."

Slowly and gently she dried her, then ran a comb of bone through Stoner's hair.

She took out a flask of oil. "High Joan the Conqueror," she explained, and touched her oil-soaked fingers to Stoner's forehead. "I purify you from anxiety. May your thoughts be clear."

She touched her eyelids. "May your vision be cloudless."

She touched her mouth. "May you speak that all may hear."

Freshening the oil, she anointed Stoner's breasts. "May the beauty of you bring beauty to your work."

She touched her hands. "May you find strength and courage."

And finally knelt and touched her feet. "May your path be firm in the ways of truth."

Taking the sheet which she had removed from the bed and folded, she draped it around Stoner's body, sculpting the folds and creases and tying it in place. She stood back and nodded approvingly. "Move around. See if you're comfortable."

She did. She was. The cotton robe felt as natural as her own skin.

"Ready?" Boneset asked.

Stoner nodded.

Boneset picked up a dagger set with semi-precious stones, and a wooden wand tipped with a glowing crystal and carved with runes. She thrust them into her belt, took her room key from the bureau, picked up Stoner's knapsack, and turned. "Let's do it."

Dinner was over, the rest of the company gone to their rooms to rest and wait for night fall. There was no one in the living room. As they crossed the patio, they saw Esther emerge from the first floor fire door, pushing Clara ahead of her.

Boneset led the way over to them.

"My goodness," Esther said, "you two look lovely."

"Nice costumes," Clara remarked. She sniffed. "Smell good, too."

"Thank you," Stoner said. "You look lovely, yourselves."

They did, too. Clara wore deep purple velvet slacks and a flowing silk blouse. A large silver chain hung around her neck, and bright rings nested on her fingers like tiny hummingbirds. Esther had chosen an off-the-shoulder cocktail dress with a net stole, and gold jewelry. She looked as if she should lounge against the piano and sing sexy-sad ballads.

"We have the stuff," Clara said. "In that bag that hangs down on the back of the chair. Don't want to risk anyone running off with it."

"Excellent," Stoner said.

"We'll look out for this for you, too," Clara offered as she took the knapsack from Boneset and hung it from a chair handle. "You don't want to spoil your effect."

"Thank you," Boneset said. "We have one more thing to do, and we'll meet you inside the barn."

With a wave, the Crones set off across the grass.

Boneset led Stoner to the woods. She went to a fallen birch and peeled off several strips of bark. Tying the ends together, she fashioned a crude necklace and placed it around Stoner's neck. "This is Artemis," she said solemnly. "She's with you. She's here."

The barn was dark when they got there. Only Esther and Clara were around, waiting for instructions. Boneset went to the light board and turned it on. She adjusted the light until the entire room was in dim blue light, then added a bright pink light to the center of the floor. Motioning to Stoner to help, she moved the chairs to the edges of the barn, leaving the floor space empty.

"Crones," she said to Clara and Esther, "your position is on the stage, under the bower. Your role in this is to keep the peace."

"I guess I know how to do that," Clara announced.

"Good. What will happen is this: when the women arrive, we'll consecrate and purify the space. Then I'll cast the circle, and purify each woman as she comes in. Next I'll invoke the spirits of the four directions and elements, and welcome their goddesses. After that, the circle is sealed and no one may enter or exit until the ceremony's completed. I'll announce the nature of the ceremony, which is to clear the air of gripes and complaints. Then each woman will be allowed to speak. While she's speaking, no one else may interrupt her."

"You run this better than a court of law," Clara said.

"In a way, it is a court of law," said Boneset. "Natural law. After each woman has spoken, the floor is open for questions, arguments, and suggestions for conflict resolution. This will be the time when you'll have to be most on top of things. We have to walk a fine line between letting women have their say, and the whole thing getting out of hand."

Clara nodded solemnly.

"We have no way of knowing how long it will take at this point. But after we come to a resolution—or decide we can't find a solution tonight—I'll invite the women to write their complaints and wishes on slips of paper, and we'll offer them up to the Goddess by burning them in the cauldron." She indicated the center of the floor, where a large black pot sat on three legs. The inside of the pot was filled with wood shavings and birch bark and shreds of incense. A pad of paper and pencil lay beneath the cauldron.

"When this is finished, I'll end the ceremony by opening the circle and inviting everyone present to feast and dance to honor the Great Mother." She looked at each of them in turn. "If you have any questions, I'll be happy to answer them."

"Yes," Esther said, "I have a question."

Boneset inclined her head in Esther's direction.

"This all sounds pretty mystical. What's the chance of ghosts showing up?"

"Very slim," Boneset said with a smile. "Though it has happened that the spirits of our ancestors have dropped by. It's more likely on Samhain, or Hallowmas. Would it concern you?"

"Not me," Esther said, "but there are some souls on the other side who don't have very good feelings toward Clara, due to past unpleasantnesses in the line of duty."

"Aha!" Boneset said. "Thanks for reminding me. I'd forgotten about the prayer for persons and spirits of good will only. That comes just before the invocation."

"That's all there is to it?" Clara asked with a raised eyebrow. "Does the Boston Police Department know about this?"

Esther gave her a little push. "Stop that. It sacrilegious."

"On the contrary," Boneset said, "humor is the role of the Crones. They know more about life, and teach us not to take ourselves too seriously."

"Let's take this one home," Clara said.

"We're not taking *anyone* home. We're crowded enough."

"We'll move that niece of yours out," said Clara. "She's not good for much."

"Well, that's true," Esther said. She turned to Boneset. "Where do you want us?"

"On the stage, under that pine bower."

They all pitched in and heaved the wheel chair onto the stage. Stoner draped the purple robe over Clara, and showed Esther how to put hers on.

The last of the light faded from behind the windows.

Stoner took a deep breath. Here we go, she thought. Anxiety surged through her. She didn't know what she was going to say. She didn't know what she was doing. She wasn't sure of her evidence. She wanted to run.

Unconsciously, she reached up and touched the necklace of Artemis. Be with me, friend, she prayed. I need all the help I can get.

Now there were voices, women coming down the hill and across the lawn to the barn.

She took a deep breath.

Boneset handed her a large sea shell and a sage smudge stick. Striking a long match, she set fire to the sage, then took the smudge and shell and walked three times clockwise around the inside of the barn. By the time the women reached the door, the air was pleasantly tangy with the odor of the desert.

"Blessed be," Boneset said to each woman as they filed in silently and formed a circle.

Barb was the last one. "Everyone's here," she said.

Boneset nodded. "Thank you for your help." She went around the circle again, waving the smoke toward each woman with an eagle feather fan. Stoner followed with the shell. When she had made the transit, she stubbed out the smudge stick in the shell, and took out a bag of salt. As the women joined hands, she walked behind them again, scattering salt on the ground.

Next was water. Lifting the flask high and facing east, she mumbled a prayer, then circled them again, splashing droplets of water on the ground.

Finally she took out her wand and made one last circle, beginning at the east and moving clockwise.

"The circle is closed."

The women began to hum, a deep, booming hum from low in their bodies. Boneset went to the east one last time, drawing her knife and wand and raising them high. "Powers of the east," she said, "spirits of air, bless our ceremony and make us swift."

She moved to the south. "Powers of the south, spirits of fire, bless our ceremony and make us strong."

To the west. "Powers of the west, spirits of water, bless our ceremony and make us wise."

To the north. "Powers of the north, spirits of earth, bless our ceremony and bring us peace."

Standing over her cauldron, in the center of the circle, she reached toward the sky. "Isis, Astarte, Diana," she chanted, "Hecate, Demeter, Kali, Inanna."

The other women took up the chant. "Isis, Astarte, Diana..."

"Oh, Great Mother," Boneset intoned, "Goddess of a thousand names..."

"Hecate, Demeter, Kali..."
"Be with your daughters as we heal our community."
"Inanna. Isis, Astarte..."
"Let each women speak the truth that is in her heart."
"Diana, Hecate, Demeter..."
"Let each of us open her heart to the words of her sisters."
"Kali, Inanna..."
"Let your wisdom guide us on this night."
She stamped her foot. The chanting stopped. "The Goddess is here."
Stoner could feel it, the room charged with energy and lightness, as though sparkling. Around the circle to her left she could see Gwen, looking at her softly and reassuringly, as if she could send waves of love through the air itself. Sherry was there, too, between Barb and Marcy. She became aware of Stoner watching her. Her mouth twisted into an unfriendly smile. Touching her Artemis necklace, Stoner looked away.
"Our sister Stoner has asked for this ceremony," Boneset explained. "But we all know there's been a lot of tension in the company lately, and we all know we have to heal before our show can continue."
Murmurs of agreement.
"Therefore, I've decided to bring us together into Stenia, the Bitching Festival. Each woman will have a chance to say what's in her heart. When we've all been heard, we'll have an open discussion and look for solutions. Our Crones..." She turned and indicated Clara and Esther. "...Esther and Clara..." Clara waved to the circle. "...aren't here as judges. They're here to see that each woman is fairly heard, and to maintain order."
"I resent that," Sherry said loudly. "You're treating us like children."
"Fault!" Clara shouted.
The other women giggled. Sherry lapsed into resentful silence.
"Because Stoner is the one who suggested this healing," Boneset said, "I've asked her to assist me tonight. I'd like her to begin the bitching. Stoner, please step into the center of the circle."
She was so frightened she thought she wouldn't be able to do it. It was only the distance of one stride, but her legs weren't going to move. Someone gave her a firm but reassuring push from behind, and suddenly she was there, with all the faces looking at her, ghostly in the pale blue light.
"Uh," she said, her mind a blank. "I...uh."
"Blessed be," someone said. The rest took up the chant, encouraging her. "Blessed be, blessed be."
"I know I haven't been with you long," she heard herself say, "but I hope I've gained a little of your trust."
She went blank again.
Words came into her head. *Just tell the truth.*
"I came here...Gwen and I came here...we aren't on vacation, as we said we were. We're here at Sherry's request." She could feel some of the women looking in Sherry's direction, surprised. "She approached me because she was

concerned about some of the things that had been happening. The mysterious disappearances and reappearances of props. The theft of the flashlights. The bench with fresh paint that wasn't marked, so that Roseann ruined her clothes. All small occurrences, but, she said, they aroused her suspicions."

She stopped for breath. The room was silent. She could feel the tension from Sherry's direction. The alertness, like a tiger watching its prey, waiting for the right second to pounce.

"After we arrived," she went on, "Sherry showed us something the rest of you don't know about. It was a threatening letter."

There was a soft gasp from the circle.

"At first we were inclined to dismiss it as a prank. A childish one. But then the note disappeared from my bureau drawer, from our locked room. Later it was returned, fastened to one of my shirts with a knife. An electrician's knife."

The room was very quiet.

She went on to detail the entire scenario. The tampering with Roseann's script. The mysterious prowler in the barn late at night. The broken ladder. The attack on Seabrook. Roseann's torn clothing. The marijuana planted among Boneset's herbs. Rebecca's "director's notes" criticizing Roseann. The missing music. The changed marks that directed Roseann too close to the edge of the stage, the silicone spray that led to her fall.

"It was obvious that someone, for whatever reason, was trying to sabotage the show. Someone was trying to make Roseann feel she wasn't welcome among you, so that she would quit and relinquish the lead to someone else."

"Hey!" Marcy squeaked.

"Fault!" said Esther.

"But, as you can see," Stoner went on, "Roseann wasn't the only target. Rita, Boneset, Sherry, Barb, Divi Divi, even Marcy was the object of mischief."

"I was?" she heard Marcy whisper.

Stoner turned to her. "You were. I'll get to that later. It seemed to us that the point of these incidents was to turn the company against itself. It almost worked. But our perpetrator made a serious mistake."

She paused for dramatic effect, feeling like a character from a detective story. Hercule Poirot grabbing center stage.

"You see, the woman who did these things wasn't satisfied to make trouble among you. It wasn't enough of a challenge. This woman is so convinced she's superior to the rest of you that she decided to increase her own excitement by victimizing the very people she'd hired to solve the case."

She caught Sherry's eye through the dim light. "Didn't you, Sherry?"

"You have *got* to be kidding," Sherry said coolly.

"Fault!" said Esther.

"The game was too easy," Stoner went on, looking directly at Sherry. "You had to up the ante. When you found out Gwen and Marcy were driving in to Bangor together last night, and Divi Divi and I would be away, you saw your chance. You had someone, one of the other guests of one of the staff, tell Marcy her ex-lover Jennifer had called, and would call her back in the evening. That got Marcy out of the way. Then you volunteered to take her place. But before you left, probably during dinner, while you were supposedly overseeing the kitchen crew, you sneaked upstairs, picked the lock to our room, and took Gwen's night shirt from behind my robe on the bathroom door. You knew I'd find it missing when I got ready for bed."

"Wait a minute!" Marcy broke in. "You mean Jennifer wasn't really going to call?"

"Fault!" Clara bellowed.

"No, she wasn't." She turned her attention back to Sherry. "You claimed the truck had developed engine trouble. That gave you an excuse to stay in Bangor over night."

"It *did* break down. I had to take it to the garage."

"I think," Stoner said, "if we call the garage, we'll find you never showed up there. Meanwhile, Gwen asked you to call and leave me a message of...well, of a personal and affectionate nature. But you didn't. Your exact message was...'See you in the morning.' You knew me well enough to know how I feel about Gwen, and how that message would make me crazy. You figured I'd blow my stack, which I did. You figured we'd have a fight, which we did. What you didn't count on was the way Gwen and I feel about one another."

"I can't believe I stayed here and waited for Jennifer to call," Marcy muttered, "and she was never going to call in the first place."

"You see, Gwen and I love each other. So, even though you could cause trouble between us for a little while, we come to each other from a position of love. Deep in my heart, I know Gwen wouldn't knowingly hurt me. When she said she hadn't done what I thought she'd done, a large part of me believed her." She turned to Gwen. "Here, in front of these women as witnesses, Gwen, I want to publicly apologize for doubting you. It was unworthy of me, and it was certainly unworthy of you."

"Stop it," Gwen said. "You'll make me cry."

"Fault!" said Clara.

She went back to Sherry. "Your plan backfired, Sherry. Today, while Gwen pretended to be so crazy in love with you she wouldn't leave you alone for a minute, I had plenty of time to do a little looking around on my own. We found your secret room, Dodder. We found the locked boxes. We found the surveillance equipment. We found the computer disk, and we found out how you managed to get into everyone's room."

"You're lying," Sherry said. "You're trying to pin this on me because you're jealous of Gwen and me..."

"You know what did you in, Sherry? Your arrogance. You really can't believe anyone could be smarter, more clever, or more attractive than you. But I'll let you in on a secret. Every woman in this room is smarter, more attractive, and just generally better than you."

"Well, I hate to break it to you," Sherry said, "but Gwen *is* attracted to me."

"Sherry," Gwen said from the shadows, "I wouldn't sleep with you if we were the last people on earth, ship-wrecked on a desert island, and I was drowning in estrogen."

Someone in the darkness laughed.

Sherry stepped out into the light in the center of the floor. She was smiling.

"Excuse me," Boneset said. "Sherry, you'll have your turn."

Stoner touched Boneset's sleeve. "Let her speak."

"Okay," Sherry said, strolling casually around the circle. "You've had your fun. Now let's talk about what really happened." She stopped in front of Stoner. "I never asked you to come here, for any reason. You were guests here just like everyone else. And I can prove it." She reached in her pocket and drew out the merchant's copy and carbon from a VISA transaction. "You paid for your own room and board. With your credit card. Here's your signature." She shoved it under Stoner's nose.

It certainly looked like her signature in the dim light. But she hadn't forgotten the Xerox of the guest register. With a little practice, Sherry could easily have made a decent forgery.

"Do you really think," Sherry asked, addressing them all, "I'd hire someone to spy on you, and then have the gall to expect them to pay their own room and board?"

There was some confused murmuring.

"That's right," she went on, "spy on you. Because that's what she's claiming I did. Hired an outsider to spy on *you*, my *sisters*. You've known me for years. I've given my heart and soul for this company. You know how generous I've been, having the rehearsals here every year. I've put a lot of my own money into Demeter. But that's not the important part. We're all sisters, and a couple of outsiders are trying to tear us apart."

She strode back and forth. "Gwen knows exactly what happened in Bangor. And it wasn't *my* doing. I think she set it up from the start, to make me look like a creep. She's the one who told me about Marcy's ex-lover calling. She's the one who insisted we stay in town because the truck was making a funny noise." She stopped in front of Stoner. "I didn't put it together until just now, but now I realize it was *you two* doing those things, all along." She faced the others. "Think about it. Before they arrived, what had happened? We'd had a couple of accidents, and some kids took our flashlights."

"And left them in your closet?" Stoner asked.

"There aren't any flashlights in my closet."

"Not now," Esther said under her breath. "We took them."

Clara nudged her. "Hush."

"But after *they* got here, it was one thing after another, wasn't it? Things disappearing and destroyed, everybody getting into a mess and turning on each other. They wormed their way into our confidence and used us. And now they're trying to blame it all on me." She came up close and put her round face inches from Stoner's. "Tell me, Stoner McTavish, if I did all these things, what was my motive? To destroy my own theater company? To make things harder for myself and my sisters? To get some kind of sick thrill out of messing up people's lives?"

"All of the above," Stoner said. "Especially number three."

"I watched you at work, cozying up to one woman after another. Intimate talks with Rebecca, trips to Green Lake with Divi Divi, you even had to get next to Marcy after you were through using her. And Rita! That was quite a number you did on her, destroying her frog and then pretending to be oh, so sympathetic."

The confusion among the women was deepening. She could feel herself losing ground.

Sherry walked away from her, to the other side of the center, then turned. "Well," she said, placing her hands on her hips, "go ahead. It's your turn."

"I have evidence," Stoner said uncertainly. She retrieved her knapsack. "Here are ladder rungs she practiced on." She threw the charred wood to the floor. "A marijuana plant, half its leaves harvested." This was sounding more lame by the minute.

"Burnt wood and illegal drugs," Sherry said. "Which you could have provided yourself. We want proof, Stoner."

The other women murmured. She couldn't tell what they meant by it.

"Okay." She took one of the flashlights. "We found this in your room."

"And you can prove that?"

She held up the computer disk. "What about this?"

"What about it? It could be Div's, or Rebecca's. Is my name engraved on it?"

The Xerox of the registration book. "You used this to practice my handwriting."

"I keep copies of *all* inn records. My accountant requires it."

"What about bugging our room?"

Sherry smiled. "Maybe you'd like to show us that. We can all go up to the house and take a look."

Damn. Esther had removed the bug.

"How about this?" It was Gwen. She was holding up the card from the roses. "You wrote this, Sherry."

Sherry took the card with a grin. She walked around the circle, showing it to each woman in turn. "You all know my handwriting. Is this my handwriting?"

Every woman shook her head.

Of course. Sherry had ordered the roses by phone. The florist would have written out the card.

She was losing ground. One by one, her arguments were falling apart, self-destructing. And the women—she was asking them to take the word of a stranger, an outsider, against someone they'd known and worked with for years.

Stoner studied their faces, silently begging them to believe her. Disappointment on Divi Divi's. Rebecca was hurt. Rage was building up in Rita. Marcy was shocked. She didn't dare look at Boneset.

Artemis, she prayed, if you have one true arrow left in your quiver, fire it now!

"I have something," she heard Esther say behind her. "I'd like to present it."

Boneset turned to the circle. "May the Crone speak?"

The women nodded. All except Sherry, who was frozen, staring at Esther.

Stoner turned and looked to the stage.

Esther came forward, carrying the locked box in one hand, and Jennifer's letter in the other. "This letter was in this box, which I stole from Sherry's room. Her *other* room, on the third floor. I'd like to share it with you." She took her glasses from Clara and read. "It's addressed to Sherry Dodder, care of The Cottage, etc., etc. 'Sherry.' No 'dear,' just 'Sherry.' 'Sherry, I know about your affair with Rita. I trusted her, and I trusted you. But I guess it's open season now. So much for your "respect for our relationship." Jennifer.'" She removed her glasses. "Can anyone shed light on this?"

From the periphery of the group came a loud, *"Affair with me? She never had an affair with me!"* It was Rita, and she was raging. "There's no way I'd have an affair with a skinny little twerp like that."

"Of course you were," Marcy shouted.

"Well, who the hell told you that, douche-bag?"

"Sherry did. She ought to know."

"You expect me to believe you? I wouldn't believe you if you told me I have blue eyes."

"Well, you *do* have blue eyes," Marcy yelled. "Ass-hole."

"All *right*," Clara said firmly. "This is getting out of hand."

"Listen to the Crone," Boneset warned.

Marcy ignored them. "Do you really think I'd have gone after Jennifer if I thought you were still a *couple*? That's not Feminist. What do you take me for?"

"A sleazy, slimy, home-wrecking douche-bag, that's what I take you for." *"You were having an affair with Sherry!"*

"Says who?" Rita demanded.

"Sherry said..." Marcy stopped dead. "Oh, Great Mother! You weren't having an affair with Sherry. But she said...I mean, 'Go for it,' she said. 'Rita and I are getting it on, and she'd be glad for an easy out.' That's what she told me."

"For Christ's sake," Rita fumed, "if you were so innocent, why did you let me call you names all this time?"

"I thought we were doing *theater!*"

Stoner nearly laughed out loud. "Instead of yelling at each other," she said, "why don't you yell at..."

She looked for Sherry.

Sherry was gone.

CHAPTER 14

"The circle's been broken," someone shouted.

A broken circle was the least of their problems. Grabbing Esther's flashlight, Stoner ran toward the door.

It was black as tar outside. She looked toward the inn, where she might catch a glimpse of Sherry's shadow against the light from the French windows.

Nothing.

Noise from the barn, women yelling, Boneset trying to keep order.

"We have to go after her!" It sounded like Rebecca.

"Don't break the circle."

"She'll kill herself. I know she will."

Stoner came to a halt. Kill herself?

"She's tried it before," Rebecca said. "She told me. She asked me not to tell, but..."

"She asked *me* not to tell." That was Divi Divi. "She said no one else knew."

"That's what she told *me*." Marcy.

"Hell," Gwen said. "She even told me."

Stoner broke into a trot. Maybe Sherry had told them all lies, or maybe not. It didn't matter. If it was true, if Sherry had indeed attempted suicide, there was a good chance she'd try it again if she found herself in a tight situation. That kind of thing happened all the time, and Sherry certainly wasn't the picture of mental health.

She didn't have time to find out the truth. She had to handle this very carefully.

But first she had to find her.

She held her breath and listened for running footsteps.

Nothing.

Okay, decide on a direction and hope for the best.

The boat house. From there Sherry could pick up the path to the wood road, and then to the main road. She could even circle back along the road behind the grounds to the parking area and get her car. There might even be a road across the lake. If she got away...

She couldn't let that happen. She didn't want Sherry dead, but she sure didn't want her getting away.

Flicking on her torch, she headed for the boat house.

The light was on, showing through chinks and separations in the walls. Sounds of thumping from inside. Sherry was there.

Stoner tried the door. It held, blocked from within. Not by the boat house lock. That lock was a hasp and padlock type, on the outside, and the hasp was empty. She thought about calling out, but that would be ridiculous. Sherry wouldn't respond. They never did. She'd seen enough television shows to know that. People in television shows were always beating on doors and yelling things like, "Let me in!" and "I know you're in there!" and "Open this door immediately!" No one ever did.

She remembered a window on the other side. Carefully, trying not to give away her moves, she worked her way around. The inside light went out. The glass panes reflected the sky. Beyond them, everything was dark. She heard an unfamiliar scraping, chain-rattling sound.

Something was going on, and it was pretty certain that that something had to do with Sherry and escape. Returning to the door, she contemplated it for a moment. Break it down. There was nothing else she could do. Break through whatever barrier Sherry had put up, and hope the woman wasn't standing on the other side with a sawed-off shot gun.

Because she had the feeling Sherry Dodder wasn't into saving *her* life.

Putting her shoulder against the wood, she pressed as hard as she could. The door didn't move. She backed up a few feet. The odd sound came again.

In the barn, the women were beginning to chant, healing their circle. The thousand names of the three-fold Goddess floated through the air.

She threw herself at the door. It held.

This wasn't going to work. Her shoulder ached.

Maybe she should go for help. But Sherry would take advantage of her absence to get away.

Stoner took a deep breath. All right, Goddesses and other ladies, I can use your help. Maiden, Mother, Crone, give me a push.

One more try. She backed up a few steps more to get a truly serious running start, and hurled herself forward.

The door cracked and creaked and swung open.

She ducked back outside and hid in the shadows beside the door, anticipating a rain of bullets.

The boat house stood empty and silent.

Cautiously, she inched around the edge of the door and reached for the light switch. Flicked it.

Nothing.

She went all the way in and turned her light toward the fuse box. The wires were ripped, the circuit breakers thrown. Sherry had disabled the electricity. And the phone. It lay in pieces, wires sprouting from the base in a rainbow of curls. Irrelevantly, it made her think of Rita.

Still apprehensive and moving slowly, she swept the room with her flashlight. Nothing seemed to have changed since the other day. Oars, paddles, and tools still lined the walls. Opposite the door, a small window. Against the wall to her right, the canoes rested in the framework of iron pipes. A wooden walkway surrounded the patch of open water where they were launched. An overhead door cut in the far wall could be raised and lowered on a chain to let them out. It was closed. The room was empty. Sherry was gone. One of the canoes was missing.

That must have been the sound she'd heard. The overhead door opening, then closing.

Sherry was out on the lake.

Well, she could follow. Granted, her canoeing skills left something to be desired, but she ought to be able to handle it. She ran to the canoe rack.

The door slammed behind her.

She whirled around.

The hasp clanked shut. The padlock clicked.

Sherry had brought her canoe around to the dock, climbed on shore, and locked her in.

There was always the boat door to the lake. That couldn't possibly be locked from the outside. She crept toward it.

Just goes to show you how wrong you can be. The door was fastened tight, locked with a dead bolt lock that could only be opened with a key. The key was missing.

She really had to compliment Sherry on her excellent security.

If she ever saw her again.

The women in the barn were continuing their litany of Goddess names.

Come on, come on. I need your help here, folks.

Damn, what if they made a mistake and had to start over again from the beginning?

She stood for a moment, listening. No sound of running footsteps, no rustling. Only the slow lapping of lake water against the shore and women's voices in the distance.

Sherry could have gotten away down the path and road by now.

She had to get out of here, had to go after her.

Okay, we have two choices. The lake or the window.

She opted for the window, and sized it up. Small, yes, but she could probably get through. Shoulders were the problem. Maybe hips. It wouldn't be comfortable or fun, not with the unfinished and splintering wood. But it was possible. And probably quicker than going into the lake, swimming around to the dock, getting out, making a lot of noise all the while...

She crossed the catwalk to the other side.

That was when she smelled the gasoline.

And heard soft rasping sound, like a match being struck.

She stood in the middle of the wooden building, paralyzed.

An ear-pounding "whump," and the boat house exploded in flames.

For a moment she couldn't think, it happened so fast. Not at all the way she'd imagined, with tiny curls of smoke seeping through a crack, then little flame fingers, and all the time in the world to make plans for escape.

But the building was old, and entirely built of wood. Even the roof. Old wood, which had dried out decades ago.

The heat was suffocating. Looking down, she saw the flames race toward her over the floor. One board, then the next, and the next, and the next. The fire jumped the small air pockets between the boards. An instant of ghost-like smoke, and the board exploded.

So fast.

The floor under her bare feet turned hot as a griddle. The edge of her robe began to steam.

Idiot, DO SOMETHING.

She whirled to her left and dove into the water. The door to the lake was smoldering. Grabbing a quick lung full of searing air, she submerged. On the other side she hesitated, reluctant to surface, certain she'd break through water into fire. Sherry was proving herself to be thorough, surely she'd think to pour oil on the water and ignite it.

But the lake water was clear and black.

She came up for air a safe distance from the shack. It was totally engulfed in flames. The roof sagged, then buckled and collapsed in on itself.

Treading water, she watched it.

It seemed she'd gotten out just in time.

Sparks flew skyward like a swarm of stars. Surely the women would see that and come to help.

Meanwhile, she'd lost Sherry, who had probably made a run for it after starting the fire. By now she'd have reached her car. By now she was probably half way to…

Something heavy and sharp hit her shoulder, sending a lightning bolt of pain down her left side.

She cried out and went under the water.

Looking up, she could see the keel of the canoe, like the belly of a huge fish, against the fire-brightened sky.

Sherry hadn't run. She'd gotten back into her canoe and paddled back toward the middle of the lake, knowing Stoner would try to save herself by diving into the water.

More than escaping, Sherry wanted to play this out.

Man, that was sick. That was truly demented. Demented and dangerous.

So it was down to just the two of them. With all the advantages on Sherry's side.

The cotton sheet she was wearing weighted her down. She struggled to untie the rope belt. It was swollen with lake water. Her left hand was numb, her fingers wouldn't work.

Her air was running out.

She stroked her way to the darker side of the canoe and slipped to the surface.

Sherry heard her break the water, and turned, paddle upraised.

Stoner gulped in a lung full of air. Pushing upward with her good hand, she forced herself back beneath the dark water.

The paddle hit the surface of the pond with a brutal smack.

That was supposed to be my head, she thought.

She held her breath and tried to come up with a plan. If she could swim under the canoe, it would be relatively easy to tip it over.

Trying not to make waves, she stroked toward the black shape of the canoe.

It backed away from her, just out of reach.

She moved forward again. It moved away.

She must be visible. Probably the white robe.

She was running out of air. Getting out of here seemed like a good idea. Maybe even better than capturing or saving Sherry and making either a hero or a fool of herself. She could swim, even in the heavy robe. There was lots of shore line. Go away from the light, where she can't see you. She struck out for the darker shore.

The robe slowed her. Too much.

She struggled forward a few yards and looked up. The canoe was still directly above her and out of reach, following her now. No chance to get away that way, then.

Confused, unsure of what to do, she floated below the surface in circles.

Her lungs began to burn.

I certainly am in lousy condition. All that city living and smog, no doubt. Can't even swim worth pennies.

Well, hell, how many city people are real swimmers? Only the health freaks with their club memberships, and they probably don't use them half the time.

Not being able to breathe, she thought, is a very painful experience.

She had to risk surfacing again. Inching close to the canoe, she moved upward through the water. Maybe Sherry wouldn't see her this time if she slipped up along the side.

Air filled her lungs in a blessing.

The canoe paddle struck the water's surface with a sound like fury. It missed her by inches.

Sherry swung the paddle again. The water exploded again. Sherry missed her again. In the confines of the canoe, she probably couldn't find the leverage to swing.

Ha! Stoner thought. Fooled you.

The canoe moved backward, away from her. She tried to follow, but couldn't make quick or easy progress through the water. And she was being drawn deeper toward the center of the pond. Sherry stood and swung, turning the paddle so the blade was like a knife. It grazed her other shoulder.

Shit!

Reacting to the pain, she lost her air.

Sherry was swinging wildly now, pounding the water with the paddle blade.

Stoner tried to swim out of reach of the canoe.

Sherry followed her.

Going deeper, she moved toward the canoe again.

The canoe floated just out of reach.

She was in serious trouble, and running out of strength. Panic swept over her in waves. If she tried to surface, Sherry would knock her unconscious. If she didn't surface, she'd die. Her only chance was to try again to swim under the canoe and tip it over.

Her lungs had become like rocks. It took all her concentration not to inhale under water.

She forced herself to go even deeper and move forward. The canoe stayed beyond reach.

She moved backward. The canoe followed.

She let herself sink, hoping to strike the bottom of the pond. There was nothing underfoot.

What do you do in a situation like this? Give up gracefully?

She didn't know how to give up gracefully.

Panic pushed her to the surface. She caught half a breath before the canoe paddle was flying toward her. She kicked her legs and propelled herself backward. The wooden blade crashed against her knee.

She managed to hold onto the precious bit of air, and sank below the surface again.

It wasn't working. She was weak with exhaustion and lack of oxygen and pain.

Maybe, if she timed it right, and grabbed the paddle blade just as it hit the water...Maybe she could pull Sherry into the water.

She made herself rise to the surface, slowly. She could see the silhouette of Sherry's head against the light. And the paddle.

Coming toward her.

All her instincts wanted her to dive. She forced herself to stay up.

Wood hit water.

She grabbed.

Pain shot through the knuckles of her right hand.

She managed to touch the throat of the paddle. It slipped out of her hands.

She couldn't hold on.

Her lungs were agony. No oxygen left.

She went under.

Time to let it happen. Time to look for the tunnel and the white lights and the bells. Time to sleep.

She let the poisoned air flow from her lungs, and felt herself drift down, and down...

The water surged like a wave. Aftershocks rippled through her. She forced her eyes open.

Against the fading light, she could see dark shapes. Struggling. Thrashing.

Somebody had come to help.

She struggled to get to the surface one last time. Fresh, cool air flowed into her lungs. Nothing struck at her.

Ahead in the darkness, two bodies churned the water. The canoe, upside down, floated nearby.

Stoner coughed up water and eased her aching body toward the boat. Grabbing the keel, she rested her head against the hard canvas.

"Give me a hand, Stoner," she heard someone call. "This one's a real little squirm."

It was Clara's voice. Clara? In the water? Fighting with Sherry?

She tried to move. Pain stabbed her shoulder. Her knee throbbed. Her left arm was numb. "I…don't think…I can," she gasped.

"Damn it, girl, I can't do it all myself."

Stoner brushed the water from her eyes. The pond boiled as if a school of barracudas were fighting over a morsel of flesh. She had to help. No matter how much it hurt, or how exhausted she was, she had to do what she could.

She didn't want to leave the canoe. It was safe here. If she left, she knew, she'd sink. She couldn't save herself again. If she stayed here…

She was afraid. So afraid. But she had to go.

Aching, sobbing a little, she pushed herself away from safety.

It seemed to take forever to reach them. Every inch of the way was anguish. The fire was dying. There was blackness everywhere. She couldn't tell sky from water. She couldn't move forward. But she *was* moving forward. Slowly, it seemed.

Horribly slowly.

Suddenly she could make out Clara's face, and Sherry's hands like claws, scratching at Clara's eyes.

"Sink her!" Clara shouted.

With the last of her strength, she drew in air, threw her one good arm around Sherry's neck, and let herself become dead weight. Immediately the water closed over them.

Sherry twisted and thrashed, pounding at Stoner's arm. The resistance of the water left her fists ineffectual. She tugged and scratched. Stoner held on.

Damn you, she thought. Damn you for everything.

They floated slowly downward, deeper and deeper.

In her anger, she went beyond fear. Beyond caring about Sherry's life, beyond even caring about her own.

If I have to drown to drown you, she thought, I'll do it.

Sherry seemed to sense her thoughts, and fought even harder.

She felt Sherry's teeth sink into her arm, breaking the skin, tearing into muscle.

She held on.